The Oasis Project

Vicki,

Enjoy the adventures of Slade Lockwood in The Oasis Project! May God bless you in all that you do!

Happiness Always!

Art Adkins

12-5-09

The Oasis Project

Art Adkins

DORRANCE PUBLISHING CO., INC.
PITTSBURGH, PENNSYLVANIA 15222

ISBN: 978-0-8059-7604-5

Printed in the United States of America

Third Printing

For more information or to order additional books, please contact:
Dorrance Publishing Co., Inc.
701 Smithfield Street
Third Floor
Pittsburgh, Pennsylvania 15222
U.S.A.
1-800-788-7654
www.dorrancebookstore.com

In memory of my Uncle Lockwood "Shorty" Adkins

and

my father, Arthur A. "June" Adkins, Jr.

Chapter One

Hurricane tracking station, Tampa, Florida, mid-July.

The overweight man bent toward the computer scope and watched the green lines trace the storm's progress across the grid, punctuated by an electronic beep every time the eye of the disturbance was located. Concern etched his haggard face and mechanically he rubbed his brow with a sweaty palm. In over thirty years this storm was the worst he had ever seen. Sighing dejectedly, he leaned back in his chair, its springs and rollers protesting audibly to the great bulk shifting uncomfortably. Several people in the room glanced his way.

The hurricane had been given birth just off the southern coast of Africa. It is there where the Indian and Atlantic Oceans meet in a chaotic battle of wind and water, each vying for supremacy. The Agulhas Current, much like the Gulf Stream flanking the eastern shelf of the continental United States, moves the warm waters of the Indian Ocean south along the east coast of Africa. The Benguela Upwelling churns the cold waters of the Atlantic against the southern and western shore of Africa, where the two systems meet in a battle of titans. Only the bravest souls dare to sail around the Cape of South Africa.

With no land mass to impede its progress, the hurricane had swept out of the southern Atlantic, gaining speed and increasing in size. When she left the open ocean, a swath of destruction was carved across the landscape. Classified as a force five, she was the worst to ever strike the Caribbean and the United States. Antiquity had provided the deadly lady an elegant name: Hurricane Cleopatra. She had already laid waste to the Virgin Islands, Puerto Rico and Cuba; she then had taken a nasty turn north and struck Key West before skirting into the Gulf of Mexico. Where would she land again?

1

Five years ago, four hurricanes had struck Florida in a matter of weeks, lying waste to vast areas of the peninsula. Along with the destruction to buildings, roads and bridges, many lives had been lost. For months, families were without electricity and water. The modern amenities a civilized society has come to take for granted were no longer there, snatched from them by the violence of nature. Federal assistance had come, but the rebuilding had taken time. These thoughts had been echoed in the room since the storm watchers had started tracking her. Would Cleopatra hit the Florida mainland? Would she be as devastating? Only time would tell. Time.

The large man in the chair looked at several sets of monitors above his head situated in a corner of the room on metal lattice work, the bigger screens on the bottom. Two of the monitors picked up images from cameras stationed on the roof. The sky was a pea soup grey, with dark clouds scurrying by in a random pattern, occasionally pausing and then rushing away. It had rained earlier, but now had stopped, with only the wind remaining. The wetness, along with the darkening horizon, gave the appearance of impending doom. The man felt a chill run up the base of his neck and the hairs on his head stood on end. Surely, they could anticipate her movements. Part of the Florida rebuilding campaign had been to upgrade storm warning stations and the latest in hurricane tracking technology was represented in this very structure. Casually, he stole a furtive look at the men and women busy at their jobs. They were the latest in technology, too. The technicians had been trained at the best schools, graduating at the top of their class.

It was the responsibility of the men and women in this room to track Cleopatra's every movement, anticipate her next turn and warn humankind of the awesome disaster spiraling their way. A large viewing screen, occupying the entire breadth of one wall, tracked the spinning monster on its erratic course from Africa to America. A second screen depicted images taken by reconnaissance aircraft, showing the whirling bands of weather comprising the storm, with the darkest rings indicating rain.

The multitude of aerials jutting skyward from the rooftop were ultra sensitive and linked to orbiting satellites. Even with the latest in technology at their fingertips, they still felt like children trying to anticipate the path of a marble over rocky ground. There were too many factors affecting the probability of a projected course: wind, sea temperature, cold fronts, the Gulf Stream. All of this information was fed into several different computers and various destination horizons were suggested. As data came in, the estimated directional line could and, generally, did change.

At least the building was built to withstand storms even more powerful than Cleopatra. The walls were over two feet thick and they were several stories underground, sequestered from the outside world, their only link the monitors. If the storm hit Tampa, at least they would be spared the devastation that had befallen Key West.

2

Key West. The overweight man rubbed his eyes when he thought about the destruction. Key West had been left in ruins. The island had been reduced to barren coral in a turbulent sea. The devastation had been total and complete. Hurricane David of years past that had struck Homestead and Miami was nothing compared to this brute. With winds approaching 225 miles per hour, nothing could withstand her fury. The seas had been churned to a violent froth and had washed completely over the islands, inundating everything in their path. The storm surge had broken all previous records and had washed away bridges, roads. The man rubbed his face a second time in just as many seconds. When would she die?

The death count was already over two thousand and rising. How many more people would lose their lives before she was recorded in the annals of history? The man looked at the cities in Cleopatra's path and a knot formed in the pit of his stomach. He was not aware he was squeezing the arm of his chair until his fingers went numb. They could not get a break.

Just when it appeared she was losing her ferocity, Cleopatra had entered the Gulf of Mexico and stalled. This was not a good sign and everyone had held their breath waiting for the inevitable. The wait was not very long. With no land mass near the storm to impede her violent winds, and the wind currents from the Gulf of Mexico and North America feeding her, she soon eclipsed her previous wind speed. She was now spinning near 230 mph and growing in size. Her appetite was insatiable, her power indescribable. She had become, in the vernacular of forecasters, a Megacane. But he knew the worst was yet to come: within the last two hours she was moving.

Scott Jones looked at the green scope on his console that seemed to be mocking him. The satellite images did not lie—Cleopatra was headed for the United States. Initially, upon entering the Gulf of Mexico, it appeared as if she was going to track due west towards Mexico. That was before she had stalled. Within the last two hours she had turned and was tracking north towards the continent. Her speed was thirty-five miles per hour. Cleopatra was only eighty miles off the west coast of Florida and currently due west of Naples. This put her on the southern southwest tip of the Florida peninsula. If she tracked true north, every coastal city on the west coast of Florida would feel her effect. Already, the constant rain accompanying her had created flooding across most of the southern part of Florida. Miami, Homestead, and Ft. Lauderdale looked like inland seas with portions of buildings protruding from the rising water. Naples was already flooded. Lake Okeechobee had breached the dykes surrounding the lake's southern side and the flooding waters had destroyed all the sugar plantations. It was impossible to navigate by roads and boats were the only means of transportation. If she moved north, the rains would come.

Turning to the map of Florida on one of the screens in front of him, Scott stared at the bright red line projecting where Cleopatra may make landfall: Tallahassee, Florida. Scott sighed once before picking up the phone. Notifications had to be made so evacuations could be started. If Cleopatra continued to gain strength she would impact Tallahassee with speeds never before faced. Scott slammed his eyes shut as he waited for a connection. He did not want to think about the possibility of death and destruction.

The connection was made. "I've got bad news." Everyone's head in the room looked at Scott as he spoke to an official in Tallahassee.

Cedar Key, Florida.

The old cuddy cabin groaned in inanimate pain as the wind turned her sideways into the teeth of the storm, the sound of tearing wood heard above the raw violence of nature. Waves, churned so dark they looked like molten onyx, unmercifully pounded her sides and shot spray over the gunnels, splashing the wooden deck that had been buffed to a high gloss. Unable to turn into the storm, she was at the mercy of the sea. With each brutal wave, the boat was pushed toward the oyster bar. Another few minutes and she would beat herself to death on the razor sharp shells lurking just beneath the opaque surface. The wood and fiberglass continued to crack and splinter as each successive wave seemed to strike her harder. Without power, she was helpless in the face of a world gone wild.

A dim-light lit the interior and it spilled onto a hooded man leaning against the door as the next wall of water struck the boat a vicious blow on the starboard side, spraying gallons of sea water onto the slippery deck. Righting himself, Bart Weiland squinted out the cabin door at the driving rain pelting him like beads of buckshot. The raincoat had done little to stop the water from running down his collar and he was soaked. The rain was increasing in intensity, driven forward by the dark clouds fleeing the wind. The storm was drawing closer, moving its dangerous force towards shore.

The sky was dark and ominous, with occasional streaks of lightning piercing the distant horizon. From a macabre perspective, the power and darkness was beautiful. There was also a primal state of fear enveloping everything and it felt as life itself was being sucked away. The storm was tracking north and was expected to make landfall by morning. A small boat advisory had been issued hours before and he was confident no one would see them. Hell, no one else would be this stupid to tempt fate and place their lives in harms way. Everybody else was boarding their homes in anticipation of the winds and rain, seeking safety indoors. Others had fled the tiny island community, moving inland in the hope of avoiding the worst.

"Are they dead?" asked Sam Andrew, his eyes riveted to the gauges in front of him, especially the depth finder. All of his life he had been at sea, piloting boats around the oyster bars and shallow inlets in search of game fish and crabs. This was the first time he had ever operated a boat under these conditions and his nerves were on end, his pulse racing.

4

"Yeah, they're dead," replied Bart, as he bent over and checked the pulse of the man lying at his feet. Removing his glove, he placed his right index finger on the man's carotid artery. Nothing. Rising, he slipped his glove on before squeezing the transmit button on his radio. "Give me a couple of minutes and then pick me up."

"Better hurry. The bar is coming up fast. I won't be able to pick you up in another five minutes." Sam once more looked at the depth finder. The rescue boat was positioned off the starboard bow of the damaged cuddy cabin and Sam had maintained a hundred yards of open sea between them. There was only seven feet of water beneath the propeller. He knew the oyster bar was directly ahead and the bottom rose suddenly to greet unsuspecting fishermen in search of redfish and trout. It was bad enough to navigate these waters during daylight. But at night and with no running lights in the teeth of a hurricane moving in? He tried to dismiss the fear rising in his throat, but failed. Nervously, he swallowed and then his eyes involuntarily moved back to his instrument panel.

"It won't take five minutes. Hold your horses," growled Bart, admiring the murderous work he had performed.

Sliding the radio into his jacket pocket, Bart bent over and grabbed the dead man lying at his feet. Straightening, he pulled the dead weight outside to the wheel, straining as the load taxed his arms. Very carefully he lifted the corpse to the driver's seat and slid the man's arms through the steering wheel. When he turned the body loose, the man's arms caught in the wheel, holding his upper torso at a grotesque angle. Gravity took over and the dead weight of the man slumped towards the deck, coming to rest entangled in the steering wheel and dashboard. The dead man's head smashed forward slashing his forehead just above the right eye. A tiny streak of blood appeared and moved eerily down his face, but was quickly rinsed clean by the rain. Pleased with his work, Bart moved to the cabin.

Once inside, he turned the propane burner to high on the stove, watching as the blue flame leapt, greedily licking through the grill. Removing a frying pan from the cabinet, he set it on the stove's burner and then turned to leave. Bart had been a seafaring man all of his life and he could not help but admire the beauty and elegance of the old boat. She was named the *Fair Rose* and he had seen her plying the waters of Cedar Key on numerous occasions, carrying the family that was now her dead cargo. This would be her last journey. Bart's eyes turned cold. There was no place for weakness in his character.

If only she had been given a chance. The old cuddy cabin was a little over twenty-eight feet in length and had been designed for rough seas. Powered by a single diesel engine, she could have fought through the hell that nature was delivering and made port. With her engine silent, her death was imminent.

Bart stole one last glance around the room. The woman was sprawled out on the bed as if she had gone to sleep and the boy was slumped over the table, his head resting peacefully on his arms. Satisfied, he left the cabin and spoke rapidly into the mike dangling in front of his face.

"Pick me up. Move in close until I tell you to stop."

Not bothering to reply, Sam kept his attention on the controls and eased the throttle forward, moving agonizingly closer to the *Fair Rose*, who was beginning to list to port. One mishap and his boat could be impaled on the cuddy cabin and both would be lost. Sweat beaded on his forehead and ran in tiny rivulets down his face, but his concentration was complete and his hands were steady. He could feel his heart pounding and swallowing was becoming difficult.

"Easy. Easy," droned Bart as Sam moved closer. "That's close enough." Crouching along the rail, Bart leapt from the doomed cuddy cabin to the rescue boat, landing on the upper deck.

Just as Bart jumped, a rogue wave, larger than those pounding the *Fair Rose*, struck the rescue boat, slamming her into the stricken vessel. Sam, trying to deftly handle the controls, had not expected this and panicked when the wave hit. Instead of moving the boat into reverse, Sam slammed the throttle forward, driving the bow into the side of the *Fair Rose* just behind the steering wheel. Regaining his composure in less than a second, Sam backed off the throttle and threw the engine into reverse. Grudgingly his boat pulled away from the cuddy cabin, struggling to free its bow from the starboard side of the dying vessel. Revving the engines, the propellers beat and flailed at the water as the prop cleaved into air when thrown free of the sea at the top of each wave. Spinning the wheel, he faced the boat into the next wave and increased the speed.

Bart was almost thrown overboard by the violence of the collision. The deck, already slick, had nearly been his doom. When the two boats struck, he was shot forward towards the rapidly sinking *Fair Rose*. The bow of the rescue boat went down as the rogue wave passed beneath her keel. The *Fair Rose* was lifted several feet over the rescue boat and loomed there menacingly. Bart knew he would be killed if he did not move fast. The *Fair Rose* was going to come crushing down when the wave passed beneath her and that would occur in seconds. Bart tried in vain to claw his way back from the impending collision, but he continued to slide forward on the wet deck. His left leg slid through the guard rail and dangled beneath the bow of the *Fair Rose* and when the collision came, his leg was snapped like a dried twig. His scream died in the teeth of the storm.

Crawling along the deck, he pulled himself into the shelter of the cockpit, fighting the waves of pain traveling through his body. Once inside, he yelled for Sam, but it took several seconds before his plaintive cries were heard.

Sam finally glanced over his shoulder, saw the stricken look of pain on Bart's face and the distorted angle of the left leg, and slid the engine into neutral. Before crossing to the injured man, he stole a quick look at the damaged cuddy cabin, barely distinguishable in the driving rain. His heart was still beating wildly from the collision.

Without a greeting, Sam pulled Bart to a seated position and placed his back against the side of the boat. There was nothing he could do here. A hospital would have to set the leg.

"We need to make land. I got to see a doctor." Bart clenched his teeth and started tying his broken leg to a small gaff. It was crude, but would serve as a splint until the leg could be set.

"We have to wait until she goes down. Those were his orders," mumbled Sam, taking the wheel and turning back to face the waves. The momentary departure of him at the helm had caused the boat to drift and it had started to pitch.

"Don't take too damn long," screamed Bart, as the rocking of the boat sent new waves of pain shooting through his leg.

It took a little over ten minutes for the *Fair Rose* to die. The relentless wind and ceaseless waves drove her port side hard against the lurking menace of the jagged edges of the rocks and marine shells. With each successive wave, the razor sharp oysters sliced into the wood, opening a wound into which gallons of sea water poured. Already damaged from the collision with the rescue vessel, the *Fair Rose* slid partially beneath the waves and came to rest against the slope of the oyster bar and sand.

During the rest of the night, the waves and wind pounded the once elegant craft, breaking her into several smaller pieces and scattering debris over a two mile area. Only the top portion of the cabin was visible when the sun lit the morning sky and cast a red glow over the low lying islands, revealing the death of another boat lost during the night.

Chapter Two

The room was full of expectant students, their pens poised above open notebooks ready to jot down pertinent points that would aid them on the final. Every seat was taken in the room, which, considering its vast size was eerily silent. The instructor was known for sudden outbursts of anger when he felt his audience was giving him less than their full attention to his unsolicited words of wisdom. Such was life on the University of Florida campus and the sociology class. Another four weeks and the class would mercifully be over.

The gray-haired professor droned intently at the front of the room, occasionally pacing to emphasize a redundant point. Dr. Samuel Krancz had been teaching this particular block of instruction for over fifteen years and knew the material better than anyone—a point he constantly emphasized to the educated and uneducated alike. Like most that have earned a PhD, he was confident and self-assured with his area of study.

Small in stature, with a graying beard and scraggly hair, he moved in nervous bursts, as if scurrying to make his next point before the echo of his voice had died on the hallowed walls. The result was a constant barrage of information spewed forth in a high, nasally whine.

The young girl seated in the middle of the class made a series of quick notes on her paper. Sociology was not her major, but this class was required in order for her to graduate. Math and engineering were her chosen fields; subjects with concrete solutions to theoretical problems plaguing her world. Not vague posturing and hypothetical questions to age old dilemmas confronting the human race that would never be solved, much less answered in the confines of this room. She sighed and leaned back in her chair. Twenty minutes more.

"There is large disagreement among scholars as to which one has more impact: the environment in which the subject is nurtured or the parenting given to the individual regardless of the environment or socio-economic status. There are, of course, documented success stories in each area. What sociologists look for is the commonality, the constant, the Rosetta Stone so to speak, that is unchanging. What factor forms the baseline leading to the identification of a pattern or constant? What does the overall analysis of different individuals with different socioeconomic backgrounds and cultural upbringings mean for their successful existence in society today? Is it influenced more by nur..."

Professor Krancz was cut short as the entry door was pushed open and a middle-aged woman wearing a brightly colored print blouse hurried across the floor and handed him a small pink note. The woman did not leave, but remained, staring at Professor Krancz in earnest. The Professor glanced at the note once and then read it a second time, slower, before conferring with the woman. Only then did he glance to where she was sitting.

All eyes were on the professor and this unexpected interruption. Without a word, Professor Krancz motioned for the young girl to follow him. Every student stared at the young woman as she gathered her belongings and walked quickly to the door, confusion registering on her face and in each step.

Not bothering to glance back, the Professor left a stunned room as he led the way out the door the middle-aged clerk had just entered, offering no explanation. The clerk was close behind and the click-clack of her heels could be distinctly heard as she followed them out of the classroom.

Once outside, Professor Krancz turned and looked at the young lady, Shirley Waterbury. She was a gifted girl, majoring in electrical engineering, with a minor in computer engineering. Her grades were outstanding and she possessed a very keen intellectual brain, bordering on the uncanny. Shirley had come within forty-seven points of obtaining a perfect score on the Scholastic Aptitude Test or SAT as it was called. That score, combined with her obviously innate intellectual problem solving ability identified her as a phenom. In university speak, that was a gifted student with very few peers. Her name had come up when he was talking with Professor Stengle, head of the engineering department. Now this.

Shirley looked from Professor Krancz to the middle-aged clerk who was busy wringing her hands in nervous anticipation. Shirley noticed the lady would not look at her, as if eye contact was suddenly taboo and she dared not enter the forbidden realm. No one had spoken.

"I do not know how to tell you this and I do not have all the details," Professor Krancz paused as he looked directly at Shirley.

A tightness formed in the pit of Shirley's stomach and she slowly, involuntarily, took a tentative step towards the professor, reaching out her left hand as if to touch him. The fingers on her hand quivered, paused and then ever so subtlety, shook again. Later, she would conclude instinct had prompted the unexpected move. A dreaded premonition enveloped her and her mouth opened, her tongue moved, but no words poured forth.

"It seems there was an accident." Professor Krancz let his words trail off. He knew the prolonging of telling her was hurting her, but he did not know how to proceed. Lecture he was prepared for, but not this. "Your parents and brother have been killed in a boating accident." Professor Krancz stepped forward and took her hands, squeezing them softly while looking directly into her confused eyes.

For several seconds Shirley never moved. Without warning, the tears flooded her eyes and she blinked in rapid succession trying to clear the mist that formed there and stung. Her mouth and lips continued to move but still no sound emerged. A large weight felt as if it was restricting her heart and making it hard for her to breathe. Her parents? And Billy? What happened? How? The thoughts raced and pounded through her head, orderly at first and then with frightening speed until it all became a blur. It was all…chaos, confusion, with thoughts flooding her every sense, threatening to overload her orderly world. With a will power she did not know she possessed, she calmed herself and wiped at the tears that would not stop streaming down her face.

"When? How?" were all she could say and then the grief took over, engulfing her in one complete moment of despair. She collapsed in the arms of Professor Krancz, crying uncontrollably, giving into the chaos that had just destroyed her orderly, mathematical world.

The ocean kayak glided smoothly across the calm water, slicing in a straight line towards the distant horizon, its bright, waxed, blue hull blending in with the sea. The target was a low reef seven miles from the Cedar Key docks. On the map it was called Seahorse Reef. To the man paddling the kayak, it was midpoint on his exercise routine.

The kayak was the latest craze in physical fitness. A New York City couple, trading in the winter snow for the Florida sun, had founded a successful business by providing daily rentals to tourists. It was an invigorating workout combining conditioning with a love of the water. By far, it was the best way to see ocean life; the silent kayak could glide unnoticed and get close to dolphins playing in the shallow waters. It also provided a platform for skin divers. A kayak designed for fishing was gaining in popularity and the man had seen several the last few months plying the water with fishing rods stuck haphazardly skyward.

The man paddling loved to see the wildlife from the low vantage point. In addition to kayaking, he had taken up skin diving. Shunning the use of scuba tanks, he practiced free diving with only fins and a snorkel and the breath he could hold. While he was still considerably off the world record mark for staying under the waves with only the air in his lungs to sustain him, he had reached a little over three minutes. Not bad for his new hobby. The man smiled to himself and dipped the kayak paddles into the gently rolling waves, using his feet to turn the rudder jutting from the rear like the dorsal fin of a shark. Glancing at some gulls following him, he rolled his shoulders with the paddles and sent the silent craft shooting through the water like a brightly colored torpedo.

When he reached Seahorse Reef, the man turned the kayak around a metal channel marker and started to glide back towards the docks. A contingent of pelicans roosting on the channel marker squawked noisily as he came too close to their perch. Splashing water at them, he grinned when several lifted off and then settled back down when he was a safe distance away, folding their massive wings neatly beside their dark-colored bodies.

He had paddled a couple of miles, the rhythm of dipping the blades into the water lulling him into a relaxed trance, when movement on his left caught his eye. When he rode to the crest of a small wave he looked in that direction. A coast guard rescue vessel and several small craft were near a low-lying oyster bar. They appeared to be fishing something from the bar and surrounding waters. Reaching into a small compartment in his kayak, he fished out a pair of small, but powerful marine binoculars and focused on the activity. His window of view was dictated by the time he spent at the crest of each wave.

From his vantage point, it appeared as if a boat had wrecked on the oyster bar and had been battered to pieces. The coast guard vessel had a winch on its fantail and was hoisting the remains of the wreck onto its deck. 'Fair Rose' was the name he made out on the stern of the destroyed boat. He did not see any bodies. Maybe they had survived. It had been a nasty storm a couple of nights ago. The hurricane had devastated Tallahassee and gone as far inland as Ohio before dying. Cedar Key had been spared, with only a couple of inches of rain as the storm moved more northwest.

Who would have gone boating in weather like that, especially with all the oyster bars? Shrugging, he replaced his binoculars and headed for shore.

It only took a few strokes before he once again fell into a steady rhythm. Roll the shoulders, dip one blade and then roll the other blade into the sea. No movement wasted. It was a calm, unhurried exercise that he liked. No need to rush. He had come here to retire and relax.

He was not an overpowering man. In his swim trunks he weighed just over 200 pounds. Barefoot, he was just over six-foot. Not exceptionally attractive, he had dark hair, almost black, that framed his face. On this particular day he had found one gray hair on his head; a renegade. Not bad, all things considered. He wore his hair in a conservative cut, neat but appealing. A pair of dark polarized sunglasses protected his blue eyes from the glare of the sun. Already, he had developed the tan indicative of Floridians, especially those who live on the coast. For a man who had just turned forty-one, he was surprisingly fit.

As his kayak nosed to his dock, he had already forgotten about the wreck of the *Fair Rose*. Pulling his boat onto the beach, he secured it with some rubber straps to a piling he had driven into the sand for just this occasion. It was a short walk up the pier to his rear door. Before walking inside he stopped to look up and down the beach. Such a beautiful place.

He had purchased the house on his second visit to Cedar Key. It had been by accident he had come to the string of low lying islands. Looking for a place to retire, he had come to Florida to visit his parents, who lived in Tampa. After visiting them several times he had decided a growing metropolis was not conducive to his idea of solitude or to pursue the quiet he desperately sought. He was trying to escape the big city and was looking for a quieter, more peaceful existence. Tampa was definitely not the answer with its accelerated growth and congestion. It was too much like Los Angeles and his memories of the California city were mostly negative.

It had been by chance he had learned of the little fishing village. The Tampa Tribune had an article on the arts festival held every year in the little coastal community. After buying a map, he had jumped into his jeep and sped off. What started out as an afternoon reconnaissance turned into a four-day exploration of the little seaside town, turned artist enclave.

Cedar Key was a quiet town still harboring a lot of the southern hospitality that had attracted northerners during the middle of the century. In the vernacular of the modern day writer, it was quaint. The large dock and pier area, that had supported a thriving fish and sponge industry of years past, had been transformed into a commercial success by the local government. Instead of fishing vessels tied to the piers, art shops and restaurants dotted the walkway. There were still charter boats catering to the weekend anglers, but with the banning of gill nets, large-scale commercial fishermen had diminished. The government-enacted ban on the nets had actually saved the community and brought several endangered species back from the near extinct list. Recreational anglers were beginning to visit in record numbers and there was talk of adding an additional boat ramp to accommodate the weekend rush. The added revenue was a boon to the small seaside town.

The downtown area had also been revitalized—antique shops gave a glimpse of the old Cedar Key and historic houses had been transformed into bed and breakfast inns. The town and the atmosphere was what he was looking for: small, quiet, with a charm that was distinctly original and southern. There were no huge shopping malls and the speed of the locals dictated a slower pace of life. The growing means of transportation were golf carts. Cedar Key was relaxed.

When he contacted a real estate agent, he really did not have a particular house in mind. He knew he was looking for something different, a house with character, and a definite uniqueness. When he first saw the older three bedroom home on stilts, with the Gulf of Mexico lapping at the back door, he knew he had found the place to hang his hat. A reclamation project at first site, the house needed work and had been listed as a fixer-upper. The first several months had been spent in restoration, which required endless hours of loving work and patience.

The only major addition he made was a screened backporch to take advantage of the warm summer nights and ocean breeze. A dock, that stretched a little over a hundred feet into the sea, had seemed like a must at the time and now he wished he had made it a little longer. The only unfinished project was a small boat house he was adding towards the end of the dock to house his kayak, and possibly, if he should decide to buy one, a powerboat. He was not sure about the powerboat. He saw them plying the waters in search of game fish and the noise was offending. Kayaking was quiet; powerboats set his nerves on edge. It was a decision he would muttle over for a while longer. No rush. There was just no need to worry about it right now.

As for the interior of the house, he had kept it simple. Aside from the master bedroom, he had turned one of the bedrooms into a computer room, complete with the latest in tech hardware. A very large twenty-five inch computer screen was located squarely in the center of a teak desk. Sporting the fastest internet connections money could buy, the man could literally be online in seconds and have access to any website just as fast. Information was knowledge. A curious sort, he would spend hours sorting through web sites on the latest world developments to keep abreast of current events.

The third bedroom he had kept for the occasional guest or so he told himself. The only people who visited were his parents from time to time. He had never been married and did not have any kids. His life had been Spartan so far and he still did not know if he preferred that. Maybe that was the reason he had come here, to learn, to evaluate, maybe to sort out. A solitary existence was okay with him. For now, he preferred the quiet. Whether that lasted or not, only time would tell.

Walking around the porch, he went to his mailbox and retrieved the latest correspondences addressed to him. Useless advertisements, which were a complete waste of money, were deposited into the trash can without a second glance. Why did the companies spend the money to send him fliers he was not going to read? A flapping of wings near his front door caused him to look up and interrupted his train of thought. A large brown pelican flapped his wings and opened and closed his mouth in a menacing gesture, creating a clacking sound as his bill repeatedly slammed shut. Old Clacker. The man disappeared inside. Several moments later he returned and tossed several small pieces of fish to the bird, which were caught in the air. Old Clacker was the only pet he had and he was free to leave. He was not so much a tenant as a guest, a winged visitor free to depart when he wanted. Several months had passed since he had first found Old Clacker. He had been on one of his early morning kayaking trips when he had come upon the pelican. The bird had become tangled in some fishing line and had almost lost his right wing. The line had restricted its movement, making it vulnerable to sharks, and unable to feed. Unable to fly, he had been drifting on the tide. Old Clacker was suffering from a lack of food and dehydration. However, there was nothing wrong with his considerable temper, which seemed to fluctuate between bad and horrible, depending on how often he ate.

The rescue of the bird had proved to be no small feat. After cutting the fishing line loose, he realized the bird would need medical treatment or he would lose the wing and starve to death. Paddling back to his house with the angry bird had been the ultimate kayak challenge, one worthy of any outdoor event to test wits and brawn. After a hefty vet bill, the bird was turned over to his care. In less than a month, the bird was healthy enough to live on his own. However, he felt home was on the front porch or rear porch of the house, depending on the bird's mood, and he made a nasty clacking sound every time he felt he should be fed, which was with startling regularity. It was a damn wonder the bird did not weigh fifty pounds or more with all the fish he consumed. It was even more of a marvel the bird could still fly considering all the fish he ate. The man was convinced the pelican violated the laws of aerodynamics.

The man laughed as Old Clacker moved back to his perch. He was the only person with a pelican standing guard. Old Clacker had already bitten the UPS driver and had chased some teenagers who had been soliciting for the high school. The mailman had learned to bring some fish to distract him so he could deliver the mail. The bird tolerated him and his girlfriend and not much else. Moody rascal, mused the man.

The interior of the house was done mostly in wood, with nautical memorabilia on the walls. Nothing was evident indicating what profession the man engaged in, but there were maritime pictures and model ships prevalent on walls and shelves. A large wheel from an old sailing vessel, glistening from the doting application of oil, stood elegantly in one corner. A small net hung gracefully on the wall behind it with several small sea stars caught in the webbing and a sand dollar he had found on one of his early morning walks along the shore. Everything indicated the man had come from the sea. That was not the case.

Walking into the kitchen, he opened the refrigerator door and removed a large glass of V-8 and a chilled, freshly cut mango. As he walked through the living room, he stopped only long enough to insert a Bee Gee's Greatest Hits CD into his stereo. Soon the sounds of one of his favorite songs could be heard coming from the rear deck where two small black speakers had been installed.

Smiling inwardly, he retired to the back porch with breakfast and the newspaper. Craning his head, he listened to the music for several minutes while watching Old Clacker. Satisfied all was well, he bit into the chilled mango and sipped from the glass of V-8. Preplanning was truly a wonderful thing. Life was quiet, simple, and totally uneventful. Nothing could have made him happier.

"How is the leg?"

"I'll be okay." Bart was not pleased. "If Sam wouldn't have panicked I wouldn't have a broken leg."

"You'll live. Just stay out of sight for awhile," replied the man behind the desk.

When he did not receive a reply, the bearded man looked up and snapped, "Do I make myself clear, Bart?"

"Yes, sir," stammered Bart, shifting uncomfortably on the crutch that was supporting most of his weight. His left leg was in a cast from the knee down.

Averting his gaze from Bart, the bearded man glanced towards Sam, who was trying not to smirk at the rebuke his partner had just suffered. "You will have to do twice the work, Sam, since Bart is out for several months with the leg." The bearded man finally relaxed and glanced back at his desk.

"Yes, sir."

For several minutes the bearded man read from a stack of papers lying scattered over his desk. They were mostly police reports and newspaper accounts of the accident involving the Waterburys. The only sound was of him shuffling through the papers as he searched for data only he deemed important. Finding the documents that intrigued him, the bearded man leaned back in his leather chair and started to read. Sam and Bart could make out the words "Cedar Key Police" stamped across the top of one of the reports.

The office they were in was part of an old warehouse bordering one of the many channels flowing around the islands comprising Cedar Key. A sponge company had been the original owner. With the demise of the sponge industry, the building had fallen on hard times and at various times in the last twenty years had been a dance hall, pool room, and a liquor store. Needing an office to house his growing interest in the area, the building had been a necessity.

From the outside, the building still had the rusty tin and weathered wood like most of the buildings in Cedar Key. On the inside, a state of the art air conditioner kept the temperature hovering near seventy-five degrees. The long rectangular building had been divided into several smaller offices, with the bearded man's office not only the largest, but at the end facing the water where he had the best view. Several heavily tinted windows installed in the wall guaranteed it.

After half an hour the bearded man looked up from the paper, removed his glasses and rose slowly from his seat. Walking carefully, he moved to one of the large windows overlooking the channel. It was low tide and he watched several small birds forage for food at the water's edge. Spinning on his heel, he turned and faced the two men, impatience stamped across his brow.

"What is the word around town?" asked the man, nervously twirling his glasses.

"A lot of people can't believe Hank was out on the water during a storm, but you know how it goes." Sam shrugged to emphasize his point.

"It's been over three weeks and the boat wreck is old news. These people move on. Hell, most of them have forgotten about Hank since him and his family was buried," added Bart, trying desperately to scratch an itch inside the cast. It felt like his calf was on fire and he had obtained a pencil and was diligently sticking the end down inside the plaster.

"The police and Coast Guard are convinced it was an accident?" The bearded man was still not satisfied.

"Yeah." Sam glanced at Bart, who nodded in agreement.

"What about the girl?" The bearded man was twirling the glasses faster, spinning them between his thumb and forefinger.

"Shirley?" asked Sam, when his employer nodded, he continued. "She talked a lot right after the...the accident. But she hasn't said anything since. Been keeping real quiet. Suffering from grief, I suppose."

"I have been told she wants to hire a private investigator." It was a statement, not a question, and both men knew their boss had information they did not. Neither spoke, but waited for him to continue. "Monitor Ms. Waterbury. If she asks too many questions she may need to meet with an accident. Do I make myself clear?" The bearded man glared directly at the two men.

"Yes, sir," answered both men.

"Good. Keep an eye on things here until I return. I have to go up north for a while. There will be other men stopping by and you are to help them. They will be operating out of here, but staying at the inn near the pier. Sam, you have my cell phone number and pager in case of an emergency, but only in an emergency." The bearded man stressed emergency with a strong backward glance as he walked out the door.

Without bothering to say goodbye, he walked to the dock bordering the warehouse. A forty-foot Sea Ray cabin cruiser was idling, ready to go, her sleek nose pointing seaward, her diesel engines humming in quiet anticipation. The minute the bearded man stepped on board, two crewmen untied the boat and the Captain eased it away from the dock. Within seconds, the boat was speeding through the Gulf of Mexico.

The bearded man seated himself on the aft deck and started to sip from a mixed drink delivered into his waiting hand by an attentive steward. Still, he could not believe his good fortune. Millions, perhaps billions of dollars were about to be his and all because of a young boy with an inquisitive mind. America truly was the land of opportunity. For the first time, he started to smile and actually chuckled as he motioned for another drink.

Chapter Three

S hirley Waterbury placed flowers at the headstone of all three graves and sat down onto a small quilt her mother had made for her when she was a child. The quilt was a bright red and vivid white, with rose patterns of various colors in each square, each delicately stitched to perfection.

A gnarled cedar tree shaped by the ocean wind cast a net of shade over her. Sunlight filtering through the branches dappled the ground and several small birds in the branches calling to each other created a soft, sweet music. It was a peaceful scene, as most cemeteries are.

No tears flowed from her eyes. They were all gone. The pain and grief of burying her family had taken its toll. There was a gaunt look lurking, hovering over her features and she could not remember the last time she had eaten. She could not even remember the last time she had a good night's sleep during the last three weeks. Events had transpired too quickly for her mind to comprehend. Family. Death. Pain. Suffering. Recovery. Recovery? When would that finally take place? Forcing a calm to take over, she breathed more slowly, slowing her pulse, clearing her mind. She must organize her thoughts and sort through the chaos that her world had become.

When Professor Krancz had told her that her family had met with an accident, she had moved through the succeeding days in a daze. It was as if she was on the outside of her body looking in, moving slowly with time slowing down, threatening to stop and envelop her. She was a spectator viewing the scene from afar; distant, yet involved. Each day had become a series of pictures embedded in her mind; still photographs resembling a photo album, some in black and white, some in color, all painful. She could remember the words of the police officer who had taken her to the morgue to identify her family. Shirley could still hear the reassuring words of the victim's advocate offering help and guidance. Everyone had been so nice. So thoughtful. Yet, it had been empty all the same, a void that could not be filled by kind words, hugs, or sympathy. It was an emptiness and only those who have lost loved ones could comprehend or understand.

Her parents had lived in Cedar Key their entire lives and everyone had known them. A small community was like an extended family and a loss was felt by all. Hank Waterbury had made his living from the sea. Hank had never asked for much or expected much, except for his family. Shirley remembered helping her dad with crab traps when she was so young the crabs looked so big they were frightening. A quick smile touched her lips and died when she remembered her father telling her they would not bite and showing her how to throw them into the crab box. So many memories, so many more pictures, so many more mental photographs, and so much more pain.

Shirley looked back at the tombstones. Her mother had been her inspiration, constantly telling her that God and fortune would smile upon her if she just applied her brain to whatever endeavor she pursued. Mary had been a middle-school teacher in Cedar Key and had made sure her two children had been given every opportunity to excel. What Mary and Hank could not provide, God had. Both Shirley and her brother were exceptional students, gifted with a mental acumen beyond comprehension for normal people. Identified early, they were both recognized as young prodigies. The word genius was used too often, but Shirley and Billy had always scored the highest on any test. Shirley had scored a near perfect 1600 on the SAT and had been pursued by every Ivy League school during her senior year. She had turned them all down to go to the University of Florida so she could be close to home and family.

As smart as Shirley was, she knew her brother had truly been the gifted one. Billy had scored a 1600 on the SAT, but he had done that this year while in the ninth grade. Math was Shirley's strong point, but academically, everything was Billy's strong point. Billy's love was the sciences: chemistry, biology, and physics. He loved them all. Billy had won every science fair he had ever entered and the list of fairs he had entered was endless. Billy was truly a genius, a boy wonder who found adventure in the mysteries of the physical world that God had left for man to sort out and unravel. Shirley realized just how much she was going to miss her baby brother.

Shirley let the thoughts of her family drift away. She could not believe they were dead. Her father would never have gone into the Gulf of Mexico with a hurricane approaching. Hank Waterbury had made a living from the sea and had come to respect and admire it. Shirley remembered her dad speaking of the sea and comparing it to a cantankerous woman; idle one moment, raging mad the next without the slightest provocation. Her father's respect of the sea was as immense as his love for his family. Respect did not translate to foolishness or recklessness in her mathematical world.

Shirley was sure her father would never have been so foolish to tempt fate, to challenge a storm on the water. Shirley, without a doubt, knew if something had compelled Hank to go to sea on the eve of the approaching hurricane, he never would have taken her mother and Billy. Her father was too much a dedicated family man and would never have placed them in peril, real or imagined. If danger was to be faced, then his family would have been safe first and then he would have moved into harm's way. No, mathematically it did not add up. It was not an orderly conclusion or a logical decision. It was not her father's way.

The police and Coast Guard reports had listed the cause of death as an accident. The autopsy had identified the cause of death as carbon monoxide poisoning and had faulted a break in the boat's deck and a leaky exhaust port as the culprit. Shirley did not believe it. Hank Waterbury made sure every vessel he owned was seaworthy, especially the *Fair Rose*. She knew he had built boats as a young man and he knew every inch of the old cuddy cabin. It had become his pride and joy and he loved taking the family for a boat ride. No, there was no faulty hose or deck on the *Fair Rose*; that much Shirley was certain.

But where was she to turn? She had tried to hire several private investigators, but they had turned her down after reading the police and Coast Guard reports. She remembered their faces, more still photographs, and could still hear their voices when they read the autopsy and the police reports. *It appears to be an accident. Perhaps your dad just made a mistake.* Shirley balled her hands into fists and stared intently at the fresh dug graves. It was not an accident and she would find someone to help her uncover the truth. One step at a time, just like mathematics. Identify the problem and start with a solution. Simple. Accurate. And final. The answer would always come.

Shirley let the thoughts surrounding her family's death dissipate and turned towards other more pressing matters. A warm feeling touched her inside. She was so much like her mother: strong, pragmatic, and resilient. Life moved forward. Shirley knew she would grieve her loss for months, but that did not paralyze her into inaction. She was a Waterbury and they had made their living from the inhospitable sea. Resolve was the cornerstone of their existence. A smile finally touched her face. She was her parent's child and she could feel that affirmation spread through her, giving her a renewed strength. That thought alone would carry her if nothing else could.

Yesterday, an insurance agent had come to visit. She had been at home instead of at school. Shirley had withdrawn from the University of Florida for this semester. It was a decision she had made to get her life back in order and it was necessary to salvage her sanity. Always thinking ahead, her parents had taken out a substantial life insurance policy. With the death of Billy, she was the sole beneficiary. The policies had been for over a million dollars, and there had been a policy for her and for Billy. Now Billy was gone, too. So much money and Shirley would have given it all back if she could have her family alive.

Shirley got up to leave the cemetery. Several times she stopped and looked back at the graves. At twenty-one she had experienced more pain and suffering than someone three times her age. But she knew she had made the most pressing decision and was moving forward toward closure. The problem had been identified; the solution was at hand. Only thing left was to solve the problem. Mathematically it made sense.

The front door chimes rattled pleasantly as the door was opened and then softly closed. Several tourists were inside the shop, browsing among items like t-shirts, coffee cups, and other take home keep sakes. In addition to the standard Cedar Key paraphernalia, there were original art works by the shop owner. Beautiful pastel scenes, depicting life at Cedar Key, hung in frames throughout the store. A northern couple were admiring a painting of a very colorful scene of downtown Cedar Key and were being attended to by a clerk. They appeared close to making a decision.

The shop was a trendy art studio located on the pier of Cedar Key, which was the most prominent feature of the small town. As part of the restoration project and to showcase the rich past of the once proud fishing village, the owner had been granted the prominent location on the dock. In the arena of small town politics, it had created quite a stir and it was months before the commotion had ceased and the gossip had dwindled to a mild chatter. The outcry had arisen because the store's owner was not a local, but the dreaded outsider. However, after several meetings, the owner had quickly been adopted as one of Cedar Key's own.

Katherine Wintergate was a striking woman in her early thirties. A wave of curly red hair cascaded down her back that was usually kept in check by a brightly colored ribbon, which framed a face with flawless features. Full lips and a small, upturned nose beneath beautiful hazel eyes complemented an outstanding figure. Katherine radiated an innocence that was instantly contagious. After several moments of talking to her, a smile quickly came to the lips of her customers. It was this innocence and enthusiasm that had captivated the City Council and won her the coveted location. The locals had quickly expressed their support to the rising artist and the murmurs had ceased. She was now one of theirs.

Her work as an artist was equally impressive. Several of her pieces had been sold for over five figures. Quickly gaining in reputation, she had already held several art shows in Tampa and Jacksonville, and word of her work was spreading. For all the fame and fortune, she remained the same sweet woman she had always been.

Selecting a color with the tip of her brush, she applied a delicate stroke to the canvas in front of her, while carefully watching the man who had just entered. Katherine smiled with detached amusement as he moved slowly down the aisles of gifts and paintings before walking toward her studio. In the last several months he had been in countless times, but always moved through the rows of knick-knacks as if he was seeing them for the first time. He appeared to be a hunter looking for a trinket that may strike his fancy.

Katherine's studio was located on a second floor loft overlooking the store. It was a unique vantage point from which to watch and work. Katherine appeared uninterested as the man climbed the stairs, moving effortlessly up the wooden steps. No word of greeting passed his lips as he stopped in front of her.

"What are you painting?"

Katherine looked up at him and smiled. He was definitely a hard man to understand; so quiet and distant, even to her. "I'm painting Old Clacker. I believe he should be immortalized in paint." This brought a smile to the man's face and he moved behind Katherine so he could gain a better vantage point. It was a painting of Old Clacker on the back porch of the man's home.

"I'm hurt. I thought I would at least have been given billing over that damn bird." The man feigned a hurt he did not feel. The painting was beautiful and he already knew he would buy it. He was rewarded with Katherine flashing a smile. When she smiled, it was as if the light from a thousands suns flooded her eyes.

"I think Old Clacker makes an excellent subject," mused Katherine, deftly applying a brush stroke as she was intent on catching the crown of feathers on top of the old bird's head in the correct combination of light and shadow.

"Yeah, but I don't see any of his meanness in the painting. He looks so, so nice," offered the man, his face briefly contorting to express his point.

"Well he is never mean to me. Maybe you should be nicer to him," responded Katherine. It was true. Old Clacker would snap his menacing bill at everyone but her. The old bird was gentle around her, never flapping his wings or showing his considerable temper.

"I thought I would invite you over for dinner. If you weren't working late." The man waited expectantly for her answer, as he changed the conversation.

She let him suffer for several seconds before responding. "What's on the menu?"

"My world famous lasagna. Of course, with a respectable wine to complement the evening." The man grinned as she turned away.

"It's the only offer I've had today, so I guess I can accept." Katherine looked down into the store and observed the tourists carrying out the painting they had been admiring. That was an expensive painting. The day had just gotten a lot brighter.

"How about six then?" asked the man, his hand resting gently on her left shoulder.

"That'll be fine." Katherine picked his hand up and kissed it gently, feeling the hair on the back of his hand tickle her lips.

"I'll see you then." The man turned and walked back down the steps without glancing back. Had he looked back, he would have seen a woman with curly red hair watching his every move, a thousand points of light dancing in her eyes.

What was it about him that fascinated her? He was a nice looking man, but not extremely so. Katherine remembered when he had first walked into the store a little less than a year ago. He had been decorating his home and was interested in purchasing some pictures to hang on the walls. She remembered him telling her he wanted the 'realism' look. By the end of their conversation he had purchased two pictures, moderately priced, of landscapes of the Cedar Key area. The next day he had returned and after what seemed like an eternity, had asked her out for dinner. Normally, she did not date men she did not know, but she had accepted. They had been an 'item', as the locals called them, ever since.

The more she got to know him, the more perplexing he became. A twenty-year veteran of the Los Angeles Police Department, he had suddenly retired at the age of forty. He gave the reason as burn out, but she did not fully buy into the answer. One thing had become evident to Katherine: he was good at hiding his emotions. His true feelings were buried so deeply she only caught bits and pieces of the real 'him.' It was as if he had locked his inner self inside a carefully guarded vault. What would make a man hide himself? Was he afraid of loving her? She did not think that was the case. Was he scared of commitment? She just as quickly rejected the idea. He did not appear to be fearful of anything.

Sighing contentedly, Katherine turned back to the portrait of Old Clacker. Like a blank canvas she would unravel his mysterious side, one stroke at a time. Katherine laughed out loud at the comparison.

"Do you have the diagrams?" asked Matt Kyle, stroking his neatly manicured beard. After leaving Sam and Bart in Cedar Key he had been constantly on the phone. The Sea Ray had docked at a private estate an hour earlier and he was on a jet streaking west for Oregon.

"I have them. I can't believe the simplicity in design. If this is functional, construction costs will be minimal."

Kyle smiled to himself. Oh, it was functional. He had seen it work on a small scale and his development team had assured him it would work on a large scale, which is what had made the Waterburys expendable.

"I'm shocked that someone else has not stumbled onto this. It's brilliant," droned Hans Klauss, chief scientist for Kyle.

"Simplicity is the product of genius, Doctor Klauss. Are we on schedule?"

"Yes. In fact we are ahead of schedule by at least two weeks." Klauss shuffled the papers in front of him. The scientist still could not believe such a simple design could solve an age-old problem. The benefit to humanity would be enormous. And so would the wealth. His portion alone would make him wealthy beyond his wildest dreams.

"Good. I'll contact Alaska and see how they're coming. Hopefully we'll all be together shortly." Kyle terminated the connection. Picking up his glass, he sipped delicately. Another couple of hours and he would be in Oregon. Marketing was the function of that team. Kyle smiled to himself as he envisioned himself on the cover of Time Magazine as man of the year. Forbes would follow with a piece about his emerging company and its cornering of the market. What a beautiful idea.

Chapter Four

K atherine had arrived at six o'clock sharp and had been greeted with a hug and a glass of white wine, slightly chilled in an elegant glass with a little metal clasp fastened around the base holding a charm. The little ornament made a soft, tinkling sound whenever she moved the glass, which produced a pleasing tone much like wind chimes and she had told him so.

After ushering her inside, he had quickly closed the door and hurried back to the kitchen to attend to some garlic bread 'tanning' in the oven. Katherine had immediately been impressed by his effort and rewarded him with expressing her satisfaction, suppressing a smile between sips. The table had candles lit. Soft, romantic music was playing in the background. Swaying to the soft hypnotic beat, she left him alone in the kitchen to continue to cook up any other surprises he may have in store for her.

Katherine went to the back porch to check on Old Clacker, who had taken control of a piling leading to the pier. The old bird guarded the pier with the tenacity of a watch dog on a short chain. When Old Clacker saw Katherine, he flapped his wings, hopped down from his perch and scurried across wooden planks towards her, shuffling like a bow-legged man who has had too much to drink. When he was at her feet, she bent down and scratched the top of his head, all the while cooing softly. The old bird cocked his head sideways at the welcome rub, his menacing posture lost.

Followed by the pelican, Katherine went to the screened porch and retrieved some fish from a small ice box. Taking several of them, she fed the old bird one at a time. Old Clacker would open his cavernous bill and Katherine would drop a fish inside. Once inside the pouch formed by the loose skin beneath his beak, he would throw his head back and swallow the fish, eagerly opening his mouth waiting for the next morsel. His appetite was enormous.

"I have to throw them to him. He won't let me get that close," commented the man, who had come in search of her.

"Do you make him do that?" Katherine rubbed the pelican on the head again. Old Clacker moved slowly back to the pier piling where he would spend the night.

"Dinner is ready," informed the host, guiding her by the elbow to the table.

Dinner was a quiet affair, with small talk breaking the silence. He asked the obligatory questions about her day and how things had gone at the store. Katherine had been interested to learn if he had developed an interest in anything other than kayaking and free diving. She was amused to learn he was considering purchasing a power boat and they launched into a discussion about fishing. After dinner, they moved to the living room. They had just settled into the leather couch when the doorbell rang. The chime was pleasant enough under ordinary circumstances, but she now found it to be intrusive, disrupting the intimacy they were sharing. Questioning, Katherine looked at him.

"Were you expecting someone?" Katherine was answered with a negative shake of the head as he moved through the living room. She left the couch and followed.

When he opened the door, he saw a young woman facing him. She looked haggard and desperate, with an uncertain look on her face. Her gaze darted around the room, lingering for a split second before moving on. The desperation however, was backed by a strength he could not readily identify. It was a glimmer that flirted across her eyes. When she spoke, she did so tentatively, searchingly.

"Are you....Slade Lockwood?"

"Yes, I am." Slade extended his hand. Slade was certain he had never met the girl before, but she looked familiar.

"I'm Shirley Waterbury. Harry Sloan told me where to find you. May I have a word with you?" asked Shirley, her confidence growing as her initial fear dissipated.

"Sure. Won't you come inside," offered Slade, shrugging his shoulders to Katherine as Shirley walked past. "This is Katherine Wintergate," said Slade, introducing the two women.

"You own the art shop on the pier," stated Shirley. "I've been in several times. You do beautiful work."

"Thank you." Katherine guided the young woman towards the living room.

"I wish I could paint like that. Your pictures are so real and vibrant," continued Shirley.

"Everyone has a talent," responded Katherine. "I'm sure you have talents I don't have, but thank you for the kind words."

When they entered the living room, Shirley glanced around the room and saw the candles and the low lighting. The soft music playing in the background further confirmed her suspicion.

"I'm sorry. I should've called first. I can come back." Shirley's face turned a bright crimson and she started towards the door. Katherine reached out her hand and stopped her.

"That's okay. It's obvious something is bothering you." The older woman guided Shirley to the couch. Katherine knew she had seen Shirley around town, but could not place her.

Slade walked over and sat down in an armchair facing the two women. Before seating himself, Slade had turned on a light, chasing the shadows created by the candles into hiding. Shirley was maybe twenty, perhaps twenty-one. Not much older guessed Slade. Whatever was bothering the young woman was dragging her down, eating away at her. Her shoulders were slouched and she kept wringing her hands in nervous anticipation, the action unconsciously repeated every few seconds. *What could have caused such torment in a person her age?* Slade's thoughts were interrupted by Katherine.

"Can we get you something to drink? Tea, coffee, water?" Katherine shot a sideways glance at Slade indicating he should have asked. She was rewarded with seeing a hurt expression briefly cross his face. Immediately, he was out of his chair and moving.

"Tea if you have it." And then as if an afterthought, "are you sure I'm not imposing? Really, I can come back." Shirley started to get up but was stopped again by Katherine.

"It's okay. Slade will get us something to drink and then you can tell us what's bothering you." Katherine smiled reassuringly at Shirley.

Moments later, Slade returned with beverages for them and again settled into the armchair facing the two women. He did not wait long to break the silence.

"Harry Sloan sent you?" questioned Slade, his eyes locking on her face. Harry was an accountant and financial investor. After moving to Cedar Key, Slade had used Harry to assist with managing his retirement account and some small investments he had made over the years. Harry was nearing sixty, weathered a dark brown from too many days fishing, and was as honest a man as you could find. At least Shirley was in good company, thought Slade. Any advice Harry gave would be good, sound, and pragmatic.

"Yes. Harry said you might be able to help me." Shirley paused and then looked directly at Slade. "You were a cop, weren't you? Not from here, but from Los Angeles?"

"I retired from the Los Angeles Police Department," answered Slade, still not ascertaining how that meant anything to her and why it should be important.

For several seconds Shirley was silent and then Katherine placed her hand on Shirley's right arm. "It's okay," reassured Katherine. Shirley smiled faintly and reached for her purse. She removed an envelope, leaned forward and handed it to Slade.

Slade took the envelope and opened it. Inside were $100.00 bills totaling a thousand dollars. Slade closed the envelope and looked up at Shirley, puzzlement on his face. Before he could ask a question, Shirley responded.

"I want to hire you. Please accept that as a deposit," stated Shirley, matter of factly. A certain edge had entered her voice and for the first time she looked directly at Slade, meeting his gaze. The tentativeness was gone, replaced by a hardness.

"Hire me for what?"

"To find out who killed my parents and my brother," said Shirley, her hands closing tightly into fists.

That was it! The boating accident! Now Katherine knew where she had recognized the name. It had happened about a month ago when the hurricane had come through. Katherine looked at Slade and realized he had also made the connection. Shirley's picture had been in the local paper and on television.

"A private investigator would be more appropriate. Besides, I'm not licensed in this state as a PI. Also, I'm retired." Slade watched the girl closely. She had lost her entire family in a freak boating accident and did not want to accept the truth. He had seen it a thousand times where victims did not accept reality. When a loved one died it was always foul play leading to murder. They could never accept that maybe it was time for them to die, that maybe God had called them. Slade did not understand it, but had come to accept it as one of life's mysteries. It was one of the reasons why he had stopped being a cop, among other things.

"I tried to hire several private investigators, but they all tell me the same thing. 'According to the police reports it was an accident.' Mr. Lockwood, I don't believe it was an accident. My father was the most accomplished boater in Cedar Key. There is no way carbon monoxide poisoning led to the death of him, my mother, and brother. I can't, no, I won't believe that." Shirley's voice had risen as she spoke and she was not aware she had moved to the edge of the couch until Katherine placed a comforting hand on her shoulder.

"Ms. Waterbury, I'm afraid I would be guilty of taking your money on a useless investigation. If the police have investigated the possible cause of death, there is little for me to uncover. Really, they are quite thorough on these matters." Slade paused before continuing, searching for another reason to offer as verbal support in his assertion to leave the case closed. "Did the Coast Guard also do an investigation?"

"Yes. They said a break in the teak deck and ruptured exhaust hose were the causes of death. The leak in the hose led to carbon monoxide poisoning the cabin air and my family becoming asphyxiated."

"The weather was bad that night, Ms. Waterbury. I don't know of many craft that would have been safe in those seas."

"Exactly. That's my point: it does not add up. My father would have never taken the boat out in seas like that. He was the most cautious man I can think of....especially....especially when his family was concerned." The last few words were choked off as tears hit Shirley's eyes. She was confused, because she thought she was through crying. Almost immediately, Shirley felt Katherine's reassuring arm around her shoulders. Shirley leaned against her for several moments before recovering.

"I'm sorry. It has been difficult. The last several weeks I mean," explained Shirley, faltering over her words, stumbling trying to explain herself.

"We understand. Losing loved ones is never easy." Katherine looked sternly at Slade, but he missed the visual cue. Where were his feelings? He was talking to her in a robotic voice. What the hell was he doing? Katherine felt the anger swell inside her breast as she comforted the young girl.

"Ms. Waterbury, I'm afraid I can't help you. This type of stuff is out of my league. If you really believe there were foul play, contact the police department and the Coast Guard and ask them to reopen the investigation."

"I've already asked them to do so and they've refused. You were my last hope." Shirley looked at him through tear stained eyes. She could feel the hope she had harbored moments before slowly slipping away. It was as if she was slipping into a watery grave where the sea was rushing over her, blocking out everything. It could not be. The problem had been identified and the solution had been given to her by Harry Sloan. Why did he not see that? He had to help her. He was the answer.

"I'm sorry. I wish there was something I could do, but there isn't." Slade stood up and picked up the envelope he had placed on the coffee table. Slowly Shirley stood up.

"Please keep that. You may reconsider," pleaded Shirley, staring intently at Slade.

Katherine had also risen and her eyes were locked on Slade's face, but he was watching Shirley and did not notice. It was Katherine who reached out and took the envelope and tossed it onto the coffee table. "Why don't you go home and get some rest. I'll have Slade call you in the morning." Katherine escorted Shirley to the front door and was rewarded with the young woman giving her a hug before leaving. On the doorstep, Shirley must have thanked Katherine a dozen times before starting down the steps.

Once the door was closed, Katherine turned and confronted Slade who had followed the two women. Katherine met his stare and her eyes did not dart or waver. The fire emitting from her was unmistakable and the anger hit her voice, lingering on every word, her tongue sliding over every syllable to emphasize her point. All her life she had been the champion of the underdog, helping others less fortunate than she. She had volunteered her time, reading to patients in hospitals, and other civic deeds. Shirley was a person in need of help and her first response was to come to her rescue regardless of what the authorities said. Katherine did not have to know Shirley to extend her hand; she was hurting and that was good enough for her.

"How damn insensitive are you? Can't you see she was hurting? She just lost her family and you refuse to help her." Angrily Katherine advanced on Slade, moving to within arms reach. It was obvious her outburst had taken him by surprise.

"Katherine, there was nothing I could do, or can do. The investigation has already been made." Before he could continue, he was cut off by his angry girlfriend.

"Nothing you could do? You cold-hearted bastard!" screamed Katherine. Without provocation she slapped Slade across his left cheek. Slade immediately took a step back, his eyes wide with wonder. He had never seen Katherine so angry, so visibly upset.

"Katherine ... Katherine ... hang on," stammered Slade, trying to tame the fire in her eyes.

"What would it have hurt for you to look into the accident, if that's what it was? What would it have hurt? What? You don't have the time? Will it take too much time from your kayaking or free diving or whatever the hell you do?" Tiny blood vessels popped out on her neck. Slade started to speak but was stopped by her upraised hand. "What the hell does it take to get to you? You don't have feelings for anyone but yourself. I've wondered if you had real feelings for me and now I can see you don't. If you can't extend a hand to another human being in need, then what kind of man are you?" The last few words were said with all the venom she could muster.

"That's not fair. Katherine." Again Slade was stopped.

"Not fair! Not fair! You know what Slade, life's not fair. And you're not being fair to that poor girl that has lost her entire family. You can go straight to hell!" Katherine grabbed her purse and started for the door.

Slade yelled her name and started to reach for her. Sensing he was about to touch her, Katherine stopped and turned. "Don't touch me. Don't ever bother me again. I care about people and I can see you can't do that. Goodbye Slade." Katherine opened the door and slammed it behind her, rattling some pans on the kitchen shelf.

Slade could hear her shoes sharply striking the stairs as she walked toward her car. Seconds later, he heard the key in the ignition and the roar of the engine. Afterwards, there was only the deafening silence of an empty house harboring a confused man.

Chapter Five

Professor Harold Johansen walked slowly through the science exhibits lining the perimeter of the gymnasium. For over thirty years he had been involved in science fairs, judging them, sponsoring entrants, and overseeing final preparations. This year the National Academy of Science, the governing body for science fairs held nationally, had selected the University of Michigan as the host site. It was an unprecedented honor and had more to do with Professor Johansen's tenure and involvement with the past science fairs than anything else. Last year the event had been held at Dartmouth College in New Hampshire.

Reaching up to his nose, Professor Johansen pushed a small pair of glasses back to a safe perch. Peering over the rims, he looked at the list of the science fair entrants and then back at the row of displays. Impressive. The brightest young science minds in the United States all gathered under one roof. Which one would be the next Einstein or Tesla? So many possibilities. So many chances. So many opportunities.

Corporate sponsors would flood the city within the next several weeks. They wanted fresh new ideas to feed the growing market technology had created. Information was the key to success in the corporate world of America and yesterday's answers were today's old news. The constant quest for the latest, best, and most promising was endless. Some of these young people would become rich or receive college scholarships.

Professor Johansen let his thoughts trail off a second time in just as many seconds. Still so much preparation to do before the science fair opened in less than four weeks. Ann Arbor was rolling out the red carpet—the Mayor had made personal announcements on television welcoming the contestants and seeking community and business support. The City Council had declared July *Science Fair Month*.

Moving towards the end of the building, Professor Johansen left the chemistry exhibits and ambled over to biology. He had moved halfway down the exhibits when he came to an empty space. Normally, the entrant would have already erected a portion of their exhibit. This space was three times the size of the others. A furrow crossed the brow of Professor Johansen and he scanned the entrant list. Realizing he did not have the biology list, he dug a small cell phone out of his pocket and dialed his office. He had liked his old phone better; it was bigger and easier to hear the person on the other end. This one was so small he was constantly adjusting and it still sounded as if he were in a wind tunnel.

The phone rang once before it was answered by his receptionist. "Good morning. Biology Department, Professor Johansen's office. Betty speaking. May I help you?"

"Betty, this is Harold. Do you have the list of biology applicants in front of you?" Professor Johansen waited while he heard the rustling of papers on the other end of the line. Several workers hurried past carrying scaffolding and waved to him as they sped away. Professor Johansen nodded at the workers and then turned to the empty spaces. On both sides of the area marked for the missing entrant, the other contestants were busy. One was on cell mutation and the other was on soil contamination. Such a wide range, mused the Professor, before Betty interrupted his train of thought.

"I have it right here, Professor. What do you need?"

"Who is occupying space….wait a second," paused Professor Johansen, moving closer to inspect the stall number assigned to each entrant. "There are actually three spaces: 1011, 1012, and 1013. They all appear to be for the same person." This was odd. Normally an entrant was allowed only two designated spaces at most. For this person to have been allocated three was highly unusual.

"Hang on while I find it." Betty shuffled through several sheets of paper before finding the space allocation numbers. "Billy Waterbury, Cedar Key High School, in Florida. This is unusual. He does not have a theme or title for his project."

Billy Waterbury. Why was his name familiar? Professor Johansen closed his eyes and tilted his head back. What was it? Why was his name echoing through his mind?

"Professor?"

"Yes? Sorry. That name sounds familiar to me but I cannot place it." After several seconds the Professor added, "Leave a note on my desk for me to check into this. I need to know why he's not here."

"Yes, sir," said Betty. "Would you like for me to call Cedar Key High School and find out if he's still planning on attending? Even though it's the summer, the Principal or someone should be there."

"Yes. Please handle that right away and let me know if you get in touch with him. Also check my day calendar and see if I judged a contest he may have attended. The name sounds so familiar but I cannot put a face with it." Professor Johansen was already mentally moving on to other concerns. He had just seen two young men carrying a portable generator towards an exhibit and he had to make sure they knew combustible engines were prohibited for health and safety concerns. Always something.

"Okay. Don't forget lunch."

"I won't." The Professor punched the off button as a smile crossed his face. Mrs. Johansen called Betty his second wife. Betty kept him on schedule and fussed over him like a mother hen. Betty said she was going to retire next year. The smile quickly faded. Professor Johansen did not want to think about life without her.

The sun beat unmercifully down on the vast expanse of white sand stretching for miles. As far as he could see, the sand joined the distant horizon in a swath of nothingness. Why would people fight over this place? Aside from oil, it was barren. As far as he was concerned the Arabs could have this forsaken desert, along with the oil and anything lying buried beneath the dunes. There had to be less hospitable sites where oil could be withdrawn from the bowels of the earth.

Clyde Sommer had his thoughts interrupted by the sound of a door opening. He was the guest of a member of the royal family of Saudi Arabia and was representing his firm on a new venture that should prove invaluable to the Saudi Government.

"Sheik Emir will see you now." The attendant was dressed unspectacular in a white wrap from head to toe. The clothing concealed a 9mm semi automatic handgun fastened on the man's belt within arm's reach. Two loaded magazines complemented the weapon and were within quick grasp.

"Thank you." Clyde failed to say that after a three day wait it was about time. Patience. He had learned long ago that sales required patience and tenacity. That was why Matt Kyle had hired him in the first place and dangled so much money in front of him he had blushed. This would prove to be the biggest sale of his life.

Clyde was escorted to a balcony encircling the second floor of a large stone structure. Probably an estate judging by its size, but one that had stood for ages. The blocks were weathered from the sun and relentless heat. Over time the windblown sand had carved patterns into the faces of the exposed blocks. Still the place exuded elegance and strength. It was a stronghold in a sea of sand dunes.

The fortress was less than a mile from the Red Sea and, by squinting, Clyde could see the timeless waves beating on the encroaching sand. The rhythm of the pounding waves on the shoreline were comforting in a strange way. The ocean's waves were the only movement in this arid, desolate frontier.

The tranquility of the scene was broken as Clyde occasionally saw armed men moving from post to post. Weapons slung over robed shoulders reinforced the sense of security.

After a brisk walk, the attendant stopped in front of two massive mahogany doors and knocked once. Clyde noticed a small scimitar on the man's belt. The hilt was made of rhino horn, a highly prized and expensive accessory personalizing the knife.

After a distinct pause, the attendant knocked a second time and continued to wait, no emotion registered on his face. The sound of footsteps could be heard and one of the huge doors hissed quietly open. A second man, dressed like the one who had escorted Clyde to the room, stood just inside the doorway. Without greeting, the second man stepped aside and Clyde entered.

The interior of the room was cavernous, the ceiling curving up and away to add to the openness. The far wall was more window than stone, and a pair of double glass doors led to a balcony overlooking the courtyard. Clyde could see several women in the courtyard lounging near a pool. Trees of every tropical variety imaginable provided a lush setting for the inner sanctuary, and Clyde could not help but think about the contrast of the courtyard to the vast expanse of sand. This fortress was a paradise in the middle of a hostile desert.

"Mr. Sommer." Sheik Emir moved forward with a cat-like grace, his shoulders flowing over his hips, his outstretched hand tanned a golden brown by the desert sun. A neatly manicured beard set off the square jaw line and razor sharp eyes gleamed. He seemed to belong on horse back waving a scimitar at an approaching enemy than dealing with matters of state.

"Sheik Emir, the pleasure is all mine. I want to thank you for seeing me on such short notice." Clyde enthusiastically grabbed the Sheik's offered hand. It was impossible to get a read on the man. His eyes darted across Clyde and moved on.

"It is I who must thank you. I am sorry to have kept you waiting, but the data your company supplied to me was impressive. I wanted to consult with other....other professionals in the field before I spoke with you." The Sheik studied Clyde's face for any hint of anger or embarrassment. He was disappointed when none was discovered.

"No problem. I will be happy to explain everything. But please remember, our invention is so revolutionary it will change everything in the field. It is truly a first." Clyde matched the gaze of the Sheik. He had expected the Sheik to confer with advisors. His company was asking for a large sum of money up front.

"Please take a seat." Sheik Emir moved towards a sofa overlooking the courtyard and pool area. Both men seated themselves and looked towards the pool where a scantily clad woman was diving into the deep end.

"I thought women must stay covered in Saudi?"

"They do, but this is my private palace and one of the benefits of staying so far away from the King." The Sheik finally turned from the pool and looked at Clyde, a knowing smile crossing his lips.

"I see. Not a bad set up."

"Tell me Mr. Sommer, can your company meet our orders in six months?" Sheik Emir tossed a look at Clyde out of the corner of his eye.

"Six months might be pushing it. The prototype is to be tested in two weeks, maybe three. If all goes well, we are prepared to start construction as soon as patents are obtained." Clyde sipped delicately from his cup, his mind racing. Where was the Sheik going with this? If he had consulted with officials then he knew no one else could deliver anything like this. Even for ten times the price.

"Where are the tests going to be conducted?"

"That information is classified."

"Your company is asking for a lot of money and a working prototype has not even been tested. Surely you can understand why I would like to see a demonstration," snapped the Sheik, using a cutting edge to intimidate Clyde. When the salesman responded, he knew such tactics would not work.

Clyde slowly placed his cup and saucer on the small table in front of him. "Sheik Emir, you and I both know that what my company proposes has never been done before. We have sufficient capital to manufacture a prototype, but we are so certain of our design, we're pushing forth with mass scale production. To do that takes money. We're going to avoid borrowing to finance this endeavor, because, quite frankly, the product sells itself. After demonstration of our prototype, we will be going global. Countries will be lining up to purchase the technology. We wanted to give your country first shot, but...." Clyde let his voice trail off and quietly folded his arms, waiting on the Sheik to speak. It was a full minute before the Arab responded.

"So your company is going to the highest bidder, playing us all for fools." No compassion entered the eyes of the Sheik when he addressed Clyde this time.

"Absolutely not! Your country is the only one we have approached at this time. The United States and Saudi Arabia have enjoyed free trade for years and we recognize the ease with which this deal can be consummated. Make no mistake about it Sheik Emir, your country is poised to become even more of a world player. Your economic output will skyrocket. Due to your unique location you export through the Mediterranean, the Gulf of Aden towards India, and overland to the European continent. And I haven't even mentioned Africa. The opportunities are endless." Clyde forced himself back into his seat; his enthusiasm had caused him to become animated.

"We are already rich," matter-of-factly stated the Sheik.

"Yes, you are. But now you will have the chance to impact world markets in another arena and become even more self-sufficient. It's an opportunity of a life time."

"An opportunity that costs one billion dollars." Sheik Emir placed his cup next to Clyde's on the table.

"Opportunity favors the rich and when they act, they become richer."

"Spoken like a true capitalist."

Clyde did not say anything and waited. If the Sheik did not go for it, Egypt would. A dozen countries would. The Sheik must have read his mind.

"The King feels we must seize this opportunity, because if we do not, other competing nations may. However, there is a condition." The Sheik paused for effect. "I must be present when the prototype is tested or we have no deal, and Saudi Arabia must always be first for technology and orders. We must never be second."

"That will not be a problem." Clyde extended his hand to cement the deal. Matt Kyle had anticipated the Saudi Government would want to send a representative to observe the prototype and would, quite naturally, want to be at the top of the food chain. Clyde was rewarded with seeing the Sheik's eyebrows arch in surprise. He had not anticipated that. Good, *surprised the bastard* thought Clyde.

"I will have the money wired to your employer's account. And Mr. Sommer," the Sheik moved closer to Clyde and was rewarded with seeing the other man squirm. The salesman was not used to close contact and the Sheik had not released his hand. "Tell your boss the prototype better not fail. It was I who persuaded the King to take the chance on your endeavor. And it would be I who would look like the fool."

Without another word the Sheik released the salesman's hand and walked briskly out of the room. Clyde was left trembling near the table, a small bead of perspiration forming on his forehead despite the efforts of the air conditioner.

The night had been a long one, punctuated by confusion and despair. The darkness had dragged for hours before the sun chased away the shadows, casting several muted rays of daylight into the room. Still it was a gloomy scene, not bright and cheerful at all.

Several empty bottles of Michelob were resting near the empty wine bottle he had shared with Katherine. More beer bottles were strewn across the floor, trailing towards the kitchen. It was an errant path attesting to a drunken journey into oblivion or temporary relief. Currently, it depended on his perspective, which was not clear at the moment.

Slade was sprawled on the couch in the same clothes he had worn the night before, finally drifting off to sleep after becoming too numb to think. One leg was propped up on some cushions and the other rested unceremoniously on the floor. His neck hurt from the uncomfortable position and, with an effort, he lifted his arm to block out a sliver of sunlight playing across his face. He then became aware of the dull ache behind his eyes, pounding away against his temples. It was a relentless pressure growing in intensity each time he moved. A hangover. He had not had one of those in a while, maybe years. A wry smile touched his face and quickly faded when another shot of pain raced through his cranium.

Moving like a dead man, Slade rolled off the couch, steadied himself on hands and knees and slowly stood erect. Luckily the walls of the hallway allowed him to careen towards the bathroom and the medicine cabinet where he found a bottle of Tylenol. The child-proof cap almost proved to be his undoing as it took him several attempts before wrestling the top off and shaking two tiny capsules into his hands. He swallowed them immediately and chased them down with water from the sink. The cup was provided by his hands.

The walk to the kitchen was less eventful, as his body was learning to compensate for his over indulgence. After starting a pot of coffee, he waited in front of the machine expectantly with a ready cup. When the coffee pot was half full, he could not wait any longer and poured a mug full. Sliding to a seat at the kitchen table he took the first sip. Bringing the cup to his nose, he inhaled deeply.

What had gone wrong? There was no point in him trying to investigate the death of a family the authorities had classified as accidental. And why was Katherine so ill-tempered about it? Surely she could see the logic in not meddling in official affairs. And he did not have a private investigator's license or any contacts in the State of Florida. His law enforcement career had ended in California.

Besides, he was retired. Slade angrily took another sip from his cup. For over twenty years he had helped the mass of victims seek refuge through the criminal justice system. For over two decades he had seen criminals placed in jail, only to see them released after a brief incarceration, or worse yet, another group of thugs take their place. Law enforcement had become a job, a relentless fight in a losing battle and he had grown to despise it. Slade paused for a moment in his reflections. He was genuinely sorry Shirley's parents were dead, but there was nothing he could do. His life was orderly, no hassles, no headaches from bosses worrying about crime clearances; no neighborhood watches to attend to explain the sudden spike in robberies; no city commission meetings to explain why a string of burglaries had not been solved. None of that. It was in the past.

Slade picked up his coffee cup and moved towards the back porch. Sitting gingerly into the porch swing he let his left foot propel him back and forth in a slow easy motion. He noticed Old Clacker was not on his usual perch. Probably out feeding.

Several minutes passed where Slade let his thoughts wander aimlessly and then he focused on the problem at hand. For him the problem was not Shirley, but Katherine. Slade had never married, devoting himself to his career in law enforcement. Only towards the end of his career, did he realize his job was an unforgiving mistress demanding endless amounts of time and energy and giving very little, if anything, in return. Slade felt the anger flush his cheeks—how could he have been so self-centered all those years? Law enforcement. It had taken away his most productive years; time he could have spent with a wife having kids. With deliberate control, Slade forced the thoughts from his mind. What was, was. Nothing he could do would change the past, but he could control the future and his future was with Katherine.

Even though he had drunk himself into a stupor last night, one thing was very clear—he did not, no, he refused to lose her. For the first time since high school, Slade felt his heart skip a beat. Was this the beginning of love? He did not know, but he knew he would do everything in his power not to lose it. If that meant doing something she wanted, even if he did not believe in it, then he would. For the first time, Slade understood why wars had been fought, friendships ruined, and careers ended over women.

Slade got up from the swing and moved towards the shower. He could at least talk to Shirley again and try to reason with her and have her accept the authorities' decision. Maybe that would appease her. Maybe that would appease Katherine, too, thought Slade, mentally preparing a logical argument.

Before closing the door, Slade heard a flapping of wings and saw Old Clacker land softly on the pier piling. Everything would be okay. For once, he was sure of it.

Chapter Six

The shower had done more than he had realized to help his spirits and to chase away the cobwebs of the lingering effects of alcohol. Slade felt almost, but not quite refreshed. The throb in the side of his head had abated and he was able to focus without squinting—a small victory.

Parking his jeep in the driveway, Slade ambled up the short walkway towards Shirley's house. The house was located on the water and Slade had seen two boats tied to a pier behind the house, both with their bows pointed seaward. One of the boats was a charter boat, the kind used by skippers to take fisherman in pursuit of game fish. The other was a crab boat, with the low sides and wide deck to provide ample working room. Crab traps were stacked neatly on the boat. It was not unusual for fisherman to have both types. The crab season could be hit and miss and a lot of the crab men supplemented their income by taking private charters.

Slade was impressed with the front yard and overall maintenance of the home. The older home had been painstakingly restored. Fresh paint glistened off the shutters and a rose garden dominated the front yard. Whatever Hank Waterbury's shortcomings may have been, laziness was not one of them.

Reaching the front door, Slade extended a hand to ring the doorbell when the door was snatched open. A smiling Shirley Waterbury stood in the doorway her hand extended. Caught off guard, Slade stood awkwardly for several seconds.

"Good morning. I wanted to stop by and talk to you about your proposal." Slade saw a sense of relief flood her face.

"Thank you so much. My prayers have been answered. I knew you would come." Shirley vigorously shook Slade's hand. Her face blushed when she realized she had not invited him inside. "Will you please come in?"

Shirley stepped aside and allowed Slade to walk past. Once inside, Slade was immediately impressed by the fresh smell of cut flowers. Slade thought it would be nice to have some at his place.

When Slade looked around, the first thing he saw was an endless array of academic awards prominently displayed on the walls. Science and mathematics seemed to dominate the accomplishments. Moving closer, he noticed the walls had been divided into sections—two for Shirley and two for Billy. Billy's walls contained the most.

Shirley had closed the door and followed him into the living room. "Mom said she and Dad wanted to always remember our accomplishments. They were very proud parents."

"It appears they had every right to be." Slade moved to the walls to inspect the awards. Slade had to hunt diligently till he found a second place finish among the plaques. The second place had been given to Shirley for a math contest she had entered in the seventh grade. The rest were all for first place.

"Would you like a cup of coffee?" Shirley took Slade's arm, guiding him towards the kitchen. There was a firmness in her grasp, assured, but not demanding. Slade did not think that firmness, that assuredness, would have been there last night.

"I would like that." Slade allowed the younger woman to lead. In the brief space separating living room and kitchen, Slade observed a family portrait. It appeared to be recent, because Shirley had the same hairdo.

Once in the kitchen, Slade seated himself in a chair allowing a view of the backyard as it led down to the pier. The same careful attention to detail that was prevalent throughout the house was evident outside. Manicured flower gardens, fresh paint, rolled up hoses, and the two boats expertly tethered to the pier indicated order. There was no haste or chaos in this house, but only order and stability.

When Shirley returned to the table, she placed a cup of coffee in front of Slade and seated herself opposite him. She did not say anything until Slade took his first sip.

"Do you like it? Mom ordered it from Starbucks. She and I had some about a year ago and she fell in love with it. She always kept some handy." Shirley smiled, sipping from her own cup.

"It's definitely different." Slade was desperately trying to track down the origin. He tasted almond and coconut. Overall, it was pleasing. Reaching into his front pants pocket, Slade withdrew the envelope Shirley had given him and tossed it onto the table in front of her. He could see the panic hit her eyes when she recognized the envelope full of money.

"But...but, I thought," stammered Shirley, her confidence eroding rapidly.

"I don't want your money. I'll offer whatever help I can, but no money or we have no deal." For some reason it made Slade feel so good to say that. Why? Was it Katherine?

"Deal." Shirley extended her hand, smiling that warm smile again.

"I want to warn you ahead of time, I may not find what you want. In fact, I may not find anything at all. It may be all a waste of time." Slade looked at her face as he held her hand. Slowly he tuned her hand loose and picked up his cup.

"I understand. As long as you look into it. That's all I ask." Shirley felt light-headed. Finally someone to talk to and confide in. He was the solution; Harry Sloan had been right. "Where would you like to start?"

"Well, for beginners I want you to tell me all you can about your Dad, Mom, and Billy. I want to feel like I know them."

"You want to know everything?" Shirley arched her eyebrows, not understanding why that was important to solving the murder of her family, for she was convinced their deaths were not an accident.

"Yup. Everything." Slade drained the last drop from his cup. Shirley took his mug, refilled it, and placed it in front of him before she started.

For the next four and a half hours Slade listened to the young woman talk about her family. Their hopes, their dreams, where they had come from, how long they had lived in Cedar Key. All the key ingredients that make a family a family. During the conversation, Shirley and Slade had moved from the kitchen to a small back porch. The coffee had been replaced by glasses of iced tea and a large umbrella offered a small patch of shade. A cool ocean breeze made the heat bearable and it seemed like the proper place for the conversation to take place. Based on the view the porch offered, Slade had a gut feeling this part of the house had been a favorite destination of the Waterbury family.

Shirley's parents, Hank and Mary, had grown up in Cedar Key. Their life was one of happiness, punctuated by family picnics and trips. Love was the barometer that marked the Waterbury success and they were a tight knit group, relying on each other and a can-do attitude. Though not rich, they still enjoyed all the amenities a middle class family in America could hope to have. Comfort was derived from family endeavors, not on the amount of money earned.

Hank's father had been a fisherman and had taught Hank how to read the tides and locate his catch. Unlike most of the other locals who had taken to smuggling the occasional boat load of dope for hard cash, Hank had remained honest to the core, true to the unwritten code of the sea. Deeply religious, Hank had truly believed that if you treated others well, that random act of kindness would be repaid ten fold in ways you could not imagine. To break the law was something that never crossed his mind, for acts of transgression would also come back. And the consequences would be far worse than the original deed. It was a cyclical philosophy and one he preached to his kids over and over. Doing well was expected; treating others poorly was never discussed, for it was not an option.

Hank had been a large man: 6'3" and strong as an ox. Shirley described how he could toss full crab traps, three at a time, onto the deck of the boat for hours on end. Slow to anger, he was always a calm man that hated knee jerk reactions and never answered without first carefully choosing his response. He believed any problem could be solved through hard work and patience. That was how Hank defined luck: patience and hard work producing desired results. A life of earning his living from the sea had instilled those concepts in him and they had become a part of him like the sun that had weathered his skin and caused lines to etch his face till it looked like a piece of driftwood. He had always told his kids the sea was an excellent teacher, if they would take the time to learn. For Hank, the sea was more than a way to earn a living; it was a way of life, a relationship of give and take, of hard work and bountiful catches. Hank Waterbury was as solid as a rock and was the foundation to which his family could turn.

Slade sipped from his tea glass as Shirley wiped a tear from the corner of her eye that had threatened to run down her face.

"Sorry."

"It's okay. It sounds like your Dad was an incredible man. I wish I had met him." Slade touched Shirley's hand and was rewarded with seeing her smile. There he was again, using words foreign to him. Katherine? Had to be. Seconds later, Shirley resumed her narration.

As small as her husband was large, Mary nonetheless had the energy and determination to match Hank's. Mary had obtained her teaching degree at the University of Florida, a decision that would later influence Shirley. Mary had taught science at the local middle and high school. It was Mary's love of science that had found its way to her children. Mary had never allowed her children to accept a solution or answer without asking why. It was this constant questioning, instilled by Mary, coupled with the work ethic of their father that had proven to be the trademark for the children's success. Failure was never considered, for given enough time and hard work, the solution would come. Mary insisted her children learn as much about the world around them as they could. School never ended for Shirley and Billy. When the formal classes at the local school were through, Mary always had a 'world of discovery' waiting for them to explore.

Mary's other passion were her roses. She could be found watering and fussing over them in her spare time. All types and varieties adorned the yard and whatever meager space may be available, soon had a rose sprouting forth.

Slade glanced around the backyard as Shirley was talking about her mother and could not help but marvel at the abundance of color meeting his eyes. There were white, red, and pink roses. In the corner in a large clay pot was a beautiful yellow rose and behind it on a lattice support was a climbing rose with small pink and white flowers. A dark, purple, almost a lavender, rose was near the white picket fence. Slade had not known roses could come in so many colors.

"Mom even had some she called double delights, because two colors of roses are in the same bloom."

"I see that." Slade poured another cup of iced tea into his glass. "Tell me about you and Billy." Slade was intently watching Shirley from behind the protection of polarized sunglasses. It was several seconds before she started.

At nine, Shirley had won her first science fair contest by proving earthworms were a natural and positive influence to prohibit soil erosion. Success in mathematics had quickly followed and she had found her niche. Recognized as a child prodigy, Shirley had quickly outgrown the academic challenges of Cedar Key High School. Her high school curriculum had been supplemented by her mother or she would have floundered and never attained the brilliance in mathematics she currently possessed. By the tenth grade she was doing college calculus, by the eleventh she had a tutor at the University of Florida teaching her differential equations. By her senior year, every major university in the nation was offering her a scholarship.

To follow in her mother's footsteps, Shirley had chosen the University of Florida. UF offered an outstanding engineering program where her math skills could be utilized. For her, it had been the best of both worlds. Plus her family was close. It had been with much trepidation when she had agreed to live on campus. It was an arrangement her mother had insisted upon so Shirley would not have to drive late at night and commute the sixty miles to the college campus on dark country roads.

Shirley's brother was a different story altogether. As fast as Shirley had mastered academics, Billy had grasped every concept quicker. It was as if he was turbo charged and could not stop; bent on a relentless quest to understand all there was to comprehend in the world. One area of discovery led to another and so on, producing a chain reaction. Billy had no favorites, though the sciences were where he excelled. His keen intellect was matched only by his observation skills and patience. He would sit and study a problem or lab specimen for hours, evaluating the differences, comparing similarities and probing for change. Only a mother who was a teacher could have withstood his constant questioning leading him to new worlds of wonder. He would have driven anyone else crazy with his pursuit to understand the hidden secrets of life and the world around him.

In the fifth grade, Billy won a science fair by comparing the differences in combustion of various materials as alternative fuel possibilities. The work had been so well researched, documented and presented, Billy had been invited and participated in the State Science Fair and he promptly won first place in his category. He was the youngest person to ever win a major science fair in the State of Florida.

43

Shirley had left her chair and beckoned for Slade to follow. In the living room, Shirley stopped in front of the two walls holding Billy's plaques and trophies. The walls were covered from top to bottom, oftentimes with plaques snugly placed beside each other.

"Mr. Lockwood, Billy never lost. He always won. You will not find a second or third place on the wall." Shirley smiled as she remembered her younger brother. "Look over here."

Slade was led to the wall behind the couch.

"This was supposed to be my wall. See, here are some of mine." Shirley pointed out a single row of plaques ending above the couch. Upon closer scrutiny, Slade realized the other plaques were all Billy's.

"How many contests did he enter?" Slade was overwhelmed by the sheer volume of awards.

"It was not uncommon for Billy to be entered into a contest once or twice a month. But he never just entered in one category. Look here." Shirley moved to the center of the wall and placed her left knee on the couch. Using the back of the couch as support, she pointed to several plaques aligned in a vertical column. "The top one is for biology. I believe he was doing work on nerve impulses in tadpoles, showing how post synaptic responses were truly chemical based. This second was in chemistry and it had something to do with metallurgy. Billy had an idea that a lot of the old gold relics from antiquity could have been covered in gold plating by utilizing simple tools available to people of ancient times." Shirley had paused as she searched her memory.

"He entered the same science fair with three different experiments?"

"Yeah and won first place in all three."

"What was the third entry?"

"It was in physics. It had something to do with quantum mechanics. Billy believed space travel over vast differences could be accomplished instantaneously. If that was so, then Einstein's equation, $E=MC2$, would have to be re-evaluated. Mass would no longer be a concern and space travel to distant galaxies hundreds, or even millions of light years away could be done in the blink of an eye. I believe he didn't hold to the theory that space was folded, like most scientist studying quantum mechanics." Shirley paused and looked at Slade for confirmation and was amused to see a look of total perplexity painted on his face. In spite of herself she started to laugh. "I didn't really understand it either, but Billy did. As a matter of fact, some people from NASA came to talk to him here at home."

"Really?" When Shirley nodded, Slade continued, "When was that?"

"Last year. About this same time if I remember correctly." Shirley wrinkled her brow to recall an insignificant date.

"I take it Billy was already being approached by universities?" Slade already knew the answer.

"Every major university in America has been courting him for the last three years and he would have been a sophomore this year."

Slade led the way back to the rear patio and slipped into his chair. Neither had spoken. Shirley was watching him intently as he gazed out at the two boats tied up to the dock. Finally she spoke

"What is it Mr. Lockwood?"

Slade turned his head towards her when he detected the change in her voice. "It is nothing and that's the problem." Seeing the confusion on her face, Slade continued. "Your dad and mom were outstanding citizens with two kids who are exceptionally bright. Your dad was a pillar in the fishing community and your mom was a school teacher—the classic American family if there ever was one. The only thing missing is the four of your portraits on a Norman Rockwell painting. There is absolutely no motive for someone to want your family dead. At least not one that I can see."

The only sound was the rustling of the umbrella as a stiff breeze fluttered the edges. It masked the sharp intake of air as Shirley fought off a wave of fear. *Did this mean he would not help? Was he going to leave?* Fighting down a wave of anxiety, she politely asked.

"You will continue to look into it won't you, Mr. Lockwood?" Shirley had moved to the edge of her seat.

Slade turned and smiled back. "Only if you quit calling me Mr. Lockwood. The name is Slade." He was rewarded with seeing a smile light her face and she quickly grabbed his hand.

"What do we do now?"

"*We* don't do anything, but I have a lot of work to do. Can I go on board your dad's boats?" Slade glanced at the pier where the boats were secured. It was high tide which would make his next task easier.

"Absolutely. I'll get the keys in case you want to start them." Shirley disappeared into the house and then just as quickly reappeared, with two sets of keys on floating key rings. "The red float is for the crab boat and the blue float is for the commercial fisher."

"What about a mask and snorkel. Do you have those?" Slade reached out his hand to accept the keys and dropped them into his pocket.

"You going swimming?"

"Maybe." Slade winked at her as he turned towards the boats.

"In either boat, you will find my dad's snorkel, mask, and dive fins in the cabinet to the right of the steering wheel. Dad believed everything had a place."

"Thank you." Slade started to walk away and glanced at his watch. It was a little past one o'clock in the afternoon. "I'm going to be a while. Do you have anything planned for the next hour or so?"

"No. Do you need something?"

"Yup. Lunch. I'll buy if you fly." Slade dug for his wallet, but was stopped by an upraised hand.

"I'll buy and what would you like? I'm supposed to meet a….a friend for lunch anyway." Shirley did not look at Slade, but avoided his stare.

Slade picked up on the hesitation when Shirley mentioned friend, but let it go. Probably a boyfriend she had not told him about. "Surprise me. I'm ravenous." Slade smiled and turned towards the boats, marveling again at the near perfect coat of paint glistening in the bright sun.

Chapter Seven

The Port of San Pedro lies directly south of Los Angeles and is one of the most congested areas in the Los Angeles Metropolitan urban sprawl. Railroads, semi-tractor trailers, and any odd combination of vehicle are employed in the hauling of freight. The port is non-stop bedlam, twenty-four hours a day, seven days a week.

Matt Kyle could have cared less about all the congestion or pollution the port was responsible for delivering into the atmosphere. The offices to World Vision Quest were housed in a converted warehouse near one of the main arteries. Kyle had purchased the building several years ago. Shipping had become a large part of World Vision Quest and Kyle liked to be near the action. Plus, having the boss nearby seemed to ensure a certain degree of diligence lacking in his absence.

Matt Kyle was a self-made man. At forty seven he was a multi-millionaire many times over. His was the typical Horatio Alger success story. At nineteen his first job was selling vacuum cleaners; at twenty-one it was computers for IBM. Kyle had peddled the old IBM 286's, competing with Wang. In no time he was the number one salesman, but his thirst for more money and power forced him to seek success elsewhere.

Technology changes fast in the computer industry. The new Pentium processor caused the 286's to become obsolete. First it was the 386's, then the 486's, then gigabytes, and competition from Dell, Apple, and Gateway started to surface. During the ensuing computer wars, Kyle struck gold with a simple, but realistic idea. Where were all the outdated computers going? Was there a computer graveyard?

America's technological success far outstripped the abilities of most countries and in their endeavor to make more money faster, the corporate computer giants were willing to feed the automated appetite of a capitalistic society. What was new today was old tomorrow. The surplus of outdated equipment reached staggering proportions and disposing of these 'albatrosses' had begun to be a problem. Enter Matt Kyle.

With an endless surplus of material, Kyle only needed a market. Utilizing his marketing and networking skills he had honed to perfection as a salesman, Kyle employed a dozen international salesman targeting third world countries. Kyle offered a product at a fraction of the cost of new material to countries trying desperately to enter the technological world. The match was perfect. To cut costs, Kyle purchased two old freighters and by the end of the first year, his company, World Vision Quest, had netted over fifty million dollars. The second year was even better and progressive growth had occurred since the first day the doors were open.

Breaking into the Fortune 500 would have been enough for most self-made entrepreneurs, but some money and power could not feed Kyle's insatiable appetite. Realizing the sale of old computers could not sustain a growing empire, Kyle had ventured into new areas. His real estate investments included strip malls and warehouses. A small Italian restaurant chain had been launched a year ago, and though sales were not what he had hoped, the future for the fifteen stores in three states was promising.

Kyle had made his money through technology and it was to technology he would turn for the long term future of his company. His goal was very simple: become the richest man in the world. Kyle's arena would be the world and his quest was to control and manipulate as many people as possible on the planet. Hence the name for his growing empire: World Vision Quest.

To access the latest trends in technology, Kyle put together a group of the sharpest minds from vastly different fields. On the Think Tank Team were chemists, engineers, health specialists, urban planners, marine biologists, geologists, to name but a few. Their goal was simple: find what people needed tomorrow, today, and before other companies could capitalize on the opportunity. Less than seven years old, already the Think Tank, or Dream Team as they called themselves, had struck it rich. A guidance system for America's latest intermediate range missile had been developed, tested, and marketed. World Vision Quest had the patent rights, manufacturing rights, distribution rights, and seemingly overnight, had thrust themselves to the forefront with such defense contractors as McDonnell Douglas and Boeing.

Genetic engineering had also proven to be highly successful. Rice is the primary food source in most underdeveloped countries and World Vision Quest had developed a strain that produced more per acre, while utilizing less water and was more resistant to bacteria than any on the market. Over fifty percent of South Korea's rice output this year would be with World Vision Quest's hybrid strain. If as successful as touted, Kyle's company would move to the front in rice production and within years could dominate the market.

Kyle stepped from the rear seat of his personal helicopter before the blades had stopped to spin, or before an attendant could rush to open his door. Passing the cockpit, he waved indifferently to the pilot before hurrying for his office.

Initially he had planned on going to Oregon when he left Florida, but he had handled that problem on the phone from his private jet. The marketing aspect for this new endeavor must be kept top secret before the prototype was tested. Secrecy was extremely important. A more pressing matter had arisen demanding his immediate attention.

The doors to World Vision Quest opened with a slight hiss and Kyle felt the cool air rush to meet him. A neatly groomed young secretary looked up from her desk and greeted him as he walked in.

"Good afternoon, Mr. Kyle. We didn't expect you back so soon. Hope you had a wonderful visit," smiled the young woman.

"Change of plans, Rebecca. Besides, I don't like to be gone too long."

"Are you going to be in your office, Mr. Kyle?"

"Yes, I'll be there for a while."

Greeting both of his personal secretaries as he strode past, Kyle seated himself at a very large oak desk. Two computer screens flanked either side of the desk and a large assortment of papers were strewn across the top. Kyle pressed a switch on the side of his desk and the doors to his office automatically locked. Kyle was paranoid about security. The doors to his office appeared to be oak, but in reality were high grade steel with oak veneer. His entire office was a vault. The windows were bulletproof and the walls were of the same high grade steel as the front doors. For Kyle, it was like being in a cocoon.

Pressing a second switch, a monitor on the far wall came to life and he was looking at the face of Clyde Sommer.

"Where are you?"

"Off the coast of Egypt. The Saudis accepted the offer, but the Sheik wants to be there when the prototype is tested." The salesman sipped from a drink. Sommer had left the Sheik's palace and boarded a helicopter that had dumped him onto the deck of one of Kyle's yachts.

"And the Egyptians?"

"I have an appointment with government officials tomorrow. Their preliminary response has been encouraging." Sommer drained his drink and motioned for someone out of camera range to get him another. The conversation was taking place in the radio room of the yacht and he could see Kyle's image on the screen in front of him.

"When you're done in Egypt, set sail for Australia. I've already been in contact with them and they're eager to hear your proposal." Kyle finished making notes and looked up at Sommer.

"I thought I was to go to Spain. What happened with them? Are we going to forget them?"

"They will be contacted in due time. You don't need to worry about that. Let me know after your meeting with the Egyptians." Without waiting on a response, Kyle turned the monitor off.

Picking up a blue phone on the desk, Kyle called a number, let it ring twice and then hung up. He waited exactly two minutes, picked up the blue phone and called a second number that was answered on the first ring.

"Bart."

"What is so important for you to page me?" Kyle could not keep the annoyance from entering his voice.

"The Waterbury girl has been seen with a cop. Actually he's an ex-cop. They been meetin' all day." Bart was in the warehouse on a phone that could not be traced.

"Who is the cop?"

"Slade Lockwood. Retired from Los Angeles, I think." Bart scratched his head with a pencil he had found on the desk in front of him. "Been living here in Cedar Key for about a year. Dating that artist that has a shop on the Pier."

"You think?" Kyle breathed heavily several times before continuing. "I don't pay you to think. I pay you to report. Is that understood?" snapped Kyle, the irritation flooding his voice.

"Yes, sir, it is. Sorry," and then as if to amend things, "do you want us to do anything?"

"Yes. I want you to watch and listen. Cedar Key is a small town and gossip flows. Is that clear?"

"What if she tells him something?"

"What is she going to tell him? She doesn't know anything, because if she did she would have already told the local police." Kyle rubbed his eyebrows. Thugs. Bart and Sam were thugs that were quickly becoming expendable.

"We'll keep our eyes open," assured Bart, flipping a thumbs up to Sam.

"You do that." Kyle hung up the phone.

So that had been the emergency—Shirley Waterbury hanging around an ex-cop from Los Angeles. Not one to overlook the tiniest of details, Kyle reached for his rolodex. It was probably nothing, but then again.

"Leonard! How are you?" exclaimed Kyle, forcing an enthusiasm he did not feel.

"Good, Matt! Hope all is well," questioned Leonard. He already knew all was not well or Matt Kyle would not have been calling. Social calls were never in abundance for him.

"I need you to check someone out for me," offered Kyle, reaching for a piece of paper in front of him. "His name is Slade Lockwood. Ex-cop from Los Angeles now living in Florida. See what you can turn up, okay?"

"How soon do you need the info?" Leonard scribbled the name down onto a piece of paper. LA cop. Not the first time he had been hired to investigate a cop. They were as crooked as the rest of society. They just hid behind a shield to protect themselves from the scrutiny of the public.

"Next week will be fine. And, by the way, keep it quiet. I don't want anyone letting him know we're looking at him. Probably nothing anyway."

"No problem. Talk to you then." Leonard dropped the phone receiver onto its cradle before Kyle could acknowledge. Reaching for a small leather address book in front of him, Leonard was already thinking about possible contacts he could use to sniff out information on this cop. What was his name? Glancing at the paper again he read the name aloud. Slade Lockwood. Odd name, thought Leonard, locating the name he was searching for in his address book and reaching for the phone. Odd indeed.

"Professor, I have the information on Billy Waterbury you requested." Betty looked up at Professor Johansen as he walked into the cluttered office.

"Excellent." Professor Johansen reached for the stack of paper she offered him.

"He's only in the ninth grade. No, actually going into the tenth grade at Cedar Key High School," reported Betty, glancing over Professor Johansen's shoulder. "You had to grant a special exemption due to his age. By the way, Cedar Key High School is the smallest high school in the state of Florida. A little trivia, for you." Betty smiled as she watched the Professor. He loved little facts and tidbits of information.

"Who requested the exemption?" Professor Johansen dimly recalled the incident.

"Professor Krancz from the University of Florida. Professor Krancz teaches Billy's sister, Shirley, at the University of Florida. His memo is in there also." Betty pointed to a piece of paper towards the end of the stack in Professor Johansen's hands.

"Thank you, Betty. You're efficient as always."

"Why, thank you, sir. By the way, I called Professor Krancz, but all I got was his answering machine. I left a message for him to call you and I gave him your home phone number. I hope that was okay?" Betty looked up as Professor Johansen moved towards his office.

"Yes, that's fine," then after a slight pause. "Betty did you read this correspondence from Professor Krancz?"

"Yes, sir. Why?"

"It would appear Professor Krancz believes this, er...Billy...Billy...."

"Billy Waterbury."

"Billy Waterbury. Professor Krancz believes he may have made a break through in biology as significant as Einstein's was in physics. Pretty hefty praise, don't you think?" Professor Johansen arched his eyebrows at his dutiful secretary.

"Especially for a kid just entering tenth grade."

"Indeed it is. I shall look forward to hearing from Professor Krancz to see what is delaying this young genius." Professor Johansen tossed the stack of papers back onto Betty's desk. "Please keep those until I can talk to Professor Krancz."

"Okay."

Professor Johansen moved into his office and quietly closed the door. *As revolutionary as Einstein's contribution to physics. Incredible.* The scientist in him was intrigued. *What had the young man stumbled upon? Was it to be displayed here at Michigan for the scientific community to see for the first time? If Professor Krancz was correct and Billy Waterbury had made a startling breakthrough in biology, then the scientific world would be coming to Michigan to see it and read about it. This science fair would be under the world's microscope in a few days. Marvelous. Simply marvelous.*

Professor Johansen leaned back in his chair and smiled to no one in particular. This was going to be a momentous occasion.

Chapter Eight

The sound of voices traveled across the back patio towards the tethered boats. Slade had just broken the surface of the water and was busy puzzling over his latest discovery when he heard them. One of the voices he recognized as Shirley's and the other made his heart flutter. For Slade it was a strange sensation and one he knew would take a while to get used to. It was a new arena for him. Strange sands indeed.

Swimming around the stern of the boat, Slade looked up at the dock as Shirley walked towards him, Katherine in tow. Slade let his eyes settle on Katherine, but she avoided his gaze.

"Find anything interesting?" Shirley stared at the mask perched on the top of his head.

"Just what I thought I would find. Your dad kept everything very tidy and neat." Slade glanced a second time at Katherine. He desperately wanted to make eye contact, but she avoided his stare a second time.

"I have some sandwiches. Why don't you get out of the water and join us." Shirley turned her back on Slade before he could respond. The two women walked back towards the picnic table where several sandwiches and soft drinks had been placed.

Slade swam slowly around the crab boat, carefully noting each detail before he got out of the water. He had already made a dive on the commercial fisherman, and had inspected the contents and engine room of both boats. Everything was in the best possible condition it could be in, almost brand new.

Using a towel to dry his head, Slade walked slowly up the concrete stepping stones towards the two women who were already seated and eating lunch. Shirley smiled as Slade walked up, but Katherine did not. Slade seated himself opposite Katherine, but next to Shirley.

"Did your dad keep maintenance records on his boats?" Slade picked up a sandwich and noisily bit off a large portion, each crunch sounding louder than the first.

"Yes. He had the engines overhauled after so many hours. It's all in his logs. Do you want to see them?"

"Not right now, but in the future." Slade stole a look back at the two boats.

"What are you looking for?" Katherine finally broke the silence she had imposed. She was secretly pleased he had decided to help Shirley and it was Katherine that Shirley had called earlier in the day to tell her Slade was at her house. Maybe there was hope after all. Katherine smiled to herself.

"I don't know," paused Slade. "I don't know." Slade repeated his statement and then looked at Katherine, meeting her gaze for the first time. It was Shirley who intruded.

"Where do we go from here?" asked Shirley. Katherine had told Shirley about their fight after she had left. Shirley also knew Katherine liked Slade very much. Katherine Wintergate was a stubborn woman and she reminded Shirley of her mother. Katherine also struck Shirley as a woman who got what she wanted. Shirley had to stifle a chuckle. Slade did not stand a chance.

"Do you have any pictures of your dad's boat that sunk?"

"The *Fair Rose*?" When Slade nodded yes, Shirley responded, "Sure do. I'll get one."

Shirley quickly left the table and disappeared inside leaving Katherine and Slade alone. For several seconds neither spoke, until Slade tentatively voiced his concern.

"Still mad at me?"

"Maybe." Katherine sipped delicately from a cup of iced tea.

"How long are you going to be mad at me?" Slade stared at her softly. Katherine really was a beautiful woman and at that very moment he knew he would do anything not to lose her. Katherine must have sensed his feelings, for she looked at him and rewarded his bravery with a smile.

"Depends on how hard and how long you help Shirley." Katherine reached out and took his hand. She raised his hand and pressed her lips to his knuckles as Shirley opened the door.

"Well I'm glad you two have made up. I was really feeling bad about the trouble I caused," beamed Shirley, dropping a picture in front of Slade.

Slade's face turned red and Katherine laughed. "Oh, he's not out of the woods yet. We'll see how well he does on this investigation." Katherine squeezed his hand a second time.

Slade nodded at both of them as Katherine released his hand. For the first time he realized why Shirley was so adamant about the death of her family not being an accident. Hank Waterbury maintained his equipment in excellent condition. Granted, Slade was not much of a mechanic, nor much of a boat person, but he could appreciate well-kept machinery when he saw it.

Slade became aware of both women's presence crowding in on him and he looked up with a puzzling expression.

"What are you thinking about, Sherlock? Care to share with us mortals?" Katherine reached out and tapped on Slade's hand.

"I'm thinking that I can understand how you believe your parents and brother were not killed in an accident. Your father was very careful and meticulous with his equipment. If he was half as careful on the sea, as he was about maintaining his boats, then..." Slade let his voice trail off and raised his hands in a questioning gesture towards Shirley, who quickly finished his thought.

"Now you understand!" the young girl exclaimed. "My father was so careful and thorough. Preparation and patience he preached to us all the time." Shirley let her voice trail off and then looked sternly at Slade. "Do you believe they were killed?"

Slade returned her gaze. So much had happened to her. He knew his next words could help or harm her. Carefully, Slade spoke. "I don't want to jump to any conclusions, because that would cloud my investigation. You're adept at science, right?" When Shirley nodded, Slade continued. "Well, it's been a long time since I conducted any experiments, but I distantly remember my science teacher telling us not to form an opinion before the facts were in. The same is true in police work. An open mind can cover more ground than one that has already closed the case. But in answer to your question, there are some questions that must be answered." Slade saw the light hit Shirley's eyes.

"Thank you so much," gushed Shirley, moisture obscuring her vision.

"Now hang on. I can't promise anything. My investigation may not reveal a morsel of information," cautioned Slade, his eyes darting from Shirley to Katherine several times, before settling on the young woman.

"That's okay, because I know you'll look and when you look, Mr. Lockwood, you'll find. You're right, it is like science." The defiance hit Shirley's eyes and stayed there this time, drying the moisture.

"Well, I'm not going to take the case if you keep calling me Mr. Lockwood. I thought we had a deal?"

Everyone started to laugh and the tension gradually left Shirley. Katherine steered the conversation away from the investigation and Slade excused himself to go and use the bathroom.

Slade could hear the two women talking in the background as he moved through the kitchen and towards the hallway. The laughter of the two women was comforting and he paused to listen to the sweetness of the sound. That is something he would not have done a year ago. Slade smiled to himself. Shirley was not the only one changing.

Slade used the bathroom and was walking back down the hall when he stopped in front of Billy's room. After several seconds of surveying the interior from the hallway, Slade moved inside. It was a typical teenager's room, in some respects. But there were no posters of Britney Spears or any other young female pop star. No sports memorabilia lined the walls. There was a small desk near the bed and Slade walked over to it. A dictionary and several pieces of paper littered the top. The drawers contained pencils and paper and a few books. Nothing to indicate a boy genius lived in the room. Slade turned and walked back to the door.

So ordinary, thought Slade. What had he expected to find? He did not know, but somehow he had the growing uneasy feeling he had missed it.

Unable to contain his excitement, Professor Johansen listened intently as the long distance connection was made. It was three o'clock in the afternoon and he hoped someone would still be at the school. Earlier, he had tried Professor Krancz at the University of Florida, but had failed to reach him. Hopefully someone was still in the office at Cedar Key High School.

The connection was made and the phone started ringing, a dull, hollow sound over the long distance line. Professor Johansen hoped it would be a good connection. He had waited the previous day for Professor Krancz to call and had then spent a sleepless night. When morning came, Professor Johansen had rushed to his office and grabbed the stack of papers off of Betty's desk. He immediately had found the memo. "A break through in biology to rival that of Einstein's in physics." What could it be? And for the world to see it at Michigan.

The phone had rung a dozen times and Professor Johansen was about to hang up when a middle aged man answered.

"Cedar Key High School. May I help you?" Dean Jones did not mind adding a little displeasure to his voice. It was summer time for crying out loud. Everyone was off. School would begin soon enough in about three weeks.

"Hi, I'm Professor Johansen from the University of Michigan. I'm chairman of the science fair committee taking place in about three weeks and I was wondering if you could put me in contact with a contestant from your school that has not arrived?" Professor Johansen heard a sharp intake of breath on the other end of the line and then silence.

Dean Jones knew Professor Johansen was talking about Billy Waterbury. He had not known Billy had entered a science competition in Michigan, but who else could it be?

"Hello? Are you there?"

"Yes. I'm sorry. Who did you say you were?"

"Professor Johansen, University of Michigan. I'm Chair of the science department and we're hosting a national science fair competition in two weeks. It will be the largest in the United States this year and is drawing world-wide attention in the science community." Professor Johansen stopped to allow the other man to catch up.

Dean Jones now remembered his science teacher talking about the competition. Of course this would be an event Billy would have entered. And won, thought Dean Jones.

"Sorry, Professor. I didn't mean to keep you holding. I'm Dean Robert Jones. I was walking out the door when I heard the phone. Its summer break and I'm the only one here."

"I understand. I was wondering if you could put me in contact with a contestant from your school. His name is Billy Waterbury."

"I'm afraid I can't do that Professor." Dean Jones slid into a chair and placed his brief case on the floor next to him.

"Why is that? I can assure you I am who I say I am. Do you need official correspondence? If so I can FAX you information." Professor Johansen had used his most commanding voice. What was wrong?

"Billy Waterbury is dead, Professor. He was killed in a boating accident about four weeks ago." Dean Jones then waited for a reply.

"I'm sorry. I had no idea," stammered Professor Johansen.

"It was a freak accident. His mother and father were both killed, too. Such a tragic loss. We're a small community, Professor, and it was like losing family." Dean Jones let his voice trail off. What more was there to say.

"I'm afraid it is a loss to us all, Dean Jones. I understand Billy was incredibly gifted."

"Yes he was. Only his sister was near him academically and she wasn't as smart as Billy. Billy just had a sense about him, an aura. I cannot even begin to describe it. It was the way he looked at things, at everything. He didn't just see something, he saw beyond it, through it, around it. His mind never stopped working, never stopped questioning. He was more special than you could ever imagine." Dean Jones had known Hank Waterbury and Mary had been one of his teachers in the Middle School. They were family.

"Was the sister killed in the boating accident?"

"No, she was attending the University of Florida and was out of town."

"If I gave you my number would you give it to her and have her call me?"

"Is it that important?" asked Dean Jones, puzzlement entering his voice.

"I don't know." And then as if to himself, "I don't know," said a confused Professor Johansen.

Dean Jones had wrestled with whether to contact Shirley and tell her about Professor Johansen's request. Why did the Professor want her to call? Would it bring back too much pain for Shirley? The last thing he wanted to do was to hurt the girl. Maybe the Professor was a friend of Billy.

The decision was made when he drove in front of her house and saw a Jeep parked in the driveway. If she had company, then she had a support group and any news would be easier to bear with friends nearby.

The walk up the drive was done slowly, as Dean Jones admired the roses Mary had planted several years ago. They were in full bloom and pedals lined the flower beds. Such a beautiful house. Dean Jones stopped looking at the rose bushes and raised his hand towards the front door. Hesitantly he knocked.

It was several seconds before the door opened and when Shirley saw Dean Jones she stepped through the doorway and gave him a hug. Dean Jones returned the embrace and then held the young woman at arms length.

"You doing okay?" Dean Jones allowed his eyes to dig into hers for the truth.

Shirley laughed and hugged him again. Dean Jones had become a friend of the family years ago and she still remembered that stern look when she was a child and he was scolding her at school. "I'm doing fine. Please come in. I have some guests I want you to meet."

Without waiting on a reply, Shirley herded the educator into the house, down the hallway and out the back door. Having been to their house countless times, Dean Jones allowed himself to be swept along. At least Shirley did not seem to be in a state of depression. Shirley was like her mother: hardheaded and strong-willed. Dean Jones smiled inwardly. There was a lot of her mother in her and he concluded that was a good thing.

Stopping in front of the patio table Dean Jones found himself staring at Katherine Wintergate, who he recognized, and a tanned man, who he did not know but had seen around town. It was Shirley who made the introductions.

"Dean Jones I believe you know Katherine, our local artist extraordinaire."

"Indeed I do." Dean Jones smiled politely and moved closer to shake the offered hand. Katherine was stunningly beautiful and became more so when she smiled.

"This is Slade Lockwood. He's looking into the death of my parents." A hint of pride touched Shirley's voice, indicating she had found someone she trusted to investigate the death of her family.

"Mr. Lockwood, the pleasure is all mine. You're a police officer, aren't you?" inquired Dean Jones. He now recognized the man and remembered the name.

"Please, call me Slade. Actually I'm retired." Slade locked eyes with the Dean. The man was protective of Shirley and Slade liked that. Obviously an old friend by the way Shirley was so comfortable around him.

"Dean Jones what brings you by? I thought you would be off on vacation this time of year." Shirley settled herself into a patio chair and motioned for Dean Jones to do the same.

"Leaving next week for the Grand Canyon. Went there two years ago and the wife and I said we must go back. Now is as good a time as ever." Dean Jones reached for a glass of iced tea that was placed in front of him by Katherine. "Thank you kind lady, this heat and humidity will dry you out in a hurry."

"I could not agree more."

After several swallows, Dean Jones looked at Shirley. "Do you know a Professor Johansen from the University of Michigan?"

"No. Am I supposed to?"

Dean Jones waited several seconds before continuing. "He called my office today and asked for Billy. He said Billy had registered to enter the National Science Fair being held at the University of Michigan's campus this year. He wanted to know what Billy was working on." Dean Jones stopped when he noticed a tremor touched Shirley's hand. She carefully set her glass down.

No one at the table spoke and the silence lingered like the quiet approach of an angry thunderhead. Of all people it was Slade who spoke.

"Why did he want to know what Billy was working on?" Slade nodded at Shirley when she raised her head and met his eyes. The silent thank you touched him.

"I don't know why. He asked that you call him." Dean Jones slid a piece of paper from his shirt pocket across the table to Shirley. "Did you know what project Billy entered?"

A negative shake of Shirley's head was followed by a faltering response. "No. No, I don't know. The last time I talked to him, Billy told me he was working on something really cool. But he always said that. You know how Billy was, Dean Jones." Shirley let her voice trail off and wiped quickly at her eyes. Billy. She missed her baby brother.

"Yes, I know. Everything was cool to Billy." Dean Jones then turned to Slade and offered an explanation. "Billy did not see the same world you and I see. Billy saw the intricate parts that make up the whole, and then he saw the pieces that made up the intricate parts. It was these pieces that so intrigued him. I have watched him glue his eyes to a microscope for hours and then ask more questions than a stadium full of scientists. Everything was a question to Billy, waiting to be answered." Dean Jones laughed out loud and was joined by Shirley.

"I wished I could have met him." Slade watched Shirley very closely.

"Have you developed anything unusual about the tragic death of Shirley's family?" Dean Jones studied the ex-cop. There was some toughness about the man, just beneath the surface threatening to break out at a moment's notice. Subtle, yet there.

"Not yet, but I'm working diligently." Slade winked at Shirley when she looked up.

Katherine sat silent, pleased Slade was showing such kindness to Shirley. There was no doubt who controlled this relationship and Katherine felt a little guilty for the way she had manipulated Slade and then just as quickly dismissed it. He had it coming.

"Well I must be off. Good to meet you Slade and good luck." Dean Jones offered his hand as he rose. "And young lady, you call if you need anything." Dean Jones gave Shirley a hug and told her he knew his way out.

As the Dean walked towards the house and the two women engaged in idle chatter, Slade's mind was racing. What science fair project had Billy been working on that so intrigued a professor from the University of Michigan? Where was the connection? Slade reached over and slid the piece of paper that Dean Jones had given Shirley towards him. Professor Johansen. What did Professor Johansen know about Billy? What was going on?

Only when he became aware of the quiet, did Slade find the two women watching him. A sly smile touched his lips and he reached for his tea.

"I think we need to call a Professor," instructed the ex-cop, rattling the ice in his glass.

Chapter Nine

The Ohio River Valley had never experienced a hurricane with the ferocity of Cleopatra. She had swept through Tallahassee, roared through Alabama and Georgia, before devastating Tennessee and Kentucky while moving north. Her violent winds and torrential rains had destroyed major areas of the country. Rivers had swelled, spilling over their banks and inundating farmland and factories. Power lines had been snapped like twigs, plunging the heart of America into darkness.

Cincinnati had not been spared. No longer classified as a hurricane, she had stalled over the city, spilling buckets of rain and pelting the city for over seventy-two hours. The mighty Ohio River had risen and then escaped her banks, sending floodwaters inland. Houses, streets, farmland, and industry, all flooded.

Weeks after the storm most factories were still without power and people were trying to piece together their lives. The governor had declared the city and the state a national disaster and was appealing to the White House for immediate federal aide. He would have to stand in line—Tennessee, Kentucky, Georgia, and Florida had already beaten him to the punch. Help would come, but not soon.

Robert Turk, Chief Engineer for Dyno Technology, looked out at the rows of idle machines. For four weeks they had been unable to produce a product. Others needed power more and had been higher on the priority list. Families temporarily relocated to government tents and emergency housing needed electricity more than he did. As a modern, industrialized society, America depended greatly on her electrical output and capacity to supply hospitals, homes, supermarkets, and factories with electricity which provided the creature comforts of a civilized country. Yesterday, power had been restored.

61

From his second story office window, he looked at the men and women performing maintenance on the rows of machines. How long before they would be in production? Luckily, the bulk of his work force owned homes that had been spared. The work helped take their minds off the problems at home. But, it could still be weeks before a product left their doors.

The shrill ring of the phone startled Robert and he looked at it a second before picking it up. In the last four weeks the phones had not rung once.

"Dyno Technology, Robert speaking." The foreman turned back to the window to stare at the workers as if his silent gaze would speed them to renewed efforts.

"This is Matt Kyle. How is everything?"

"Not well. We just got power yesterday and the floodwaters have finally receded to a level where we can start clean-up. We may be down another two to three weeks before we start milling the parts." Robert involuntarily rubbed his forehead. He had only met Kyle once after the millionaire had purchased Dyno Technology. His dislike for the man had been immediate.

"I can't wait two to three weeks," snapped Kyle, the frustration cracking into his voice. "I need those valves and fittings in three weeks. If you wait two to three weeks to start production that places me behind schedule."

"Sir, the hurricane has put us all behind schedule. We ma..." Robert was cut off.

"I don't give a damn about a hurricane! I don't care about storms, floodwaters, lack of electricity, or any damn thing else! What I do care about is the order that Dyno Technology is supposed to deliver to San Pedro in three weeks. If you can't get that done, then maybe you need replaced and I'll get someone who can. Do I make myself clear, Mr. Turk?" Kyle had been screaming into the phone and he had risen from behind his desk to pace the floor in his San Pedro office.

"Yes, sir, you do. But I can't do the impossible. I'll put us on twenty-four hour shifts, but we may still be late," countered Robert, wondering what was so damn important about a set of valves and fittings. If they had been standard size he could have produced them in several days. But the specifications he had been given by Klauss did not conform to anything they had manufactured in the past.

"There is where you and I differ, Mr. Turk. I can do the impossible. And make sure you're not late on those parts." Kyle slammed the phone onto its cradle with a resounding crack.

Robert Turk looked at the phone in his hand and gently placed it back down on his desk. Opening his top drawer, he pulled out a small rolodex. He flipped to the "A's". Might as well start calling the employees not here and inform them of the new schedule. Slowly his fingers began to punch in the first number. When the phone started to ring, Robert closed his eyes and waited for it to be picked up.

The steel hull of the freighter had been painted cobalt blue, the color of World Vision Quest. A yellow lightning bolt adorned each stern, standing out vividly in contrast to the blue background. It was noticeable from a considerable distance and drew the attention of several people on the dock as the freighter moved into Alaska's inland passage. A blue flag with the same lightning bolt flew from the bridge.

Captain Ari Theopolous stood watch on the bridge as the pilot expertly moved the large ship into the main channel. The sailing would be smooth until they hit the Gulf of Alaska and turned south towards California. Unexpected rough seas were the norm in this part of the world; they could be both unpredictable and considerable in their fury. Ari turned back to the coffee pot and poured himself another cup of the jet-black fluid. Sniffing the cup and the sweet aroma, he slurped noisily.

Ari was not worried about his ship performing. She had just been retrofitted in Valdez with both engines receiving a comprehensive overhaul. The work had been furious, going around the clock. Workers had completely overhauled the interior of the ship, replacing vast storage bins for wheat and other produce, with a series of 50,000 gallon tanks. Captain Theopolous had never seen a ship designed like this, but his job was to captain the vessel, not ask the owner why he wanted it constructed a certain way. Besides, Matt Kyle had called him personally to check on the progress and had been most pleased when Ari had told him the vessel would reach San Pedro on time.

Moving to a chair beside the pilot, Captain Ari Theopolous leaned back and propped his feet on a steel beam just below the bridge windows. Ari watched a large bald eagle glide across the Inland Passage on silent wings, its massive white head scanning the water below for an unsuspecting fish. Alaska. He would miss this place. It was beautiful, still the last rugged frontier. There was something totally American about the state—the vastness, the hidden secrets, the sheer magnitude—its immensity defied words.

Sighing once, he engaged the pilot in conversation, the thoughts about the wondrous country and strange modification to his ship forgotten.

The open curtains allowed moonlight to drift softly into the room, causing shadows to dance seductively over the two lovers. Katherine was snuggled into the right side of Slade, her leg bent ever so slightly, her beautiful hair cascading down the pillow. With small movements she traced tiny patterns on Slade's chest, moving her hands with delicate precision. It was as if she was painting a picture on living skin; an image only she could see.

The last few hours had been priceless to her. She wished she could stop the hands of time or strangle the sands slipping through the hour glass. Content to be locked in this moment for eternity, she wanted it to last forever, to dominate her thoughts, consume her emotions. Squirming slightly, she burrowed against Slade even closer, inhaling his aroma as she rubbed the tip of her nose against his neck and upper shoulder.

Never before in their relationship had Slade been so tender, so caring, so revealing. She felt she had opened a hidden door of emotions and feelings long buried. It was only in the quiet conversation that followed did she confirm her suspicions. Slade was a man of many dimensions. Dimensions easily overlooked by the casual observer because he never allowed anyone to get close, keeping those around him at arms distance. Until now, till this very moment, he had kept a space between them. But now, he was letting her in, closer, nearer to his heart where he was vulnerable.

Finally, she was getting to know 'her man.' Katherine smiled at the thought. Slade was so distant, so evasive about certain things and she was just now beginning to understand. Who was 'her man?' In halting words, he had tried to tell her.

When Slade was twenty-one he had applied to LAPD. Being a cop was a life-long dream he had nurtured from his earliest memory. As a kid he had watched all of the cop movies and television re-runs of *Dragnet, Adam 12, TJ Hooker, NYPD Blue*, and the real life version of *COPS*. The danger and allure of pursuing criminals had so appealed to him he had majored in criminology at UCLA and, upon graduating, had applied.

Slade quickly proved the agency had made a wise choice and graduated number one in his Academy Class. His career afterwards was the envy of many. Slade did his probation in the Hollywood Division. He was promoted to Corporal and transferred to South Bureau Vice. While working vice, Slade had been involved in three shootings, killing two suspects. For his bravery he was awarded the Medal of Valor and had become a two-time winner of the coveted award. Not many resided in that elite category. Still his quest and desire for perfection was not sated and he pushed harder, faster to be the best.

Supervision quickly followed for the young officer. He made sergeant, lieutenant, and captain in rapid succession. His next command assignments saw him move from one trouble spot on the agency to another. If there was a management problem, Slade Lockwood was called in to solve the issue and get the Big Blue Machine back on track. At the end of twenty years Slade was a Deputy Chief and his future was bright. The opportunity to be Police Chief was around the corner and beckoning, no longer a dream, but a tangible picture on a not to distant horizon. He had played the game and made all of the correct political decisions both inside and outside of LAPD. He was the consummate cop, from street officer to administrator.

For the young adolescent dreaming of being Joe Friday's partner to management star had been a fast and dizzying ride. For twenty years Slade had lived, eaten, and breathed LAPD. He would joke later that even his blood had turned blue. And for twenty years it had slowly consumed him, from his personality, his mannerisms, his attitude, his feelings, and, he would argue, his soul. Slade had given it all to a cause he had believed in, only to realize he had lost himself in the process. His identity had vanished, swallowed by his aspirations in law enforcement.

Katherine had remained silent as Slade had talked endlessly about how the political game on LAPD is played with all the subtle subterfuge that takes place in private industry for capital gain. In the public sector, promotion and recognition replaces financial reward, but the method is the same. You learn to hide your emotions to out fox the person vying for the same promotion or assignment. Bottle your feelings, remain stoic and poker-faced. And most importantly, do not ever show weakness. To succeed, you had to be ruthless. And Slade had succeeded.

And then it had all changed.

Revelation had come in the morning newspaper. A growing uneasiness had been developing inside him for several years. Was Los Angeles any different now than when he had signed on? Slade could make a convincing argument it was worse. The violent crime had increased. Political maneuvering by corrupt city officials was at an all time high. Had he made an impact? Joe Friday had changed the face of TV, but Slade Lockwood had not changed Los Angeles.

But what scared him the most was reading about a woman who had been killed when a crack addict shot her in the face for her purse and $40.00. She had been killed in front of her two daughters. She left behind a husband who would now have to assume the role of both.

The nothingness Slade felt was the fear awakening him to the truth. To him, she had become a crime statistic. She was an 'incident' he would have to explain to the news media and assure scared mothers it would not happen to them. And, most importantly, he would have to make sure the Big Blue Machine was not placed in a bad light.

For the first time in his life, Slade was terrified. No feeling of anger flooded his body. No sorrow for the children. No sympathy for the dad. Where was the young Slade Lockwood that had promised to right the wrongs and bring criminals to justice? Where had he gone? Where was the young Joe Friday? Had he died too?

It was then and only then, that Slade realized he had been consumed by the LAPD. It was a sleepless night, but the next morning Slade resigned. And, not surprisingly, LAPD never missed a beat. Someone else stepped into his position and the Big Blue Machine rolled on. Katherine had detected a note of resentment and anger in his voice and squeezed him tight. Several minutes would pass before he would continue.

Slade had moved to Cedar Key to 'find himself.' Katherine had laughed when Slade told her he had heard if a man starts out on a journey and walks far enough and long enough, he will come face to face with himself and have his true soul revealed. Slade had started his journey in the little island community.

"So have you walked long enough and far enough?" Katherine raised her head to stare down at him. His blue eyes were soft and he examined every inch of her face before responding.

"Not yet, but I have hope." Slade reached up a hand and moved Katherine's hair from her shoulder.

"You have changed," mused Katherine. "What was the reason?" asked the artist, snuggling into his chest and being rewarded with his arm encircling her waist.

"You. I could not stand the thought of losing you."

Katherine raised back up and looked at him when she heard the doubt enter his voice.

"You will never lose me, Slade Lockwood. That is as long as you can put up with helping the needy when they call."

"I should never have told you my weakness. Now I'm vulnerable." Slade tried to sound stern.

"I already knew your weakness, Mr. Lockwood. Woman's intuition." Katherine leaned down and kissed him gently.

"I don't suppose you would want to share? The intuition I mean."

"Not a chance. Not a chance under the stars."

Chapter Ten

The wooden floors creaked ever so slightly, but it was enough to awaken Slade, who lifted his head to stare in the direction of the sound. Slade saw Katherine's silhouette drift in from the bathroom. She had only taken a couple of steps when she stumbled into his clothes, which had been discarded in a rush during the heat of passion hours earlier. It was his shoe she hit, bending her toe back at an odd angle.

"Ouch."

"You okay?"

"Yes. Sorry. Didn't mean to wake you." Katherine stopped long enough to rub her foot. "You better clean this place up, Mister, or your bedroom is going to look like a work room." Katherine had started to laugh when she was cut short by Slade.

For a split second several emotions tried to wrestle for dominance on his face. First, it was humor to join Katherine in laughter. And then curiosity as a thought struck. And lastly realization as the answer hit. In the span of that split second, Slade's heart constricted and his mind became clear. His leaping out of bed sent Katherine's laughter into a shriek and she took several involuntary steps backwards, bumping into the dresser.

Realizing he had startled her, Slade stopped, looked at her, started to move in her direction, and then froze. Raising his hand to speak, he stopped again and then looked frantically around the room. Katherine never moved during his strange antics.

"The phone. Where's the phone?"

"Here it is." Katherine offered the phone at arm's length.

Snatching the phone from her, Slade quickly began to dial a number and then slammed his thumb on the disconnect button when the connection was not made.

"Shirley's number?"

Katherine stepped forward and pulled the phone out of his grasp and looked him in the eye. She had regained her composure.

"Slade it's almost two o'clock in the morning. What's wrong?" Katherine hung onto the phone when he reached for it.

"Billy's room. Too neat, too orderly. I knew something was bothering me about it when I saw it yesterday, but I couldn't place it."

"What are you talking about?"

"No work space. If Billy is entering all of these science fairs, then where was he doing the research? His bedroom is not big enough and there was no evidence of any research in his room. It was too orderly."

"Then where was Billy doing his resear..." Katherine was cut off by Slade.

"That's why I'm calling Shirley. I don't care if it is two o'clock in the morning." Slade reached again for the phone.

It was Katherine who dialed the number and handed it to Slade when it started to ring. Luckily it was a cordless phone, because the minute the receiver was in his hand he started to move around the room. It was the fourth ring before Shirley picked up.

"Shirley! This is Slade. Are you awake?"

"I am now. Is something wrong?" Shirley rubbed the sleep from her eyes and squinted at the alarm clock perched on the night stand. 1:47 AM. Was Slade losing his mind?

"Listen to me carefully, Shirley. Are you listening?" Slade was not aware he was yelling until Katherine touched his arm and pointed to her ear.

"Yes, I'm listening," answered the confused girl. "What is it, Slade? You're scaring me."

"I'm sorry. Where did Billy do his research for his science fair projects?" Every muscle in Slade's body was tense.

"Oh my gosh! I didn't even think of that. I'm such an idiot." Shirley was now out of bed and moving towards the light switch. Any sleep cobwebs were gone and seconds later the room was bathed in light.

"That's okay. Where did he do research?"

"In a detached garage of an old house that my grandparents owned. When they died they willed it to my mother, and mom and dad rented out the house, but turned the garage into a lab for Billy. He has all of his stuff there." Shirley paused and started to tremble. A tear gathered in the corner of each eye and started to build. How could she have been so stupid to overlook this? But what was the significance? "How is this important?"

"I don't know. I do know a Professor from Michigan is calling and even after he's told Billy is dead, he still wants to talk to you. And after we call him, he's even more curious about what Billy was working on. And now, I want to know what Billy was working on. It may be nothing, but it may be what we need. Now where is Billy's lab?"

Less than a minute later Slade slammed the phone down after telling Shirley to stay home. Turning towards Katherine, who had remained standing in the middle of the room, Slade said, "Want to go on a bike ride?"

"At this hour?"

"We'll beat the traffic."

They both started to laugh as they grabbed shorts and shoes.

Egypt, Libya, and Spain all within two weeks. The countries were agreeing to terms and placing deposits with World Vision Quest. Clyde Sommer stared out the window of the jumbo jet and saw his face reflected back to him. It was mid-afternoon and the sky was bright, cloudless. How many miles had he logged?

The only reward was money and he was about to become a millionaire many times over. Just his commission was going to make him rich. The total deposits were quickly reaching two billion dollars and once production started that number would explode.

Five weeks ago he would never have believed this possible. But now? Clyde leaned his head back and stared at the cabin ceiling in disbelief. Even now it was hard to comprehend. So much money in such a short amount of time. One day a computer salesman and the next, riches beyond belief. So much, so fast. Unbelievable.

Forcing himself to focus on the job at hand, he reached for his briefcase and unlocked the clasp. Australia was next. Kyle had called and changed his itinerary again. Sommer had been instructed to deal with Spain and several smaller countries first, before going 'down under.' The Aussies represented a prize as large as Saudi Arabia, maybe even larger. Kyle was convinced the Aussies would recognize an opportunity and seize the initiative. It would give them a chance to become more of a world player because they already had production lines in place to handle bulk shipping. Clyde had wanted to go to Australia first, even before the Saudis, but Kyle had decided otherwise.

Matt Kyle. The man was possessed with this project. Kyle was convinced this was his ticket to stardom and immortality in the world of business. But how much was enough? The man was already a multimillionaire. How much more did he need? Money was power, but how much power did Kyle want? Enough to influence or direct neighboring countries with technology? Was that his game?

Clyde let his eyes drift to the stewardess walking slowly towards him wearing a perpetual smile. After declining a beverage, she moved on and Clyde focused back on the proposal for Australia. Whatever his egocentric boss was up to was his business. Clyde was just a salesman delivering a product.

Reaching into a back pocket of the briefcase, Clyde produced a small folder with the word 'Australia' printed across it. Better check the numbers and production output a second time. Preparedness was a salesman's ticket to success and this deal alone could net him over a million dollars in commission.

The bicycle tires crunched on the small gravel lining the roadway from Slade's house. Glancing over his shoulder, Slade made sure Katherine navigated in safety. The small rocks could torque the handlebars if she was not careful and the darkness did not help. He was rewarded by a smile from her as she pedaled alongside.

"You really know how to show a girl a good time," chided Katherine, easily keeping pace with Slade. She could sense he wanted to go faster, but kept the pace slow so she could follow.

"One of my many traits." Slade let his bike sweep into a shallow curve that led to downtown Cedar Key.

The address Shirley had given Slade was on the outskirts of town. Once the house was described to him by Shirley, Slade remembered it vividly. It was a turn of the century two story home painted yellow and white. The garage was not visible from the roadway, but the original design had not called for a garage to house automobiles. The original intent of the detached structure was to house horses. The small stable had been converted to a garage when cars replaced the horse. Later, the Waterbury's had converted the old stable into work space for Billy.

The ride had taken less than five minutes. Nothing was very far on Cedar Key. Slade was impressed with how Katherine had kept-up. Initially he thought she would have complained, but she had eagerly wanted to go, despite the lateness of the hour.

"We'll leave the bikes here. Shirley said you get to the garage on the far side of the house. I think she meant the west side," instructed Slade, leaning his bike against a fence in the front yard. The house was rented to a retired couple from New Hampshire. They were both in their mid-sixties and had moved to Florida to escape the cold.

As they walked down the path to the back of the house, they both spoke in hushed tones. Slade had forgotten to ask Shirley if the couple owned a dog. If they did, hopefully it was a sound sleeper.

"If a big mean dog shows up, you jump in front of me," directed Katherine, moving closer to Slade.

"Gee, thanks."

"Won't the door be locked?" Katherine was trying to follow in Slade's footsteps in the limited light.

"Shirley said Billy kept a key under a planter just to the left of the door."

"Oh."

Katherine was about to speak to Slade and tell him how he was going to have to make breakfast for dragging her out in the middle of the night, when she felt his hand grab her forearm and squeeze. Katherine immediately felt the tenseness in his grip and pressed her body against his. Without knowing how, she knew something was wrong.

Just as he was about to round the corner of the house, Slade had moved slightly off the trail. A large camellia bush had grown a prodigious girth. The old bush was at least fifteen feet high and nearing twelve feet in diameter. Slade saw a stepping stone to the side of the bush providing a detour between the camellia and the fence. He was about to tell Katherine to watch her step when he noticed light.

The garage was approximately forty feet behind the house and slightly to the left. The path leading to the garage had been the old buggy road and, at one time, had been about twelve feet wide.

The doors on the front of the stable had been replaced with walls. What appeared to be the door was near the side. A tiny window was located high on the door and it was from this window that Slade had seen a beam of light. After several seconds he had seen the beam of light a second time. Someone was inside the garage, quite possibly with a flashlight.

Moving deep within the shadows, Slade pulled Katherine to him. Pressing his lips to her ear, he whispered, "Go call the police. There is a public phone about a half mile up the road. It's closer than the house."

"Who do you think it is?" Katherine's heart was pounding.

"I don't know, but I know it's not Shirley or someone who belongs there."

"How do you know that?"

"If they belonged there, they would have turned on the lights. Whoever this is, they don't want to be seen."

Picking up on his change in demeanor, Katherine whispered back, "You be safe. I'll have the police here as soon as I can." Without another word she turned and moved quickly down the path, expertly retracing her steps.

Slade watched her disappear. At first he had thought about waking the couple inside the residence, but had just as quickly dismissed the idea. Whoever was inside the garage would hear him knocking. Besides, the old couple was probably hard of hearing and it would take a considerable amount of time to wake them. Slade needed to know the identity of the person inside the garage now, not later.

With considerable care, Slade moved to the garage door, being careful to stay in the shadows. Once at the door he moved ever so slight until he could peer inside. The door was open about ten inches and Slade had to flatten against the wall and crane his neck.

The building was bigger on the inside than he had anticipated. At one time there had been two stalls for the horses and a separate place for the buggy. Hank had redesigned the interior for Billy. Slade could see a computer and a file cabinet along one wall. A large table dominated that side of the room and papers were scattered haphazardly. A file cabinet was next to the computer and Slade saw a man carefully opening each file before tossing them onto the table top. It appeared as if the man had already gone through the top file drawer as it was partially open and appeared empty.

"Hey, Sam, I think I found it." The man at the file cabinet turned to look towards the back of the room.

"Make sure. We don't want to leave anything." Sam moved towards Bart as he answered, a two gallon gas can in his hand.

"He has a lot of shit in here. That kid wrote about everything," muttered Bart, tucking the file he had just taken into the top of his pants. Bart's cast had been replaced by a rubber walking boot, causing him to move slowly.

"If we got what we need let's go. Unplug the computer. We'll take it. He'll want it," ordered Sam, taking the lid off the gas can.

Slade expectantly waited for the police. It was obvious they were going to burn the garage. Whatever the Waterburys had been killed for, the answer resided in this room. If Katherine did not hurry, the answer would be lost.

Taking a chance, Slade leaned more into the doorway and peered into the garage. It took several seconds for his eyes to adjust. Only when Sam swung his light to the rear of the room did Slade get a chance to see the rest of the interior. There were different science fair projects lining the walls. Closer to Sam and Bart were fifteen gallon buckets with small trees growing in them. Slade did not recognize them, but they were all about six to eight feet tall. They each had a piece of tape on them, with some type of writing.

Apparently the older projects were towards the rear. Slade looked back at the two burglars when he heard the splash of gasoline. Any moment now and they would strike the match. Where were the police? What was taking Katherine so long? Slade mentally cursed himself for not bringing a weapon.

His name was Walter. He was a Jack Russell Terrier and the prized pet of the old couple. Walter had a doggie door at the back of the house and had complete run of the house and yard. Walter was the old couple's 'baby' and was pampered. His sleek coat and pronounced belly was testimony to the care he received.

Walter had been asleep on a small mat in the bedroom, when he heard a sound at the rear of the house. At ten years of age, his hearing had diminished, but his inquisitive nature had not. Moving as quietly as he had when many years younger, Walter made it downstairs and out the doggie door. He was rewarded with seeing a man peering inside the garage. Only the old couple and a young boy who brought him doggie bones used this door. Walter immediately tensed his body. The youth from years past flooded his tiny frame and his senses became fine tuned. He moved stiff-legged towards his quarry.

This was his house and his yard and this stranger was about to find that out first hand. With every hair on his small body standing on end, Walter moved silently closer to the back of the strange man.

Katherine had pedaled with all her might and was slightly out of breath when she made it to the public phone. It was at a convenience store in the center of Cedar Key. Dropping the bike on the sidewalk, Katherine sprinted to the phone and snatched it off the hook, frantically punching in 911. After pressing the receiver to her ear and not hearing anything, she dialed 911 a second time. All the while she had been staring back at where she had left Slade as if her eyes could penetrate the darkness. It was not until she looked at the phone a third time did she see the 'out of order' sign taped to the booth.

Panicking, Katherine hung up the phone and silently cursed. What should she do? Where was the nearest phone? Her heart leaped! Her studio was close by, less than a quarter of a mile. Just as quickly her hopes died. She did not have her keys to the front door.

Grabbing her bike, Katherine straddled the seat and placed a foot on one of the pedals. Slade's. It was the only answer. Making up her mind, Katherine started to pedal towards his house. A silent urgency caused her to pedal with a fury she had never known. Katherine knew Slade was in danger. She did not know how she knew this, but she just knew.

Chapter Eleven

Shirley Waterbury walked from her bedroom to the kitchen and back again, her bare feet padding noiselessly on the hardwood floor. Each step was punctuated by her staring at the cordless phone held tightly in her hand. Twice she had tried to dial Slade's cell phone, but received no answer. When she tried Katherine's cell phone, she received a recording. Finally she had tried Slade's house with no results. Where were they? Were they alright? A thousand questions, with a thousand possible scenarios flooded her worried young mind.

Shirley moved back towards the kitchen and stopped in the hallway to stare at a portrait of her family. Her eyes locked on the face of her mother. Her mother's eyes were calm, steady, yet thoughtful and insightful. What would she do right now? Shirley knew she would not be standing here when the answer was somewhere else. Smiling, Shirley turned and fled to her bedroom, discarding her robe in an untidy heap as she ran. She was a Waterbury, and like her mother, she was not afraid to confront and find the answers she sought.

Walter lowered his body and felt the grass rub his belly. His nose had picked up the scent of the other two men inside the garage, but he was focused on the immediate target. There would be plenty of people to bite tonight. Silently Walter curled his lip, revealing impressive teeth for a dog his size.

Just as he was about to charge the leg in front of him, the man shifted his weight, causing Walter to stop.

Slade moved further into the doorway to peer into the old stable that had masqueraded as a lab for a young genius. The door opened silently, the hinges moving quietly as Slade leaned into the door. The door lock had been pried off by a crowbar. What was left of the twisted metal was hanging on the

74

door jam by a single screw. Slade found the crowbar propped against the outside wall, its usefulness for the moment gone.

The faces of the two men looked familiar. What was their interest in Billy's stuff? They were methodically conducting a search for particular items. Slade did not risk moving into the room any further.

Walter had waited long enough. With a wild rush, Walter rushed forward biting Slade on the left calf. Simultaneously with the biting, Walter barked and growled, sounding more like a rottweiler, than a Jack Russell. The desired effect was achieved, as the man jumped forward, banging into the door.

Slade had been caught completely off guard by the dog's attack. Later, he would admit the dog had scared the wits out of him. He was already tense from peering into the garage and trying not to be seen.

When Walter bit him, Slade had involuntarily jumped forward, slamming into the open door and causing it to swing violently outwards. The two men in the room snatched their heads up and looked at the door, focusing first on Slade, then Walter, and then back to Slade. It only took them a split second to recognize what had occurred.

Slade was framed in the doorway when he looked directly into the eyes of the killers. For a second their eyes locked, riveting on each other in silent combat. When the tension broke, the next several seconds happened in slow motion, even though it occurred in the wink of an eye. Both Sam and Burt reached quickly for hidden weapons, massive Glock 40 calibers outfitted with menacing silencers. Both killers dropped what they were holding and swung the guns up to get a bead on Slade, both hands wrapped around the butt of the weapons to steady their aim.

Slade moved with incredible speed and certainty, his animal instinct dominating his mind and body. He knew there was one way in and one way out. When he saw the two men reach for weapons, his desire to survive took control. Walter's attack had forced Slade several feet into the doorway until he realized it was not a large dog. Walter he could deal with; the gunmen were a different story.

Without hesitating, Slade propelled himself backwards into the door that had swung shut. The broken lock is what saved his life. Meeting no resistance from the locking mechanism, the door rocketed open from Slade's weight. Due to his momentum, Slade hit the door and went backwards onto his back, his feet driving like pistons to shove his body out of the line of fire. Out of the corner of his eye, he saw repeated muzzle flashes from the guns and heard the silenced spits. The sound of bullets raced towards him and buzzed past his head, angry bees on an errant path. Any one of the silenced rounds would tear him to pieces at such close quarters.

Slade rolled to his right searching for darkness. Light was his enemy, an enemy that silhouetted him to the gunmen. He felt a searing, burning sensation in his left rib cage and he knew he had been struck by one of the massive rounds. No time to access the damage, he had to move or die. Clawing with both hands and feet, Slade cleared the doorway as he heard both men drop empty magazines and slam new rounds into their weapons. These men meant business. If the police did not arrive in the next several seconds, he may die. Unarmed, he was no match for two killers.

To get to Billy's lab, Shirley had the option of taking a route leading her past Slade's house or a shorter route straight through the center of town. For some strange reason, Shirley had taken the route leading to Slade's. Later, she would say her decision to take the long route was an act of God.

Rounding the curve slightly faster than she should have, Shirley almost did not see Katherine pedaling furiously in the dark. Slamming on the brakes, Shirley's car slid to a stop several feet in front of Katherine who had slid her bike sideways to avoid being hit.

Shirley was out of the vehicle and sprinting to the front of the car, where both frantic women met. Katherine was out of breath, but grabbed Shirley tightly when she recognized her.

"Are you al-" Shirley was cut off by the artist.

"Your cell phone. Do you have it? Men are in Billy's garage and I left Slade. Need the police," shrieked Katherine, her voice trying to gain control as she tried to catch her breath. She had been pedaling as hard as she could to get to a phone and her lungs burned from the exertion.

"Come on! You can call on the way," instructed Shirley, pulling Katherine off the bike and shoving her towards the passenger side front seat.

Once inside the car, Katherine grabbed the cell phone and punched in 911. The call was answered on the third ring by a late night police dispatcher.

Shirley listened with one ear as Katherine told the police dispatcher about the burglars inside Billy's lab. With both eyes glued to the road, Shirley pressed the accelerator to the floor and skidded around the curve, both rear tires churning up gravel and dust as the car shot forward. Katherine slammed the cell phone shut and looked at Shirley.

"Hurry. Please, hurry. I should've never left him." Katherine's eyes were riveted on the roadway and the bouncing headlights. Slade! He was all she could think about.

Dodging out of the doorway, Slade rolled into the crowbar left by the two assassins. Grabbing the work tool now turned lethal weapon, Slade stood and moved into the shadows by the door. The dog had retreated to a bush in front of the door and was continuing to bark. His only chance was to even the odds slightly when they rushed the door. He was hoping they would think he had run from the garage. All he had to do was spring the trap if they took the bait.

"Grab the computer." Sam lit a match and dropped it to the floor. The fumes from the gasoline had drifted over most of the room and they ignited first, bursting into flame and filling the interior with a fireball. Both killers were temporarily engulfed in flames. Bart screamed and stumbled towards the door, dropping the computer as he tried to find his way to safety. Sam threw the gas can away from him and it exploded, sending a stream of fire towards him. Some gasoline had dripped down his pants leg and now it caught his clothes on fire.

Outside the door, Slade could feel the rush of heat from the initial fireball and he heard the screams from the two men inside. He tensed his body when he heard one of the men rush towards the door.

Just as Bart cleared the door, he started to turn to his left, directly into Slade's path. For a brief instant he saw the silhouette of a man, holding what he thought was a baseball bat. Too late he knew he should duck, but could not move fast enough. The crowbar impacted right above his eyes in the center of his forehead with a sickening, dull thud. Bart was lifted off of his feet and propelled back through the doorway. The folder he had taken from Billy's cabinet was still in his waistband.

When Bart was knocked backwards, the file came loose and the contents scattered into the entranceway. One piece of paper landed near Slade and he quickly picked it up, stuffing it into his pocket.

Sam saw Bart fly back into the room, the Glock .40 still clutched tightly in his left hand and he saw the blood gushing from Bart's head. Without taking time to aim, he fired several rounds towards the door and wall. He only had moments before the building would be engulfed. Already the smoke was stinging his eyes and obscuring his vision.

Slade had reached for additional papers, but when Sam started firing Slade knew he would have to retreat. Luckily Slade had been crouching near the door, because the bullets carved holes into the wood above his head before disappearing into the night. Slade turned and fled down the wall towards the back. Reaching the end of the building, he turned the corner and sprinted for a low fence.

He had been hoping to get the gun from the man he had killed, but when the killer fell back into the garage all hope disappeared. The second killer would not be as careless as the first. Time was everything now, each second precious. Slade had to retreat fast and continued to run, his arms and legs pumping wildly.

Stepping up next to Bart, Sam pried the remainder of the file from the dead man's hand and moved to the door. There was no time to gather the remaining pages. How many pages did the man get? Sam stepped into the doorway, firing as he moved.

Sam heard the sounds of Slade running from the garage. Turning towards the road, Sam moved towards the street and safety. They had parked

Burt's old pickup truck around the corner. Sam knew he needed medical attention. The fireball had singed his eyelashes off and burned most of the hair on his head. The gasoline from the can had burned his pants legs to the skin. But first, he must escape without being seen. That was proving to be more difficult by the minute.

All of the noise had awakened people. Lights were coming on in the house and he could hear the residents calling for "Walter." Sam moved onto the street, tucking his gun into his waistband. Pulling his shirt over the weapon, Sam walked towards his truck and slipped quietly inside. Just as he closed the door, he saw a dark colored, older Toyota Camry slide into the driveway and two women jump out. Both of them looked in the direction of the garage and both screamed simultaneously when they saw the fire and smoke billowing from the old horse barn. Sam recognized both of them. He had seen Katherine around town and he had known Shirley Waterbury for years. That meant Katherine's boyfriend was the man who had killed Bart.

Without pausing to think any longer, Sam started the truck and eased away from the scene. He waited until he was several blocks away before turning his lights on. Already he was thinking how he was going to tell Matt Kyle about this, his medical needs taking second stage. A large knot formed in the pit of his stomach and started to move towards his throat. His palms were sweaty and it took a considerable amount of effort to regain some semblance of control. What would Kyle say or do?

For the first time since he was a kid, Sam Andrew found a lump of fear had settled deep inside his bones and his body grew cold. Matt Kyle was not to be taken lightly.

Chapter Twelve

The hospital lights were unusually intense. The directional lights shined directly onto Slade, illuminating him in a harsh white brightness. There was also the smell that accompanied hospitals. It was an antiseptic, prescription smell. It also had the nasty habit of lingering long after you were gone. The nauseating odor drifted into the weave of most fabrics and he knew he would have to wash his clothes to rid himself of it.

The injury to his ribs had required several stitches, but no surgery. The bullet had cut a groove from his hip area, up towards his pectoral muscle, tucking tightly against his ribcage. It had torn the skin and a little muscle. Slightly deeper and the damage would have been severe. Still, he would have a nice scar.

During the entire proceeding, Katherine was hovering around him, watching with concern, eying every move the doctor made. Several times the doctor had to ask her to move back. Slade smiled inwardly at her obvious concern. She was a remarkable woman and when their eyes met, he smiled. She nervously smiled back and quickly glanced at the monitor tracking his blood pressure and heart rate.

Shirley was just as bad. Shirley continued to wring her hands in apparent grief and anger at forgetting to tell Slade about Billy's lab. With all she had been through, he could not let her continue to blame herself. As soon as the doctor was done, Slade wanted out of the hospital.

When Sam had burst out of the garage, Slade had already made it to the rear of the building and across the fence. He stopped to see what direction Sam would take. When he heard Sam run towards the front of the yard, Slade moved in pursuit, more to observe than to apprehend.

Concealing himself in the bushes by the front of the house, Slade watched Sam run to the old pickup. At the same time, Shirley and Katherine had arrived and started to scream. Slade quickly calmed them down and obtained Shirley's cell phone. A quick 911 call and the fire trucks were on their way. Cedar Key had a volunteer Fire Department and their response was not as quick as a fully staffed, full-time unit. By the time they arrived the garage was gone. All information relating to what Billy had been working on was up in smoke.

The police arrived along with the Fire Department and Slade had repeated the story several times. They became extremely interested when told about the dead man. Cedar Key Police Chief, Bubba Singletee, admonished Slade not to leave town.

"Well I think you will be okay. Next time don't cut it so close." Dr. Wagner had come to Cedar Key to relax and semi-retire. This was the first gunshot victim he had tended since his arrival three years ago.

"Any special restrictions, Dr. Wagner?" Katherine moved to Slade's side.

"No physical activity that would directly affect the area for several days. I'm giving him a prescription for an antibiotic to fight off infection. Other than that, he will be as good as new," reassured Dr. Wagner, scribbling some notes on Slade's chart. Lifting his eyes, he looked directly at Slade. "Come and see me in a couple of days and I'll remove the stitches. I'm giving you a small quantity of pain killers. After that, use aspirin or Tylenol."

"Sure will. Am I ready to check out, Doc?" Slade moved to a sitting position. Katherine immediately steadied him and Shirley moved up as well, even though he did not need their help.

"Yes, you are," laughed Dr. Wagner. "You seem to have a good support group."

Thirty minutes later, Slade was being driven home by Shirley with Katherine in the front passenger seat. Katherine turned every couple of seconds to look at him. The drive to his house was done in silence.

The pain killer Dr. Wagner had given him had not worn off and Slade was able to walk up the stairs without assistance. It was not until they were seated in the living room that the silence was broken.

"I don't want you to look into this any longer, Slade." Shirley stared straight at him as she spoke, her eyes wide and defiant. A sternness was enveloping her he had not seen before. She was discovering an inner strength, her mother's strength thought Slade.

"Why?" was all Slade asked, sipping from a chilled glass of mango and orange juice.

"Because I've lost my entire family and you and Katherine are all I have left and I'm not going to lose either of you. That's why." Shirley's brow wrinkled in frustration. That was the most stupid question she had ever been asked and if he was not injured she feared she would have slapped him.

80

"So we're going to let the killers get away? We're not going to bring them to justice?" Slade's voice was level, his tone flat. No expression hit his face; no tenseness entered his body.

"Let the cops take over. We have enough information for them. Surely they don't think Shirley's parents died in an accident. Not now. Not after what happened." Katherine moved closer to Slade. It was almost like he was a machine, a robot trained and devoid of emotion. And then she remembered what he had said about being in management on LAPD when he played the game. *You hide your feelings, you look for the most expedient, viable alternative to succeed and then you put your plan into action.* Was this the man Slade had run from? Now she was beginning to understand.

"Yeah. Let them take over, Slade. You said so yourself you're not trained in this area. I almost got you killed tonight." Shirley let her voice trail off and lowered her eyes. A quietness settled over the room, causing a stillness to envelope them.

"Let's look at the facts. First, you did not almost get me killed. I should have asked the proper questions to begin with. To be honest, up until tonight I still thought there was an outside possibility your family had been killed in an accident. The phone call from the professor at Michigan alerted me somewhat, but not enough. If he was interested in what Billy was working on, then it should've clued me in someone else may be, too. Someone that may kill to get it or keep it. It wasn't until I was outside the doorway to Billy's lab that I realized whoever killed your family wanted to make sure they found all the information Billy had. Besides, I didn't tell the cops everything."

For the next half an hour, Slade told them what had happened, up to and including seeing the man get into the pick-up truck.

"Why didn't you tell the police this," asked Shirley.

"Because if they don't find a silencer, then I can't trust them."

"You mean they could be in on it, too?"

"Exactly. You said so yourself: the police classified the death of your parents as an accident. Their report was sent to the Coast Guard, but without some suspicion on the part of the local authorities, the Coast Guard investigators are not going to look too closely. I bet they didn't even conduct a thorough investigation." Slade drained the last of his juice and started to get up, but Katherine motioned him to stay seated and quickly retrieved the carton of mango/orange juice.

"Thank you, gorgeous."

"You're welcome."

"But we still have nowhere to go." Shirley did not mean to, but she sounded dejected.

"Not exactly. Whatever Billy was working on was of such importance someone is willing to kill for it. We need to find out what that was. Did Billy keep any other files of his work?"

"No. Mom and Dad made him keep everything in his lab. He had so much stuff it would have taken up acres of shelf space. He was always looking at things and conducting research. It could be anything."

"Not anything." Slade reached for his front pants pocket. "I was able to get one piece of paper from the file the two killers were trying to make off with." Carefully Slade unfolded the piece of paper and slowly read the contents. Part of the page was full of a formula that meant nothing to Slade. Katherine had moved to a position behind his shoulder.

"What do you make of this?" Slade handed the piece of paper to Shirley.

Shirley took the paper and stared at the writing. It was definitely Billy's.

"This appears to be the chemical makeup of a plant. Here on the bottom of the paper, Billy is describing where it grows, mostly around the edges of salt marshes. The rest of the description is cut off. I wish you could have gotten more of the file."

"So do I. Can you identify the formula?" Slade shifted his weight.

"It will take time, but yes." Shirley lifted her head from the paper and looked at Slade. "You said there were plants in Billy's lab. Can you describe them? How many were there?" The scientist in Shirley was taking over and the questions started to flow.

"There were four to five of them. They were about five to six feet tall, with dark green leaves. The leaves were not real big, and kind of tear shaped. I wouldn't have noticed them, except they were close to the door."

"They were in buckets?"

"Yeah. Appeared to be fifteen gallon buckets."

"Can I change your thought process for a minute?" Katherine entered the conversation. When Slade nodded yes, she continued. "How do you know the guys were amateurs?"

"Because they set the fire while they were still inside the lab. The gas fumes, especially in a closed space, created a small bomb. When the one killer dropped the match, he had to have been engulfed in flames. The one I hit with the crowbar screamed like he was being burned alive. A pro would have thrown the match from outside."

"You're basing it all on that?" Katherine curled her legs under her.

"Not entirely. When I jumped back out the doorway, they both fired at the door and not to either side. It wasn't until after I hit the first guy that the second guy fired near the door. They both should have done that first. It would have increased their chances of killing me." When Slade finished, Katherine buried her head on his arm and squeezed softly.

"Well, I'm glad he missed." Katherine tried to add a tone of bravery to her voice.

"You okay?" Slade kissed her on the forehead. When she said she was, he said, "Good. Can you miss a couple of days at the studio?"

"Yes. Why?"

"Because I want you and Shirley to go through Billy's room with a fine tooth comb. I want anything relating to that formula or anything that may tell us what he was working on. I also want a copy of the last six months of phone records," Slade paused as Shirley had grabbed a piece of paper and was writing down his instructions. When Shirley glanced up at him, he continued. "Also, did Billy have any friends he may have invited over to talk with? Dean Jones at the high school, maybe? Anybody. I need their names and phone numbers."

"Slade, I would feel better if we gave this to someone else," droned Shirley, her pencil poised above the paper.

"Who knows Billy better than you? After tonight, who has more of a motive to see justice than me?" Slade arched his eyebrows. "Shirley, I don't know who we can trust, but I know we can trust each other."

"While we're doing this, what are you gonna do?" Katherine rubbed Slade's shoulders.

"I'm going to look at a boat," smiled the ex-cop, sipping again from his chilled glass of juice.

"I thought I told you to do nothing unless you checked with me? Didn't you understand that, you fucking idiot!" screamed Kyle, tiny veins popping out all over his neck and face. He was so close and yet so far. These bumbling buffoons in Cedar Key could ruin the whole thing, could kill his dream and destroy World Vision Quest.

"We only found out about it a couple of hours ago. An old friend of theirs was drinking with us at the bar and we were talking about Hank and his family going out the night of the 'cane. That's when he told us about the kid working in that old building. We destroyed everything that could be linked to the kid." Fear touched the very corners of Sam's heart.

"Did the cop ... what's his name ..."

"Slade Lockwood."

"Slade Lockwood." Kyle had heard that name enough. "Did he get anything out of the garage before it burned down?" Kyle purposely lowered his voice and exerted a calm he did not feel. Great men flourished in adversarial circumstances. Great men do not make history; great history makes great men. Kyle lowered himself into his large leather chair in his office, reaching for his rolodex of names even as he was speaking to Sam and repeating the quote he had chanted all of his adult life.

"I don't think so. He was running for his life." Sam was pleased his boss had lowered his voice and calmed down.

"Did he overhear anything?" pressed Kyle, his fingers stopping at a card marked 'Leonard.'

"There was nothin' to overhear. We never said nothin'," answered Sam, trying desperately to think about the conversation from hours earlier. He had treated his burns. They were not as bad as he had first believed. His hair was another story. It would be weeks before it all grew back.

"Good. I want you to sit tight. Mr. Lockwood may have over stayed his welcome. I'm sending someone to help you remove our problem, but I don't want any action taken until he arrives. Do I make myself clear?" Kyle could not keep a small amount of irritation from entering his voice.

"You certainly do. I will wait here until I hear from your guy."

"Good. You do that." Kyle waited several seconds before dialing the next number. The phone was answered on the second ring.

"Hello."

"Leonard. Kyle. You were supposed to get back to me about this Slade Lockwood."

"It's four o'clock in the morning. Didn't want to wake you." Leonard rolled out of bed and reached for a cigarette. A half empty pack of Marlboros was on the table, next to an empty bottle of beer.

"Well I'm awake now, so bore me with the details." Kyle propped his feet up on his desk. Leonard did not hesitate but started to narrate from memory.

"Left LAPD suddenly after twenty years. Was a rising star and had just been promoted to Deputy Chief two years before retirement. Everyone I talked to spoke highly of the guy. Most people thought he had a shot at making police chief if he had stuck around."

"Why did he quit?" There had to be a reason, mused Kyle. No one walked away from power and glory unless there was a good reason. Everyone was affected by greed, especially cops.

"No one knows why and he never really gave an answer. Just said it was time."

"Bullshit. No one leaves just like that unless there's a reason. Did he have any skeletons in the closet? Any old girlfriends? What about his financial picture?"

"No skeletons I could find. Had very few enemies and even they speak highly of the guy. His financial picture is good, solid. In addition to his retirement, he invested some money in stocks and quite heavily in a 457 program that will yield him a considerable sum over time if he manages it properly. He should be able to live in ease the rest of his life."

"Wife? Kids?"

"Never married. His parents are still alive and live in Tampa. Doesn't really have a hobby or outside interest." Leonard shuffled through the rest of his notes on the coffee table in his one-bedroom apartment.

"Well, this non-descript guy is nosing around in our business. It seems he needs to meet with an accident. I want you in Cedar Key by tomorrow morning. Let me know if you need anything." Kyle hung up.

Leonard reached for a photograph he had gotten of Slade from the newspaper. Leonard eyed the picture carefully, committing the image to memory. In less than two days, Slade Lockwood would be dead if all went as planned. Leonard placed the photograph back onto his coffee table and got up. He had to pack for a cross country trip.

Matt Kyle spun slowly in his leather chair until he could look out of his office window at the port of San Pedro. Slade Lockwood. With him gone, the girl would have no one to turn to and would be paralyzed. If not, she could be removed too. The decision made, Kyle reached for the phone again. He had not heard from Sommer since he had arrived in Australia.

Asking for an international operator, Kyle had already forgotten about the death warrant he had just put into motion for a man he had never known. He was concerned with history and where he would be remembered in the business archives.

Shirley and Katherine had spent the better part of the morning looking through Billy's room. They had stumbled across novels. Everything from science fiction to anatomy to biology to the exploration of space. Katherine had flipped through some of the books and had become quickly lost in the technical information.

"Don't feel bad, I don't understand some of the stuff either. Billy was way ahead of all of us when it comes to this stuff." Shirley sounded very much like a proud, older sister.

"Did he ever just read for pleasure?" Katherine deposited an issue of Science America on the bed.

"This was enjoyment to him. He would read an article then come and talk to me about it for hours, especially if it interested him. Billy was a walking, talking encyclopedia of facts. He could name every country in the world, along with the capital, the minerals mined there, population, etc. When he read something it became permanently engraved in his mind, much like information on a computer chip. Except Billy processed information far faster than any computer."

"Raising him must have been difficult." Katherine took time to glance at a chart of the elements above Billy's bed. Most young teenage boys would have had a cheerleader or bikini model on the wall. Billy was more concerned with atomic weights.

"Not really. Mom was in tune to him. Even though she did not understand a lot of what Billy worked on, she encouraged him to explore the vast reaches of his intellect." Shirley paused and stared out of Billy's window at the rose bushes lining the drive. "She did the same for me, except I don't have Billy's intellect."

"You seem pretty smart to me, kiddo." Katherine laughed, trying to ease the pain creeping like a thief into the young woman's voice.

"Thank you for saying so, but like I've told you and Slade, Billy was the genius. I just wonder how smart he really was." Shirley lifted Billy's mattress.

85

She found several magazines and was about to drop the mattress when a thought occurred to her. "Katherine help me get these magazines."

Both women alternately held the mattress as the other would gather the magazines and pile them on the floor.

"What are we looking for?" Katherine stared at the small pile.

"I don't know. But I do know Billy was an avid note taker and he would write on books and magazines. He always kept pencils and pens nearby so he could jot down his latest thoughts." Shirley motioned to a quart jar on Billy's lamp stand containing about two dozen pens and pencils.

"Well, let's get started," moaned Katherine, and then as an afterthought, "I think Slade conned us. I bet his job is not as tough as this one."

Both women started to laugh as they carried the magazines to the patio and put them on the table. Armed with large glasses of iced tea, they both picked up a magazine and started to thumb through the pages, ready to mark any area where Billy had made notes.

Chapter Thirteen

The drive to St. Petersburg had been enjoyable. Slade had taken the top and doors off of his Jeep. A dark pair of polarized sunglasses adorned his face and a baseball cap was pulled snugly down to his ears. The heat from the sun felt good, especially as it permeated his skin. The injury to his left side was feeling better and he was not near as uncomfortable as the night before.

The drive down old country roads had appealed to him and he knew he needed the time to think and put things in order. Though Slade knew he was no private investigator, he had been a detective and a damned good one. This investigation had turned into police work: simple and straight forward. Uncover the reason for the deaths and catch the killers. First and foremost he had to find the motive. The obvious had to be explored; the immediate leads pursued and eliminated. After that, it was back to searching for the clues he had missed.

Slade was convinced Billy had been the focus from the very beginning. Hank and Mary had been average, honest, working people struggling to raise a family, albeit an extremely gifted family. Hank and Mary were average. In middle-class America, Hank and Mary were poster-parents for the fading working class. Maybe the effort they put into their kids did not make them average. Their kids, from what Slade could gather, were not average in the least.

What had Billy stumbled upon? It could have been a thousand different things. A young boy, nurtured by parents who supported his quest for knowledge and encouraged him to explore the world of science, could have discovered any of a hundred things of interest to humankind. But what had he found? Had it threatened someone? Billy's research would surface soon enough. If it was as important as Slade believed, Billy's research would force the killer to reveal himself.

Slade did know one thing for certain: the killer would try again. They did not know how much Slade knew. Doubt in the mind of a cunning killer was a dangerous thing. Theirs was a shadowy world of living on the run. Trust was nonexistent, allies nothing more than future adversaries. A killer's psyche dictated they control as much as possible in their arena of illusion and distrust. Control was essential. Because none of them, not even one, wanted to spend the rest of their life on death row waiting for the inevitable curtain call. Taking someone else's life was inconsequential, but ending their own was a different story.

Surprisingly, the thought of being hunted did not frighten Slade. He accepted it as a cold fact and nothing more. He would have to prepare for the confrontation, but no panic infused his thought process.

The welfare of Shirley and Katherine concerned him more. If the killers knew about Slade, then they knew about Katherine. It was a logical mental step of deduction to recognizing Shirley had appealed to Slade for help. Slade knew he was prepared for the inevitable confrontation, but he knew the two women were not. He would have to insulate them from danger and he had already taken the first steps by insuring they were together. A killer was less likely to target two people. It did not appeal to their cowardly nature. His sense of security left him when he remembered the killers had killed Hank, Mary and Billy.

No time to dwell on it now.

Taking a moment to consult his AAA map of the St. Petersburg area, Slade turned off the main highway and headed for the coast. It took less than twenty minutes for him to reach the Coast Guard headquarters. Finding a suitable parking space in the lot, Slade walked inside the brightly painted building. The glass doors hissed when they opened and a wave of cool air rushed over him. The counter was directly in front of the doors and was staffed by a young woman in a Coast Guard uniform, every crease starched to a razor's edge.

"Good morning. May I help you?" The eyes of the young officer quickly surveyed him.

"Yes you can. I understand you have a boat here that was involved in a tragic accident off the coast of Cedar Key about a month ago. Is the boat still here?"

"Do you have a name for the boat?" The young officer had her fingers flying over a computer terminal. When she had the desired screen in front of her, she looked up at Slade and waited expectantly for the name.

"The *Fair Rose*." Slade watched as the woman typed in the name and within seconds she was scanning the screen.

"Yes, we do. It has been scheduled for destruction and is to be hauled off tomorrow. Are you a relative of the owner?" The young woman's voice took on a note of compassion. Information on the screen said the family had been killed while trying to escape a hurricane.

"I'm a friend of the boat owner's daughter. Is there any chance I could see the boat?"

"Sure. Hang on while I get someone to staff the desk."

Within minutes Slade was being ushered through the halls of the Coast Guard building to the back door. The young woman led him past a dozen boats, each tucked nicely into a designated space, much like cars at a shopping mall parking lot. Most of the boats were badly damaged, while some appeared to be in pretty fair shape. Slade estimated at least forty percent of them would float again, provided the owners decided the effort was worthwhile. If not, they would be auctioned to salvage yards and gutted.

"Why are all of these boats here?"

"They have either been seized for drug smuggling or involved in an accident warranting our review." She stopped in front of a flatbed trailer. On the trailer was what was left of The *Fair Rose*.

Slade moved alongside the young woman and stared at the remains. The *Fair Rose* had been broken into three pieces. From the cabin forward and above the water line represented one section; the cabin and most of the upper deck was together; and the engine compartment above the water line and stern made up the rest. The only section intact was the keel running the length of the boat. The boat had been positioned on the flatbed trailer as if someone was trying to piece her back together, a giant puzzle lacking a few key parts. Countless smaller fragments were scattered over the deck and on the boat itself.

"Did they find what caused the accident?" Slade carefully walked around the boat.

"There was nothing wrong with the boat. The police report said they died of carbon monoxide poisoning. The accident was attributed to operator error." The young officer looked directly at Slade through a pair of dark sunglasses. "I'm sorry, sir, but you can tell the daughter her father should have never been out at sea with a hurricane rushing up the coast. We try not to go out in seas like that and our boats are designed for the worst weather on earth. This boat is thirty years old. We can only speculate that the torque and strain from the pounding caused the deck to rupture. That, coupled with an exhaust leak, allowed carbon monoxide to seep into the cabin." She held her hands up in a defeated gesture.

Slade did not say anything, but continued to walk around The *Fair Rose*. She still maintained a certain dignity about her and Slade could see why Hank Waterbury had bought and restored her. The decks were wood and still held some of the luster of his painstaking restoration, reflecting the bright sun skyward. Her bow was sleek, capable of handling the sea with grace and stability. She was a boater's boat and Hank must have been at home at the helm. Slade guessed her length at about twenty-seven or twenty-eight feet.

"She is twenty-seven feet six inches from bow to stern. A beautiful boat. You just don't see them like her anymore," said the young officer, guessing his thoughts.

"Who owns the boat?"

"What do you mean?"

"Does the owner's daughter still have ownership or has that transferred to the Coast Guard? I'm not familiar with how this works," prodded Slade, peering at her from behind the safety of his sunglasses.

"The daughter would still be the owner. No one contacted us regarding claiming the boat and we were going to have her auctioned. Why?"

"Because I want her."

It took over three hours for Slade to complete all the paperwork and it cost him $1,100.00 to have her shipped to his house.

When he was finally done, he realized he was hungry. He found a Denny's not too far from the Coast Guard headquarters and ordered lunch. An overweight, middle-aged woman, continuously calling him 'Hon' served him a club sandwich. On her third trip to the table, Slade convinced her to leave the pitcher of tea on the table. Happily, she obliged and patted him on the arm before scurrying to the kitchen.

On the table in front of him, he spread out the paperwork on The *Fair Rose*. It was a brief account of her history, size, engine capacity, and the report filed by the Coast Guard. Everything he wanted to know about the boat was confined on the eight and half by eleven inches of paper.

The *Fair Rose* had been custom built by a small boat company in Ft. Lauderdale in 1974. She had been sold to an attorney who used her to impress clients. On weekends, the *Fair Rose* plied the waters of the Intracoastal Waterway, with brief forays into the Atlantic to shoot up and down the coast. An old newspaper article had a picture of her in the Ft. Lauderdale Christmas Boat Parade.

With his success and growing practice, prestige dictated the attorney have a bigger boat. Due to the attorney's success, the *Fair Rose* became expendable. Over the next twenty-five years she was sold to several owners before ending up in Steinhatchee, Florida, a little coastal community north of Cedar Key. Steinhatchee was known for scallops and every summer thousands of vacationers flocked to the area to harvest the tasty bivalves. It was at Steinhatchee that Hank Waterbury had first seen the *Fair Rose*.

Slade gazed out the window, his mind's eye recalling the conversation where Shirley told him how her dad had found the boat. Hank had taken a couple north of Cedar Key to Steinhatchee in pursuit of game fish. The day had been long, hot, and humid. During the early part of the morning the anglers had not met with much success. Hank had taken his clients into the town of Steinhatchee in the hope of restoring their spirits. A local restaurant, specializing in clam chowder, was the destination to revitalize them and put a bright spin on a dismal day

90

of fishing. During lunch at the restaurant, Hank had seen the *Fair Rose*. She was out of the water and residing on wooden blocks, her graceful bow pointed seaward, itching to feel the rush of water slide past her hull. It was clear the *Fair Rose* was not in the best of hands. The restaurant owner had bought the boat with the idea of restoring her, but did not have the time or expertise.

Two weeks later, Hank made the trip back to Steinhatchee and offered to buy her. The restaurant owner was more than happy to sell, ridding him of a project he would never undertake. Hank made sure she would float and towed her to Cedar Key where he spent many an evening restoring the *Fair Rose*. Shirley said Hank spent most every night working on the cuddy cabin. Oftentimes, Mary was the only one who could pry him away from his hobby. The *Fair Rose* had become his pride and joy.

Now she was coming home again. Only Slade did not know if she would ever be put back together. He wanted another opinion on the condition of the *Fair Rose* prior to the 'accident.' Carbon monoxide poisoning may have killed them, but was it an accident?

Slade motioned towards the waitress and indicated he wanted another pitcher of tea. After she left, Slade went back to looking through the papers on the *Fair Rose*. Everything the Coast Guard found indicated the boat was in excellent condition prior to the accident. 'Operator error.' Slade had never met Hank Waterbury, but he did not buy that explanation. Two killers in a garage had convinced him.

Picking up a picture of the *Fair Rose*, Slade let his eyes trail over the boat, taking in every detail. The picture had been supplied from the manufacturer the day she had been sold. There was a timeless aura to the boat and Slade could see why Hank had so carefully restored her.

Slade slowly closed the file and stared out the windows at two young girls walking by. The *Fair Rose* may still provide some information, but Slade knew he had to look elsewhere. Draining the last of the iced tea, Slade rose from his seat and motioned for his bill. There was still a lot of daylight left and still a lot to do.

"Anything?" Katherine rubbed her eyes. It was late afternoon.

"I found a lot of Billy's notes, but nothing of substance. Usually, his notes were about the article he was reading. Nothing more." Shirley tossed the last magazine onto the table.

They had eaten lunch on the patio and now the afternoon sun was slipping gracefully down the horizon.

"What do we do now?" Katherine glanced over at Shirley.

"We still need to find out what that formula was Billy wrote down. You know, the one Slade got from the garage. Maybe that will tell us something."

"How do we go about that? Is there a reference book for that type of stuff?"

91

"Sort of. I know the formula is for a plant, I just don't know which one. Maybe one of the biology books Billy has in his room can help. If not, we can check the computer and internet sites on plant classification. First we have to identify the species, then narrow it do-" Shirley was cut off by Katherine.

"Sounds like a long night," moaned Katherine, rolling her eyes in exhaustion.

Shirley busted out laughing. "Welcome to the world of science: ninety-five percent research and boredom, with five percent discovery and exhilaration."

"Sounds wonderful. Where do I sign up?"

"Right here, right now." Shirley stood up and gathered an armload of magazines.

"I tell you what. Why don't you get started on tracking down this plant formula, and I'll call Slade and see how he's doing. Then I'll get something started for dinner. Deal?" Katherine stretched as she stood.

"Deal." Shirley disappeared towards Billy's room with the magazines.

Katherine grabbed the cordless phone and dialed Slade's cell phone.

"Hello?"

"Hi, sweetie. Thought I would see how you were doing." Katherine cupped her free hand over her other ear to hear better. The sound of wind blowing past Slade's phone was making it difficult to understand him.

"Doing just fine. Tell Shirley I'm having the remains of the *Fair Rose* delivered to my house. I want someone else to look her over and give an opinion as to the condition of the boat. Make sure Shirley knows the boat is being delivered, so she is prepared when it arrives. Should be there tomorrow." Slade had put the top back on the Jeep, but not the doors. The wind noise was still considerable and he had raised the level of his voice to compensate.

"I understand. When are you going to be back?"

"Not till tomorrow, maybe the day after. I want to meet with Dr. Krancz. Professor Johansen said it was Dr. Krancz who told him about Billy and this revolutionary project he was working on. I've already called and spoken with his wife. She said she is sure Dr. Krancz will see me when I get to Gainesville. I'll be staying at his place tonight." Slade swerved to miss a rabbit bolting across the road.

"Okay. I'll call if we find anything. I love you."

"I love you, too. Be careful and stay at Shirley's tonight," cautioned Slade.

"I will," answered Katherine, before hanging up.

Katherine held the phone near her breast and then leaned heavily against the door frame. Slade. He was so much what she was looking for. Her love and admiration for him was growing daily.

Katherine started to hum a song as she went to the pantry in search of dinner.

Sorority Row is a long line of student housing in Gainesville, Florida. The proximity of the sororities to the University of Florida campus makes them an enviable choice for students attending classes. Most of the undergraduates can walk to class, thereby eliminating the need for a car. For young girls living on their own for the first time, the ability to sleep late after partying most of the night, and still be able to make it to class on time is priceless.

At the east end of Sorority Row are the older dorms, with Greek lettering adorning the entranceway of most of the red brick buildings. A small pond is at the center of the cul de sac and is frequented by a local brood of ducks, which are in turn fed by the young girls living in the sororities. The setting is very university-like and appears on several brochures. Moms and dads love the pictures for the innocent quaintness they portray.

The largest sorority on the street does not have the traditional Greek lettering, and the only indication it is a sorority is by the large number of young women coming and going. The rooms are spacious and easily accommodate two students, who are usually paired together their freshman year and remain so until graduation. The sorority caters more to the serious student, who has already predetermined their major and is intent on pursuing a Masters or Doctorate.

Mandy Chambliss sat on the edge of her bed and folded the last of her laundry, placing her shirts neatly into a dresser at the foot of her bed. She had already hung up her slacks and dresses, organizing them in her closet by color. A chemistry book was open and several pages of notes were scattered across her desk, indicating a final was close at hand.

Mandy walked over to her chemistry book and scanned the notes a second time. Redox equations. She hated those and was having difficulty balancing the formulas. The transfer of electrons was confusing. If only her roommate was here to help. Shirley could do them in her sleep.

Walking over to her friend's bed, Mandy sat down and looked at Shirley Waterbury's desk. Shirley had left her computer on and a light in the upper right hand corner blinked intermittently indicating someone had sent her e-mail. A picture of Cedar Key was Shirley's screen saver and it continuously tracked across the screen from left to right every seven seconds. It was a moving picture of Shirley's hometown. Smiling, Mandy looked at the picture on the dresser of her and Shirley sitting on the Cedar Key pier throwing bread to the greedy gulls. That had been last year when Shirley had invited her to Cedar Key for Thanksgiving.

A tear rolled slowly down Mandy's cheek and she wiped it away. She had been friends with Shirley for almost four years and they had become extremely close. Mandy had sent Shirley a sympathy card two weeks ago, but had not heard from her friend. The last time she had seen Shirley was at the funeral. Had it been that long? Shirley had withdrawn from the Summer B term at UF to get things in order. Mandy knew she must be busy.

She knew how close Shirley had been to her family and was wondering how she was coping. Three more weeks of classes and she would go and visit and help her friend get her life back together. Mandy had offered to withdraw from classes to be with Shirley, but Shirley would not hear of it. She had insisted Mandy continue and make-up chemistry so she would not get behind. Always the pragmatic one laughed Mandy, to no one in particular. Shirley was the big sister she had never had and she missed her.

The computer light blinked again, indicating Shirley had a message. Whoever it was could wait, thought Mandy, rising from the bed and moving to her desk. Her friend had more important things to worry about than answering an e-mail from someone.

Chapter Fourteen

The Aussies had been less than receptive. The list of demands by the Aussie officials had surprised Sommer and he had used every tactic to convince them of the feasibility of the project. Only when he was frustrated and ready to leave, did they concede and meet him halfway.

Development of the prototype had been the key stumbling block. The Aussies wanted to see a working model before they would ink a deal and sign. Sommer had to admit the Aussies lived up to their reputation as being fighters, both physically and mentally. They were expert negotiators and had commanded his respect. So far, they had represented the toughest challenge and had put up the most resistance.

Clyde walked out onto his balcony over-looking the Sydney harbor. In the distance he could see the distinct lines of the opera house, its series of half dome roofs breaking the monotony of the shoreline, the whiteness of the building shimmering in the sun.

Still Clyde did not understand the reluctance. The benefits to their country would be enormous. Only Saudi Arabia would benefit as much as the Aussies. Both countries would become overnight world players, impacting their respective geographic sphere on the economic level, overwhelming less developed nations and creating a clear superiority in production.

In the end, Clyde's logic had won out. The Aussies had agreed to deposit $500 million with World Vision Quest, refundable if the prototype failed and another $500 million after a successful demonstration.

Moving to the closet, Clyde continued to pack his clothes for his next trip. Where would Kyle send him this time? Back to Europe? The Middle East? Clyde still felt China represented a hidden treasure, but Kyle was leery of dealing with the communists. It did not matter, because in a couple of years, once they were at full production, China would come to them and beg to be included. Only Clyde would not be around to see it. Commissions alone had made him a millionaire and he intended to retire. Let someone else do the bidding of Matt Kyle.

Clyde zipped his suitcase shut and headed for the door, a new found enthusiasm in his step.

Gainesville is a town that exists because the University of Florida allows it to breathe. The nationally recognized learning center employs the most people in the county and drives the economy and dictates local politics. Without the university, Gainesville would be a series of small farms dotting the land-scapes, with pine trees planted in neat rows for miles, like other less fortu-nate cities in Florida that have neither a major university or the coast as a calling card. The pursuit of higher learning has been good to the city and the blue and orange of the Gators is on everything.

It is a city not without some natural wonders. Several crystal clear springs dot the countryside and one spring fed river, the Itchtuknee, attracts both tube enthusiasts and scuba divers. The tube ride is scenic and while floating down the river, Florida as it used to be, before tourists and develop-ment, unfolds along the banks. The occasional gator and snake brings cries of excitement and large mouth black bass cooling in the crystalline depths defy description. Upon completing the river run, most go back for a second trip, intent on seeing what they thought they missed, but mostly to enjoy the peaceful tranquility of the water and to feel the pulse of the river.

Slade was familiar with the Itchtuknee and had been down the river sev-eral times in the last year. Unfortunately, he knew he would not be able to take advantage of sight seeing this time around. He was here to see a profes-sor; one he hoped would help solve the mystery as to what Billy Waterbury had been working on.

Professor Krancz lived near the UF campus in a quiet residential neigh-borhood, with long serpentine drives and perfectly manicured lawns. Consulting his notes, Slade found Professor Krancz's house at the end of a dead end street. A large fountain, complete with three porpoises rising on a concrete pedestal, spewed a steady stream of water from their mouths and was strategically situated near the front door. Currently, two morning doves were taking a free bath.

A large golden horse head adorned the oak door. A ring was held in the horse's mouth and Slade used it to knock. The resulting sound was hollow and distant and Slade had a feeling the house was bigger than it appeared. When Mrs. Krancz opened the door and ushered him in, his suspicions were confirmed.

During his lifetime, Slade had met very few people he immediately liked. Professor Krancz and his wife, Joanne, were two of them.

96

"Well I hope you are at ease, young man. If not, what kind of hosts would we be?" Professor Krancz gestured with a corn cob pipe as he spoke. Slade noticed the pipe was not lit.

"You have arrived just in time for dinner." Mrs. Krancz was delighted she had someone else to cook for other than her husband.

Dinner was grilled pork roast covered with apple slices. Mrs. Krancz had also prepared corn on the cob, lima beans in a sauce to which she would not share the secret, and mashed potatoes so creamy and smooth, Slade ladled two large spoonfuls onto his plate. Only when he was about to bust did he stop, much to the delight of Mrs. Krancz who watched his every fork-full.

"Mrs. Krancz, this is the best dinner I've ever had. I couldn't eat another bite."

"A cook always likes to see a satisfied diner, Mr. Lockwood." Mrs. Krancz was gathering the dishes and Slade moved to help her, but was shooed away.

"Well your dinner was fantastic, Mrs. Krancz. I'm going to have to get my girlfriend to pay you a visit and learn how to cook like that."

"What does your girlfriend do?" Professor Krancz pulled his pipe from his pocket and stuffed it with a cherry scented tobacco.

"She is an artist and quite good, if I must say so myself. I have a couple of her paintings in my home."

"Oh, really? What is her name?" Professor Krancz inhaled deeply as he lit the bowl of his pipe.

"Katherine Wintergate. She owns a studio in Cedar Key." Slade stopped when Professor Krancz glanced at his wife and they both stared at Slade.

"Katherine Wintergate?" asked Mrs. Krancz.

"Yes."

"Come with me young man," instructed Mrs. Krancz, drying her hands on an apron around her waist.

Slade followed Mrs. Krancz into a den area. It was apparent the Krancz's collected art, as evidenced by the number of paintings hanging on the wall. Mrs. Krancz stopped in front of a fireplace and looked up at a large landscape scene prominently displayed in a beautiful cherry wood frame. Slade moved alongside and stared intently at a painting of Cedar Key. The artist had signed the painting in the lower left hand corner. Katherine Wintergate.

"We go to the Cedar Key Arts Festival every year and this year we fell in love with Katherine's work. She is very talented." Mrs. Krancz flipped a small light on that quickly illuminated the painting, casting a soft light over the picture. The scene was of a small fishing boat leaving the dock and heading to sea. Gulls were winging ahead of the boat and the way the light was cast brought them to life. Slade expected them to explode from the canvas at any moment and fly across the room.

"Yes she is." Slade was pleased Katherine's work was in their home.

"Tell Katherine she will be seeing us again this year. We're planning on taking the motor home and spending some time there." Professor Krancz moved to a chair and motioned for Slade to sit down.

Mrs. Krancz turned the light off the painting and headed back to the kitchen, telling the two men a blueberry cobbler was cooking. Slade could already smell the dessert and his taste buds kicked into high gear. A good thing he was not staying here for a week or he would weigh 300 pounds.

"So how can I help you, Mr. Lockwood? I thought the death of Shirley's parents and brother had been ruled an accident. Is there an active investigation?" Professor Krancz was studying Slade over a pair of glasses perched on the end of his nose.

"No investigation. I'm looking into the matter myself. Kind of conducting an informal investigation." So far he had not heard the Professor launch into the nasally, didactic style of speech Shirley had described.

"Have you found anything? Do you suspect murder?" pried the Professor, finally succeeding in lighting his pipe.

"I do now, but didn't at first." Seeing the perplexed look on the Professor's face, Slade added, "let me explain."

Slade explained everything to Professor Krancz, from checking on the condition of Hank's two boats, to going to the Coast Guard, to recovering the piece of paper, the two killers in the garage, the phone call from Professor Johansen, and finally his trip to the Professor's house hoping he could tell him what Billy had been working on.

The Professor sat for several seconds before saying anything. When he did speak, Slade could pick up on the sadness in his voice.

"I'm afraid I cannot help you, Mr. Lockwood. I never knew what Billy was working on."

"But Professor Johansen, from Michigan, said you told him that 'Billy was working on something in biology that was as revolutionary as Einstein's contribution to physics.' Did you tell him that?"

"Yes, I told him that. I believe it, too. Whatever Billy was working on would have been that revolutionary."

"How can you say that if you don't know what it was?"

"Because I know Billy's sister, Shirley," answered the Professor, briefly being interrupted by his wife who came into the room carrying a steaming pot of coffee and two plates of blueberry cobbler.

"Mr. Lockwood, I want you to try this cobbler. A young man outside of town picks me seventy pounds a year and I freeze them so I can have blueberries regardless of the season. These berries are all organic and taste delicious." Mrs. Krancz shoved a spoon into Slade's hand and he dipped into the cobbler. The rich, creamy berries melted in his mouth and Slade momentarily forgot about his conversation with Professor Krancz.

"This is delicious, Mrs. Krancz. I bet I have gained five pounds here tonight."

"Glad you like it. Let me know if you want some more." Mrs. Krancz hurried back to the kitchen.

"Where were we?" asked Professor Krancz, setting the cobbler down in front of him.

"You were talking about knowing Shirley, but not Billy." Slade finished the last of the cobbler and sipped from his coffee cup. He already knew he was opting for seconds on the blueberries.

"A university is a closed society, Mr. Lockwood. Even one as big as UF. Professors talk and share stories, especially about gifted students. Shirley Waterbury was the most gifted student we had ever seen." Professor Krancz was interrupted by Slade.

"Who are we?"

"My fellow professors. Shirley was a rare combination of brains and focus. A lot of students are smart, but not focused. Shirley was not only smart, but extremely focused. She also had an intangible, an ability to see through a problem in a way very few students ever achieve. Shirley could see the problem, analyze possible solutions, and arrive at a conclusion faster than anyone I have ever taught and that spans almost forty years. She is, for lack of a better phrase, academically insightful."

Slade looked at Professor Krancz. "Her brother, Billy?" Slade had a feeling he already knew the answer.

"I never met Billy, but from what Professor Gordon told me, he was smarter than Shirley. As far ahead of other students as Shirley is, that is how far ahead of Shirley that Billy was."

"Billy was enrolled here? I thought he was still in high school?"

"I'm sorry. I didn't mean to confuse you. Billy is in or was in high school. Professor Gordon, like myself and other professors judge science fairs all over the state. Professor Gordon met Billy at a science fair about six months ago. Naturally, Billy won his category and in talking with Billy, Professor Gordon learned Billy's sister Shirley was a student of mine."

"So Professor Gordon looks you up when she gets back on campus to tell you about Billy and the fact Shirley is his sister." Slade let his remarks trail off.

"Precisely. Needless to say, we were all quite impressed."

"Why was that?"

"Because Billy had entered a science fair for college students. He had been granted a waiver by the National Board of Science Fair Judges so he could enter the contest and he won. Well, you can imagine the stir this caused, especially for the second place finisher. They wanted Billy's project thrown out, but it wasn't and Billy was awarded first place." Professor Krancz leaned forward in his seat and gestured towards Slade. "Here is the truly awesome part, Mr. Lockwood. Billy entered in three different categories and won first place in all three."

Slade had involuntarily leaned forward towards the Professor and found himself lowering his voice. "What were the categories?"

"Biology, chemistry and physics. By the way, Shirley entered the same science fair and won first place in math." Professor Krancz leaned back in his chair and smiled like a proud parent extolling the accomplishments of his kids.

"Now I remember Shirley telling me Billy had won first place in three divisions in a science fair. She didn't tell me she had entered and won." Slade sipped again from his coffee cup and as if on cue, Mrs. Krancz appeared with a steaming pot and another helping of blueberry cobbler, which Slade could not wait to accept.

"Shirley was very modest, Mr. Lockwood. If you have gotten to know her at all, you know that. She is an extremely proud young woman. Her intelligence is a gift that sets her apart form others. From what she has told me, her brother was truly a genius, a young Einstein. It is a shame her brother is gone. I can only hope Shirley continues her education and achieves her full potential. It would be a tragedy for her not to."

Slade could hear the concern and despair in the Professor's voice when talking about Shirley. "She'll get her education, I promise. I think her best days are yet to come," replied Slade, surprised at the forcefulness with which he said it. Shirley was becoming the sister he had never had and he would make sure he was there to guide her and give advice. It was not a role for which he had asked, but, surprisingly, he did not mind.

"This piece of paper with a formula on it, do you have a copy?"

"No. Shirley has it. She said it appeared to be a plant."

"That makes sense. Professor Gordon was judging the biology section at the science fair and when she returned she told me about Billy and the wonderful things he was doing."

"Is that when she told you that 'Billy's contribution rivaled that of Einstein's in physics?'" Slade felt his pulse quicken.

"Yes, it was."

"Where can I find Professor Gordon?"

"You have a long trip ahead of you, Mr. Lockwood, if you want to see Professor Gordon."

"Why is that?"

"Professor Gordon is in Borneo cataloguing rare fauna. She is not expected back for two more months and there is no way to contact her."

Chapter Fifteen

The distress call came over the marine frequency as a may day, any ship in the area please respond. It was the universal call for help ships at sea send when needing immediate assistance, when life hangs in peril and death looms in the murky depths. The unwritten rule of the sea was to respond. It had been that way since the first day man set forth on the sea on a plank of wood driven by oars or the winds. Modern technology had not changed the unwritten law of the sailors.

All eyes on the bridge turned towards the Captain.

"Position."

"She is about seventy-five nautical miles west, northwest of our location, Captain. We can reach her in a little over four hours at maximum speed." The navigator looked up and then glanced back at the charts in front of him. They were just off the northern coast of British Colombia. The distressed ship was a fishing freighter in the middle of the Bering Sea. Her engines were out and she was being swept towards a rocky shoreline of an island inhabited by migratory birds. If help did not arrive soon, she would be lost.

"How long before she runs aground?" The Captain cradled his favorite coffee mug in his hands, channeling the delicate aroma towards his nose.

"At their current drift and prevailing wind, they may have six hours, maybe seven if lucky."

"Any chance they will miss the island?"

"I don't think so. Not based on my charts of the area." Brian Loveall, navigator for *Quest 1*, looked expectantly at the Captain.

Captain Ari Theopolous stared out the fog shrouded glass surrounding the bridge. Why now? He had assured Matt Kyle that *Quest 1* would be delivered on time in San Pedro. If they responded to help the distressed freighter they would lose at least two, possibly three days. If they had to tow her to shore, then it could be a week, possibly longer. Up until now, the voyage had been uneventful.

"Where is the nearest ocean going tug?" All eyes turned to a young man staffing the radio.

"The two tugs in the area are assigned to a mobile drilling platform off the Alaskan coast. They cannot be in route for at least three, possibly four days. They are asking for our immediate assistance. We are the closest ship." Kevin Long let the earphones dangle around his neck. He could still hear the May Day request being transmitted by the stricken vessel.

"Notify the Captain of the stricken vessel *Quest 1* is enroute to assist." Captain Theopolous turned towards his helmsman. "Plot a course for intercept." Captain Theopolous reached for a button that had 'engine room' on it. "Chief, we need maximum revolutions. A fishing freighter is headed for some rocks if we don't get there first. I need whatever you can give me."

"The engines are purring like a kitten, Captain. Just say the word and we are at full-throttle." Chief Engineer Jody Parker lovingly rubbed the gauges on his display panel with a rag kept always within reach. The overhaul of the engines in Valdez had been done under his supervision. Every nut and bolt had been replaced or tightened under his watchful eye. The engines were running flawlessly.

"Thank you, Chief. The word is given. Maximum speed."

Everyone could feel the deck on the massive vessel quiver as the revolutions to the huge propellers were increased. Slowly the gigantic freighter turned towards its new target, San Pedro momentarily forgotten.

Captain Ari Theopolous stayed on the bridge for several minutes weighing his options. Matt Kyle would not like this turn of events. It would be best to notify the eccentric millionaire from the safety of his cabin. Captain Theopolous did not want any of his crew to hear the outburst from his boss that was sure to come. In the privacy of his cabin, Ari could save face; on the bridge, his men would hear the outburst and question his leadership. The sea had its own laws governing man and the men who spent their lives sailing the deep waters lived by them.

Turning towards the bridge door, Captain Theopolous nodded towards his second in command, indicating he was in charge. Silently, he left the bridge and headed for his cabin. A phone call had to be made.

"Have you been up all night?" Katherine walked around the corner of the desk and placed her hand on Shirley's shoulder. A sleepy, red-eyed young woman looked back at her. A lopsided grin was on Shirley's face, indicating a tell-tale sign of discovery. And fatigue.

"It's morning already? I knew it was late, but I didn't know it was that late." Shirley stretched in her chair. She had spent all night on the computer tracking down the elusive formula. Finally, just before dawn, she had cracked the 'code' and identified the species of plant.

"Did you find out anything?" Katherine tugged on Shirley's shoulder and directed her towards the kitchen. Shirley needed coffee.

"Yes and no. I found out what the chemical formula is, but it doesn't make any sense. I think Billy was attempting to alter the genetic make-up of a plant. I just don't have enough to understand what he was doing or why." Shirley stretched and yawned for the third time since leaving her bedroom.

"What kind of plant is it?" Katherine slid a cup of coffee towards Shirley.

"Mangrove. Specifically the black mangrove." Shirley smelled the rich aroma of the coffee. It tasted so good.

"I didn't know there were different kinds." Katherine's voice took on a new found respect for Shirley.

"I knew there were different kinds, but I never really studied them. There is a red, white, and black mangrove. They are facultative halophytes, which allow them to grow in fresh or salt water, but they seem to prefer salt rich environments. That is evidenced by the fact that all three species grow in brackish, marsh areas or on the edge of saltwater. They actually grow in designated areas along a shoreline. The red mangrove grows near the waters edge; the black mangroves are usually found growing immediately inland of red mangroves. White mangroves grow immediately inland of the black mangrove. So you have the red growing near the shoreline, the black immediately behind it, and the white mangrove farthest from the water." Shirley looked up to see if Katherine was keeping up. "Pretty cool, huh?"

"Yeah, I guess. I never really thought much about them. Why was Billy interested in them?"

"I don't know. The formula Slade found was to the black mangrove, but Billy was trying to change the cellular structure. Kind of like messing with the genetic make-up in a strand of DNA. Change the DNA, you change or alter the species."

"I'm no scientist, but aren't we doing that already? I hear about hybrid plants all the time. Is that what Billy was trying to do?"

"We do genetically alter plants to bring out the best qualities in them. For example, take corn production. Scientists have modified the genes in the plant to resist disease and parasites. Almost all the food you eat has been genetically altered."

"Do we eat mangroves?"

"Not that I'm aware of. Their real benefit is to the creatures inhabiting the coastal fringes—shrimp, small fish, etc. Not to mention the mammals, amphibians, and other small animals that live near or in the root system. The root system provides a safe-house environment for the species hiding there. The predators can't get to them because of the tangle of roots. Also, the mangroves help prevent erosion and release nutrients back into the sea if the area is properly flushed."

"What do you mean, 'properly flushed'?" Katherine took a seat next to Shirley. If Billy had been as smart as Shirley said, then he would have been scary. Shirley was recalling information she had just read hours earlier as if she was a computer and doing it while suffering from a lack of sleep.

"If the tidal area where the mangroves grow are not subjected to a good exchange of water coming in and out due to rising tides, then sulfides and other elements non-conducive to a healthy eco-system can proliferate. Remember, where most of the mangrove forests grow is where a lot of the nitrogen from fertilizer and other heavy chemicals are washed into the ocean. The mangroves help to process some of this material, but again it hinges on the ability of the system to be flushed." Shirley started to get up to refill her coffee cup, but Katherine motioned for her to remain seated and retrieved the coffee pot. After filling both cups, Katherine sat back down.

"So do you have any idea what Billy was trying to accomplish?"

"No. I do know he was trying to alter the chemical structure, but there is not enough of the formula to determine what characteristics of the plant he was hoping to enhance or eliminate. Billy could have been exploring the possibility of improving the growth rate of mangroves for possible production as timber."

"Do they grow tall enough to be a viable timber resource?"

"The black mangrove grows to twenty meters in height. But I don't know if the wood is favorable for construction. Also, I don't know anything about the growth rate. And then again, Billy could have been looking at the mangrove for something totally different. This is just a guess."

Katherine did not immediately reply, but instead continued to sip from her coffee cup. Shirley had succeeded in identifying the formula, but still the answer was hidden. It was like having a road map with no cities or states on it. The road led somewhere, but where? Only the cartographer knew and in this case he was dead and could not tell them.

"Well maybe Slade is having better luck," sighed Katherine, moving towards the refrigerator. "You hungry?"

"Yeah, a little." Shirley felt the fingers of sleep tug at her.

"Let's get you something to eat and then off to bed with you. Waffles sound good?"

"Excellent choice."

Both women giggled, one because of exhaustion and the other to hide her frustration.

Sam had picked Leonard up at the Orlando International Airport. That was the only airport accepting a direct flight from Los Angeles. The flight had lasted a little over five hours and Leonard was in no mood for conversation. Sam had met him once before and remembered the aloofness, the cold part of the man. Little had changed. Leonard did not offer conversation and Sam did not press for any.

The drive back to Cedar Key took almost three hours. By the time they arrived at the office, Leonard seemed refreshed from the nap he had taken. Sam went to pull into the driveway but was stopped by the Los Angeles killer.

"Show me where the cop lives," ordered Leonard, sliding down in the seat a little lower.

Without a response, Sam swerved out of the driveway and drove slowly to Slade's house. After they passed, Leonard had Sam pull over on the side of the road. After adjusting his rearview mirror, Leonard sat there for over an hour watching the house, committing everything to memory.

The sweat had already soaked Sam's shirt and was running in tiny rivulets down his back. His seat was damp from all the moisture and the temperature inside the van was stifling. If Leonard was as uncomfortable as he was, he was doing a good job of hiding it. Sam glanced towards the passenger seat and watched in fascination as Leonard's eyes remained glued to the mirror. What was he looking for? What could be so interesting?

The only visitors to the house besides the mailman were Shirley and Katherine. Leonard had asked who they were and after learning their identities, had retreated back to his solitary silence. The two women had taken in the mail and fed a large brown pelican roosting on the pier. The bird had allowed Katherine to rub its head.

Leonard had instructed Sam to follow the two women when they left Slade's house. First they had gone to Katherine's art studio and then to a local grocery store. Their last stop was back at Shirley's, where Leonard had Sam take up a quiet vigil again. The women stayed inside and, as the sun drifted slowly down the sky, Leonard realized they were staying put for the night. After another hour Leonard informed Sam he was ready to go to the office.

Once at the refurbished warehouse, Leonard told Sam to call Kyle. When Kyle was on the line, Leonard reached for and pulled the phone out of Sam's grasp.

"The cop is not here, but I followed the two women. They're at the young girl's place. Probably waitin' on him."

"Where is the cop?" Kyle gently rubbed his temple. A late afternoon board meeting had drained most of his energy. Even though he was on the verge of an astounding breakthrough that would catapult his company into the upper echelons of corporate America, he still had to manage the existing assets of World Vision Quest.

"I don't know. Our local help doesn't seem to know either." Leonard did not even bother to look at Sam.

"That doesn't surprise me. I'm surprised he was able to find the airport to pick you up."

Leonard did not reply and waited for Kyle to speak. Whatever the next move was going to be, his boss would have to make it. He had been called in to make sure the cop met with an untimely accident.

"If the cop is not there, then he has learned something or he would still be in town. I have a bad feeling and I have learned to trust my feelings. Why don't you pay the young women a visit and see what the cop has learned. Maybe they can shed some light on what he is up to."

"What was the name of the boat that sunk?" Leonard turned towards Sam as he spoke.

"Why?" asked Kyle, clearing some fatigue from his voice.

"It was something *Rose*," said Sam, trying desperately to get a read on the conversation.

"Because there is a boat on a flatbed trailer parked next to the cop's house. Looks like it just got put there. When the two women were at the cop's house, the younger one started to walk towards the boat, but the older one stopped her."

Sam squirmed uncomfortably in his seat. He had been so preoccupied with Leonard he had not even noticed the boat. Everybody in Cedar Key had a boat in their yard or one tied up to the dock.

"Okay, that solves it. See what the women know and then make sure they don't have the opportunity to learn anything else." Kyle had turned to stare out the window at the Port. Calmness. Great men exuded calm in the face of chaos and uncertainty. That is why they were great and others followed them. Kyle intended to be the greatest of all.

"The cop?"

"Make sure he joins them," Kyle paused and then added, "See to it that our local helper leads the way for them to the world of the dead." Without waiting on a reply, Kyle hung up the phone. Time to start cutting his losses and look towards the future. Financial rewards beckoned.

Leonard hung up the phone and turned towards Sam. "What do you have in the way of weapons? I prefer a semi-auto with a silencer. Have anything like that?"

"I've got just what you need. Be right back."

Leonard watched Sam disappear to the back of the office and return within minutes. Sam was carrying a Glock .40 in his hand, a long silencer attached to the end. It was a menacing weapon, one that was utterly reliable and deadly in the hands of a trained assassin.

Sam handed the gun to Leonard and stepped back. Leonard hefted the weapon and then quickly dropped the magazine into his palm. After inspecting the rounds, he slammed the magazine back into the butt of the gun and brought it up to eye level, training the sights on an imaginary spot on the wall.

106

"Who else knows about your role in the deaths of the Waterbury's?" demanded Leonard, lowering the weapon to his side and turning a penetrating gaze on Sam.

"No one. Well, no one now that Bart is dead." Sam carefully watched the gun in Leonard's hand. For the first time, fear invaded his throat and he felt butterflies dance around his stomach. Involuntarily he took a step back.

"Good. Less loose ends." Leonard looked directly at Sam with absolutely no remorse in his eyes. After all, to him, it was just a job. "Thanks for all your help, Sam. By the way, I'll take it alone from here on out." Leonard raised the gun and trained it on Sam's chest.

"Please. Please don't kill me. I can be use..."

The words died in Sam's throat. The first bullet was fatal, impacting Sam in the center of the chest and hurling him backwards into a chair. The second and third rounds were for effect only. One bullet struck Sam directly in the heart; another between his eyes.

Leonard walked up to the dead man and watched the blood leak out of him, spreading a bright crimson path across the floor. Why did they all have to beg? Show a little backbone, thought Leonard. In his profession death was around every corner.

Going to the back of the office, Leonard found several large plastic bags and began the unpleasant work of cleaning up the mess he had made. Anyone walking by would have thought it was a janitor inside mopping floors, as Leonard started to hum a song.

After cleaning up the blood stained floor, Leonard wrapped Sam in a series of garbage bags and carried him to the van. The cover of darkness hid his activities from anyone who may have been out walking. The other factor working in his favor was the remote location of the remodeled warehouse.

Next on Leonard's priority list was fare. The airplane flight, in addition to being boring, lacked any type of quality food. A brief drive to a small diner just outside of town satisfied his hunger. The waitress had tried in vain to engage him in conversation, but had finally given up. Retreating back to the counter she had glared at her non-talkative patron from time to time, frustration evident on her face. Some people were just rude.

It was a brief drive to Shirley Waterbury's house. Lights were still on in the house, which meant the women were awake. Leonard parked down the block and slid down in his seat, prepared to play the cat and mouse game as he began his surveillance. This was nothing new for him and he let his mind wander.

It was almost midnight before the lights went out. Leonard would give them another hour to fall asleep and then he would make his move. But first, it was essential to get a feel for the neighborhood.

Leaving the van, Leonard walked down the sidewalk, being careful to note every alley and dark spot along the road. If something went wrong, he would need to have a place of retreat.

After circling the house twice, Leonard felt he had committed the layout to memory. Shirley did not own a dog, he was certain of that. Two houses down a golden retriever had barked at him until he had crossed the street. If there were other dogs on the block they were inside and already asleep for the night. That was a big plus. Dogs could ruin everything.

Moving into the shadows next to the house, Leonard rechecked his weapon, moving the slide back until he could visually see a cartridge in the chamber. Satisfied the weapon was loaded, he slid the gun back into his waistband, the long silencer sliding down his trouser leg to mid-thigh. He would have preferred a custom holster, but there was no way he could have brought it on the plane after 9–11.

Stepping gingerly out of the shadows, Leonard opened the white gate set in the center of the small wooden fence framing the yard. Rose bushes were everywhere and even in the limited lighting, he could see the bright blooms. Briefly, he wondered who had been the gardener. The woman probably. Women always liked flowers.

Leaving the sidewalk, Leonard moved quietly along the side of the house to the back yard. Two boats were tied to the dock behind the house. One was a sport fisher, but he was not sure what the other was. It appeared to be some type of work boat. The boats were not his primary concern at the moment, but gaining entry into the house was.

The kitchen door was dead bolted into a very secure frame. It was going to take time to open this door. Whoever had installed the lock had known what they were doing. The dead bolt had been specially made and slid deep into the frame of the door, anchoring into the studs. There was absolutely no give or play in the lock. Leonard had a feeling the rest of the house was as secure.

Reaching into his back pocket, Leonard extracted a small, cylindrical item resembling a tooth brush. On one end was a small circular disk about half the size of a dime. Leonard had used the glass cutter to cut more than one window. Placing the cutter on the pane of glass nearest the lock, Leonard slowly started to trace a circle on the glass. The scratching sound could not be helped and he moved as quietly as he could, listening carefully for the occupants inside lest he should awaken them. It took three passes with the cutter before the pane was cut through. Using the end of the cutter, Leonard inserted it into the cut glass and gently pried. A brief pop and a perfectly round piece of glass sprung into his hands.

Moving back to the door, Leonard reached inside and unlocked the door, swinging it open on silent hinges. When he stepped through the door, the gun was in his right hand and aimed at a forty-five degree angle. Wherever his eyes moved, the weapon moved, its menacing silencer tracing a path across the kitchen.

Swinging the door shut, Leonard started to move silently down the hallway. From his surveillance, he remembered which light had gone off last and he had committed the location of the light in the house to memory. This was an older home, which meant the bedrooms were probably all on one end.

Testing the first bedroom door he came to, he felt the doorknob turn easily under his hand. Moving close to the door, Leonard eased it open and stepped inside, pushing it partially shut behind him. On the bed in front of him was a young woman with flowing red hair, spread out gracefully on a pillow. One leg was protruding from beneath the blanket and was curled slightly. Some light from the moon filtered softly into the room and Leonard could make out her face. She was a beautiful woman. Too bad she was about to die.

Raising the gun, Leonard sighted down the barrel of the weapon and centered on her head. Two quick shots should do it.

Chapter Sixteen

It had been a frustrating day. After having breakfast with Professor Krancz and his wife, Slade had called Katherine. Shirley had told Slade about the chemical formula belonging to a species of mangrove, but could not tell him much else. Billy had been trying to alter the genetic make-up of the plant, but why?

The only person who may know something about why Billy would be altering the genetic code was in Borneo and was not due back to the United States for two months. To complicate matters, there was no way to contact Professor Gordon as she was in a remote area of the jungle and despised cell phones.

Professor Krancz had suggested Slade go to Professor Gordon's biology department and speak with her graduate assistants. Perhaps one of them had been with her when she was judging the science fair Billy had entered. Professor Krancz had agreed to be Slade's chaperone and escort him around, a move that proved to be beneficial as the professor was well known on campus.

Once on the campus, Slade realized just how big the University of Florida was and how possessed the university was with expansion. Every corner was under construction, with new buildings being erected or remodeling taking place. Professor Krancz informed him that for the university to maintain its national status as a premier learning center, space was needed.

The biology department was housed in a main building away from the main part of campus. Due to the size of UF and the foresight of early administrators, there was still enough land to avoid congestion, even though with increasing yearly enrollments, some would argue the university was becoming crowded. Current enrollment was well over 50,000 and growing. The biology department had not yet felt the housing squeeze and occupied two city blocks.

The main facility, where most classroom teaching and lecturing occurred, was a three-story monolith designed like a maze. If it had not been for Professor Krancz, Slade would have been lost the minute he stepped inside. They drifted down several well lit hallways and took countless turns, moving deeper into the cool interior. They finally stopped outside an office with Professor Gordon's name prominently displayed in gold lettering. Professor Krancz motioned Slade inside and then followed.

A middle-aged woman was seated behind the desk reading a stack of papers, but looked up when she heard the two men enter.

"Hi, Sally. How are you this morning?" Professor Krancz moved forward.

"Quite well, Professor, and you?"

"I'm doing fine. Sally, I would like for you meet Slade Lockwood."

Slade stepped forward and shook Sally's hand. "Pleased to meet you."

"I know this is not a social visit, Professor, so what can I do for you?" Sally slid back into her seat.

"That hurts. You think I wouldn't stop by to say hello and chat?" queried Professor Krancz, smiling at Sally over the top of his glasses. The small educator had moved around the desk.

"Not when you have a visitor." Sally met his smile and then turned towards Slade. "He's a perpetual charmer, you know."

Slade laughed. "I don't blame him." The compliment seemed to brighten Sally even more and she instinctively moved her left hand through her hair, arranging locks already in perfect order.

"Well, what can I do for you gentlemen?"

"If you insist on being so business-like," moaned Professor Krancz. "Sally, Professor Gordon judged a science fair about one or two months ago, just before she left for Borneo. It was near Winter Park, just outside of Orlando. Do you know if she took any of her graduate assistants with her?"

"I believe she took Paul Kim with her. Why?"

"What's his particular field of study?"

"Genetic mutation and engineering. One of the brightest young minds here. Professor Gordon's star pupil."

"How come he didn't accompany her on the Borneo expedition?"

"He has a term paper due when Professor Gordon returns. He's close to finishing his Masters and wants to start his PhD. It simply killed him not to go. She took a handful of students, you know." Sally rifled through some papers in her top left drawer. "She only takes the brightest and most well-deserving on her field trips."

"Yes, I know. She always takes her best students into the field," repeated Professor Krancz, more for Slade than Sally.

"Here it is. It was Winter Park," Sally was reading from a travel order. "They stayed at the Sheraton. The science fair was over a three day period, starting on Friday and ending Sunday afternoon. It was in May. The ninth through the twelfth."

"As always, your record keeping skills are impeccable," flirted Professor Krancz.

"Did Professor Gordon make any mention about any of the participants in the science fair?" Slade interrupted the flirting.

"As a matter of fact she did. I heard her and Paul talking about the event. A young man won the biology section and was extremely gifted, or so she said. There was something odd about him though, but I can't remember what it was." Sally gazed towards the bookcase, trying to pry into her mind's eye. After several seconds, she smiled and turned her gaze back to them, focusing on the present. "He was a high school student. Made a tad bit of a stir because the competition was supposed to be for college students."

"Sally, your memory is as wonderful as you are."

"You said Professor Gordon and Paul talked about this kid. Did he ever visit here?" asked Slade.

"Not that I'm aware of. I know he called Professor Gordon several times and she called him. I believe he called Paul, too. He was going to enter the National Science Fair Competition in Michigan this year. That's the biggest competition to be held in the US. Professor Gordon was torn as to whether to go to the science fair or Borneo. I think she will fly back early to attend, but that's only speculation." Sally snapped her fingers and continued, "You could probably find him there if you wanted to meet him."

An uncomfortable silence followed and the smile slowly faded from Sally's face. "What? Is there something wrong?"

"The young man is Billy Waterbury. He's dead." Slade watched her face closely. He saw her hand fly to her mouth and a sharp intake of breath caused her to sit up straight in her chair.

"How? What happened?" Moisture was crowding her eyes. "Professor Gordon had spoken so highly of the talented young man. She will be devastated when she returns and learns of his death."

"I believe he was murdered, but currently I can't prove it. That's why I'm trying to gather as much information as possible about him."

"How can I help?"

"Did Professor Gordon bring anything back from the science fair, especially anything Billy was working on? A research paper or anything?"

"Yes she did. I know this because she and Paul were discussing it for days. I heard bits and pieces of the conversation, and even though I'm not a biologist, I've learned to pick up on some of the 'lingo' after all these years." Sally rose from behind her desk.

"Do you remember what it was about?"

"Genetic engineering if I remember correctly. I believe Billy was trying to enhance the cellular structure of plants to restore the eco-system of contaminated environments. Pollution is a large problem, Mr. Lockwood, especially near urban fringes, where chemicals may escape holding or retention facilities. Professor Gordon has been a leading activist for some years in helping to clean up areas like that. Tampa Bay is a classic example. Due to over building and over crowding, run off from industry had threatened to turn the bay into a cesspool. Luckily, environmentalists, along with the scientific community, stepped in and the eco-system is thriving today. It has become a model in Florida for habitat restoration."

While sharing the information with the two men, Sally had moved to Professor Gordon's office and was looking through a stack of papers on her desk. After several seconds, Sally looked up.

"Sorry. The paper is not here. But I know Paul can fill you in. Professor Gordon probably took it with her. She does that with articles or papers that are extraordinary. She likes to read and re-read until she has dissected every bit of possible information."

Slade felt his heart sink. So close. At least he knew more now than he had minutes before. Still there was hope with the graduate assistant.

"Do you know if Paul is at school today?" asked Professor Krancz.

"Oh, I bet he is. He practically lives here. Probably at one of the green houses. I would start with the facilities out back and go from there. Somebody will know where he is." Sally slid back behind her desk.

"Thank you for your time," offered Slade.

"You're quite welcome. I wish I could've been of more help."

"You were wonderful and thanks again."

Professor Krancz waived at Sally and then led the way out the door and through the remainder of the building. Both men lapsed into silence as they negotiated the labyrinth of hallways and stairwells. It took five minutes before they made their way out the back door to the green houses.

The two green houses behind the main facility were football field size, in both length and width. They were huge, domed glass structures, with automatic fans and water to control the temperature. The parking lots were filled to capacity and a steady stream of students was walking to the greenhouses. The bicycle rack next to the front door was also full.

The first thing Slade noticed upon entering was the smell. The fertilizer was strong, and combined with the high humidity, created a challenging environment. It only took him a couple of minutes before he became accustomed to the odors and then he was able to survey the orderly green world.

The plants were in straight rows running the length of the building. Each row had layers of plants in pots, all properly tagged and marked identifying them by name. The bottom tier contained the larger plants, with another tier hanging five to six feet off the ground. This second tier consisted mostly of ferns. Above this second tier, were the vines and orchids.

Following Professor Krancz, Slade walked slowly to the back of the green house. Students were busy pruning plants, checking thermometers stuck in containers and adjusting spray nozzles on hanging PVC pipes to adjust the water to a fine mist. It was a busy, yet organized scene.

Once at the back of the building, Professor Krancz walked straight to a young oriental man wearing a pair of blue jeans and a UF tee shirt proclaiming he was proud to be a Florida Gator. The young man was instructing several students on how to properly plant a small bush.

"Don't plant the root ball so deep it can't breathe. The roots need room to grow laterally as well as vertically. If the root ball is too far below the surface the plant will slowly suffocate. The next time you drive around town, pay attention to the crepe myrtles in the median. Every now and then the city workers will plant one too deep and after six or seven months, the leaves will turn brown and the plant will slowly die. Most people think you must bury the plant deep, when in fact the opposite is true. Now each of you try it."

The young man turned to Professor Krancz and smiled. "Professor! How are you?"

"Good Paul and you? How is it going?"

"Good. I wish I was with Professor Gordon in Borneo."

"Paul, I want you to meet Slade Lockwood." Both men stepped forward and shook each other's hand.

"Pleased to meet you." Slade judged Paul to be about twenty-three or twenty-four.

"Likewise." Releasing Slade's hand, Paul turned back to Professor Krancz. "What can I do for you, Professor?"

"Slade needs to ask you some questions about a participant in a science fair you and Professor Gordon judged back in May. I'll let Slade fill you in."

"Let's go into the back office. It's quieter there." Paul turned and led them to a small glass enclosed office at the very back of the building. A desk, with two small folding chairs, was crowded into the tiny space. A hanging vine was suspended from the ceiling and was gracefully wrapping around every object with which it came into contact. Slade motioned for Professor Krancz to sit, while he remained standing.

Slade gave Paul a brief account of why he was there and what he was hoping to learn.

"And you think Billy was murdered?" Paul shifted uncomfortably.

"Yes. Especially after the incident at the lab. Burglars don't act like that. I need you to help me with what Billy was working on. His sister identified the formula on the piece of paper I got from one of the killers and she said it was a mangrove. She also said the formula was being manipulated by Billy, but she could not tell how with the limited amount of information."

Slade looked expectantly at Paul and there was silence in the room for several minutes. Finally, Paul looked up at Slade, a blank expression on his face.

"Forgive me, Mr. Lockwood, but I find this all very frightening. It seems like yesterday Professor Gordon and I were in Winter Park judging the science fair. I spoke to Billy on the phone about a month ago. He was preparing for a contest in Michigan that was to take place this month. This seems so sudden."

"It is sudden, Paul. But that is why we need to help Slade. Whoever did this must be brought to justice." A bitterness and a hardness had entered the small man's voice. "Billy's sister is convinced, as we are, that Billy's death was not an accident. Neither was the death of his parents." Professor Krancz stopped and looked directly at Paul.

"I just don't know how I can help." Paul gestured with his hands and met the stern gaze of Slade.

"I think Billy was killed because of what he was working on. I think he discovered something that was either new and revolutionary or embarrassing to someone. I don't know which, but that's where I need your help. Can you tell me what he was working on, what discovery he may have made?"

"Maybe. First, Mr. Lockwood, let me tell you about Billy. He was doing stuff that I haven't even studied at UF. Genetic splicing, genetic manipulation, and cell enhancement were just some of the things he was doing. We have tenured professors here that can't do those things. The funny thing is I don't think he realized just how important his accomplishments were to the field of biology. He just kind of shrugged it off, you know, as if to say, 'hey, anybody can do this.' He was definitely way ahead of most us."

"Is that what he was doing with the mangroves, genetic alteration?"

"That's putting it mildly. Billy had identified the specific chemicals within mangroves that allow them to process fluids. You know mangroves grow in conditions that would kill most any other plant. Their ability to filter out toxins plays a large part in their survival. Well, Billy not only found the chemicals allowing the plants to process out toxins, but more importantly, he discovered the sequence that allows this to occur." Paul looked at them, expecting them to relish in this new found discovery. Blank looks and raised eyebrows greeted him.

"I don't understand. What is so important about the sequence?" asked Slade.

"It's like notes on a page of music. If the laymen were to pick up a sheet of music and look at it, they would see a bunch of jibberish that made no sense. By consulting a musician, they could identify the individual notes and understand the corresponding representation. But only a musician could make the notes turn into a beautiful harmony when they picked up an instrument because they understand the rhythm. The same is true in biology. Understanding what chemical reactions take place in a plants cell is one thing; understanding the sequence or rhythm, for lack of a better word, of how these chemicals react and in how much quantity and why is an entirely different matter. A biologist needs to know when these different chemicals interact, how much, and for how long. Scientists spend years trying to determine how this occurs and often never discover the secret." Paul saw some understanding.

"Billy discovered how the mangroves worked? How they processed these toxins by understanding the chemical interaction in their cells?" clarified Slade.

"Yes. Not only did he discover how it worked, but he was able to enhance their properties. Remember, all plants process nitrogen and other essential elements to obtain nutrients necessary for growth. We, as scientists, have learned over the years how to genetically alter some aspects of a plant's internal process to produce or enhance the qualities we desire. The food you eat in the supermarket is not the same food your great grandparents ate. It has been modified, changed to be bigger, more nutritious, and resistant to disease."

"But mangroves are not processed for food, are they?" Professor Krancz looked over at Slade who shrugged.

"Not to my knowledge," said Paul.

"I find it hard to believe Billy would be killed for advancement in genetic biology as it dealt with mangroves." Slade was trying desperately to see a connection.

"I disagree. I mean, I don't have any idea about Billy being murdered, but the part about the genetic enhancement of mangroves is pretty impressive. If Billy did find a way for mangroves to process toxins at an efficient and high rate, then it would have commercial applications. Think about all the brackish water where mangroves grow. There are a large number of these areas near urban developments where runoff from industry contaminates the eco-system. Mangroves, especially those enhanced to recognize and target toxins could purify the water and soil. This would be of great benefit, especially to industry."

"He has a point. Think of all the money manufacturers spend to clean up an area that has been contaminated by mercury, phosphates, or other elements used in industry. Theoretically, the business could plant genetically altered mangroves and have them do naturally what would cost industry millions, perhaps billions, of dollars to accomplish." Professor Krancz looked at Paul for confirmation.

"Precisely and there would not be the scars left from dredges or heavy equipment. Genetically enhanced mangroves could be planted in case toxic elements escaped from a factory. Theoretically, several different types of mangroves could be planted, each targeting a different element. It would be a type of toxin net, capturing poisonous chemicals before they reached the environment. It would all be very efficient and aesthetically pleasing."

"So is this what Billy accomplished?" Slade was still not convinced.

"You mean the genetic alteration itself?"

"Yeah. Is that what he won the science fair for?"

"No. He won the science fair for depicting the specific ratio of chemical reactions or interactions that take place inside a mangrove's cellular structure. More specifically, he determined when and how long each chemical reacted and was identifying the sequence of chemical reactions to determine what element or nutrient the mangrove was after at a particular time. By understanding this process, Billy theorized he could genetically alter the cells inside of mangroves to target an element of his choice."

"He had not perfected this technique?"

"Not at the science fair. When I spoke to him about a month ago, he said he had successfully altered a mangrove's cellular structure to target specific elements." Slade watched as Paul's face contorted in thought and Slade left the young man to his memory. After several seconds, Slade prodded him.

"Was there something else?"

"I believe so. I think so. Billy always called when I was in the middle of doing something and our conversations were usually disjointed. He was still a kid, if you know what I mean." Paul looked at Slade and Professor Krancz for understanding. When they both nodded he visibly relaxed.

"Did he discover something else?" asked Professor Krancz.

"He asked me if I was going to the science fair in Michigan. Professor Gordon and I try to go to as many science fairs as we can. He told me he had discovered something 'really cool' with the mangroves. I asked him what it was, but he said he would show me. Until now, I just thought it was something to do with the cellular structure and internal chemical reactions."

"Do you know if he said anything to Professor Gordon about what he was working on?"

"No. She would have told me. We both talked about Billy a lot. His work was revolutionary. More so his approach, than his work. A lot of people are working on identifying cellular properties of plants, but very few approach it like Billy did."

"What do you mean?"

"Scientists are told to never form a hypothesis, but to remain open and let the research lead them to a conclusion. The truth is that seldom happens. Everyone has an opinion, an idea. Most scientists spend their time conducting research to support a hypothesis. Money is at stake, grants to be awarded. Billy did not approach research in the same manner. Billy would conduct research to see what would happen and then would go from there. His mind was truly open. Plus he was still so young. His mind was free from any of the academic restraints a scientist encounters through the education process."

"I appreciate your time, I really do," smiled Slade. "Do you know of any companies that would benefit from the research Billy was doing? Did he ever mention any to you?"

"There are a considerable number of companies that would benefit from the research. But Billy never mentioned any of them to me."

"If I remember correctly, most major companies attend science fair projects all over the country. They are interested in obtaining patents to promising new ideas. That may be a place to start." Professor Krancz looked directly at Slade.

"Do they keep a list of the companies attending?"

"Yes. The person, college, or university sponsoring the science fair keeps a log of companies attending. These same companies are contacted for donations to help offset costs and to help with advertisements. It's a small price to pay if they find a product worth millions."

"Well, good luck and thanks for your time." Slade rose to his feet and shook the young man's hand.

"Tell Professor Gordon to give me a call when she returns." Professor Krancz, opened the door and stepped back inside the main part of the green house. After saying good bye a second time, Paul hurried off.

They stopped back by Professor Gordon's office and spoke to Sally. Slade wanted to know who had sponsored the science fair Billy had attended in May. After a brief search, Sally told him it had been sponsored by the University of Central Florida. Sally did not have a list of companies attending the event, but said the UCF science department would. Sally called to have the list FAXed. The FAX machine lit up and a list of companies materialized. There were 377 companies listed on the dozen pages. Slade felt his heart sink.

"Are they arranged by fields of study?" inquired Professor Krancz, looking over Sally's shoulder.

"Some are, but most have multiple fields of interest. Like this company." Sally stabbed at a company halfway down the list. "They're a local company just north of Gainesville. They produce prosthetics and some regenerative skin products. They have also purchased a chemical plant. So they would have interests in both biology and chemistry."

"How do you know so much about them?" asked Slade.

"I own some of their stock. They have done quite well, all things considered with this turbulent economy. Earnings are up and operating costs are down. Turned a substantial profit last quarter," said Sally.

"You sound like a stock broker," chided Professor Krancz. "Any other local companies?"

"Just two. Both are in town, but they're engineering firms. They probably don't have a need for biology."

"Did the companies indicate who would be attending the science fair?"

"No. They have a person to contact, but that doesn't mean that person attended. I'm sure UCF would have more information. Each university tracks that kind of information, because they may approach the company for donations or a financial gift. Which one did you want me to find out about?" Sally looked questioningly at Slade.

118

"At this point, I don't know. I'll have to conduct some field work and get back with you. If you don't mind, that is."

"Not at all. Here, take this. You have a lot of work to do." Sally handed Slade the list of companies.

After thanking Sally again, Slade left and drove Professor Krancz home. Professor Krancz insisted Slade call him if he needed any additional information. Slade assured him he would.

It took Slade almost four hours to check the three companies that had attended the science fairs in Winter Park and he met with a dead end at each. None of them had visited the biology section. Slade knew he needed a different approach if he was to narrow the field of 377 companies.

As he was sitting in his Jeep preparing to leave the last of the locations, it occurred to Slade he could check the list of science fairs Billy had entered in the last year and cross reference it with the companies attending. By narrowing the list of companies interested in biology with the frequency of their interest in science fairs might be a logical place to start. It was a long shot, but for the next two months until Professor Gordon returned it was all he had. At least it was better than trying to check on each one personally.

Ari Theopolous had not called and that was incredibly significant. It was no trivial matter. The Captain had been a full day off schedule before Kyle had become aware of it. A fishing trawler was headed for certain disaster had Captain Theopolous not intervened. As it was, the fishing trawler was safe and his company was poised to become heroes.

Matt Kyle rose slowly from behind his desk and moved to one of the large windows overlooking the Port. From his vantage point he could see the empty berth awaiting the arrival of Captain Theopolous and the retro-fitted freighter, the sea doors open beckoning her inside. They would be delayed another week at best.

The delay of the vessel was not his immediate concern. Information was what made a company successful. That and trust in leadership. The realization his employees were terrified of him had hit like a hammer. Without trust, he could not count on information or dissenting opinions forcing him to consider every option, every angle to success. He had learned that as a salesman. The path to riches was his ability to harness the creative energies of his employees and reap a small profit from each of their efforts. The collective sum far outweighed the efforts of what one man could accomplish. It was the colony approach: each component part giving a little towards the overall needs of the whole.

Kyle knew he was obsessed with riches and the subsequent power. The fact he wanted more was of no surprise; his desire for power was an insatiable hunger. Neither was the fact he would kill to achieve success a surprise to him. The ends justified the means.

The unthinkable had occurred and a dark cloud hovered around him, casting him into a shadowy realm. Kyle had allowed himself to slowly spin out of control, like a top losing its momentum and entering the final chaotic wobble before toppling. Once the momentum was lost, it was difficult to recover and re-start the process. Only through self-control could he regain his momentum.

The current project represented such a huge monetary potential, Kyle had allowed himself to become entrapped by the possibilities. Untold wealth beckoned like an expensive mistress, intent on trapping and controlling him with her charms. Billy Waterbury had truly discovered the greatest gift to Twenty-first Century man and it was a gift World Vision Quest now controlled and would share with the world when the time was right.

But first Kyle must control his desire for success, or like a cancer it would slowly consume him. No one else moved at his speed, with his clarity of mind, with his singular purpose. It was a gift and a curse. How could he expect others to understand when they did not possess his insight? Patience was a virtue he must have now more than ever. Set backs were inevitable in the business world and he knew the most successful businessmen catapulted themselves to success when confronted with obstacles; they did not become paralyzed by a hurdle, but stronger, more determined.

Inhaling deeply, Kyle moved back to his desk and slid into his chair. Pushing the intercom button, he asked his receptionist to get Captain Theopolous on the line. Ari need not fear him. It was success that needed to fear him, for he would succeed despite all the odds. It was his destiny.

It was almost five minutes before the connection was made. Kyle immediately detected the hesitancy and uncertainty in his voice.

"Mr. Kyle?"

"Ari, how are you? You have made our company heroes in the eyes of the world and you, yourself, deserve all the credit. I cannot thank you enough," shot Kyle, his words exploded forth as if he was making the sales pitch of his life.

Taken by surprise, Ari Theopolous hesitated. This was not what he had expected. "Thank you. I'm sorry I didn't call sooner, but we were busy." Ari let his voice trail off. He had gone to his quarters with the intent to call, but could not find the courage. It was a realization he had lived with for the past twenty-four hours.

"No need to apologize, Ari. Is the crew safe?" Kyle smiled to himself and at his masterful manipulation of transpiring events. This was how leaders responded—with self-assurance in the face of adversity. The great leaders turned a losing hand into a winning one; they drew an ace when one was needed to trump the opponent!

"The crew is safe and so is the trawler. We should be making port in about six days. Unless a tug can come and take over." Ari was shocked. There were no expletives from Kyle urging him to steam forward at break neck speed.

"Excellent. I would prefer if you towed the trawler to port. Are you taking her to San Francisco?" Kyle jotted a note down onto a piece of paper.

"Yes. It depends on how fast our Chief Engineer can plug a leak in her engine room. She's not in danger of sinking, but we don't want to take a chance. As a result, we're moving slowly."

"Fantastic. Please keep me posted. I want to be there at dock side to greet you. I'll have the press there. This is a shining moment for the company, Ari, and I hope you realize that."

"Yes sir, I do. We won't let you down." Ari had taken the call in his room and he found himself reaching for his map and double checking the projected time to San Francisco. With Kyle in such a good mood, he wanted to be sure of their arrival.

"Be safe, Ari, and I will see you in San Francisco."

"Thank you, sir. See you then," replied the perplexed Captain.

Kyle hung up the phone and continued to stare out the window. The media opportunity was incomprehensible. It would give World Vision Quest the opportunity to show they were good stewards of the seas and gain the respect and envy of rival companies. Kyle knew they were entitled to salvage fees, but he had no desire to collect them. It would be World Vision Quest's gift back to the trawler company. Kyle laughed out loud at the grand design. His ace-in-the-hole had been found. Never fold; up the ante and grab the pot.

The extra week in San Francisco would not harm the Project. Robert Turk had called and left a message with the receptionist that several weeks were needed to complete production. It would take at least a week to ten days to outfit *Quest 1* with the other machinery. Plenty of time for Turk to complete the order. Klauss had to double check the storage containers and the machinery that had already been shipped.Picking up the phone a second time, Kyle called Turk in Ohio.

"Turk here." Robert Turk rubbed his eyes with the back of his hand. The factory had been working twenty-four hour shifts, seven days a week to complete production on the order for Kyle. No one had seen a day off since the hurricane had struck and tempers were beginning to flare. Fatigue was setting in and he was trying to do his part to lessen the strain.

"Robert. Matt Kyle here. How is everything going?" Kyle realized the look of surprise that must be on Turk's face.

"As well as can be expected. I called your office the other day and told your receptionist we would need at least two more weeks to complete the order. I have everybody working as hard as they can." The foreman waited for the violent retort from Kyle.

"That's what I wanted to talk to you about." Kyle paused to let his words sink in, before adding, "Why don't you give the employees some time off. They've had a chance to earn some overtime money that I'm sure they can use with all the flooding in the wake of the storm. They probably need rest more than anything. A day or two is not going to hurt, do you think?"

Stunned into silence, Turk pulled the receiver from his ear and stared at it for several seconds. Was this the same man who had called yelling and screaming demanding a twenty-four hour, seven day a week schedule?

"Are you there?" Kyle fought to keep the laughter out of his voice. Once again he was in control, just like when he was a top-flight salesman keeping the customer guessing as to his next move. Control. It was all about control. And timing.

"Yes, I am and I'm a little confused. One minute you call up demanding I place the employees on shifts around the clock and then you call back and tell me to give them a day off. I don't get it," said Turk, his lack of patience, caused by fatigue, piercing through his voice.

Kyle smiled again. Turk had courage and would speak his mind. Perhaps he should look at the foreman for a position on the company with more responsibility.

"We all make mistakes, Mr. Turk. Myself included. Sometimes I have a tendency to push too hard. Give the employees a couple of days rest and thank them for me." Kyle had lowered his voice as he spoke, a tactic he had learned years ago when presenting a delicate proposal. As then, it worked now.

"Yes, sir, I'll do that. And thanks. I know they could use some time off." Turk leaned back in his chair and closed his eyes. Rest was what everyone needed and deserved.

"Good. Then call me in a week and let me know how things are going. Take care." Kyle hung up the phone without waiting on a reply and started to laugh. Slow things down and control your actions which in turn control the actions of others. So simple and yet so profound.

Kyle spent the rest of the day going over schedules, laughing with employees, and dealing with issues in the company he had been neglecting. By the end of the day, he felt he had accomplished a great deal and, for the first time in weeks, slept soundly all through the night.

Chapter Seventeen

Slade had contacted Sally at Professor Gordon's office for help with sorting through the companies. The eager secretary had jumped into the assignment with a relish. Sally had a knack for extracting information from computers and the two of them worked on the project until late in the evening, her fingers flying over the keys in a blur. For their effort, they succeeded in eliminating forty-two of the 377 companies. But most importantly, they had a system Slade knew he could use to finish the research.

The system they had devised was quite simple. First, they would locate the company's internet web page. Every company had a catchy web page serving as an information browser to tease the reader. Each introductory page listed the company's officers, locations, and products or services. By checking the directory, companies were eliminated that were not connected to biology.

If the company did have an interest in biology, then Slade and Sally would narrow the search to see what branch of biology. If it was dealing with regenerative tissue or human genetic engineering, then it was not likely they would have been interested in Billy's work. But if the company was interested in plant biology, then that company had an asterisk placed next to it for Slade to follow up on. So far, none of the companies interested in biology had met the narrow criteria.

It was after nine o'clock when they called it quits. Slade thanked Sally and escorted her to her car. After she had left, Slade realized he had not eaten since lunch and the first signs of hunger pains were readily recognizable. At this hour, Slade knew there would not be much open. Denny's was always his first choice when traveling and there was one near the campus. Besides, they served breakfast twenty-four hours a day and he felt like eggs and bacon.

Dinner was a leisurely affair. It was an opportunity to realize just how out of touch he was with fashion. Tattoos seemed to be the latest craze and the women as well as the men were indulging. Some of the designs were intricate and brightly colored. He would have to remember to discuss this with Katherine when he got back to Cedar Key.

Thinking of Katherine, Slade glanced at his watch. It was almost 10:30 PM. She was probably in bed. A tinge of guilt hit him as he realized he had not spoken with her since the early part of the afternoon. Slade let his thoughts drift around her image in his mind for some time. How had he managed to live alone for so long? Was it too late to start a family with Katherine?

Shaking his head in disbelief at the thought, Slade finished his cup of coffee and rose from the booth. As late as it was, it would be prudent to get a hotel room in town. Cedar Key was over an hour away and the two lane road leading to the small town could be treacherous at night. There was a Holiday Inn near I-75, just a few miles from campus.

After paying his bill, Slade jumped into his Jeep and backed out of the parking space. So much more work to do on trying to find out who killed Billy and his family.

Leonard was beginning to squeeze the trigger when he heard the bed springs in the adjoining room creak. Seconds later, he heard the bed springs creak again and then the sound of a body shifting weight. Leonard quickly moved into the shadow of one corner of the bedroom, his head craned to the not too distant sound. Sound could mean movement and detection.

The adjoining bedroom door was opened and he could hear footsteps down the hall. Raising the gun, the assassin trained it on the bedroom door he was hiding behind lest it should open. The footsteps moved closer and then retreated down the short hallway, continuing to the bathroom he had passed. A split second later he heard the door being closed. The distinct sounds of the young woman going to the bathroom reached his ears. In less than a minute she was done and on her way back to her bedroom, the soft patter of her feet echoing off the wood. The sound of the toilet bowl refilling finally quit and all was quiet again. All the while, Leonard never moved, the gun held steady towards the door.

He would now have to wait. There was no way he could take a chance on the girl in the next room hearing him when he pulled the trigger, even with a silenced weapon. Kyle had asked him to interrogate the two women and see what they had learned. That was always a dangerous proposition and too much could go wrong. He would kill them and search the house. If they had any information they would have probably written it down. If not, then he would tell Kyle they had not known anything.

Leonard could hear the even breathing of the young girl as she started to resume the nightly chase of her dreams. She had probably slipped back into a peaceful sleep, but he had to check. Moving out of Katherine's bedroom he crept down the hall to Shirley's door. Leonard leaned his head against the door and pressed his ear to the wood. The smell of fresh paint came to him and he could feel the soft texture of the wood against his cheek. With his right hand, Leonard reached down to grip the door knob. Since he was here, he might as well kill the young girl first; because he knew the other one was asleep.

The next set of events happened so quickly, Leonard was caught totally by surprise. A bright light was switched on and aimed directly at his eyes. The sudden brightness was followed by the hysterical shouts of the red haired woman he had thought was asleep.

"Shirley! Shirley! There's a man with a gun in the house! Call the cops!" Katherine was screaming at the top of her voice.

Katherine had been asleep when Leonard had first entered her bedroom. She had been dreaming of when she was a child and playing with her brothers on the porch of her parent's home many years ago. But something was different. It was the smell of aftershave. An aftershave her dad had never worn. Slowly, as sleep had receded, she became aware of another presence in the room, an unfamiliar presence.

Fighting the panic threatening to envelop her, Katherine trained her ears on the spot where she thought the stranger was. At first, she was not sure what she was hearing and then realized Shirley was going to the bathroom. Now she could pick out the sound of the stranger breathing, even though it was quite shallow. Katherine fought the terror clouding her mind and continued to breathe as if she was asleep, somehow knowing that may buy her a few precious minutes. Taking a chance, Katherine slowly opened her eyes to the merest of slits and from her angle, strained to see into the corner where the stranger was. Her heart almost stopped when she saw the gun raised towards the door. If Shirley opened the door, Katherine knew the stranger would kill her.

When Shirley closed her door the man lowered the gun, but continued to listen. After several minutes, he left Katherine's bedroom and moved towards Shirley's room. Katherine knew he was there to kill them and she had never felt so helpless in all her life. Exercising a control that was foreign to her, Katherine moved slowly, but steadily to the side of the bed, being careful not to make the bed springs squeak. She had heard Shirley's bed groan in protest when Shirley had lain back down and rolled over. The killer had heard it, too.

Time seemed to stand still. The only weapon at her disposal was a flashlight with a powerful beam of light. Shirley said her dad had used the light on board the boats to see at night when he was fishing late or running crab traps. The battery was the latest lithium powered rechargeable model and was equivalent to over thirty thousand candle power. Shined directly into someone's eyes it could temporarily blind them.

Creeping to her door, Katherine peered out until she could see down the hallway. The stranger was frozen at Shirley's door, the ugly looking gun held downward in his left hand, his face pressed hard against the wood. Katherine was desperately trying to formulate a plan of action when she saw the man's hand reach for Shirley's door knob. At that point instinct took over.

Katherine aimed the powerful light at the man's face and squeezed the button, simultaneously yelling so hard her lungs hurt. The man had jerked upright and spun to face the light, raising his right arm to shield his eyes. Too late, Katherine realized the killer was swinging the gun towards her, but she could not move. Her eyes locked on the gun, rooting her to that very spot. The only thing she remembered was yelling for Shirley.

Just as the gun reached shoulder height, Katherine slumped back against the door frame, her body and mind momentarily paralyzed by the fear she felt, believing she was about to die. Just as she thought the inevitable was about to happen, two rapid bursts of gunfire echoed behind her, the roar temporarily deafening her. Katherine immediately dropped the light she was holding and grabbed her head, her ear splitting scream adding to the chaos. The hallway did not retreat to darkness, because someone had switched the light on.

Katherine was aware of another presence, a familiar man moving abreast and then past her, a gun held at a forty-five degree angle, a determined look on his face. Katherine had slid to a seated position in the doorway.

Leonard was knocked back and down towards the hallway floor, two bright crimson holes in his chest. Leonard looked up at the man approaching and tried to focus on the image of the stranger, finally settling on the face. There was no compassion in the eyes, no feeling. Leonard knew this man would kill him. Without immediate medical attention he would die. Leonard summoned all of his strength and started to raise the Glock, the ugly silencer moving slowly up towards the advancing man. Just as Leonard was about to squeeze the trigger, the man fired twice more and Leonard entered the world of darkness, never to return.

Slade's last two shots hit Leonard in the head, spewing brains and skull across Shirley's bedroom door. The would-be assassin was dead immediately. Shirley could be heard inside screaming for help. Slade only paused at Leonard's body to kick the gun free from his grasp and then he quickly opened the door and calmed Shirley by letting her know it was him. Pausing for only a second, Slade turned and faced Katherine, who had risen to her feet. In three short steps Slade covered the distance separating him from her and gathered her into his arms, pressing her tightly against him. Within moments, Katherine was sobbing uncontrollably, her head buried against his shoulder.

Slade moved Katherine to Shirley's room. Tersely, he told them not to make any noise or open the door unless it was him. Before they could respond, Slade was moving, his semi-automatic Beretta .380 held at eye level.

Where his eyes looked the gun followed. It was a merging, a one-ness and Katherine felt a tinge of terror touch her when she realized the man she loved was capable of such acts of violence. Before she could dwell on it, Slade locked them inside and proceeded to search the house.

It took less than two minutes, but to the two women it felt like eternity. When Slade knocked and said it was alright, Katherine ran to the door and flung it open, desiring to see him with her own eyes. She noticed his gun was gone and briefly wondered where he had put it, before he slipped his arm around her waist.

"Come on. We need to move outside before the police arrive." Slade motioned for Shirley to follow. Neither woman looked at the dead body as Slade led them down the hall.

In the distance, sirens could be heard rapidly approaching and within minutes the place was swarming with police and paramedics. The front street was alive with flashing lights, a sea of red, amber, and blue all competing for visual prominence. Uniformed personnel were streaming in and out of the house, until yellow police tape was strung across the front door. A young police officer had taken a position there and was busy logging everyone in and out of the crime scene.

Shirley, Katherine, and Slade had retreated to the patio. Another uniformed officer was standing nearby. None of them had spoken since the shooting.

Finally Katherine had regained enough of her wits to speak.

"How did you know? I mean, how did you know a killer was here?" Katherine wiped a wayward tear from her face.

"I didn't. I was going to stay in Gainesville and come back tomorrow, but something kept telling me to come home and see you. I can't explain it." Slade stared at Katherine and then at Shirley.

"What alerted you?" Shirley's hand was shaking as she reached for a glass of water. Nothing had prepared her for this. Not the death of her parents or Billy. Nothing. Her orderly, sane world was still being turned upside down, threatening to envelop her in a perpetual world of chaos. When would it end? Would it end?

Slade cleared his voice and started to tell them what had happened, trying not to leave anything out. He knew he would have to repeat it to the cops later, probably several times. After deciding to leave Gainesville and come back to Cedar Key, Slade had driven as fast as he could, a weird sense of impending dread settling over him. When he entered the tiny island community, he had driven to his place first, thinking the two women might be there. When he failed to locate them, he had driven towards Shirley's house.

Slade paused as the Police Chief arrived on scene and walked towards the patio where they were. When the Police Chief stopped, Slade nodded towards him and then continued. The streets were deserted and when Slade

127

rounded the corner, he had seen the white van parked at the end of the block. Realizing he had never seen it before, Slade turned his lights off and parked his car behind a cedar tree about a block and a half away. Utilizing all the cover he could find, Slade had crept up on the van and found the keys in the ignition, a sure sign someone was coming back for it, wanting to leave in a hurry.

Raising his eyes, Slade looked directly at Chief Singletee as he continued to speak. Slade told them how a brief search of the interior of the van revealed a dead body wrapped in plastic bags. Before he could say anything else, Slade was stopped by the upraised hand of Chief Singletee.

"Where is the van?" asked the Chief, his eyes narrowing.

"At that end of the block," motioned Slade, indicating towards the pier.

"Get over there and don't touch it. I'll have the detectives get a search warrant when they get here." The uniformed officer that had been standing beside the table, bolted for the door to carry out the request of the Chief. Turning back to Slade, Chief Singletee said, "Go ahead."

"I then sprinted for the house and found where the killer had cut the door glass out." Slade motioned to the door leading to the kitchen and the Chief, along with both women, looked at the perfectly round piece of glass lying on the windowsill next to the door. "I was creeping down the hallway when I saw Katherine turn on your dad's flashlight and start screaming he had a gun. By then I had found the light switch and when he turned on Katherine, I shot him." Slade let his voice trail off. Katherine got up and walked over, kissing him lightly on the cheek.

"All of you need to come down to the station and make a statement," instructed Chief Singletee. He started to move forward when he was stopped by Slade's voice.

"No," was all Slade said.

"What do you mean, 'no'?" snapped the Chief, squaring off on Slade and meeting his stare directly.

"Just what I said. I thought I was perfectly clear. No means no. Which means I'm not going and neither are they." Slade met the eyes of the top cop and did not blink. A coldness entered his eyes and lingered in his voice.

"You just killed a man, mister, so you may want to cooperate. I could have you arrested if you-"

"If I what? You and I both know you're bluffing. You have nothing to hold me on. I just gave a statement and for now, that will have to do. If you have charges, let's see them. Put up or shut up," snarled Slade, taking a step towards the lawman.

Chief Singletee did not say anything, but returned Slade's glare. It was the chief who looked away and adopted a more docile tone.

"Where will you be?"

"At my place. And make sure you knock and identify yourself. I'm getting tired of people trying to kill me and the ones I love." Slade reached out and took Katherine's hand and then grabbed Shirley's upper arm as he directed them to the front door.

"Slade, I don't have any clothes," pleaded Shirley.

"We'll bring you some," responded the chief and then he added, "I'm placing a guard on your house and giving you an escort, whether you like it or not." Before Slade could respond the chief motioned for two of his officers to accompany them. Chief Singletee did not move until Slade and the women were in his Jeep, with a police cruiser in front and one in the rear. Even then, he remained there until they disappeared from sight. The man had a set of balls, mused the chief. It was time they talked, but not right now.

Turning back to the crime scene, Chief Singletee started yelling for his detectives. It was going to be a long night and he did not even have a cup of coffee, much less the proverbial donut.

Chapter Eighteen

The remainder of the night had gone by swiftly, finally chased away by the early morning rays of the sun peeking over the horizon and the sound of water birds calling to each other. Shirley had been given the guest bedroom and Slade had heard her tossing and turning, trying desperately to find the elusive realm of sleep. It was a losing battle and the bags under her eyes proved it.

Katherine had not fared much better. She had snuggled up next to him and faked like she was in slumber, but Slade had felt her hand rub his shoulders repeatedly through the early morning hours, making sure he was there. It was a safety blanket for her and he did not let on he was awake.

During breakfast, he had tried his best to cheer them up and they had played along. It was obvious they were both still very scared. Slade was scared, too. He just hid it better. The thought of losing them was something he did not want to consider. Shirley had become like a sister to him. And Katherine, well, she was the woman with whom he knew he would spend the rest of his life.

"Why are you looking at me like that?" Katherine sipped slowly from a cup of coffee.

"Just thinking." Slade turned to look out onto the back porch. "Hey! Look who is here." The excitement in Slade's voice caused both women to turn around. Old Clacker had somehow managed to enter the screen porch and was staring inside the house, occasionally opening and closing his massive beak, indicating they were late with breakfast.

"He's probably hungry." Katherine moved to the refrigerator and returned with a plateful of fish.

"Will he bite?" Shirley looked distrustfully at the large bird.

"Yes," said Slade, rising from the table.

"No, he will not," countered Katherine opening the back door and reaching down to rub Old Clacker's head. The bird craned his neck to direct her fingers around to the most sensitive spots. Smelling the fish, the bird opened his mouth and Katherine dropped a small fish towards him. Old Clacker caught the fish in one deft movement and swallowed quickly.

"Can I feed him?" asked Shirley.

"Sure. Come on over here." Katherine instructed the younger woman where to stand.

Old Clacker watched the approach of the younger woman and when she drew near Katherine, the feathers on the top of his head stood up and he started to lower his wings, a sure sign of anger indicating attack was imminent. "You stop that," scolded Katherine, reaching down to rub his head. She motioned for Shirley to do the same. Once Shirley touched his head, the old bird calmed down and eyed the plate of fish.

"I'll be damned," stammered Slade.

"See. I told you to be nice to him," laughed Katherine, handing Shirley a fish.

Shirley deftly dropped the fish and Old Clacker made short work of the morsel. Greedily, he opened and closed his mouth in rapid succession, indicating he wanted more. Both women each dropped a fish to the waiting bird. A cry of glee emitted from them when Old Clacker showed no signs of slowing down. It was hard to tell who was having more fun, the bird or the two women.

Slade quietly retreated to a chair in the corner of the porch. Old Clacker had succeeded where he had failed. The hungry bird had them thinking about events other than those of last night. A wry smile crafted itself carefully across Slade's face. He was never happier than right now that he had taken the time to rescue the pelican.

"Does he always eat this much?" Shirley dropped the last fish into the bird's cavernous pouch.

"Sometimes." Katherine bent down to rub the old bird again. Old Clacker lowered his head exposing his neck to the gentle touch of the woman. Old Clacker waddled after the two women, settling down between them, when they moved to a bench. Within moments he rested his bill over his right wing, closed his eyes and fell asleep.

"You have literally fed him off his feet."

"He needed a good meal." Katherine smiled at Slade. Somehow things seemed brighter and she could tell Shirley felt the same way.

Before anybody could say anything, the doorbell sounded. All three of them snapped their heads up and rose at the same time. Motioning for the women to stay in the living room, Slade walked over to a cypress wet bar that also housed his stereo in addition to some liquor. It appeared as if Slade reached under the front portion of the protruding lip of the bar and pulled down. The front part of the bar slid down, recessing into the panel beneath it. Inside the hidden drawer were several handguns, placed into neat cutouts. Slade selected one, slipped it into the back of his pants and then closed the bar. Turning, he met the stern gaze of Katherine.

"Just in case."

"When were you going to tell me about your hidden arsenal?" Katherine did nothing to mask the hurt in her voice, indicating she was not happy he had not shared the secret.

"I thought I had." Slade glanced back at her twice as he walked to the door. Just as he reached for the doorknob, the door bell chimes sounded again. Slade slipped his right hand behind his back and gripped the handgun hidden in his waistband and opened the door with his left. Standing in front of him was Chief Singletee.

"Good morning, Mr. Lockwood. I assume Ms. Wintergate and Ms. Waterbury are here?" The chief was in a very jolly mood.

"They are." Slade stood silently in the doorway and waited for the chief to speak.

"May I come in?" asked the Chief, looking at Slade's right arm and noticing it had disappeared behind his back. "Unless you're going to shoot me."

"Should I?" Slade stepped back and allowed the lawman to enter.

"Not hardly. I believe we can help each other. It's time you and I share our resources," smiled Chief Singletee.

Slade directed the chief into the living room area where Katherine and Shirley were still standing. After pleasantries were exchanged, Slade motioned for him to have a seat. The chief selected a large leather armchair that enveloped him. Shirley and Katherine took the sofa and Slade seated himself across from the chief.

"How can you help us?" asked Slade.

"You don't trust me, do you?" When Slade nodded he did not, the chief smiled. "Is it because of this?" The chief unbuttoned his uniform shirt and reached inside, withdrawing a dark blue cylindrical object. When the chief looked up, the smile fled from his face. Slade had his 9mm Beretta, the same gun he had carried on the force in Los Angeles, trained on the chief's chest, the barrel held steady by experienced hands, the muzzle dancing across his heart.

When Katherine and Shirley saw the chief's expression change, they both looked at Slade and inhaled quick intakes of breath. Both women remained silent, staring at the cold light in Slade's eyes. There was no doubt in the room he would pull the trigger if provoked. That startling truth was also not lost on Chief Singletee. At that moment, Katherine was fiercely proud of him and a little afraid.

"That would be the main reason. I assume that's the silencer from the man I killed at Billy's lab." Slade waited for the chief to answer. When the chief nodded yes, Slade continued. "Does it match the one of the man I killed at Shirley's?"

"An exact match. I think it belonged to the dead man we found in the van. The serial numbers have been filed off, so there is no way to trace them. I think the dead man in the van was the partner of the man at Billy's lab who tried to kill you. I also think the man you killed at Shirley's was sent in to clean up the loose ends, including the man you missed at Billy's lab."

"But why?" blurted Katherine.

"For the same reason they killed Billy and his parents." Chief Singletee spoke slowly.

"I thought you were of the opinion the deaths of the Waterbury's was an accident?" Slade's gun barrel was still leveled at the chief's chest.

"I never said that. You assumed that. I knew Hank for over fifteen years. He helped me become police chief here and he was the best damn sea captain I have ever met. There is no way under the sun he would have gone out in the middle of a hurricane." The chief paused and turned to Shirley. "Your dad was a fine man. I didn't know your mom that well, but your father was a friend and a confidant. I'm sorry I've remained silent for so long, but I've been waiting for more to go on. Maybe now I can help." The chief stopped and looked back at Slade, his eyes inadvertently dropping to the weapon that was still trained on his chest.

"Go on," was all Slade said.

"What is your next move? I know you went to the Coast Guard in Sarasota and I know you have the builder of the *Fair Rose* coming to inspect her. What is it going to prove? I also know you have gotten close to the truth or the person pulling the strings wouldn't have sent that hit man to finish the job. I think it's the first time he or they have panicked and made a mistake. It might be our chance to capitalize on their error." The chief smiled at Slade but it was not returned.

"How do you figure?" Slade rested the barrel of his gun on his knee. The chief may be who he said he was, but he was not taking any chances. More than his life depended on it.

"Track him down to his source. It is our only chance. Unless of course you have another angle." Chief Singletee settled back in the chair.

"I do have another lead I'm tracking down and hopefully they will both end up at the doorstep of the person who started this whole mess." Slade decocked his gun and slid it back into his waistband. Only then did a smile touch his lips.

"What changed your mind?" Chief Singletee visibly relaxed.

"You think too much like a cop." The point was lost on Katherine and Shirley. If the chief was bad, then he had been fooled. Chief Singletee was a diehard cop. It was evident in everything he said and did.

"Occupational hazard."

"Let's catch each other up," instructed Slade. The two lawmen exchanged information in a very crisp, non-wasteful type of conversation. Katherine and Shirley were able to keep up with ninety percent of the conversation, but every now and then the chief and Slade would lapse into police-speak.

"Leonard Woodman. You got a match on him quick."

"He's been in the system for some time. The locals in your old neck of the woods know of him, lived just north of Los Angeles in Pasadena. You familiar with the area?"

"Yeah. Do you have an exact address?" Slade's mind was racing.

"Yup, sure do. Here." Chief Singletee dug into his shirt pocket and handed Slade a small piece of paper.

"Can we keep all of this out of the media?" Slade was already mentally preparing himself for a cross country trip. Los Angeles—he had not thought of the place in a long time. So many memories. Slade let the thoughts trail away. Glancing out of the corner of his eye, he saw Katherine watching him. She would not like this.

"Nobody cares what happens in a sleepy little town like Cedar Key. I have already squashed the media. The reporter owed me a favor and I promised him an exclusive once we sort this whole thing out." Chief Singletee drained the last of his tea and politely asked Katherine if he could have another glass. "You'll want to leave so nobody sees you or knows that you're gone."

"And how will I accomplish that?"

"Leave that to me."

Why had Leonard not called? Matt Kyle moved across the room and robotically straightened some books on a bookshelf. Leonard was always punctual. Was he dead? Kyle dismissed the idea. He had used Leonard in the past and the man was ruthless. Leonard would make sure the odds were in his favor before striking. Maybe it was taking longer than he had expected to dispose of the cop and two women.

Kyle let the thought leave him. With more insight, he was gaining greater understanding of himself, his surroundings and his purpose. It was all becoming so clear, so vivid, so alive. The future was bright and promising.

Kyle pressed the monitor near his phone and instructed his secretary to have his private jet ready for a trip to San Francisco. Ari Theopolous was still at sea towing in the stricken fishing trawler, but would be arriving in San Francisco Bay in four to five days. Kyle wanted to make sure he was there. It was a grand opportunity to showcase his company. Until Turk sent the new valves there was nothing Klaus could do. The valves were pivotal to construction and were the final pieces. He might as well capitalize on the slow time to garner media attention.

There was another reason Kyle wanted to fly to San Francisco. Silicon Valley was close-by and he wanted to visit several micro-chip manufacturers. Always alert to grab technology for his growing export company, Kyle had heard rumors about a new chip that was soon to make the current processors obsolete. If he could swing a deal to purchase existing technology for pennies on the dollar, then he could export to Latin and South America and recognize a substantial profit, perhaps into the tens of millions.

Moving back to his huge desk, Kyle picked up a secure phone and called Sommer. The salesman had been incredibly efficient and successful. It was time to see how he was doing with Israel. The phone connection was made and a limited amount of static filled the receiver.

"Hello? Matt?" Sommer cupped one hand over his other ear to hear his boss better.

"Clyde! Can you hear?"

"Yes I can." Sommer cradled the phone with his shoulder while retrieving a notepad from his briefcase. "The Israelis have a counter-proposal."

"What is it?"

"They have offered one billion dollars for exclusive rights in the Middle East, with the exception of Saudi Arabia of course."

"What type of exclusive rights?" Kyle quickly calculated the amount of deposits already logged into World Vision Quest's accounts. Over four billion dollars. He had been right—the demand was there. A large demand.

"They don't want the technology shared with the Syrians, Iraqis, Iranians, and most certainly not the Palestinians. Also, they want to be there when the prototype is tested. Is that acceptable?"

There was a long pause before Kyle answered. His mind was working quickly, shrewdly calculating the costs earned versus the potential for earnings in the future. If Israel held exclusive rights to the Middle East, then they would monopolize the area, controlling a large corner of the market. The balance of power would once and for all shift in their direction. A billion dollars was a cheap price to pay for such a stranglehold. For the first time in the last eighty years, oil would no longer be the number one marketable item in the Middle-East.

"That's not acceptable. They need to sweeten the deal. Maybe tie us in to a percentage of profits for the next twenty years or substantially up the initial entry price. Either way, a billion dollars is cheap for them to attain such a huge advantage. Remember, we have not even talked to Kuwait and they are always looking for new technology and have the money to pay for it. A billion dollars is not enough."

Clyde Sommer slowly closed his brief case and sat down on the edge of his bed. Reluctantly, he had to agree with Kyle. The Israelis were getting off lightly. Who would have ever thought a billion dollars would be considered a small payment for services?

"I agree. I'll go back to the Israelis and tell them. They are shrewd and know a good deal when they see one. I think they'll do business." Sommer was already thinking of the new proposal he would present.

"Excellent. Thanks for all of your hard work on this, Clyde. I know you have been away from your family for some time, but the reward will be worth it. As a matter of fact, when you close the deal with the Israelis, I want you to come home. We have more than enough start up capital for this project. Once production starts and publicity hits, we'll be hard pressed to keep up with demand. Your job is almost over." Kyle propped his feet up on his desk. There was a moment of silence before there was a response on the other end of the phone.

Sommer did not immediately say anything. Something was wrong. Kyle had changed. Sommer shrugged his shoulders to himself and engaged Kyle in conversation.

Kyle and Clyde talked about Clyde's family, the weather, traveling and all the non-descript things two people talk about that have not seen each other for some time. Sommer was left with a renewed sense of loyalty to Kyle and World Vision Quest and Kyle had detected it in his voice. Hanging up the phone, Sommer grabbed pen and paper and started writing out the new proposal. A new vitality surged through him. Whatever had changed Kyle had changed him for the good. Good for him and good for the company. In addition to being rich, Sommer now felt like his work was meaningful. For the life of him, Sommer could not determine which meant more.

Kyle hung the phone up in his office and once again closed his eyes. Control. Everything hinged and pivoted around control. Control the variables and you control the outcome. Sommer was a variable, just like Ari Theopolous and Robert Turk. Each crucial to the success of World Vision Quest. Each playing a part he had pre-destined for them. He was like a marionette and they were puppets, with their strings being pulled at his whim and desire.

Professor Johansen ambled slowly down the aisles. Only a little less than three days left before the exhibits were completed. Students were buzzing around display cases and erecting poster boards. Soon judges would hover in front of their displays, ask pointed questions, and decide if their effort was worthy of a first place vote. All the work and preparation would be decided in less than thirty minutes of evaluation. Somehow it did not seem fair. All the toil, for a few brief moments of fame.

Professor Johansen stopped in front of the three empty stalls that were to have housed Billy Waterbury's project. What had the young man done with mangroves that had been so important? A Slade Lockwood had called him to see if Billy had possibly mailed a paper to him detailing what he had been working on and the exact nature of his exhibit. Professor Krancz and

Professor Ruth Gordon, both UF peers, had vouched for Billy and no paper had been sent. Their words of recommendation and strong praise had been enough.

As powerful as Einstein's work in physics. The thought kept traveling through his mind, tormenting him and depriving him of sleep. What had the young man discovered? Professor Johansen could not help but continue to feel grief at the loss of the young life that had been so promising. Surely, there was a record somewhere of his work. Someone as intelligent as Billy would not have left his work to chance. There would be notes, a journal, something.

Making up his mind, Professor Johansen removed his cell phone from his breast pocket and dialed Betty.

"Yes." Betty recognized the cell phone number as it flashed across her phone pad.

"Betty, I want you to book me on a flight to Cedar Key as soon as this science fair is over." Professor Johansen continued to stare at the empty spaces. If he had been killed in an accident, he would want someone to bring his work to light and share it with the scientific community. From one scientist to another, it was the least he could do. The young man's work would not end in vain.

"Cedar Key? Can I go?" asked Betty.

"Absolutely. I will need your help. Make sure we get a couple of graduate assistants wanting to do some field work. And Betty," added Professor Johansen, "Make sure we have computers and all the other stuff we'll need. We have a lot of work to do and a mystery to solve." Professor Johansen snapped his phone shut before his confused secretary could reply. He had one more field assignment in his old bones. He could feel it.

Betty looked at the phone receiver for several seconds. A field trip? It had been years since Professor Johansen had gone on a research field trip. It had to be the Waterbury boy. The death of the young man had hit Professor Johansen hard, which was weird considering he had never met the young man. Professor Johansen had asked her a dozen times if she was sure Billy Waterbury had not submitted a position paper. Only after assuring him Billy had not and showing him all of the biology position papers for the science fair, had the professor let the subject drop. But Betty knew it had not gone away.

Professor Johansen was the brightest mind she had ever encountered in her tenure at the University. He was also the most stubborn. Once Professor Johansen had an idea planted in his mind, it would take irrefutable evidence to sway him. And then it was only a fifty-fifty proposition. Billy had obtained a champion to further his cause, to complete his work, and bring it to light of the science community and mankind. Betty could think of no one better.

Picking up the phone, Betty started dialing the Professor's wife, Elaine. If the Professor was true to form, he had not yet informed her they were about to go on a trip. For that matter, Betty realized she had better call her husband. Frank had some vacation time coming and had always enjoyed going along on field trips. Besides, they had been talking about a vacation to Florida.

Grabbing a piece of paper, Betty started to make notes as Elaine Johansen's phone started to ring. A lot to do in three days.

Chapter Nineteen

The knock at the door was done softly. Looking over at Shirley, Katherine carefully got off the sofa and moved to the door, listening intently as she went. A third soft knock prompted her to respond.

"Just a minute," called Katherine, pausing to look out the window. A smallish, heavy set man was at the door. A straw hat was pulled down on his head hiding a bald spot that was circled by a two inch band of defiant brown locks. The man was staring over his shoulder at the *Fair Rose*.

Moving to another window in the living room, Katherine found the policeman standing near his police car. The police officer could see the heavy set man and the doorway. Making eye contact with Katherine, the police officer gave the thumbs up sign. Making a mental note to herself, Katherine knew she should have given the officer Slade's phone number.

Katherine opened the door and confronted the stranger, with Shirley close behind.

"May I help you?" Katherine used a flat tone in her voice.

"I believe you can. I'm Willard Mayes, original builder of the *Fair Rose*. Slade Lockwood called me about three days ago and asked me to come and look at her. Is Mr. Lockwood here?" Willard offered a beefy hand for Katherine to shake.

Katherine liked the little old man. He had a certain fatherly quality to him and Shirley sensed it, too. Both women visibly relaxed.

Sensing their pent up apprehension, Willard apologized. "I'm sorry if now is a bad time. The police officer told me about some of your misfortune. After he verified who I was and called the Chief of Police." Willard laughed a deep throaty laugh and his face turned bright red.

"I'm glad to hear he is being efficient." Katherine immediately knew who Willard reminded her of. "Have you ever been told that you look like the Skipper on *Gilligan's Island?*"

"Yes, I have, especially when I laugh," said Willard, bursting into laughter again with the two women.

"Why don't you come in?" Shirley prompted Katherine to open the door.

"I would rather have you ladies join me while I look at the *Fair Rose*, if it is okay with you?" The portly man smiled and turned a brighter red in the face. When both women nodded, Willard started back down the steps.

"Why did Slade call you?" Katherine was trying to keep up with Willard.

"He wanted me to look at the *Fair Rose* and see if I could find if she had been tampered with. Slade does not believe the boat owner allowed her to fall into disrepair and I don't believe he feels there was any faulty equipment on her."

The conversation stopped as Willard stood quietly in front of the *Fair Rose*, his practiced eye taking in her bow. Carefully, Willard bent over and looked at her keel and let his eyes travel the length of the hull.

"My dad bought it for my mom." Shirley moved forward and placed her hand on the starboard gunnels. "My mom had a thing about roses and Dad thought the name and the boat would make her happy." Shirley rubbed the boat with her hand and then added, "It did."

"Your father took real good care of this boat, maam." Willard moved slowly around the hull. "You can tell your father knew a thing or two about boats. I assume the engine was the original Volvo I had installed?" Willard arched his eyebrows and was hoping the answer would be yes.

"Yup. I remember when Dad overhauled it. He was so particular about it, he almost drove us crazy."

"What do you hope to find?" Katherine was listening intently to the conversation between the two.

"I don't know, but I'm going to have a look if it is okay with you ladies?" Willard smiled a toothy smile under his straw hat.

"It's fine with us." Shirley moved back as Willard climbed aboard.

"How about if we make some ice tea and bring you some?" Katherine placed a hand over her eyes to shield the sun. It was barely ten in the morning and already hot.

"Thank you, maam, but please bring lots of it. I believe I'll sweat up a storm." With that, Willard started his throaty laugh and disappeared towards the rear of the boat, lifting the engine cover. "Hello, lady," said the boat builder, dropping down into the hold.

Katherine and Shirley headed back up the stairs. The little boat builder was eccentric, but cute. Both women did not speak the unthinkable, but both knew they hoped he would find nothing, which was the something they needed.

Chief Singletee had sneaked Slade out of Cedar Key in the middle of the night. The mode of travel was a twin engine 1984 Cessna T303 Crusader a retired Navy officer kept at the Cedar Key airport. The airplane had been painted white with blue stripes. A pink Flamingo, complete with sunglasses and a straw hat adorned each fuselage. The birds were eye catching. She had been named *The Pink Flamingo*.

She was fast and functional. Cessna had only built 297 of the planes from 1978 to 1982. Larger single engine planes with better fuel economy and competition from other airline manufacturers had spelled the end for the Crusader. Only a handful existed. *The Pink Flamingo* was capable of 250 miles per hour with a cruising altitude of 18,000 feet. With the capacity to carry six passengers, she was sleek, strong, and roomy.

The owner was a fifty-one year old ex-Navy fighter pilot, but still had the swagger and brashness of a younger combat man. June Stenger was slightly taller than Slade and kept a wad of chewing tobacco in his jaw, spitting every so often or whenever he needed to make a point. Being a retired military man, the plane was spit and polish.

The plane had gotten its name by June's former Navy buddies. When asked what he was going to do after retiring from the military, June had told them he was going to move to Florida and fish. They had all laughed and said he would buy a house in a retirement village, complete with fake flamingos on the lawn. In the end, the love of flying had won out and the only flamingos were the ones painted on the plane. For a man used to flying off the decks of aircraft carriers and still feeling the longing to kick in after-burners of a thirty million dollar fighter, the turbo-charged Cessna had filled the void. *The Pink Flamingo* had found the right man to handle the controls.

Katherine had opposed the idea from the very beginning and it had taken all of Slade's persuasive powers to convince her he would be okay. The deciding vote came when he looked her in the eyes and told her he loved her more than anything else on Earth. The fact that Shirley and Chief Singletee were present when he confessed his feelings seemed to seal the deal. Reluctantly, Katherine had agreed, but only after making sure he would call at least once a day while he was gone.

On the ride to the airport, Slade had told Chief Singletee that calling daily may be out of the question. Chief Singletee had agreed, so they established a second, more clandestine form of communication.

"You have everything?" Chief Singletee placed his right hand on Slade's shoulder. The Chief liked this man. There was a certainty about him, a solidness. Something inside told him he could trust Slade Lockwood.

"Yeah, I think so." Slade smiled and then his face grew sober. "Please keep an eye on Shirley and Katherine. I can take care of myself, but don't let anything happen to them."

"Don't worry, Slade. Nothing is going to happen to them. You find out what's going on and I'll track things down on this end. By the time anyone finds out you're gone, you'll have a leg up on them. Do you have a gun?"

"Yeah, I have one. Extra ammo, too." Slade turned towards the plane.

"Be careful," yelled the Chief, moving back as Slade slipped inside the Cessna and the engines increased in revolution.

"Buckle your seatbelt," instructed June, sliding his headset on and motioning for Slade to do the same.

After they had been cleared for takeoff, June eased the plane onto the runway and gunned the engines. The only runway at Cedar Key leads directly into the waters of the Gulf of Mexico. Miscalculate and within seconds you are swimming instead of flying. Slade sat stoically as the lights from the plane danced across the asphalt and the runway disappeared beneath the belly of the craft. Just when he was sure they were not going to make it, June pulled back on the yoke and the plane nosed into the air, sprinting up and away. Slade looked over his shoulder and saw the lights of Cedar Key fading quickly. It was only then that Slade looked around the cock pit and into the interior of the plane. She was bigger than he had thought.

"She's a beauty isn't she?"

"Yes, she is. Can she get us all the way to California or do we have to refuel?"

"We'll have to refuel in Texas, probably Dallas-Ft.Worth. We'll see. All depends on a tail wind." June spoke briefly to the radio tower.

"I want to thank you for all your help. Keep up with expenses and I'll pay you when I get back."

"No charge, Mr. Lockwood. Hank and Mary Waterbury were personal friends. So is Chief Singletee. You just find out what happened. That's payment enough for me." June looked at Slade with a stern look in his eyes. "You might want to get some sleep. The chairs fold into a bed. Not the Hilton, but they ain't bad either."

"Thanks."

Kicking off his shoes, Slade laid down on the bed, but not before sliding his Beretta beneath his pillow. From here on out he was entering enemy territory and it was best to think that way. Slade cradled his head, his fingers resting on the butt of the gun. The drone of the engines lulled him into a shallow sleep.

June looked over his shoulder at Slade who was snoring contentedly. He knew they had considerable flying time to get to their destination. Somehow, he hoped it would be enough time for Slade to get sleep and get refreshed. An uneasy feeling formed in the pit of June's stomach, but there was a warm feeling coursing through his body at the same time. He had not felt like this since the last time he had flown in combat.

June glanced at his sleeping passenger one more time. Whatever was ahead, he would make sure he was there to help. Hank Waterbury had been a friend. He deserved that and much more. A wry smile touched June's face. Checking the controls of the *Flamingo*, he moved her back on course. All the gauges indicated the old bird was flying just fine.

Adjusting his headset, June started to softly whistle a tune his dad had taught him many years ago.

San Francisco was a beautiful city. The rolling hills circling the famous bay; the massive bridge spanning the water, arching high into an early morning fog. Even modern development had not spoiled the natural allure the place held. What were the words in the song, "I left my heart in San Francisco." Matt Kyle could not remember all of it, but he had always liked visiting here. It made him feel alive. It was here during the sixties the hippie movement had started. Clint Eastwood and Dirty Harry had made the city unique in the seventies and it had just never gone out of vogue.

Kyle slid back in the posh leather recliner that had been specially installed in his private Learjet. An attentive hostess poured him another glass of chilled orange juice and he sipped from the frosty cup, tasting the pulp as it coursed over his tongue.

Quest 1 would be docking in another day, perhaps two. Ari Theopolous was making good time towing the stricken fishing vessel to port. Per the laws of the sea, World Vision Quest, though not a salvage or tug company, could claim rights and demand compensation for saving the damaged trawler. Kyle had no intention of milking the owners for a few hundred thousand dollars. The publicity he would receive from the generous and heroic acts of *Quest 1* would far outweigh any monetary compensation.

The publicity trail had already begun. Before leaving San Pedro, Kyle had started his marketing department on the task of generating information to feed the insatiable appetites of the news media. Journalists could not help themselves. This was the type of story for which they lived. 'Prominent company saves those less fortunate and asks for nothing in return.' Kyle could see the headlines now depicting him as a hero.

The news surrounding the saving of the trawler would serve as a launch pad for him to visit Silicon Valley. Everyone loved a hero and he was sure to be splashed across all the papers.

Forgetting about the trawler and the news interviews awaiting him in San Francisco, Kyle turned his attention to more pressing matters. Why had Leonard not contacted him? Was he dead? With each passing hour, Kyle feared the worst. He was fighting an urge to send someone else to check on Leonard and finish the job if he had failed.

After carefully reviewing all of the information at his disposal, Kyle was convinced it had been a mistake to send Leonard to kill the two women and the cop. Foolishly, he had listened to the local thug in Cedar Key. He should have trusted his instincts and waited. To act rashly always had negative consequences. Patience. Patience was always needed in the ruthless jungle of the business world.

Too late, he had realized that if the women or the cop had any information they would have gone to the authorities. Why wait? They had nothing. Lockwood had the remains of the boat on which the Waterbury's had been found. So what? It would not show anything. It was a busted up relic. A tomb for a stubborn, ignorant, backwoods family.

What had made the Waterbury's unable to see the benefits of signing a contract with him? They would have become multi-millionaires. World Vision Quest would have manufactured and marketed Billy's invention and they would have reaped untold wealth. It was a win-win scenario for everyone.

The conversation with Hank Waterbury still echoed in his brain. *"My son wants to perfect his idea and conduct some further tests. If it is as beneficial as you believe, then your company will have an opportunity to compete."* An opportunity to compete. To compete for what? Second string? A backseat while someone else cornered the rights to the greatest invention to ever benefit mankind? A chance to be left out of the history books?

If only they had co-operated they would have been alive today. Kyle let the tenseness leave his body and sunk lower in his seat. Hopefully, all information Billy Waterbury had pertaining to his model was destroyed or in the hands of World Vision Quest.

Reassuring himself, Kyle slid lower in his seat and motioned for a pillow. Everything would be okay. Through his will power alone, he would ensure it.

Chapter Twenty

"There is no way carbon monoxide poisoned the passengers in the cabin. When the engine was reworked, Mr. Waterbury added two stabilizers to the exhaust system to make sure the diesel engine vented outside. Even in a storm and even if the deck ruptured, the exhaust lines would have never burst and entered the cabin. It's a physical impossibility." Willard Mayes looked directly at Chief Singletee.

"Are there any smaller lines leading to the cabin that could have carried exhaust fumes?"

"There are no small lines. Everything is self-contained in the engine well."

"What about if one of the exhaust lines sprung a leak? Could the carbon monoxide have traveled through a natural channel to the cabin and seeped up through the floor? I mean is that possible?"

"Perhaps, but I would need to conduct further tests to determine if that happened. That is a highly unlikely scenario anyway, because for the boat to have twisted and turned to create a channel in the superstructure means the boat was being torn apart. Cause of death on the autopsy report was asphyxiation from carbon monoxide. I don't think anyone is going to wait around to die from carbon monoxide poisoning when a boat is being torn apart around them."

"Where would you conduct further tests?" Katherine adjusted a pair of dark tinted sunglasses.

"At my plant. My oldest son runs the operation now, but I kept a small bay in the back so I can tinker around. Keeps an old man out of trouble." The little old boat builder smiled.

"Do you need any money? Any up front costs?" Shirley took a step closer. Here was another man willing to help prove her family had been murdered.

145

"I don't need any money." Willard stopped, turned and looked at Shirley for a long time before addressing her. When he did, he removed his straw hat and wiped his head with a dark blue handkerchief. Placing his hat back on his head, he finally spoke. "You have gone through enough Ms. Waterbury. Besides, I built this boat and know her better than even your dad did. I'll have her towed to my boat yard."

Shirley stepped forward and kissed Willard on the cheek before giving him a hug. For several seconds there was an awkward silence. When Shirley finally let the portly little man loose, she smiled at him through misty eyes.

"Thank you for all your help."

"Don't mention it."

"Why don't we go inside? Shirley and I will make some sandwiches." Katherine turned and led the group up the stairs and inside Slade's house.

After they were seated and at the table chewing on thick slices of cold cuts, the Chief directed his first question to Shirley.

"Any more luck with what Billy was working on?"

"Not really. So far I know Billy was attempting to change the genetic structure of black mangroves. As you know, this was confirmed by the conversation Slade had with Professor Gordon's intern at the University of Florida. Apparently Billy had spoken to him several times about genetic cell manipulation. The problem is I don't know what quality Billy was hoping to improve. It could have been reproduction, growth rate, or any of a number of things."

"Why are we assuming it was Billy's work on mangroves these people were after?" Katherine placed a half eaten sandwich on her plate and selected a very large and plump pickle. "If Billy was half as prolific at entering science fairs as you're telling us, then it could have been something from an earlier discovery. Not necessarily what he was working on now."

"We found the remains of several plants in the garage. Five to be exact. What we have found supports what Shirley is suggesting. There was no evidence to indicate the two thugs were interested in anything else," added Chief Singletee, reaching for another sandwich.

"You're forgetting Slade recovered a piece of paper from the one gunman and it had the formula for the mangrove on it," clarified Shirley. "All roads lead to Rome and all evidence points to Billy's work on mangroves as the target."

"I had forgotten about the piece of paper. Was there anything left in the garage that could be checked or examined?" Katherine directed her question to Chief Singletee.

"No. The computer hard drive was burned by the fire and our lab techs were unable to retrieve any data."

"Where is all the stuff?" Shirley looked over her glass at the chief.

"In our evidence room. I've put a hold on all the items until this case is over. No need to throw anything away until we know exactly what we're dealing with. You never know what might be evidence."

"What about the list of companies Slade was going through? Any luck with those?" Willard looked up when the room grew silent.

"I didn't mean to eavesdrop, but I've heard you talking about it the last two days." Willard smiled reassuringly.

"So far nothing has developed. We found several companies that attended all the science fairs Billy entered. However, there is nothing to indicate these companies had a great interest in biology or gene manipulation. I can't find any record of these companies calling the house. We're still checking, but it looks like a dead end." Shirley sipped from her glass.

"I hope Slade is having better luck." Katherine had a far away look enter her eyes.

A sharp tap at the rear door caused them all to jump and the chief spun quickly around, reaching for his gun. Peering in the back door was Old Clacker and he was letting them know he was hungry.

"That damn bird tried to bite me yesterday," growled the chief, rubbing his hand across the butt of his gun.

"Old Clacker? He would never do such a thing," laughed Katherine, retrieving some fish for the hungry bird.

"How is he getting in the porch? I locked the door this morning," questioned Shirley.

"I don't know, but as long as Old Clacker is standing guard, I feel safe," giggled Katherine, opening the door and tossing the bird a sardine. A quick flip of his head and the morsel was gone.

"Does he ever stop eating?" asked Willard. "I have seen you two feed him pounds of fish."

"He's keeping his energy up." Shirley moved beside Katherine and selected a medium sized sardine and deposited it in Old Clacker's waiting maw.

"Energy for what?" The chief arched an eyebrow.

"Guard duty, of course." Katherine looked over her shoulder as she said it.

With Katherine's last remark, Old Clacker extended his wings and the feathers on his head stood on end. With short rapid steps, he moved towards the chief who had come too close for his comfort. The chief beat a hasty retreat.

"See, I told you," scolded Katherine, tossing another fish to Old Clacker.

"Well I'll be damn." Willard shook his head. "I've seen it all. A pelican as a watch dog. My family is not going to believe this. How did you get him?"

Everyone moved back into the living room and Katherine started to tell the story of how Slade had rescued the old bird. Only Shirley caught the note of longing in Katherine's voice each time she mentioned Slade's name. Crossing her fingers, Shirley said a silent prayer Slade would be okay.

Ari Theopolous had made magnificent time in towing the fishing trawler to port. *Quest 1* had performed as admirably as an ocean going tug and when they steamed into San Francisco Bay, thousands of people lined the docks cheering. The crew of *Quest 1* was on the rails of the large ship and confetti rained down in buckets. The festive aura was accented by blasts from horns and trumpets.

The wave of media coverage had been slickly orchestrated by Kyle and when local interest in the event took hold, the arrival of the stricken trawler took on a life of its own. Matt Kyle was escorted to the head of the gangway and met Captain Ari Theopolous when he descended to greet the media horde. Matt Kyle pumped the astonished Captain's hand and gave him a hug and slap on the back. Light bulbs flashed and cameras whirred as the media spectacle was beamed into the homes of those not fortunate enough to attend 'history in the making.'

Matt Kyle was the first to speak and he extolled the virtues of his brave Captain and crew and reminded everyone of the law of the sea not to leave any stricken vessel in time of need. The loudest applause came when he announced World Vision Quest would not be claiming any salvage rights. The owner of the fishing trawler broke down in tears and Matt Kyle seized the opportunity to place his arms around the shoulders of the man. The fishing trawler, *Monterey Bay*, named after its famous landmark, was the only vessel the old man had left, misfortune having claimed the others.

The interviews lasted for almost two hours. Kyle never tired of the camera. He tirelessly answered questions and stayed close to Captain Theopolous to assist with clarifying a point. By the end of the afternoon, Kyle was certain World Vision Quest's name would be splattered across every newspaper in the country. It was a major promotional accomplishment and incredibly timely.

After giving his last interview, Kyle asked Captain Theopolous to accompany him as he boarded *Quest 1*. Once safely up the gangway and on board, Kyle turned to the still awestruck Captain.

"Mr. Kyle, I never expected such a reception. I don't know what to say." Captain Theopolous looked wide-eyed at his boss.

"Ari, you are a hero. You and your brave crew. Rejoice." Kyle burst into laughter and slapped the broad shouldered Greek on the back. "You have made the company very proud. Tell the crew that I will estimate what salvage costs would have been and make sure each man gets his share. It's the least I can do." Kyle had already estimated the earnings of rescuing the tug.

Ari looked at Kyle in bewilderment, confusion and then shock registering on his face. "You're going to pay us the salvage money?"

"Of course. I made the decision not to claim the money, you and your crew didn't. Besides, I'm sure the crew can use a little extra cash." Kyle smiled again. It was so easy to impress those that were poor. Throw a few coins their way and they would work themselves to death. How simple and disgusting the minds of simple men.

"Thank you, Mr. Kyle. This has truly been a day full of surprises."

"Ari, I would like to see the modifications that were made. If you have time, would you mind showing me?" Kyle was rewarded with seeing the Captain draw himself up to his full height like a beaming father. *So predictable, so utterly predictable.*

"Of course, Mr. Kyle. Please, follow me. I oversaw the entire project in Valdez. I made sure they went exactly by the blueprints supplied by Mr. Klaus. There was not one deviation."

The tour of the ship took over three and a half hours. Kyle spent a great deal of time in the mid-section of the ship looking at the most extensive of the modifications. To verify Ari's statements about the construction adhering to Klaus' demands, Kyle asked for the blueprints and then compared the completed work to the illustrated diagrams. Everything had been adhered to scale, even down to the smallest detail.

"Ari, you have done a fine job." The ship would perform magnificently. When Turk had the new valves constructed and they were shipped to San Pedro, Klaus could have the last of the modifications installed. The remainder of the material was already in San Pedro.

"When do you plan on leaving for San Pedro?" Kyle wiped his hands on an offered towel.

"I was planning on leaving tomorrow morning, if that's okay."

"That's fine. We're still waiting on some parts to arrive to finish the retrofit. No need to rush." Kyle turned and led the way back to the bridge, ending the conversation and the inspection. Once on the bridge, Kyle stopped to look at the front part of *Quest 1*. Over 1200 feet long, she dwarfed any boat next to her. The bright yellow lightning bolt on the blue background could be seen in all directions. Looking around the bridge, he noticed it was spotless and told Ari so.

"Thank you, Mr. Kyle. I have been on ships all my life. I always said that if I ever was captain of a vessel, she would be clean."

"*Quest 1* is certainly clean, Ari. I will give you that." Kyle noticed there were two junior officers on the bridge. Both men were also Greek. Probably relatives, thought Kyle. "Ari, I must leave you. I have business in Silicon Valley I must tend to, but it has been a pleasure." Kyle stepped forward and shook the Captain's hand.

"Thank you, Mr. Kyle. It has been a pleasure for us, too. I will see you in San Pedro in about four days." Ari walked with Kyle to the gangway.

"See you then, Ari." Kyle did not look back as he left the ship and headed for his waiting limo.

Captain Ari Theopolous watched his boss until he disappeared into the waiting limo and sped away. The attention Kyle had spent examining the modifications to *Quest 1* had been interesting. *What did Kyle intend for this ship to do? Quest 1 could no longer haul grain, produce, or any other goods. The changes to her internal structure would prohibit that? What was Kyle planning on using the ship for?*

Ari turned and started back towards the bridge, his head bent slightly downward. Whatever it was, Kyle was not going to share it with anyone. Even the Captain of the vessel.

The landing was as soft as a gentle caress. June brought the Cessna in without a hitch and taxied her to a nearby hanger. The airport was a small one near Upland, California, about thirty-five miles east of Los Angeles on Interstate 10. Slade was familiar with the area and actually knew some fellow officers who lived there.

"Come on, let's get something to eat." June stepped down to the ground. When Slade joined him, June shut the door to the plane and locked it. "Can never be too safe."

"Where is there something to eat around here?"

"You must be kidding. The best damn breakfast you ever sank your teeth in is waiting for you right around the corner, my friend. It's called *Wings and Wheels*. Old buddy of mine from the Navy bought the place when he retired, married a gal, and settled down out here."

The restaurant was in an old converted aircraft hanger and the inside was decorated with various parts of airplanes that had not graced the friendly skies for decades. From the looks of the place, it appeared as if the customers had been bringing the proprietor airplane parts for years.

Once seated in a corner booth, an attractive brunette sidled noisily up to the table and asked if they wanted coffee. They both did and June asked her if the owner was around. After being told he was, June asked if she could have him stop by.

Slade was on his second cup of coffee, when the largest black man he had ever seen parked himself in front of their booth and let out the loudest bellow he had ever heard.

"June Stenger, you old fox! How the hell are you!" BJ Watson pulled June out of his seat and gave him a monstrous bear hug.

"Good BJ. And you? How is the family?" June slid over so BJ could sit down.

"Doing good. My oldest is attending USC. Got a scholarship on the football team." BJ smiled a wide, toothy grin and then turned his attention to Slade.

"BJ, meet Slade Lockwood. Gave him a ride out west." June sipped from his cup and watched as Slade's hand disappeared in BJ's huge mitt.

"Pleased to meet you."

"Likewise," responded BJ. "What brings you out west?" BJ leveled his eyes on the smaller man.

"I have some things I need to check on for a friend."

"BJ, do you think Slade could borrow your car? I would deeply appreciate it." June smiled at the waitress as she slid a plate full of food in front of the hungry pilot.

"Sure. I have a brand new Toyota Forerunner he can use. When you're done eating I'll get the keys for you."

"I appreciate the offer, but do you have anything a little older? Maybe an old car or truck?" asked Slade. Before BJ could answer, Slade added, "This is the best damn ham and eggs I've ever had."

"Thank you. Recipe my momma taught me." BJ looked quizzically at June.

Feeling the eyes of the large man on him, June returned his questioning stare and arched his eyebrows. "I'll explain it to you later."

"Good enough for me. I have an old Ford pickup that has seen too many miles and too many minor fender benders. She still runs well, though." BJ raised his enormous bulk to an upright position. "I'll go get the keys."

Slade watched as BJ disappeared to the rear of the restaurant. The man had to be 6'4" or 6'5". BJ had shoulders rivaling those of an NFL lineman.

"BJ is 6'6" and about 315 pounds." June read Slade's thoughts. "He wanted to be a fighter pilot but was too big. Ended up working on the B17's as navigator and even then a General had to pull strings because of his size. Cockpits aren't made for a man as big as him."

Slade nodded silently. Apparently BJ's heart was as big as he was, because he walked back up with a set of keys dangling from his hand. Before Slade could say anything, he tossed them to him. Slade caught the keys and slipped them into his pocket.

"She's parked out back with a full tank of gas. Dark green. Can't miss her."

"Thanks. I owe you one."

"Don't mention it. Let me know if I can be of anymore help."

"You've done enough. Thanks again."

"What are you doing this afternoon?" asked June.

"What did you have in mind?" BJ flashed his warm smile.

"Thought we might catch up on old times," winked June. "You know, share stories and lies."

"Well, we'll do just that. Let me get this breakfast crowd out of here." BJ shook Slade's hand again and ambled back to the kitchen, greeting and laughing with patrons as he met them.

"He's really a nice man," commented Slade.

"The best. I could always depend on BJ. Still can," mused June, his eyes taking on a faraway look, seeing missions flown in the past.

"June thanks for the ride. I could've never slipped out of Cedar Key if it had not been for you." Slade slid quietly out of the booth, while June remained seated.

"No problem. Besides, I haven't seen BJ and his family in a while. Good excuse for a trip." June shook Slade's hand but stopped him as he started to walk away. "Here Slade, just in case you need some help." June handed Slade a small piece of paper with his cell phone on it.

"I hope I won't, but if I do, I'll call." Slade turned without another word and walked to the door, disappearing around the corner of the restaurant.

In less than two minutes, June saw an old green Ford truck with Slade at the wheel, heading for the freeway. June did not think Slade would call if he got into trouble. It was not in the man's nature to involve friends or others in what he thought he could handle on his own. That was okay. Slade Lockwood was not alone. June had a way of finding out if he would be needed in the future. For Slade and those depending on him, the hunt had officially begun.

Chapter Twenty-One

The freeways were just as Slade had left them over a year ago: crowded, slow, and frustrating. Slade took the 210 west to Pasadena. In order to move fast, he had carried a small duffle bag with several changes of clothes.

Slade still questioned if he was the right choice for this investigation, but until he had some concrete evidence pointing at someone in particular, he had to play detective. Shrugging to himself, Slade tried to remember Pasadena. Other than the Rose Bowl, Slade was not that familiar with the city, despite having lived in southern California for twenty years.

It was almost 10:00 AM before Slade crawled off the freeway and drove into the heart of Pasadena. It took him less than twenty minutes to locate Leonard Woodman's address. The killer had lived in an apartment complex in a questionable part of town. There was a seediness to it, an unkempt air permeating the grounds. It was the perfect place for someone trying to hide. While nicer than other parts of Pasadena, it was still someplace where Leonard would have gone unnoticed.

Slade found an empty parking space four blocks from Leonard's apartment. Before getting out of the truck, Slade slipped on a dark green button up shirt. It was the type apartment maintenance repairmen wear. A matching ball cap completed his ensemble. The Beretta found a resting spot inside the front of his pants and the shirt, which was untucked, concealed it.

Feeling he was ready, Slade left the truck and started back to the apartment complex, noting alleys and buildings as he moved down the sidewalk. If things did not go well, he would need a ready made escape route. For the first time in his adult life, Slade wished he had the resources of the LAPD at his disposal.

Reaching the apartment building, he entered a small mom and pop store across the street to buy a Pepsi. Moving around the store and acting as if he was trying to decide what to purchase afforded him an opportunity to study the complex. Very little activity. The parking lot was in the rear, which cut down on people near the front of the building.

Paying for a Snicker's candy bar, Slade unwrapped it as he moved away from the apartment and towards a traffic light. Crossing the street at the light, Slade walked back towards the apartments and into the inner courtyard. A Hispanic woman was trying desperately to keep an eye on several small children playing soccer.

Selecting the stairs to his left, he went to the second floor. Leonard lived in 205. The complex was two stories and shaped like a square. Leonard's apartment was a corner unit, with the back of the apartment facing the parking lot.

Moving to the door, Slade knocked softly and turned to watch the kids and mother in the courtyard. No one had paid him the slightest attention. Knocking louder, Slade waited several seconds before reaching inside his pocket and selecting a lock pick. To the casual observer, it appeared as if Slade removed a key. Deftly, Slade inserted the lock pick and sprung the lock after the third attempt. Less than ten seconds had elapsed before Slade opened the door and stepped inside.

With his right hand Slade pulled the Beretta from his pants pocket and moved to a combat position. Scanning the living room and kitchen, Slade eased down the hallway. A check of the bedroom and bathroom confirmed he was alone.

Sliding the Beretta into his waistband, Slade walked back to the front door and wedged a chair beneath the door handle. Satisfied the chair would act as a barricade and buy him time if needed, Slade turned to the task of searching Leonard's apartment.

Slade decided to start with the areas holding the highest possibility of success. During his career, Slade had been to a lot of schools teaching different search techniques. He had taken the advice of one of his earlier instructors and developed his own method based on fundamental, sound principles. It was like firing a gun—everyone had their own particular nuances and habits.

Slade selected the bedroom and started with the closet. A trunk in the corner contained several weapons and specially designed silencers. The trunk was rather plain, the contents were not. Slade knew he was looking upon the tools of a cold-blooded killer and wondered how many people Leonard had killed. Slade closed the trunk and resumed his search.

Other than a few pieces of paper with mindless writing, Slade did not find anything of value. He did stuff the pieces of paper into his front pants pocket.

The next stop was the living room. Starting clockwise, Slade moved his eyes around the room, stopping at the telephone. Strolling over to the phone, Slade picked up the receiver and dialed *69. The phone automatically dialed the last number Leonard had called. Slade hung up when a pizza shop answered.

A pile of magazines were stacked haphazardly near the phone and a loose set of notebook papers had been tossed on top of them. Slade took the top piece of paper and held it horizontally at eye level. Small indentations were clearly visible in the paper. Selecting a pencil that was lying near the phone, Slade lightly shaded the paper with the side of the pencil. Though faint, a few brief words could be read. Slade's heart stopped when he recognized 'Cedar Key.' For several seconds, he could feel the tightness in his throat. With renewed vigor, he scanned the piece of paper but was unable to locate any additional discernable words.

It took him less than twenty minutes to finish his search of the living room. There was nothing indicating a human presence resided here. What was wrong? What was he missing? There was no answering machine. No newspaper. No mail with Leonard's name on it. Nothing.

Slade walked over and sat down on the couch and jumped to his feet when the phone rang, his hand reaching for the Beretta. The phone rang seven times before stopping. Who was that? Slade could only wonder. If Leonard had an answering machine he could have cross-checked the name on the recorder with the rolodex. Slade immediately scanned the room a second time. Where was it? Leonard had survived through contacts. Contacts were information and there was no way he could have remembered them all. Where was the journal of phone numbers? Names and numbers were his path to safety and work. Something of that value would have been carefully hidden.

Taking a deep breath, Slade started his search a second time, this time paying particular attention to areas that may hide a small book.

Fatigue is the enemy of an insightful mind; it can whittle away at your senses until they become dull and tired. Slade had been at it for over three hours, constantly searching an area sometimes two to three times. Sweat was beaded on his forehead and had stained his shirt, creating damp areas beneath his armpits.

With fatigue had come frustration. The only decorative item in the living room was an artificial tree about six feet tall. New it would have accented a living room with grace and color. But now it had fallen into neglect; most of the leaves were gone and the wicker base was torn and ragged in places, much like the furniture in the room. Passing by the tree, Slade lashed out in anger with his foot, catching the wicker base and propelling the tree across the living room. When the tree hit the floor, it burst into several pieces, the wicker basket rolling one way and the trunk of the tree the other. Revealed between the two pieces was a five inch by seven inch small black notebook with weathered pages. Slade stood in disbelief. Leonard had carved out a space beneath the trunk of the tree in the wicker basket to hide the book.

Scooping up the book, Slade scanned the pages and was rewarded with seeing countless names and addresses. Slade started to move towards the sofa, when a noise at the door caused him to freeze. The door knob was being turned. Slowly, the knob turned until the tumblers caught and the door was unlocked. Next, the person on the outside started to push against the door and met the resistance of the chair. Slade could hear muffled voices on the outside and the door was shaken back and forth several times, before the weight of the person on the outside was brought into play.

During the entire time, Slade had stood frozen, paralyzed into inaction. He was in an apartment without a search warrant breaking the law. For the first time in his life, he was the criminal and was on the other side of the legal system. What had prompted him to take such foolish action? Streams of disjointed thoughts raced through his head, crashing into dead ends before he could sort them out. Stop it! Now was not the time to worry about what had been done. He would have to move or be discovered.

The door was beginning to yield to the advances of the two men who were applying weight to the door frame. Wood could be heard cracking and tearing. The door itself would cave in at any time, seconds were all he had.

Slade turned and grabbed the magazines on the coffee table, stuffed them into the front of his pants and sprinted towards the rear of the apartment. His eyes had the look of a trapped animal, but amidst the chaos the mind of a trained professional was asserting itself, forcing control on a situation threatening to spin out of control. The whirling vortex of panic was subdued and a careful, albeit quick, plan was taking shape. Necessity is the mother of invention, and Slade was desperately trying to figure a way out of the apartment.

The splintering of wood was growing louder and Slade could hear the excited voices of the two men as they neared success. Time was running out. Removing the screen in the bedroom window, he forced the bottom half of the window pane up and open. The opening was small but it would have to do. Slade hoisted himself up and through the bottom half of the window.

With a loud bang, the door crashed open and the two men were sent sprawling into the living room, falling over the now broken chair. Both men sprung to their feet and reached inside the folds of their jacket removing silenced firearms. A quick silent sideways glance assured each of them the other was okay. The two killers, brothers employed by Matt Kyle, swiftly stepped towards the bedroom as they heard the sound of breaking glass.

Slade heard the door when it was broken. Forgetting about silence, Slade forced himself through the window, shattering the pane of glass. Sliding down the side of the building, Slade tried the best he could to pick the spot where he would land. When he heard the two men moving towards the bedroom, he dropped the dozen feet to the ground, rolling when he hit to lessen the impact. Not daring to look back, he was on his feet and running towards the rear wooden fence.

Jeremiah and William Henderson made it to the window just as Slade was scaling the fence. Jeremiah raised his weapon to fire, but William placed his hand on his shoulder, stopping him. Just as Slade reached the top of the wall, William motioned for his brother to shoot. The wood next to Slade's right hand exploded and the ex-cop catapulted himself over the wall, landing heavily on the other side. Jeremiah turned to William as they both stepped away from the window.

"Make the call," instructed Jeremiah, sliding his weapon back inside his jacket.

William extracted a cell phone from his pocket and dialed 911. Within seconds, he had a communications call taker on the phone and excitedly told her about a man breaking into Leonard's apartment. With startling accuracy, William gave Slade's description and told the young woman on the other end of the line what he was wearing. William also told her Slade had been surprised inside the apartment and was now running from the location. When asked, he told her the direction. When the call taker asked for his name, William disconnected.

"Do you think he found anything?" William looked at his younger brother.

"I don't know how long he's been here. Besides, Leonard may not have had anything here. One thing's for sure, his fingerprints will be all over the apartment." Jeremiah slapped his older brother on the shoulder with a gloved hand.

Slade cleared the back yard of a house and moved to the sidewalk, slowing his pace to blend in. With a nervous hand, he pulled the ball cap lower. Slade had walked about a hundred feet, when he heard sirens approaching. As the sound neared the complex, his heart constricted when they were turned off.

They had called the cops! The thought sent electrical shots of adrenaline pumping through him. It was standard procedure to get to an in progress crime as quickly as possible. As you neared, you needed to turn your siren off lest you alert the culprit. Slade knew the officers would be responding from several locations, all converging towards the apartment. No doubt they had called in his description as well.

Slade had moments. Before he could react, a police cruiser with two uniformed officers turned the corner directly ahead. There were not a lot of people on the sidewalk and he felt naked, isolated on the wide expanse of concrete. There was no convenience store or business to duck into. Slowing his pace, Slade appeared to be looking away, but kept one eye on the slow approaching police car.

There were two officers inside the vehicle, both scanning their respective side of the street. It was the passenger officer, a young Hispanic female that saw him. Apparently she was a rookie, because she grabbed her partner's arm with her left hand and pointed towards Slade with her right. A veteran officer would have remained calm and nonchalantly told his partner so they could move closer in case the suspect ran. It was a lesson in law enforcement to never alert the criminal, but to use surprise to your advantage.

The roar of the engine accelerating towards him decided Slade's course of action. There was no way he could be caught. Hopefully, Leonard's address book contained information he could use. If he was caught, the address book would be confiscated and he would never get it back. And he would have to deal with a burglary charge. There was only one thing to do: run.

Slade waited for the patrol car to draw within twenty feet. When he heard the doors to the sedan open, he sprinted through the front yard of an old style Mexican home towards the back fence. The fence was wooden and about six foot high. Slade grabbed the top rail and swung over, pausing just long enough to hear if the officers were in pursuit. Their excited yells to each other and hurried exchange of information over the radio told him they were. The senior officer was taking charge, directing officers to where he thought Slade would appear on the opposite street. In the distance, Slade could hear sirens and the sounds of approaching police cars. They were trying to box him in.

Slade started across the back yard and was halfway to the outer fence, when he realized he was not alone. A large Rottweiler had been asleep, lolling in the afternoon sun, when he had been awakened by the commotion. The dog had heard sirens and cars before but had never had anyone enter his compound. One sight of him had always turned back would be interlopers. But this man dared him, taunted him. The hair on his back stood on end and he zeroed in on the man as he shot out of an ornately decorated dog box and sprinted for the fleeing man.

Not bothering to glance over his shoulder, Slade redoubled his efforts and leaped for the back fence. His fingers closed over the top boards and he was hoisting himself up and over. The dog saw his prey getting away and flung himself through the air in an act of desperation. His massive jowls closed on Slade's left lower pants leg and slid down towards his boot. Only the thick leather canvas saved Slade from serious injury. The dog sunk his teeth into the boot, tearing through to the skin beneath. Slade's weight wrested his ankle free and he fell to the ground.

Some skin had been torn, but no serious damage. The dog would work to his advantage because the cops would have to go around. Turning his head, he listened to see which direction they would take.

They had split up. One to each side of the back yard. That was not good for him. Already, he could hear the other officers on the far street giving directions and taking up perimeter locations. The net was set and now it was up to the pursuing officers to either flush him out or call for canine. The other danger was an air unit. If a helicopter was winging their way, it would be minutes before they arrived and activated the infrared tracking device.

The FLIR, Forward Looking Infrared device, targeted body heat. There was no hiding from it. With a canine unit and the FLIR unit, he would be found.

Moving along the fence of the back yard with the dog, Slade carefully looked around the corner. A large shrub afforded some degree of cover. The female officer was working her way down the fence, her gun held steady between two hands.

Officer Monica Montoya was still on probation. Patrol Officer III John Bartley was her first training officer and one of the finest officers on Pasadena PD. Already she had made five felony arrests this month while working with him and the adrenaline was pumping as she thought about making her sixth.

Officer Montoya had attracted the dog on the inside of the fence. The dog was following her down the fence, growling and barking with each step she took. She knew he was alerting anyone to her presence, but she had no choice. Her partner was clearing the other side and she had a responsibility to clear her side. Honor dictated she uphold her end of the bargain. She had already earned a lofty reputation while working with Officer Bartley and she had no thought of letting him down.

Slade had found a slit through the wooden fence and would be able to see her when she neared the corner. A brief touch of sympathy went out to her, but Slade quickly squashed it. For now, she was the enemy. Officer Montoya was making a tactical mistake Slade was quickly capitalizing on. Instead of moving four to five feet from the fence, she was right against it, using it as support as she walked. To the new officer, it gave her a sense of security, when in reality it could be used as a trap, as Slade was about to use it now.

Sounds to his rear. Her partner was nearing the end of the wooden fenced yard and would turn the corner quickly. If Slade did not act soon, he would be seen. Tensing his muscles he waited.

Officer Montoya's radio squawked, her partner checking on her progress. Grabbing the mike, she told him she was about to clear the corner. That was the last transmission she made until she was found.

Just as Officer Montoya cleared the corner, Slade stepped forward in a rush of movement. The suddenness of his attack startled her and there was a brief moment of paralysis. Before she could react, Slade slammed the blade of his left hand into the side of her neck and she dropped to the ground. Slade drug her into the bushes and removed her radio and gun. Making sure she was okay, Slade tucked her gun into his waistband and walked rapidly back towards the street, her radio turned down low but pressed against his ear.

Slade neared the police cruiser. It was parked haphazardly across the sidewalk where the two officers had jumped out to chase him. The major obstacle of getting to his truck was still in front of him. The truck was over two blocks away. With the police around, it might as well have been two

miles. Slade's heart sunk when he saw another police cruiser turn the corner. They were backfilling positions. He needed a diversion.

When radio traffic paused, Slade keyed the mike and screamed out instructions as if he was in foot pursuit. "He's crossed the road! Get a unit north of me! He's broken the north perimeter! Move units! Move!" Slade let up on the mike and listened. The roar of engines met his ears, followed by everyone trying to talk at once. The prey had been sighted. Time to move the net.

The police cruiser that had just entered the street, accelerated with lights and siren. There was no need for silence, the suspect had been seen, his whereabouts known. Time was of the essence. Only seconds before the suspect may escape north and be lost.

Slade stepped out onto the sidewalk and hastily walked to his truck. Removing the hat he was wearing, he also removed his shirt and put on a white t-shirt. Using a towel, he dried himself and mopped the sweat from his face. He must blend in and appear to be a member of the community. Less than a minute later, he was driving past the abandoned police car.

Slade did not allow his mind to focus on anything but escape for the next thirty minutes. Instead of heading back towards Los Angeles, Slade drove north, away from Pasadena. Distance was his friend.

The radio crackled next to him. The female officer had been found and paramedics called. The radio traffic had become much more heated and then ceased. They had discovered her radio missing and knew he was monitoring their channel. He tried other frequencies, but they had stopped all radio traffic. Slade turned it off and slipped it into the glove box, along with the officer's hand gun.

Catching Interstate Five, Slade drove north for over an hour before he turned off the freeway and stopped at a diner. It was constructed to look like a diner from the fifties, complete with black and white checkerboard tile and plenty of chrome. Slade sat in an available booth. Out of nowhere, a middle-aged waitress strolled up next to him, her pink outfit somehow fitting for the location.

"What'cha need?"

"How about a cup of coffee. With cream and honey."

Slade watched her jot it down on her note pad.

"Anything to eat?"

"Got anything in the way of desserts?"

"Dutch apple pie to die for, peach cobbler, New York Cheese Cake, and blueberry pie. Any of those touch your taste buds, Hon?"

"A slice of the Dutch apple sounds nice."

"Coming right up."

The waitress returned with a steaming cup of coffee in an old fashioned cup. Deftly, she deposited the cream and a plastic bear shaped jar of honey. Slade emptied two of the creamers in his coffee and measured off a teaspoon full of honey.

Slade placed the address book he had taken from Leonard's apartment on the table in front of him. Were the answers he was looking for inside the dusty pages? Were there any notes to identify who had hired Leonard?

It was obvious to him he had been set-up. The killers had adopted a different tactic and were using the legal authorities to their aid. It was an interesting change, with the fox alerting the farmer.

Reaching for his coffee cup, Slade took another sip and moved his arms as the waitress slid a large piece of apple pie in front of him.

"If you need anything else Hon, let me know." She patted Slade on the arm before turning back to her other customers.

They were one step ahead of him. They must have been watching when he entered the apartment or arrived shortly thereafter. Either way, they had trapped him inside. The realization he had been out-foxed infuriated him. Slade had banked on the element of surprise and it had back-fired.

Tentatively, he reached out and took hold of Leonard's address book. Shoveling a fork full of pie into his mouth with his left hand, he opened the cover and started to scan the pages. He could only hope the answers he was looking for were inside. If not, he had committed felonious acts in vain.

Chapter Twenty-Two

She had been stripped down to the keel, the outer decks peeled away like an onion. The damaged parts had been discarded into an untidy pile, the remaining portion sitting like a half-clothed model, elegant, yet past her prime. The hint of the classic lines still commanded attention and deserved, demanded, more than a casual glance. Elegance was not easily lost, even on a damaged vessel like the *Fair Rose*.

Willard walked over to a three-ton chain hoist and positioned it over the engine. Lowering two chains, he hooked them onto the Volvo engine and activated the automatic wench. Slowly, the diesel engine was lifted clear of the hull, the whir of the hoist the only noise. The engine was placed on a metal rack specifically designed for such work.

Willard removed the valve cover gaskets and shined a light onto some of the internal parts. The salt build-up was not as bad as expected. Shirley had told him her dad had recently overhauled the engine. It just needed a good bath and rinsing. The oil was clear and clean. Hank Waterbury knew how to maintain a marine engine and a glow of satisfaction settled on Willard. The *Fair Rose* had been one of the first large vessels Willard's boat yard had ever been commissioned to build. The love and care he had taken to craft the boat was still evident. The *Fair Rose* would never lose her beauty or the warm place in Willard's heart.

Leaving the diesel engine, Willard climbed back on board the *Fair Rose*. The keel and part of the boat still intact were resting on movable metal stanchions that could be raised and lowered, depending on where Willard was working. It was a simple, yet innovative design that had served him well when working on large craft. It also meant he did not have to spend hours bent over in a crouch, inviting exhaustion and muscle cramps.

162

Willard walked around the remains of the *Fair Rose* like he had several times during the past two days. She was a tough old boat; sturdy and dependable. All the pre-requisites he demanded of any boat he built. It was amazing she had not been destroyed beyond recognition.

A sudden thought hit Willard and he walked back to the engine and started to examine the exhaust manifold of the diesel engine. Reaching for a light on a retractable cord, Willard flicked on the powerful beam and directed it to the fittings along the manifold where the exhaust ports and the engine joined. Reaching for magnifying glasses that he used when doing trim work, Willard carefully examined the exhaust ports and fittings. No leaks. Leaning back, he gazed out at the Intra-coastal Waterway, the early morning sun causing him to squint as the light danced off the water.

Rising from his stool, Willard proceeded to the exhaust system that was still in the keel. The engine resided in the hold, about five feet from the stern. The exhaust ports for the engine had been routed from the engine to the stern. Two parallel lines of two inch steel comprised the exhaust lines and had been constructed in a straight line to the rear. It had been the cleanest and safest way to route the diesel emissions and it insured no contamination of the engine compartment if the skipper needed to check on the engine while at sea.

Once again, Willard retrieved the powerful light and magnifying glass. Carefully, and with a jeweler's precision, he inspected every square inch of the lines. Finished, he was as perplexed as when he had started. Not one to accept things on the first try, Willard double-checked the exhaust manifolds and lines. When he was finished he retrieved a bottle of water from a small refrigerator in the corner of the work shop.

Satisfied there were no breaks in the metal, Willard moved to the engine compartment itself. The engine compartment had been constructed of several bulkheads, designed to isolate the engine and cut down on the noise it emitted. The bulkheads had also acted as reinforcement to stabilize the engine well.

Climbing down into the engine area, Willard shined the powerful light onto the timbers and carefully examined the seams where the keel and bulkheads joined. Willard had constructed the interior beams from old growth live oaks. The wood was dense, strong and hard to come by. Because the beams were so thick, it had added considerably to the weight of the *Fair Rose*, but the compromise had been durability and safety, trade-offs Willard would take any day.

With this last inspection complete, Willard slipped to a sitting position inside the engine well and leaned his head against the forward beam of the compartment. The upper super structure had been damaged and torn off in places, but the lower portion of the boat had been spared the damage inflicted on the upper side by the wind and oyster bar. A smile touched his weathered face. The *Fair Rose* could have ridden through the hurricane without a scratch if the skipper had been alive. The occupants may have been seasick and happy to reach shore, but if running and with a seasoned skipper at the helm, she could have made it.

Willard opened his eyes and looked straight at the ceiling of his work shop. He had learned enough about Hank Waterbury to know the man could have piloted the *Fair Rose* and brought her safely to port in any kind of weather. Without another thought, Willard reached inside his top pocket and extracted a cell phone. Scanning through the list of pre-set numbers, Willard selected the second from last and pushed the automatic dialing function.

"Hello?"

"Shirley. Willard Mayes here. I have some news about the *Fair Rose*."

The formula was proving to be elusive and deceptively complicated. Shirley knew Billy had been trying to manipulate the cellular structure of the Black Mangrove, but why? What was he hoping to attain? She had tried several different combinations based on her knowledge of the plant species, but to no avail. Other than to environmentalists and fishermen, the mangroves held no particular allure.

Sighing, she reached for a glass of iced tea when her cell phone rang. Only a couple of people had the number. Picking it up, she was quick to recognize the voice of Willard Mayes. After a brief conversation, Shirley hung up her cell phone and went in pursuit of Katherine, a new spring in her step.

Katherine was seated on the back porch with Old Clacker near her feet and Slade's phone tucked tightly against her ear. The list of companies Slade had given her to check on was in her lap and she was crossing off one of them while talking to someone on the other end.

"So your company does not do any research in biology?" Katherine looked up at Shirley. "All right. I appreciate your help. Thank you."

"Another dead end?"

"Yup. I'm only a third of the way through this list. I don't know what Slade had hoped I would find, but so far I've drawn a blank. What about you?"

"As far as the formula goes, I'm no further along now than when I started. I just can't find what Billy was hoping to enhance in the mangroves. From the research I've conducted and the recent literature I've read, I still believe it may be growth enhancement or growth acceleration. As a shoreline protector, it makes the most sense, especially with development taking place in Florida at such a rapid pace. Most of these eco-systems are fragile to begin with and when contractors start developing and disturbing this system, it only makes sense that a natural buffer would prove invaluable in keeping the environmentalists at bay while the businessmen reaped enormous profits. Plus, it would provide a natural habitat for countless marine species and I know that would appeal to Billy."

"Billy never mentioned this to you?"

"No, and that bothers me. Billy always told me what he was working on and would bore me to tears with the details. I was one of only a few that could comprehend and understand him. He would go off on tangents that would confuse the best educators. I don't know how dad and mom tolerated him." Shirley laughed as she remembered her baby brother.

"I'm sure you'll crack the code." Katherine smiled at the younger woman whom she had grown so close to in such a short period of time.

"Any word from Slade?"

"No. He was supposed to call me every day, but he didn't call yesterday. Maybe he will call today and let me know what's going on. Hopefully, he's having better luck."

"He's only been gone two days. That's not much time." Shirley picked up on the longing in Katherine's voice. For the thousandth time, Shirley had regrets about dragging Katherine and Slade into this mess. They were such good people—sincere, honest, and dependable. A lot like her mom and dad. Shirley fought down the lump trying to rise into her throat.

"Well, I need to go and check on the shop. Betsy has been running it in my absence, but I need to check on things. Want to go?"

Both started to get up, when Shirley remembered her conversation with Willard.

"Oh! I almost forgot. Willard called to tell me about his investigation of the *Fair Rose*. There are no leaks in the exhaust system or the diesel engine. If my parents and Billy died from carbon monoxide poisoning, then it was not on board the *Fair Rose*." Shirley looked sternly at Katherine, the toughness of her family once again asserting itself.

"Then that means they were killed somewhere else and moved aboard the *Fair Rose*." Both women were silent. "We need to contact Chief Singletee and tell him."

"Come on, we can stop by his office on the way to your shop." Shirley was already turning and moving towards the door.

Old Clacker watched as the two women left and then moved to his favorite piling. Flapping his wings he flew up to the top and settled softly on his perch. From here, he could see the women when they returned. He tucked his bill into his wing to wait.

Quest 1 had set sail at night, her massive bow easing out of San Francisco Bay and turning south once she was free of the channel. The media circus had finally died. Now the ship was back on course and would only be four to five days late in arriving. Captain Theopolous watched as the lights from San Francisco disappeared in the background.

The wind was stiff outside the bridge and Ari buttoned his captain's jacket up to his throat and pulled a knit cap down around his ears. Matt Kyle had told him the future modifications to *Quest 1* may take two to three weeks. After that, Kyle had told him to be ready to travel at a moment's notice and be ready to be away from home for months at a time. When Ari had asked about tentative ports, Kyle had told him their destination were 'the ports of the world'.

Ari had taken the time to have the Chief Engineer go over the engines once again when they were docked in San Francisco. Everything checked out. *Quest 1* would function as good as she ever had. Beneath his feet, Ari could feel the quiver of the huge freighter as she increased speed.

Taking his time, Ari walked the entire ship from bow to stern. It was something he did every time they left port. Call him superstitious, but Ari believed in being thorough. Maybe that was why Kyle had hired him in the first place.

'The ports of the world? Maybe they would dock in his beloved Greece and he would get to see loved ones and family members. With that thought occupying his mind, Ari completed his self-appointed rounds and hurried back to the bridge. There was a pot of strong coffee waiting for him and it would take the chill out of his bones.

"So the authorities have a description of him?" Kyle was unable to hide the enthusiasm entering his voice.

"They have his description and fingerprints. He wasn't wearing gloves when I saw him. He was taken totally by surprise." Jeremiah Henderson looked at his brother for confirmation.

After shooting at Slade and calling the police, they had quickly left the apartment and watched as police cars streamed into the area. Luck had allowed them to drive down the street where the ambulance arrived to take the female police officer to the hospital. Later, mingling with the crowd who had gathered to watch, they caught bits and pieces of conversation between the officers. That was how they had learned Slade had knocked out the female officer and stolen her gun and radio. It was turning out better than they could have hoped.

"You've done a wonderful job. Stay in the area and I'll call when I discover what his next move is going to be. I'll probably need you to help him have another run in with the authorities."

"No problem. Contact us on our cell phone." Without waiting on a reply, Jeremiah hung up.

Kyle leaned back in his chair and stared out the window at the clouds. The Silicon Valley business was finished. The rising publicity had afforded him the degree of importance he had hoped, and with his face on the television and his interview carried by every major news channel, negotiating the deal for the computers had been a virtual snap. With shipment dates in hand, Kyle was flying back to San Pedro to make sure everything was ready on the distribution end.

The idea to use the authorities to hunt Lockwood had come like an inspiration in the night. It had flitted across his consciousness, taken shape, and then crystallized into an idea, a plot he found to be both ingenious and fool proof. Moments like this came only every so often and he was quick to realize this.

The Henderson Brothers had been employed by him in the past. With the death of Leonard, because he was sure Leonard was dead now, the brothers had moved into the number one position on his list of 'enforcers.'

The two women were still alive in Cedar Key. That had been confirmed by one of his lesser talented people. Lockwood was also alive but had not been seen in a couple of days. That tidbit of information had almost come too late. When Kyle had realized Slade may have found out Leonard's real name and was moving on Leonard's apartment, he had sent the Henderson Brothers to intercept him, but not to kill him.

The death of the cop would raise too many questions. Legal entanglement, however, would sufficiently crush Slade's endeavor to pursue any investigative leads he may develop. Without huge reservoirs of capital, Slade could not hire attorneys to extricate him from legal snares Kyle would throw at him. It was so clever. Use the system the cop had worked in for twenty years against him.

Information was the key to success. Kyle needed up to date information on Slade. With the assault on the female officer, Slade's picture was sure to be on the news. There would be an all out manhunt. The resulting media circus would supply the much needed momentum to pursue Slade to the ends of the earth. This time Kyle laughed out loud and his private stewardess looked at him suspiciously.

Reaching for his phone, Kyle placed a phone call to Randolph Myers, his head computer technician. Randolph had been convicted of computer piracy for trying to steal corporate secrets from Microsoft. For his efforts, he had spent six years of a fifteen year sentence in Federal prison. Kyle had gotten Randolph's term shortened and had hired him. Randolph had a knack for getting information no one else could, legally or illegally.

"Randolph here." The computer technician was small in height, but extremely obese. Folds of fat dropped over his entire body, from his double chin to his ankles. An unkept string of brown hair drifted down to his shoulders, settling in dirty piles on his shirt. He was always dressed in sweats, as they were the only thing that fit him.

"This is Kyle. Are we on a secure line?"

"Give me a minute." Several minutes passed while Kyle waited. Finally, the overweight computer technician came back on. "Go ahead."

"I need to know the constant whereabouts of a Slade Lockwood. He just committed a burglary in Pasadena and assaulted a police officer. He is ex-LAPD and lives in Cedar Key, Florida. He might try to communicate with them. Understood?"

"Understood. Give me about an hour and I'll have everything ready. You want me to call you on your cell?" Already Randolph's fingers were flying over the keyboard in front of him. Information on Slade Lockwood started to pop up immediately.

"Yes. Let me know as soon as you hear something. I want twenty-four hour monitoring on this, but only you need to know."

"I got it. Will talk to you soon." Randolph hung up and turned his attention back to one of the four screens in front of him.

The officials in Cedar Key must know what was going on to have kept Leonard's death quiet. That meant the bumbling Police Chief and Slade were working together. That might be an angle he would need to exploit. Kyle leaned his head back and let his eyes close, his brain plotting angles of destruction.

"Are you sure about this?" screamed Commander Rich LeFleur. "I can't take this to the Chief unless you're dead certain. I know Slade Lockwood and I don't believe this for a second."

"I know him too, Rich. We worked together in South Central Los Angeles years ago, before I left and became Chief here. He's a good man. I don't know what he's involved in, but his fingerprints are all over the apartment." Pasadena Police Chief Mike Van Gant looked back at an old photograph on his desk. It was a picture of Slade and him as young officers working a narcotics task force. Dropping the picture down on his desk, Mike rubbed his head.

"Who did the apartment belong to?" Rich LeFleur picked up a pen and started to write.

"Leonard Woodman. He has a rap sheet as long as your arm. Did time and has been suspected of murder in the past, but nothing we could tie him to. Been living in this apartment for about a year. A no good type."

"Does the press know about this?"

"Not yet. I'll have to brief them in an hour or so. Word is sure to get out. I have a call in to the Police Chief in Cedar Key, Florida, where Slade lives now, but I haven't heard anything back."

"Did you try his house?"

"Yes, but all I got was a recording. No one home." Chief Van Gant paused as he listened to the heavy breathing of his friend. All of them had worked together and had become close. "Rich, I know this is hard to take, but Slade assaulted one of my officers, for crying out loud. I don't know what the hell he is involved in, but he needs to come in so we can help him."

"Whatever it is, it must be damn important. Slade was the most level headed person I've ever met in my life. If he would've stayed here, he would've probably been an Assistant Chief by now." Commander Rick LeFluer was desperately trying to figure out what his friend had become tangled up in.

"Call me after you brief the Chief. Okay?" asked Van Gant.

"Yeah. I'll call you. And Mike, thanks. I damn sure wouldn't have wanted to hear about this from anyone else."

"Don't mention it. We have to look out for our own," replied Van Gant, before hanging up. Picking up the picture of him and Slade, he shook his head. Every cop in Pasadena was looking for Slade. Slade had assaulted another cop and, whatever the motive, it would never be good enough for them. Slade had crossed the line and they wanted blood. Mike Van Gant knew Slade could have killed the young officer, but had deliberately placed her so she would be found. Things were not adding up, but this early into a mess like this, they never did.

Commander Rich LeFluer got up and walked to the elevators, his aids growing quiet as he passed. It was a short ride to the Chief's office. When he closed the door, Chief Brad Hummerman looked up and removed his reading glasses.

"You don't look good, Rich. Pull up a chair, because when you have that look on your face it's usually bad news." Chief Hummerman leaned back in his leather chair and waited for his subordinate to speak.

"It is bad news. News I never thought I would bring to you." Commander Rich LeFleur looked his boss in the eye and started to relate the story Pasadena Chief Mike Van Gant had told him. LeFleur watched as the Chief's face turned pale.

"Oh my God," was all the Chief could initially say.

169

Chapter Twenty-Three

The public library was small and quaint, but it did have the one item he needed most—a computer with internet access. In this age of automation, a computer and information via the world-wide-web was a foregone conclusion if someone wanted to conduct research. And Slade needed additional information on a company he had identified.

Slade had gone through Leonard's entire address book and had found one company listed: World Vision Quest. At first, he thought it had been some international foundation created to save endangered species, but then he remembered he had found the name in the address book of a killer. Leonard Woodman was not a philanthropist.

The company's name had been penciled in next to a man's name in the book, Matt Kyle, but he did not know if they were related. Other than the man's name and the name of the company sharing the same line, there was no other information in the address book to denote a connection. Hopefully, the company had a web page and he could learn what type of business or product they manufactured.

Deftly, Slade's hands flew over the keyboard and within seconds the web page for World Vision Quest popped up, filling the screen. The computer he was using was not as powerful as the one at his house, but it would suffice.

The artist who had designed the web page had spared no expense and the screen was not only filled with images, but accompanying sound as well. Slade turned down the volume when another person in the library looked his way. No need to attract attention.

Matt Kyle's picture, as founder and CEO of the company, dominated the home page of World Vision Quest. Slade stared intently at the man. Was this the person responsible for the killing of the Waterburys? Was this the man who had tried to have Shirley and Katherine murdered? Pushing aside the rage that was building, Slade focused on learning more about the company, its product, its history and anything else of value.

The main market for World Vision Quest was the sale of computers to third world nations. To accomplish the shipping and to cut costs, the company had purchased some old freighters that had been overhauled in their shipyard in Valdez, Alaska. According to the article, this hefty acquisition had already paid handsome dividends. Recently, the company had also bought into strip malls in various states and opened a small chain of restaurants. The company was diversifying, but the sale of computers was their largest revenue generator. According to the article, additional freighters were being purchased to accommodate the growing demand for technology.

There was no information on the company being interested in or conducting research in biology. Slade felt his heart sink. It had been a long shot.

Slade moved the pointer to Matt Kyle's picture and clicked on it. Instantly a bio of the founder and CEO of World Vision Quest filled the page. It chronicled Kyle's early career as a salesman and his founding of the computer company, from a fledgling start-up to international player. The story ended, noting that World Vision Quest was now a Fortune 500 company servicing over twenty-five foreign countries. Quite a success story: from rags to riches and more riches.

Moving back to the main page, Slade clicked the pointer on a title 'recent news' and a picture of *Quest 1* filled the screen. It was a shot of the freighter steaming into San Francisco Bay towing a fishing trawler, flanked by numerous smaller vessels. The picture had been taken from the air. The entire tragic incident of the fishing trawler and the rescue by *Quest 1* was well documented. The generosity of Matt Kyle, in not claiming salvage rights, was mentioned four separate times. Slade clicked back to the main screen.

Taking his time, Slade carefully read everything on the main page and any information provided by links. The article on Kyle, as nauseating as Slade found it, was read again. After forty-five minutes of non-stop reading, Slade leaned back in the chair and stared dumbly at the screen. What was bothering him? What was he missing? Why did the company and Matt Kyle annoy him? Was he reaching for a hidden meaning or clue that was not there? Was he too close? Was he trying to make a connection where none existed?

It was also not lost on Slade that he had mentally condemned Matt Kyle without so much as a shred of evidence. Slade was convinced the man was guilty on nothing more than 'gut instinct.' As desperate as he was to find the person or persons responsible for killing the Waterbury's, Slade knew he had to take a step back and reexamine the evidence. Slade would have to pursue the case as if World Vision Quest and Matt Kyle were innocent, as hard as that may be.

Clearing the screen, Slade logged onto AOL and sent an e-mail to his house in Cedar Key. In the e-mail he asked Katherine to check the list of companies that had visited science fairs Billy had entered, to determine if World Vision Quest was one of them. Slade also instructed Shirley to query phone records to see if Matt Kyle had ever called her mom and dad. Slade closed by telling Katherine he missed her and loved her. Logging off, Slade stood up and stretched.

Two little old ladies hurried past Slade, talking excitedly, and he heard one ask the other, "I wonder who they are looking for?" Looking out the window, Slade saw a police car slide to a stop outside the front of the library, its red and blue lights flickering in the evening shadows. Moving to a window near the rear of the building, Slade saw a second police cruiser. He was surrounded. But how? How did they know he was here? The truck was parked over three blocks away at a grocery store, just in case someone had seen him leave Pasadena. Before entering the library, he had conducted a brief surveillance. The approach and entry had been clean, sterile.

Slade was certain they were here for him. There had been no other activity around the library and aside from him and the two old ladies, the only other people inside were some kids. A chill moved from the base of his neck down his spine, causing his hair to stand on end. Slade knew he was trapped, with nowhere to go. This was not a scenario he had considered and, once again, he had been outfoxed. Someone was manipulating him, trying to remove him from the picture and take him out of the equation.

Think! The thought screamed through his mind, piercing the darkest corners in desperation to form a plan of escape. Within the next few seconds he needed a distraction, an event to channel the attention of the officers away from him.

The kids! With a vile lump in his throat at the thought at what he was going to do, Slade walked rapidly to the main entry area leading to the front doors. Two uniformed officers were already at the desk talking to an elderly clerk who was nodding emphatically at a picture the young officer was showing her. Seconds were now precious. Slade could hear the young officer on the radio asking for additional help. The net was being tightened, the trap about to be sprung.

A courtesy desk was in the middle of the library, staffed by an elderly gentleman wearing a camel colored sweater, complete with leather elbow pads, who appeared to be unaware of the activity taking place. A frock of grey hair and large handle bar mustache made his appearance appear genuine. Slade had smelled the distinct odor of cigar smoke on the man when he had asked him earlier if there was a charge to use the computers. The man was where Slade had left him, sorting through books and placing them on a rolling dolly for return to the shelves.

172

"Excuse me, do you have a light? I wanted to step outside and enjoy a smoke and I left my lighter in the car." Slade patted at his pocket to emphasize a point.

"Sure. Be my guest. I prefer cigars, myself," smiled the elderly man, extending a silver plated lighter to Slade. According to his name tag, he was Adolph.

"Thank you, Adolph. Do they have a designated smoking area?" Slade turned towards the entrance. So far his luck was holding as the officers had not yet started their search.

"That is so kind of you to ask. Not everyone likes cigarette smoke these days, especially in or around the library. Go down the flight of stairs and there is a small door that lets you out near the dumpster. Be sure to prop it open, because it shuts automatically." Adolph pointed to a small door opposite the main entrance.

"Thanks again. I'll bring this right back." Slade walked as fast as he dared to the door without arousing Adolph's suspicion. On his initial scan of the library, he had missed the fire exit. Silently, he cursed himself. Avenues of exit were of paramount importance to him now and he could not be this sloppy in the future if he wanted to survive.

Reaching the door, Slade pressed it open and looked at the clerk. Adolph was already sorting books. Slade descended a short flight of stairs and entered a basement that smelled old and musky. The building itself was probably a hundred years old and the lighting had only recently been added. Single bulbs housed in protective metal grates to avoid breakage provided illumination.

The basement was used to store and sort books not in circulation. Tables were lined in close rows with piles of books. Paperbacks and magazines were separated from the hard covers. There was an orderly method to it, but Slade did not pause to discern what it was.

Slade found the exterior door exactly where Adolph had told him it would be. It was a heavy metal door with a push bar emergency exit handle. He leaned into the door and eased it open. A police car, complete with an alert young officer, was in the rear parking lot seventy-five feet away, the red and blue lights rotating, casting mottled lighting across the building and surrounding area. Darkness would be his friend, but he was caught between sunset and evening.

Moving back to the middle of the basement area, Slade searched for and found the fire sprinkler system. It was a standard design, with the nozzle suspended from the water supply line about six inches from the ceiling tiles. Slade had noticed the same system in the main part of the library. The sprinkler system was activated by heat when the detector on the end of the nozzle reached a certain temperature. A one inch water pipe fed the outlets, which would allow water to flood an area.

Near the door was a fire extinguisher and Slade removed it from its wall mount and pulled the pin. Standing it upright, he moved back to the fire sprinkler system and removed the lighter Adolph had given him. Grabbing a book lying on a table near him, Slade ripped out some pages and rolled them into a funnel shape. Lighting one end, he raised the flame to the sprinkler system just beneath the temperature gauge on the nozzle and waited. The wait was short. Within seconds of the flame touching the nipple on the water nozzle, a loud alarm sounded throughout the building and the sprinkler system activated. Immediately, he could hear the confused shouts and footsteps of people above him.

Stomping out the pages of the book that were on fire, Slade ran for the back door. Picking up the fire extinguisher, Slade half opened the door and pressed the release valve, spewing the contents into the room. Glancing over his shoulder, Slade saw the young officer looking around in confusion and craning his head to hear his radio. Slade forced the door open and wedged a book beneath it so it would not close. Holding down the handle to the fire extinguisher, Slade sprayed the area continuously, a white cloud enveloping everything. The smoke from the fire extinguisher rolled out of the door like fog and Slade backed out with it, partially obscured.

Turning towards the young officer, Slade yelled, "Help me! There are people here! Hurry!"

The sounds of kids screaming had the desired effect. Abandoning his post, the young officer ran towards Slade, intent only on rescuing and saving anyone trapped by the fire. Slade waited until the last second. Turning the fire extinguisher, Slade sprayed the officer in the face, causing him to stumble backwards, temporarily blinded. Slade quickly shoved him inside the building, closed the door and bolted towards the police car.

No one had noticed, as most of the attention was focused on the front of the library and the 'rescue' attempt. Apprehending a fugitive was now the second priority; saving innocent lives was the first. Young children... He let the thought trail off. Hopefully none of them had been hurt by the false fire alarm and resulting panic.

It was easy for him to get lost in the descending darkness and the walk back to his truck was uneventful. Slade slid behind the wheel. Staying here would accomplish nothing. He had to move, put distance between him and his pursuers.

Leaving the library behind, Slade once again headed north. There was no plan to his action, just a desire to place as many miles between him and the library as possible. Realizing he had used Interstate Five after leaving Pasadena, Slade turned onto a junction road that carried him to the 101 freeway. A sign for Paso Robles indicated the town was not too far ahead and he felt he could make it in several hours. Paso Robles was noted for fishing and hunting and Slade had fished Lake San Antonio many years ago.

Night caught Slade long before he reached Paso Robles. Nearing the outskirts of a town, he found a small motel with perhaps a half dozen rooms and the majority of those did not have vehicles parked in front of them. It looked a little run down. It was a motel where questions would not be asked and no answers given if there were inquiries.

Parking in an empty space in front of one of the end rooms, Slade headed towards the office at the other end of the motel. The motel was painted a drab olive green. It took Slade two rings of the bell on the front desk and after a short conversation with a drunk hotel clerk, he paid $55.00 for the night.

The clerk may have been disheveled from booze, but the room was not. The motel was called the Pine Forest Inn and smelled of fresh cut pine. It gave him the feeling of being at a hunting lodge or fishing resort and the room was decorated to maintain the illusion.

The bathroom was his first stop and his eyes went wide when he saw his reflection in the mirror. A stubble of beard was growing on his face, giving him the appearance of a vagrant. Some grey hairs protruded from his chin. The bloodshot eyes and haggard appearance added to the picture. Deftly, he removed a shaver and shaving gel from his gym bag and lathered his face. His next stop was the shower.

The hot water pounding softly on his muscles relieved the tension from his body. Mentally and physically he was exhausted. He had not had any sleep since June had flown him to California over thirty-six hours ago, other than what he had gotten in the cabin of the *Pink Flamingo*.

Once the door had been locked and dead bolted, Slade slid the Beretta beneath his pillow. Turning the air conditioner setting to seventy-two degrees, he slipped into a deep, troubled slumber.

The bank of computer lights blinked off and on in rapid succession, throwing tiny shadows onto the face of Randolph Myers. The obese little man scanned the screens quickly, his pudgy fingers darting across the keyboard sending multiple commands to query unseen data bases.

Randolph had moved to an inner office deep within the bowels of World Vision Quest at the San Pedro office. It was here where Matt Kyle allowed his computer wizard to indulge himself. The latest in technological hardware was in this windowless room resembling a tomb. At his fingertips was the ability to tap into any computer in the world. It did not matter to Randolph how information was obtained. The thrill for him was in the obtaining of the information. What Kyle did with it was his business, as long as he got paid.

This latest endeavor was proving to be the ultimate in hunting. It was like a reality game show. The prey, Slade Lockwood, would surface and he would put the predators, the police, on his trail through an anonymous tip. Of course he could always count on the police to screw it up, like they had at the library. So close, but yet Lockwood had slipped away, again. He had also assaulted another cop. It only made the game that much more fun.

A pile of computer printouts littered the desk near his right elbow. Within hours he had learned everything about Slade Lockwood. Where he had his investments, the type of car he drove, the type of clothes he wore, even which restaurant he frequented the most.

The data on Slade had largely been obtained through the tracking of his social security and driver license numbers. Fingerprints are required for most licenses, especially to carry a concealed weapon like Slade in the State of Florida. The centralized medical clearing house in the northeastern United States, just outside of Dover, Delaware, gave Randolph an up to date medical profile. The man was in top physical shape, aside from some stomach pains he had last year.

The real information had been gleaned from his credit cards, especially his check card. The check card allowed lending institutions to track electronic activity pertaining to a specific account immediately. 'The check was in the mail' was now truly a cliché. A quick check of account activity could tell a lender if a bill had been paid, where you had eaten, if you paid for your cleaning bill, etc. It was all available. Of course, the information that was supposedly guarded, with encryption safeguards. Randolph smiled a wicked grin. Encryption safeguards did not stop him; they were only an inconvenience.

It had been a credit card that had led Randolph to Slade's internet account and screen name. From there it had been easy to place a search on his computer to alert him when Slade accessed the internet utilizing his screen name, Clacker1. What the hell did that mean? It did not matter since Slade had been found and was on the run again.

Picking up the top paper from the stack on the table, Randolph read the e-mail Slade had sent his girlfriend. It appeared to Randolph that Slade had no concrete evidence about the involvement of World Vision Quest or Matt Kyle. The troubling aspect of the equation was that Slade was on the right track and it would only be a matter of time before he would find the evidence needed to link World Vision Quest to Cedar Key.

Before Slade could find evidence, the authorities needed to 'find him.' If only he would use his credit card. The ringing of the phone startled him. Only one person called him here.

"Speak to me," droned Randolph.

"I read the e-mail. The idiot is still in the dark, but as you said, dangerously close to the truth. Has he surfaced again?" Matt Kyle was back in San Francisco attending to details on the computer purchase he had cemented in Silicon Valley.

"Not yet. He hasn't used his card. Must be using cash. Lucky him."

"He can't keep this pace up. Have you figured out how he got out of Cedar Key?"

"No and the local cops aren't saying. An anonymous tip to the local paper did not stir up any interest. They must be in with the cops. We need our boy to mess up again so we can make headlines. Sooner or later we will get what we need."

"We need it sooner rather than later." Kyle reached for another glass of champagne. He was staying in the penthouse suite at the Hilton, overlooking the bay. Money took care of everything, even problems. "Well, stay at it. I'll be back tomorrow. Let me know if anything develops."

"He's as good as caught." Randolph hung up and started another trace to find Slade.

Chapter Twenty-Four

Professor Johansen was admiring the ribbons hung on displays. Excited parents were everywhere, talking in frantic tones to their 'young scientist.' A smile touched the old man's face and lingered there, traveling all the way to his eyes before dying. Maybe that is what he liked so much about science fairs, that moment of discovery and recognition. Maybe that is why he had stayed on so long as chair of the science department.

A sudden longing touched his heart and he felt an uneasiness course through his very veins. Billy Waterbury would never be allowed to have that feeling again. Whatever Billy had planned to share with the world had died with him. Or had it?

Reaching for his cell phone, Professor Johansen called Betty.

"Yes, sir?"

"Have all the arrangements been made?"

"Yes. The Dean was not happy about losing you for a prolonged period of time, but did acknowledge you have not been on a field trip in quite a while." Betty reached for a notebook lying on her lap and crossed off item twenty-seven, route all incoming calls to Jaunita Gonzalez.

"What did you tell him was the reason we were going?" The Professor realized he had never ventured forth an explanation to his superiors as to why he must go on this field trip.

"To pursue the study of invertebrate, specifically, the snail mollusk which happen, incidentally, to populate the waters of Cedar Key. The Dean told me he did not know you had an interest in them." Betty crossed another item off of her list.

Professor Johansen chuckled. "Excellent call young lady, excellent. Remind me to put you in for a raise."

"I will. Just before I retire so I can get it in my pension. Anything else?" questioned Betty, dropping the last of the items she would need into a box near her desk.

"When do we leave?"

"Tomorrow morning. We fly down and the equipment and graduate students will drive down. It should take them a day, maybe two."

"See you in a couple of hours. They're wrapping up here. The awards have been handed out and the students are breaking down the exhibits."

"Bye." Betty hung up. It had been many years since she had seen this kind of academic fervor in the professor. Something had stoked his fire.

Professor Johansen stopped in front of the three spaces that should have been occupied by Billy Waterbury. For some unknown reason he had refused to issue the space to other students.

Why was Billy's death torturing him? He had never met the young man. What was the unseen connection tugging at him? Why did he feel compelled to go to Cedar Key and bring to light the scientific discovery Billy Waterbury was going to share with the world? Was it his dedication as a scientist? Was it because he was getting old and did not have many more field trips left in him? Was it a combination of all of these things?

Professor Johansen knew sometimes science could not explain everything or account for the emotions roaming freely in the minds of humans. Impulsive behavior had led to many scientific discoveries, even though the methodology to arrive at the conclusion was not the least bit scientific. Call it human whim.

Moving into the empty spaces that had been reserved for Billy Waterbury, Professor Johansen turned and looked out at the other displays lining the vast hall. Brightly colored paper and brilliant streamers beckoned the eye and stopped the curious, inviting them into a world of discovery. Billy Waterbury would never have the opportunity to stand in a hall such as this again and share his knowledge, his discoveries with the world.

With a purpose in his stride that had been subdued in years past by the weight of academia, Professor Johansen moved towards the exit, waving to those he knew and nodding to those he did not. Billy Waterbury, though gone, had one last story to tell the world. He only needed a narrator. Professor Johansen intended to be that narrator.

Chief Singletee nodded at Shirley and Katherine, smiling politely, as they related the information Willard Mayes had told them about the *Fair Rose*.

"So she was in tip-top shape, no breaks or anything?"

"Not even a crack. My dad knew boats. Knew them better than anybody."

"I know he did. Everybody in Cedar Key knew he did. Willard found what I thought he would find." Chief Singletee looked over at Katherine. "Have you heard from Slade?"

The sound in the chief's voice alerted Katherine that something was wrong. A tightness formed in her stomach. "No, have you?"

"Not yet."

"Why do I get the feeling you know something you're not telling me."

"Slade is in a little trouble. Now, don't worry. You and I both know he can sort through most anything. I'm sure he's okay." Chief Singletee had seen the color drain from Katherine's face. To her, Slade Lockwood was indestructible, the white knight who could conquer all. He was also the man she loved.

"What happened?"

"I only have the details the local police out there have provided me with. Seems Slade was detected going into Leonard's apartment and the police were called..." Chief Singletee was cut off by Shirley.

"Who called the police? A neighbor?" Shirley's computer mind kicked into gear.

"An anonymous caller alerted the police and that's cause for concern. Slade escaped, but narrowly. He had to assault a female police officer. Took her radio and gun. There's a state-wide BOLO, Be On the Look Out, out for him in the State of California." Chief Singletee stopped to let them catch up. Too much information, too fast, could throw them into a tailspin.

"Was he hurt?" Katherine asked the question cautiously.

"Apparently not. He set a fire in a little library north of Pasadena to escape from the police when he was found a second time."

"How did they find him so soon?" asked Shirley.

"I don't know. I do know it was an anonymous caller again. According to the clerk at the library, Slade was using a computer." Chief Singletee paused before asking, "Did he send you an e-mail or anything?"

The chief looked at Katherine.

"Not that I'm aware of. We've been gone all afternoon. I had to check on the studio. Shirley had to check her mail. We left early this morning. Do you think he sent me an e-mail?"

"It would explain why he was in the library. Most libraries have computers with internet access."

"That still doesn't explain who called the police." Shirley wrinkled her brow.

"Is there anyway someone could have tracked his internet usage and traced it back to him?" Katherine asked the question slowly, fearful of the answer.

"Some large agencies can track actively via a credit card. I know a subscriber service, like AOL, can track you, but I don't know about anyone else. It's possible, I guess." Chief Singletee peered over his tea glass at Katherine.

"Let's go to Slade's. If he sent me an e-mail, it's on his computer." Without waiting for a reply she stood and headed for the door.

The drive was short. If it was true Slade was being tracked by someone with the ability to access computer systems, then he was truly alone. His every electronic move would be monitored and reported to the authorities. This new curve could prove deadly to Slade and was one they had not considered. Before leaving, Slade had told Katherine he would send her e-mails if he could not get to a phone. Internet services had proliferated in recent years and the ability to find a computer terminal and modem was easier than it had ever been. This avenue now appeared to be closed.

Chief Singletee followed the two women to Slade's and into his office. Katherine seated herself at Slade's desk and quickly typed in his access name. Within seconds, the screen came to life and an electronic beep informed Katherine she had mail.

No one spoke until each of them read the e-mail. Katherine then clicked on the printer button and the ink jet printer spit out three copies in rapid succession. Shirley grabbed them and handed Katherine and Chief Singletee one. Each of them read the e-mail a second time.

"World Vision Quest? Never heard of it," mumbled the chief.

"I have," stated Shirley, matter-of-factly.

Katherine looked at the younger woman and noticed her knuckles were white from gripping the paper. When Katherine saw the look on her face, she finally understood: Shirley was putting a name to the people who had murdered her family. There was something tangible to go on, and to hang on to.

"How do you know of the company?" Katherine rose and moved next to her.

"I remember them from several of the science fairs Billy and I entered. There was always a group of them. Like most companies, they wanted to be the first to buy the next invention or find the next discovery. I remember one kid who sold an idea to enhance the performance of a jet engine. I heard my mom and dad talking about it and about the money. It was enough to put him through college."

"Did they ever express an interest in anything you or Billy did?" Katherine continued to hold her hand.

"Not that I remember. But if they had, then Dad would have handled that. He made sure to screen us from the business types."

"Were they on the list that Slade gave you?" asked Chief Singletee.

"I don't know. I'll get the list." Katherine disappeared.

When she returned, the Chief and Shirley were in the living room. Katherine scanned the list as she walked. Her finger stopped in mid-air and then she stabbed the paper.

"Here it is. Near the bottom." Katherine handed the list to the Chief.

"It gives us a start and nothing more," cautioned Chief Singletee. "We need to know all we can about this company. Who runs it, what there interests are, if they have offices here in Cedar Key, everything. Can you girls handle that?" The Chief already knew the answer to that question. It was written all over their faces. The hunt was in their eyes, much like a rookie cop on their first big case.

"You betcha," laughed Shirley.

"By the way, who called you about Slade? You never did say." Katherine's eyes met the Chief's.

"LAPD. A Commander Rich LeFluer wanted to know what Slade was up to. I don't believe he bought the story I gave him, but he didn't press it either. Call it professional courtesy."

"And that was all?" pressed Katherine.

"Not exactly. He wanted to know about Leonard Woodman and if he was alive or dead. I told him Slade killed him while saving your life and Shirley's. If this Commander LeFluer is half as smart as I think he is, he's probably on a plane right now and flying this way. I would."

"Why?" asked Shirley.

"Because he and Slade were friends. Besides, I don't know Slade as well as Commander LeFluer or either one of you, but if you knew he was involved in something, wouldn't you think it was something big and something with purpose? I know I would." When he saw a questioning look from them the chief added, "Some men make friends that are nothing more than casual acquaintances or professional associates. Slade is one of those people others are drawn to, that they depend upon. Slade is a doer, a man who can be counted on and won't let you down. When you become friends with someone like him, you find yourself trying to do better, to achieve more, to go the extra mile, because you know that's what he would do. Trust me, Commander LeFluer is on a plane headed to Cedar Key right now."

"Good. Then maybe he can help us." Katherine pulled the piece of paper with World Vision Quest's name from Shirley's grasp. "Slade has given us a glimmer of hope and I say we move on it, instead of standing around and talking."

"Agreed." Both the Chief and Shirley said it simultaneously.

The Israelis had agreed to up the price. It was an awesome amount of money: 1.5 billion dollars of up-front money plus eighteen percent of the gross for development in the region. A tidy sum when added to the coiffures of World Vision Quest. With all the contracts front end loaded, the up-front money was nearing six billion dollars. And the monetary iceberg had just been scratched, with untold wealth still to come. The awesome potential of the invention could lead to a hundred billion dollars within ten years.

Clyde Sommer leaned back in his seat and closed his eyes. Matt Kyle had called him home. Sommer's work in the field was done. Later, when the product was being mass produced, he may need to venture forth again to negotiate some smaller contracts, but, for the immediate future, his work was complete.

Home was in Arkansas, near Little Rock. Clyde had three weeks of vacation before he was to report to San Pedro, California. Kyle wanted him there for the first demonstration.

Removing his calculator from his breast pocket, Clyde estimated his commission again. It came to just over two million dollars. The numbers looked almost obscene on the tiny green LED screen. It was more money than anyone in his entire family had ever made. His wife would not believe it. It would be financial freedom for the entire family.

The British Airways jetliner dipped its starboard wing as it climbed to cruising altitude. Clyde looked out the window at the darkness of night and smiled. All of his troubles were over.

Finally the valves and special fittings were complete. The employees had needed the rest and time had healed many of them. Their sickness was not a physical ailment, but mental and emotional fatigue. Robert had seen it in there eyes, in their walk, and in their speech. They had been tired and pushed to the limits of exhaustion.

The days off had given them a chance to get their life back together. For many of them, that meant finally hiring a contractor or settling with an insurance company to get much needed home repairs started. That little sense of stability had righted their course and allowed the healing process of accepting a personal loss to begin. With their homes now taken care of, they were ready for work.

The employees had not asked for overtime this time to complete the job. It was their way of thanking Matt Kyle for having trust in them and allowing them to attend to personal issues. The around the clock work had completed the job in record time. With clear minds, the valves and corresponding couplings had been manufactured. All was ready for shipment.

Robert Turk had already spoken to Kyle and informed him the shipment was leaving. Once again, the eccentric millionaire had surprised him. After thanking Turk repeatedly, he had informed him to start manufacturing five duplicate sets of valves, fittings, and couplings. Kyle wanted them in four weeks, if possible and had given him unlimited overtime to complete the job. The employees would love this. It was a chance to earn extra income when most needed.

Turk paged his two shift foremen and told them to report to his office. Good news should be delivered first hand.

Breakfast had been an egg sandwich from a local diner and generous amounts of coffee. Slade had returned to his room and taken a shower and shaved. Sleep had done a lot to restore his faculties and the man staring back at him in the mirror finally looked familiar. Slade had also removed the stitches to his left side with a pair of tweezers. He still did not think he had ever needed stitches, but he had not wanted to argue with Katherine.

Moving to a chair near the bed, Slade turned on the TV and surfed through the channels until he found a local news station. The pretty blonde anchorwoman was talking about the weather forecast.

Lying on the bed was the stack of magazines he had taken from Leonard's apartment. He could not bring himself to think of it as stealing, because he still considered himself one of the good guys, regardless of his recent actions. The fact he had a lot of explaining to do was not lost on him.

Slade picked up the first magazine and started flipping through the pages, not sure what he was looking for. The sound of his name on the television caused him to snap his head up.

"Ex-Deputy Chief Slade Lockwood of the LAPD has been identified as the suspect in a burglary in Pasadena. While making his escape from police, Lockwood assaulted a Pasadena police officer, taking her radio and duty weapon. Miles up the road, in a rural library in a tiny town Lockwood made a second daring escape when police were alerted to his presence. Setting off the fire alarm, Lockwood assaulted another police officer and vanished into the night. Authorities are unsure as to his whereabouts, but a BOLO has been issued for him as well as an arrest warrant. The LAPD has declined to comment and a motive for these senseless crimes has not been given. If you have any information where this dangerous fugitive may be, please contact your local law enforcement agency."

Slade stared in disbelief as his picture was flashed onto the screen. Luckily, it was a picture of him in police uniform wearing a hat from several years ago. Still if someone looked at him closely, they would recognize him.

How had the police found him in the library? No one recognized him there, because his picture had not been on TV. The only thing he had done was send an e-mail to Katherine on the internet. The internet! The thought rocketed through his head like a bolt of lightening. He was getting close to the killers and it had scared them. Whoever had the power to monitor the internet was influential and wealthy, with considerable resources. The computer systems and software needed to accomplish that feat was no laughing matter.

Slade rose from his chair and paced the room. The change in position was a beautiful tactical move on the part of the killers. Why live being the hunted, when with a simple twist of fate, you could use the system against the person pursuing you? That meant they knew he had killed Leonard and would go to the killer's apartment to seek information. So far, the authorities in Cedar Key and the State of Florida had abandoned Shirley, listing the cause of death as accidental. If the professionals had been so helpful in the past, why not utilize them now? It made sense.

Was there a leak in Cedar Key? Chief Singletee? Slade did not think so. It was more likely they had rolled the dice and waited for him to make the next move. Unwittingly he had underestimated his adversary and walked into a trap.

For the first time in years Slade felt truly alive and invigorated. This game was forcing him to utilize all of his skills. It was the thrill he had gotten as a rookie cop when he had chased his first criminal. The adrenaline rush had pushed him to an all time high and he could remember it like it was yesterday. Until now, he thought he would never know that feeling again.

They were hoping to drive Slade to the ground, where he would hide from authorities. Fear is a powerful weapon and could paralyze most; incapacitating them until they could be dealt with at a later time. Slade had no such intention of remaining out of sight. This situation could be reversed, but he still needed information. Knowledge was power in this the ultimate chess game.

Moving back to the chair, Slade picked up Leonard's address book and thumbed through the pages again, reading everything. The only name next to a company was a Matt Kyle, penciled above World Vision Quest. He had Shirley and Katherine checking on that. A pang of fear momentarily grabbed his heart. The e-mail! The killer may have intercepted that as well. If they had, and they were one and the same, then they would know he suspected them. It was up to Chief Singletee to protect the two women.

Undoubtedly Katherine and Shirley had shown Chief Singletee the e-mail and, more than likely, Chief Singletee had already been contacted by authorities from Pasadena and Los Angeles. The knot slowly let loose its grip on his heart. The women were safe. Chief Singletee knew the stakes and would not let him down.

Grabbing all the magazines, Slade placed them on his lap. In the second to last magazine, near the middle, Slade found a few words written in the margin of an article. The writing had been done in pencil and had grown faint with the passage of time. The light on the dresser provided the necessary light and he was able to make out some of the words.

'Kyle' was penciled in at the top. In a flurry of excitement, Slade placed the magazine back on the desk top and ran back to the chair to retrieve the address book. Hurriedly he fanned through the book until he found Matt Kyle's name. An exact match!

The next words on the page were placed one after the other: Valdez; Alaska; *Quest 1*. What did all that mean? If he could recall geography properly, Valdez was a city in Alaska. An oil refinery port, if memory served him correctly. Dimly, he remembered a story about an oil tanker running aground many years ago off the coast of Alaska and spilling crude into the Bering Sea. If he was right, the ship had been named the *Valdez*.

Slade flipped through the rest of the magazine but found nothing. Were the answers in Valdez? When he had searched the internet, he did not remember seeing anything in Alaska that World Vision Quest owned....*Quest 1*! Was *Quest 1* the name of a boat for World Vision Quest? The possibilities seemed to match, but it could not be this easy.

Something else was bothering him about *Quest 1*, but he could not pin it down. Until now the name had held no meaning, no significance. It seemed like he had heard something on the news about it, but he was not sure. The harder he tried to peer into his mind, the further the information slipped away, like night's shadows fleeing the rising sun. It could have been something he had read on the Internet about the company, but, for now, it was gone.

Slade went to the closet and started to pack. Wherever the truth may be, he knew it was not here in this motel room. Valdez seemed like as good place as any to start.

The drive up Interstate 1 had occurred without fanfare or detection. Every time a police cruiser had passed, his throat had gone dry and he nervously watched them in the mirror until they were out of sight.

Once he entered Oregon, Slade moved back to Interstate 5 and spent the night in Eugene. His hope was to make Portland and catch a flight to Valdez. If that did not work, then he was prepared to drive through to Seattle. Valdez was on the coast and offered shelter from the hostile Bering Sea. This time of the year, there would be no ice, so he did not expect problems in chartering a float plane to take him there.

If he had too, he could catch a flight to Anchorage and drive to Valdez. The roads in Alaska were not the best, with the constant freezing and summer thawing. He was also getting low on cash. For some unknown reason he had brought $1,500.00 with him, but he had cut into that considerably. With gas, food and lodging, he had a little over $1,100.00 left. With the killer monitoring his electronic activity, accessing an ATM was out of the question. Within minutes, it would give away his location and the authorities would be summoned.

Morning found Slade back on the road and heading north. Portland was made by early afternoon and an unusual chill filled the air.

The first restaurant he stopped at proved to be beneficial in several ways. The food was great and the waitress knew where there was a small airport where planes routinely flew up and down the Pacific Northwest.

After lunch Slade found the airport. It was small and the planes when viewed from a distance looked like remote control toys weaving and bobbing across the skies. A large red and white sign indicated flying lessons were available. The airport, in addition to asphalt runways, butted up against the Colombia River and the roar of float planes could be heard as Slade walked towards the office. Several hangers were visible near one end of the largest asphalt runway.

Pushing open a rusty door, Slade stepped inside. An elderly, fat man was on the phone and a younger man was talking to a couple seated at his desk. It was the younger man that looked up and spoke.

"Be with you in a minute."

"I'm in no rush." Slade moved to a window near the back. Lined on the river in orderly rows were dozens of float planes. Looking down the river, Slade watched as one accelerated, spraying water in all directions and then gently lifting into the air, wagging its wings to shake off the last droplets clinging to its metal skin.

"What can I do for you?" The younger man extended his hand.

"You have a nice place here." Slade enthusiastically shook the extended hand. According to the embroidery on the man's shirt, his name was Paul.

"Yeah, it's nice and quiet. Family run for the last forty years. My dad started the business and I'm kinda taking over." Paul had gestured to the older man on the phone when he mentioned 'dad.' "You interested in flying lessons?"

"No, salmon. I would like to know if any of your pilots are heading to Alaska. I was hoping to catch a ride."

"Alaska. A lot of people love to go up there. Been there myself quite a few times. Where you headed, Ketchikan? They have excellent salmon fishing this time of the year."

"No, I have a friend working in Valdez. Thought I would surprise him and go fishing at the same time."

"Valdez? Not much there. An oil refinery and the cruise ships stop by to refuel. Some of the locals set up shop on the dock and sell their stuff to the tourists. Never fished there. Should be good fishing though." Paul moved to his desk and Slade followed.

"How much do you think it would cost?" Slade sat down.

"That's up to the pilot. The problem is going to be finding someone going that far north. Generally they all fly to Sitka, Ketchikan, or one of the other closer coastal towns. Every now and then you find one heading up there. I'll probably have to check and see if any of them have a flight planned. Might take a day or two. Where can I reach you?" Paul glanced from the computer screen.

"I'll call you. I haven't found a room yet and I wanted to sight see a little." Slade extended his hand as he stood up.

"Call me in the morning. I should know something by then." Paul returned the hand shake and then sat back down, clicking onto a different page on his computer screen. The whine of a plane could be heard gaining speed and, seconds later, it roared over head.

"I'll call you about nine. Is that okay?"

"Yeah, that'll be fine."

Without another word Slade walked out of the office and moved towards the pick-up truck. Hopefully, he could find a pilot to take him to Valdez.

"Is that the last of it?" Professor Johansen walked over to the crates still to be loaded onto a truck. About a dozen students wearing blue jeans and sweat shirts were placing the items onto a covered trailer.

"That should do it, Professor." A young woman with a large blue 'M' across the front of her shirt had answered. Angela Caruso was a grad student studying chemistry and was delighted the Professor had asked her to come along and head the student team. It was an honor carrying a lot of responsibility, but also showed the confidence the Professor had in her.

"Good. Everything has been double checked?" Professor Johansen handed Angela back the neatly typed pages of supplies that had two check marks by them.

"Yes, sir. Actually, everything has been triple checked," Angela paused before adding, "I'm a little confused Professor. We have brought a lot of different equipment. Are we limiting ourselves to the study of just snails or are we branching off into other areas?"

Professor Johansen looked directly at Angela for several seconds before answering the eager young scientist. "No one knows what the future holds. It is best to be prepared for any eventuality." Professor Johansen slapped the young woman on the shoulder.

"Are you and your wife flying down, Professor?" Angela called to the Professor as he was walking away.

"Yes. Betty, her husband, my wife and I are flying down to make arrangements. We will need a base of operations. The Dean is already yelling about the expense budget I turned in." Professor Johansen held his hands out palm up in a plaintive gesture of humility. "I raised a large portion of that money to fund research, so he better not yell too loudly." Everyone burst into laughter.

Professor Johansen had spear-headed an effort by the University of Michigan to raise needed capital to fund research in the field. By calling on local businessman and wealthy alumni, money for field research had soared into the millions. The funds were watched over by Dean Haskins, who treated the account as if it were his own. However, Dean Haskin had not bickered too much when the travel and lodging request had come across his desk and had been signed by Professor Johansen. No need to bite the hand feeding you.

"Everyone has cell phones, right?" asked Betty, waving a list at the students.

Four trucks, two of which were towing trailers brimming with equipment, would be driven to Cedar Key by the graduate students. Two additional cars were being brought as well to carry passengers. It was a modern caravan on a quest seeking knowledge. The lead vehicle was being driven by Angela. The others would follow, staying in contact by cell phone. Each vehicle had two drivers and a person responsible for communication.

"Don't rush. We have all the time we need," grinned Professor Johansen. A pain touched his heart and shot through him in the form of realization. He had stayed too long behind the desk and had not spent enough time in the field doing what he loved best—research, uncovering the mysteries of the world. His research now was to help a young man he had never met bring his dream to the eyes of the world.

"All right, let's move out," yelled Angela, sounding like a wagon master from the pages of history.

All of the students hurried to their vehicles and clamored inside. There was much yelling and shouting and the last vehicle had placed a cardboard sign in the back window: "Florida or bust." Young minds, young ideas, unlimited enthusiasm.

"We have a plane to catch," droned Professor Johansen, spinning on his heel and walking to a dark blue Chevy Tahoe. The spring in his step was obvious and the Professor's wife squeezed Betty's arm in recognition. This was going to be a marvelous trip.

Chapter Twenty-Five

"World Vision Quest representatives have been at every show Billy has entered in the last year." Shirley tried to keep the excitement of discovery out of her voice, but failed miserably.

"When was the most recent?" Both women were on the porch. Old Clacker was asleep on the deck next to Katherine's chair and had raised his head, when she had gotten up. Detecting no immediate threat, the old bird placed his bill back beneath his wing.

"About two months before he died." Shirley let her voice trail off.

"Where was the science fair held?"

"It was in Tampa at the convention center. Billy won first place in engineering based on a system to enhance the performance of the engines used to power the space shuttle. I remember because he called and told me all the boring details. Billy had designed a series of valves to enhance the thrust of the engine, while cutting fuel consumption. It created quite a stir from what mom told me. People from NASA were interested in the technology."

"Nothing about mangroves?"

"Not that I remember. We may be off track, Katherine. It might have nothing to do with mangroves. Maybe the killer picked up the wrong piece of paper. There was another science fair in April or May and I believe Billy may have entered it. I was busy with finals at UF and we didn't talk much." Shirley shrugged.

"Maybe, but I don't think so. Perhaps Billy was still working on the mangrove project and told someone about it..." Katherine was stopped.

"Someone from World Vision Quest! That's a distinct possibility. Billy loved to talk about what he was working on. You couldn't shut him up. That could very well be, but it certainly doesn't help us much. It doesn't put us any closer to unraveling what Billy was doing with the mangroves."

"No, but the pieces are beginning to fit. It's much like when I'm painting," explained Katherine. "I start with a blank canvass and when I start to fill the picture with color, shapes start to materialize. Vague at first and then they come into focus with greater clarity until the entire picture is clear and can be seen. It's the same here, but we are at the stage where color is being applied, the image is not clear."

"You sound like, Slade," said Shirley, regretting she had said it the minute it left her lips. "Sorry."

"It's okay. I'm sure he's okay. Slade probably figured out his e-mail transmissions were being monitored. When he needs to, he'll contact us when he finds something." Katherine tried to sound courageous. "Let's get something to eat and tell Chief Singletee what you have found. Any news is good news."

Both women abandoned the porch and moved inside, an uneasy quietness settling on them. Where was Slade?

Holiday Inn had provided Slade with a room. It was more than he had wanted to spend, but he did not complain as sleep was something he desperately needed. After breakfast, Slade had called Paul Lewis at Busy B Airport to see if he had located a flight. Paul had booked Slade on a one way trip to Anchorage and that was the best he could do. From there, Slade would have to find his own transportation to Valdez. The flight left at noon.

At 11:45, Slade wheeled the old pick-up into the parking lot of Busy B Airport and parked it near a fence in the corner. A short walk and he was inside Paul's office, where he paid for the ticket. The price was $145.00.

"Go to Hanger Three and ask for Randy. You can't miss him." Paul gave Slade a receipt and Slade turned for the door. "What about your truck? When are you coming back?"

Reaching into his back pocket, Slade pulled out his wallet and handed Paul a hundred dollar bill.

"For parking my truck here. I'll be back to get it. Just look after it." Slade saw the confused look hit Paul's face. "Thanks, and I appreciate your help."

"Don't mention it," muttered Paul as Slade walked out.

Slade found Hanger Three right where Paul had told him. The large bay doors were open and an old aircraft with oil streaks on the fuselage greeted him. A large man with a dark black beard appeared from around the wing.

"You the guy going to Anchorage?"

"Yeah."

"Put your stuff in the plane. I'm leaving in ten minutes. If you're not on board I'm leaving without you."

Slade moved to the open door and tossed his bag into the cabin area. Supplies in various boxes were piled from floor to ceiling. Most of them had been lashed down with rope. Climbing over the boxes, Slade slipped down into the co-pilot's seat and buckled himself in.

Randy climbed into the plane, which groaned from his weight, and he slammed the door shut, cursing every second. Moving over the freight, he deposited himself in the pilot's seat and started scanning gauges. Satisfied, he attempted to start the engine and she coughed in protest and belched a plume of black smoke before catching life. Randy let her idle for several minutes, his eyes intently glued to the gauges. Finally, a certain rhythm could be discerned.

Slade could feel his heart pounding a little faster than he would have cared for. Slade noticed the plane was not in the same mint condition as the *Pink Flamingo.* Torn upholstery, dirty carpeting and a questionable pilot had Slade thinking about waiting for a second flight.

"Let's see what she's got," smirked Randy, easing the throttle forward. The tiny plane belched another billow of black smoke.

Instinctively, Slade reached down and tightened his seatbelt. Not to appear nervous, he folded his arms across his body and leaned back.

Randy got clearance from the tower and moved the single engine plane onto the runway. A stiff breeze was coming off the river and he made the necessary adjustments. Later, Slade would say the mad rush down the asphalt was the scariest thing he had ever done. The wind constantly tried to push the little plane into the grass. Randy cursed violently and fought the stick, all the while increasing the rpms to gain enough speed. With the fence and end of the runway rapidly approaching, Slade was about to suggest they were not going to make it, when the nose pointed up and the heavily laden aircraft clawed into the air.

"Didn't think we were going to make it there for a moment. I probably have too much weight on board. Ah, the hell with it. We made it anyway." Randy burst into laughter and dipped the starboard wing in a sharp bank.

"Yeah, it was close," replied Slade.

The landing in Anchorage was less eventful. Slade grabbed his gym bag while the plane was being tied down. During the flight, Randy told him he knew of several guys going to Valdez and if they had not left by the time they landed, he would see if they could give him a ride. Fortune was smiling and a little over an hour after landing, Slade was sitting in the back seat of an old Chevy Impala listening to the banter of three oil workers.

It was late at night when they made Valdez. Slade was dropped off at a little string of cabins and rented a room.

Leaving his few possessions, Slade headed for a restaurant the oil workers had told him about. The town was small and everything was within walking distance. When he entered, cigarette smoke was as thick as fog and he moved towards a table near a window that offered some relief from the tobacco smell.

"You made it! Have a beer." A bearded man that had driven the Chevy was the first to speak. He was already well on his way to a good drunk. A bottle of native beer was slammed down in front of Slade.

"Thanks, Keith." Sipping from the bottle, Slade asked, "What type of beer is this?"

"Made from spruce leaves and some other damn stuff. Not real sure to tell you. Gets you plenty drunk though."

"What's good to eat?" Slade smiled at a heavy set waitress.

"The prime rib is awesome, honey. The steak is good. Salmon is always a favorite." Brenda smiled at Keith as he looped his arm around her ample hips.

"What about you and me, Hon?" Keith looked up at her and turned his beer towards the ceiling.

"Maybe some other time, Doll."

"Prime rib it is and include a potato." Slade closed the menu.

"What about a salad?"

"Sure," and then as if an afterthought, "Do you have Michelob? This Alaskan beer takes getting used to."

The remainder of the night passed with Slade, Keith, and the rest of the gang drinking and sharing stories. Slade learned about the businesses in town and how most of the folks made their living. It was well past midnight when Slade stumbled back to his cabin. It took him less than two minutes to bolt the door and fall asleep, his right fingers curled protectively around the Beretta beneath his pillow.

Randolph Myers queried the computer screen in front of him and accessed a program he called "Random Probability Matrix." Randolph had created the program while in prison. By entering a set of data and establishing the probable scenarios, he could estimate an eventual path or outcome. Other more expensive and highly classified variations were available in the Pentagon and other remote think tanks, but not even he had access to those.

For the last several hours, he had been entering data about Slade Lockwood. There was no tidbit too small or insignificant. If there was information on Slade, it was entered. The tricky or "random" part involved proposing the possible scenarios. This was based on what information Slade had learned and this was mere speculation for the most part by Randolph. A lot of this information had been gleaned from the e-mail Slade had sent to Cedar Key. But even then, there was a large degree of guesswork. For example, he knew Slade was aware of the company because he had accessed the company's internet web page. But how much had he read? Had he just casually glanced over the pages and scanned the subtitles? Or had he taken the time to read every page.

Sliding back from the console in front of him, Randolph punched his right index finger on the 'enter' button before rubbing his eyes. His eyes were tired and he could feel it. A cot was in the corner of the room and he would try to get some sleep as soon as the program had spit out some possible solutions.

At first, Randolph thought Slade had blindly fled Pasadena in an attempt to throw authorities off his trail, but now he was not so sure. The incident at the library confused him. If Slade was innocent or had a lot of information, then he would have surfaced and given it to the authorities. But instead, he had remained hidden. Also, he had not used any credit cards or logged onto the internet. Was he that smart?

A beep at the computer console caused Randolph to re-adjust his glasses and he leaned back to the screen, selecting the appropriate key. Immediately, the screen was filled with two possible outcomes. After reading them both, Randolph picked up the phone and dialed Kyle.

"Yeah."

"The Random Probability Matrix indicates he will make one of two moves: San Pedro or Valdez. The percentage for error is approximately fifteen percent, based on the limited information we have."

"Estimated time to move." Kyle had swung his feet over the edge of the bed and was now wide awake.

"Based on time and distance, and his ability to adapt, he could already be at either location."

"What about the probability he has learned anything of significance?"

"Only fifty-five percent, but again, I don't have all the information on him and I don't know who he has spoken to or what he took from Leonard's apartment."

"Okay, I'll make the necessary calls to alert security. Any electronic activity?"

"None. He must be using cash or has an incredible network of friends."

"Get some sleep. We'll talk in the morning."

Was Slade already in Valdez or San Pedro? It was a scary proposition and he did not want the ex-cop snooping around. In all likelihood, he did not know anything, but he could not take that chance. Kyle picked up the phone and dialed San Pedro first and then Valdez. Preparations had to be made.

Chapter Twenty-Six

"I was wondering when you were going to get here. Pleasant flight?" Chief Singletee watched as Commander Rick LeFleur tried in vain to stop the sweat from streaming down his face.

"Slade and I go way back; all the way to the academy. You want to tell me what the hell is going on?" Commander LeFleur seated himself in a chair opposite Chief Singletee.

"Sure." Chief Singletee poured his guest another glass of water. It took him almost forty-five minutes to bring LeFleur up to date.

"I wonder why he didn't call me. I would have helped him..." Commander LeFleur let his voice trail off.

"Help him do what? Tell you that he thought Leonard Woodman was responsible for the death of the Waterbury's and he thought there may be evidence in his apartment? Do you think you would have gotten a search warrant on that?" Chief Singletee looked directly at the younger cop, his eyebrows raised questioningly.

"I don't know. Maybe. Maybe not. We could have tried," was all Commander LeFleur would say.

"And if you didn't? What then? Do we just forget about this? You and I both know Slade is not going to do that, and neither am I for that matter."

"What can I do to help?"

"Go back to California and wait. Sooner or later Slade will contact you. I understand his name and picture is plastered all over the news media. See if you can exercise some influence and get the media types to lay off the story for awhile. Give our man some breathing room. Right now that is all we can do."

"You give me your word you will keep me informed?" Commander LeFleur looked sternly at the chief.

"Word of honor from one lawman to another." Both men shook hands to seal the deal.

BJ's green pick-up had gone unnoticed in the lot of Busy B Airport and would have remained just one more vehicle had a teenage driver, with a brand new driver's license, not backed into it. The father was taking flying lessons and was allowing his son to drive him around. The father was understanding, because the damage to his Cadillac was far more severe than the dent in the bumper of the old truck.

When notified of the accident, Paul had called the local police and they had run the tag when filling out the report. When BJ's name came back as the registered owner, the police officer asked Paul where BJ was.

"I didn't know that was his name. As a matter of fact, he never gave me his name."

"Well, where did he say he was going?" asked Officer Justin Strama.

"Valdez, but I could only get him a flight to Anchorage."

"Anchorage, Alaska?"

"Yeah." Paul looked over at the pick-up truck. It had never occurred to him to ask the man for his identification.

"Can you describe BJ?" asked Officer Strama and when he noticed the strange look on Paul's face, he added, "It's for the police report. Not all of the information is on the registration."

"Oh. About six feet tall, black hair, blue eyes." Paul was cut off.

"Blue eyes?"

"Yes. Why?"

"This registration says BJ is a black man."

"Black? No way, he's as white as I am. And he had blue eyes."

Reaching for his radio, Officer Strama asked for records and a detailed description of BJ Watson. Confirming BJ was black and not white, the young officer looked back at Paul.

"I'll have the local police in Upland pay a visit to BJ. The vehicle is not reported as stolen. Maybe he doesn't know it's missing. Did this white guy seem odd or act like he was hiding anything?"

"No, paid for his trip in cash, which I thought was unusual, but it was really not that much money."

"We'll get to the bottom of it. We always do." Officer Strama snapped his book shut and walked towards his patrol car. He would have to call a tow truck and have the vehicle towed to the police impound yard.

Within twenty minutes, a bright orange tow truck arrived.

"Have you done an inventory yet?"

"No. Waiting on you," answered Officer Strama to Clyde, owner and operator of Clyde's Towing Service. "Go ahead."

It was standard procedure to inventory a vehicle when police impounded a car or truck. Clyde started the inventory, but called to Officer Strama the second he opened the glove box.

"You need to take a look at this." Clyde had moved away from the passenger door of the pick-up and the tone in his voice brought Officer Strama immediately to his side.

The glove box was open and lying inside was a handgun and police radio. Officer Strama recovered the gun and contacted records a second time. Within seconds of entering the gun's serial number, the dispatcher hit the alert tone and asked him if the suspect was on scene.

"Negative. No suspect." Officer Strama looked directly at Clyde and then at Paul. What had he stumbled into?

"10-4. That weapon, I repeat, that weapon is stolen. It was taken from a Pasadena police officer. Is the radio there?" Tiffany Holmes looked at the computer terminal. Reading from the teletype transmission, it said the officer had been assaulted, knocked unconscious and her gun and radio taken.

"10-4. The radio is here. Dispatch, notify my supervisor and have him respond. Also, I will need prints." Officer Strama immediately instructed everyone to move away from the truck, this case was far more important than a minor accident.

Officer Strama moved his police vehicle closer to the pick-up and activated his emergency lights so responding personnel could find him easier. The truck was tucked away in an obscure corner of the lot and now he understood why.

There was silence on the radio for ten minutes while notifications were being made and then Officer Strama's world erupted into a frenzied, talkative bedlam. In addition to his radio going off, his cell phone was ringing and his beeper was activated.

Within thirty minutes of the original notification, Sergeant Mayes and Lt. Huckster arrived, along with a forensic team to dust the truck for prints. Two detectives pulled up and immediately cornered Paul Lewis, who was now a very alarmed owner of Busy Bee Airport. The questioning was pointed and relentless—they wanted to know anything and everything about the person who had driven BJ Watson's pick-up onto the airport parking lot.

"He said he was meeting a friend of his in Valdez to go fishing. That's all he said. People come here all the time and ask to go fishing. There was nothing unusual about the request. Honest that's all I remember about the guy, aside from the description I've given you."

"We'll be in touch." Detective Douglas handed Paul a business card.

"I'll be here. Am I free to go?"

"Yes," yelled Detective Douglas over his shoulder.

Paul turned and hurried back to his office. His wife and father were not going to believe this.

Lt. Huckster listened intently to the report provided by his two detectives. When they were done, he nodded silently to himself. What made a cop go bad? The Communications Center had notified him the Pasadena Police officer's weapon had been taken by an ex-LAPD Deputy Chief named Slade Lockwood. When the name had been mentioned, he remembered reading about it in the paper. Anytime a cop did anything wrong it made the headlines, no matter where it occurred.

"I've already called Upland PD. They're sending over two detectives to talk to the owner of the pick-up truck. Maybe he knows this guy Lockwood. Hopefully, he can shed some light on this mess." Lt. Huckster looked around. "Why don't you guys interview anybody else that may have come into contact with Lockwood. Also, notify the authorities in Valdez. If memory serves me correctly, that's not a very big town to hide in."

"Will do." Detective Douglas hurried for the nearest hanger.

The car tires crunched on the gravel and slid to a noisy stop. Shirley and Katherine could hear several doors slam shut and they both peered out of Slade's living room window to see who it was. An older gentleman, with a grey beard and close cropped hair, was obviously in charge. He had confronted the young officer Chief Singletee had appointed as security and was pointing to Slade's house. After several minutes of the young officer talking on the phone, he handed the grey haired man back his identification and motioned towards the stairs.

They could hear the entourage walk up the steps and then a soft knock echoed from the door.

"Did you recognize any of them?"

"No. I thought you might know them." Katherine moved to the door.

All four of the occupants of the vehicle were gathered on the doorstop. The grey haired gentleman spoke first.

"Shirley Waterbury?"

"No. I'm Katherine Wintergate. This is Shirley Waterbury." Katherine stepped back so the man could see Shirley.

Without waiting on a response, the grey haired man stepped inside and extended his hand towards Shirley. "I'm so pleased to meet you. I'm Professor Johansen from the University of Michigan." When he saw the look of puzzlement cross Shirley and Katherine's faces, he added, "I have some explaining to do, don't I?"

"Yes, you do," smiled Katherine. "Why don't you come inside."

Katherine led the small party to the living room and when they were all seated, she looked directly at Professor Johansen.

"You called about Billy's entry into the science fair in Michigan, didn't you?" asked Katherine.

198

"Yes, I did. And that's why I'm here. But first, let me extend my deepest heartfelt sympathy to you for the loss of your family. I know words can never bring them back, but I am sorry for your loss." Professor Johansen had started out answering Katherine, but had turned his attention to Shirley with his last remarks.

"Thank you, that is very kind," acknowledged Shirley, her eyes locking on the Professor's.

"So tell us why you are here," prodded Katherine.

"Professor Ruth Gordon, from the University of Florida, said Billy had made a discovery in biology as 'revolutionary as Einstein's in physics,' if I remember the wording exactly. However, according to you and a Mr. Lockwood I spoke to, no one knows what that discovery is since Billy is no longer with us. No research papers, no evidence, nothing. Well I am here to help piece together and re-discover what Billy was working on. I have a team coming from Michigan as we speak bringing all of the latest equipment and technology we can cram into two trucks. I have also assembled some of the brightest young minds in science to help. Your brother's discovery will not slip unnoticed into the annals of history to be forgotten; I will make sure the world knows what he has found and he will be recognized for his achievement. I make that as a promise from one scientist to another."

"I'm touched, but you didn't know my brother." Shirley arched her brow in bewilderment. Why would a total stranger be so willing to help discover what Billy had been working on? Why?

"No, I didn't. But let me tell you a story, young lady. For the last forty plus years, I have toiled in science, focusing on biology, mainly. I have conducted research, led expeditions, chaired science fairs, talked to leading experts in the field of biology, and traveled the globe in search of knowledge. And not once in my entire forty years have I been able to discover something as significant as what I am being told your brother was working on, whatever it was. Realizing how difficult it is to make a breakthrough in science, much less a significant contribution, do you think I'm going to stand by and see your brother's efforts go to waste? This has been plaguing me since our telephone conversation. I owe it to your brother as one researcher to another!" Professor Johansen had stood up and was looking down at the two women. It was his wife who ushered him back to his seat.

No one spoke for some time. Katherine watched Shirley closely. She was staring intently at the Professor, her eyes scanning him for a hidden truth only she could see; searching for a tell tale clue on his face only she could discern. It was Shirley who broke the silence and it was then that Katherine was aware everyone else had been watching Shirley, too.

"You remind me of Billy. So passionate, so intense about science and knowledge. He was always on the journey to discovery, oblivious to everything else." Shirley's voice had trailed off and the last part of her comments had been done in a whisper.

"Then you understand why I must attempt to do this," stated Professor Johansen.

"Yes, I do. I think Billy would have understood, too. You scientists are weird." Shirley laughed and everyone joined her. Only Katherine noticed the joke made by Shirley was to hide a tear. "Katherine, can you call Chief Singletee? They might as well hear it from the top and we'll probably need his help."

"I'll call him now. I have some tea in the refrigerator if you want to get our guests some." Katherine picked up the phone and moved to the porch.

Small talk and formal introductions were made as they waited on the Chief to arrive. By the time Chief Singletee had come inside and been brought up to speed, they had all moved to the porch. It was the Chief who briefed the Professor and his small entourage on the circumstances, including that Slade was in California trying to track down the people behind this.

"You must be very proud of your boyfriend." Betty smiled tenderly at the younger woman.

"You will never know," stated Katherine, gazing out the screen towards the distant horizon as if she could somehow see Slade on the faraway waves.

"Well, we have a lot to do. I would like to see the garage Billy had turned into a lab. There has to be something there we can uncover that will tell us more about his research. Shirley, can you make a copy of the piece of paper Slade obtained? I want to make sure we go over everything that holds the slightest chance for us to unravel this mystery." The Professor smiled reassuringly at Shirley and Katherine.

"I'll get you a copy right away." Shirley disappeared towards the second bedroom.

"Do you think it will be okay for us to erect tents at the lab site?" The Professor turned towards Chief Singletee.

"Sure. The old couple that lives there rent from Shirley and I don't think they will mind."

"Then let's get rolling." Professor Johansen headed towards the door with everyone in tow.

Katherine held back and cornered Chief Singletee. The jovial cop spoke before Katherine could ask.

"No, I haven't heard from Slade." The chief touched Katherine on the arm.

"Am I that obvious?"

"Written all over your face." Chief Singletee shoved her towards the door.

Katherine looked back at the pier as she was entering the living room. Old Clacker was taking his noon rest on his personal piling. She was sure Slade would be all right.

The two Upland PD Detectives strode purposely into BJ's restaurant. One was a cocky youngster still green behind the ears and the other was older, but not by much. Neither had ever handled a big case and they were unsure about how to approach this interview. They had discussed it on the way over, but could not settle on who would do the talking and who would do the note taking.

The teletype from Oregon had asked for immediate assistance. Their Captain had sent them to BJ's to see if he had loaned his truck to a Slade Lockwood.

It was the shorter of the two that approached the counter and flipped out his shield, like he had seen it done in the movies.

"BJ Watson here?"

"Depends on who's asking." BJ looked menacingly at the shorter man.

To impress BJ, the short detective pulled himself to his full height and just cleared BJ's armpit. Realizing his tactic had failed, he tried the tough guy routine.

"Tell him the law is asking and if he doesn't get his ass out here there will be trouble," snapped the shorter man.

"Well, his ass is out here, because I'm BJ Watson. Now what kind of trouble am I in?" BJ folded his massive arms across his chest and glared at the detective until he turned away.

"We would like to ask you a few questions about your pick-up truck." The taller of the two men had walked up and had moved his partner aside.

"What about my truck?" BJ motioned towards his new truck parked just outside the window of his restaurant.

"Don't you have another truck? An old Ford?" asked Detective Mayo.

"Yeah, sure do. Parked out back in the hanger." BJ glanced over at June Stenger who was seated in a booth listening to the conversation. June caught his glance.

"Are you sure about that?" asked Detective Mayo.

"Yeah I'm sure. It's been there about a month now," feigned an angry BJ. "Unless you want to buy my old pick-up, I got work to do." BJ picked up a dish cloth and started to wipe the counter.

"Your pick-up turned up in Portland, Oregon at a Busy Bee Airport. Seems it has been used in a series of crimes." Detective Mayo watched the large black man with curious eyes. It was obvious that if BJ knew anything, he was not going to tell them.

"My pick-up truck? Are you sure?"

"Yes, I'm sure. It had a stolen radio and a stolen gun in it."

"I don't know anything about that stuff. Heck, I didn't even know it was gone." BJ rested his elbows on the counter.

"Don't you want to go and see if it is missing?" asked Detective Pollard.

"Why would I want to do that? Did you boys come all the way down here to mess with me? Unless you're lying, I believe you."

"Do you know a Slade Lockwood?" queried Detective Mayo, his eyes riveted to BJ's.

"A who?"

"Slade Lockwood."

"Never heard of him. Am I supposed to?" BJ smiled again at the taller detective.

"He's the man who was in possession of your truck."

"Well, where is he now? Did you guys arrest him?"

"No, not yet, but we will. He has fled to Valdez, Alaska, but we'll track him down," snapped Detective Pollard. Reaching up, he tugged on the shirt sleeve of Detective Mayo. This was a waste of time. The stupid owner did not even know his truck had been taken.

Unnoticed by everyone but BJ, June Stenger quietly left his seat and walked outside.

"If you hear anything, please give us a call." Detective Mayo handed BJ his card.

"I sure will, Detective. Hey, how do I get my truck back?"

"We'll have it shipped to you."

"Thanks."

BJ followed the two men to the front door and watched as they walked to their car. The roar of a prop airplane engine could be heard and he looked up as the *Pink Flamingo* gained altitude and climbed into the clear blue sky. BJ smiled when he saw the wings wag a 'thank you.' BJ waved back.

June smiled out of his cockpit window. BJ Watson was a good man, but that was not what was bothering him. Slade needed help. The authorities and the killer were looking for him and closing in. June smiled and set a course for Valdez, Alaska and asked the tower for permission to climb to 15,000 feet. Might as well head there as fast as he could. He had a feeling time was of the essence.

Chapter Twenty-Seven

❝Valdez, Alaska. I can't believe this guy. He just doesn't give up." Randolph Myers was shaking his head in disbelief. Earlier, he had intercepted the police transmissions from Portland concerning BJ Watson's pick-up truck. "He's probably already there."

"Good. Valdez is a small city and no one likes outsiders. Alert Jeremiah and William. It seems they have a job to do. Alaska is a remote country. A man could get lost there and never be found." Matt Kyle headed for the door. He had only taken four to five steps when he stopped. "Send Lockwood's picture to the plant foreman and have them double security. Tell them he's trying to sabotage World Vision Quest."

"Consider it done." Randolph Myers pulled up an e-mail account and quickly downloaded a picture of Slade. After typing a brief text message, Randolph sent the electronic message to the shipyard in Valdez. Within moments the message was received.

Dustin Surface, night assistant-foreman for World Vision Quest in Valdez, read the e-mail a second time before pushing the print button. After opening the attachment, Dustin printed off ten copies of Slade Lockwood's picture. Better inform the foreman and start posting pictures so they could be on alert in case the man arrived to cause trouble.

During the summer, darkness is a brief phenomenon in Alaska, especially the farther north. In Valdez, it was daylight for more than nineteen hours a day during late summer. Slade was having problems adjusting to the eternal sun as he left his cabin just before midnight. If he was lucky, dusk would descend in the next thirty minutes or so and he would have four to five hours of darkness to conceal him. Hopefully, that would be enough.

Earlier in the day, he had reconnoitered the shipyard owned by World Vision Quest. There was only one guard at the entrance in a rundown shack. There was no need for an abundance of security due to the remoteness. The walk was brief and Slade made good time. The shipyard was just off the main channel and towards the back of the fiord, but still near deep water. A large container ship was anchored in the main channel, near the dry dock, but out of the way of the main shipping lanes. The dry dock was currently occupied by a large tanker, her vast bulk evident from a considerable distance.

The back fence had seemed like the best choice to gain access onto the grounds. It was eight feet to the top, with a strand of barb wire added as a secondary precaution. Removing a pair of gloves from his pocket, he slipped them on, cast a look around, grabbed the fence and heaved himself up. Surprisingly, he went up and over quickly, landing softly on the other side. The backpack had been hidden where it could be easily located on his trip out. He was getting pretty good at this detective stuff.

The first building he came to contained parts for the ships. The shipyard was on a twenty-four hour schedule, but the midnight shift was not as large as the day or evening shift. Slade peered through a dirt smeared window and watched a half-dozen men load a large cylinder onto a flatbed trailer. Minutes later, they were snaking through the warehouse.

Slipping alongside the wall, Slade moved silently inside and disappeared into the shadows. Lighting was bad and he took full advantage of the darkness, staying away from the any light, no matter how dim. He was aware of the smell of diesel, oil, and other foul odors all vying for prominence.

Leaving the main warehouse, Slade moved through a small courtyard to a second, smaller warehouse adjacent to the ship in dry dock. This was the first time he had the opportunity to see her up close. Men looked like ants swarming over her; suspended by ropes or working off scaffolds. The errant sparks of welding torches cascaded down the sides of the massive monolith, dying before they reached the ground. The hum of grinders and engines straining as steel beams were lifted to her decks, deafened him.

Time was running out. He had to find the offices. It was his hope there was information on the retrofit of *Quest 1*. And he hoped the information would somehow tell him why a family had been murdered in Cedar Key. It was the longest of long shots, but Slade dismissed the odds.

Skirting the work crews, Slade worked his way around the ship to the back of the dry dock area. Suspended on a steel platform several stories high was the office complex. It gave a commanding view of the deck of the ship and the work taking place.

Retracing his steps, Slade moved back to the smaller warehouse. Every employee was attired in a blue jumpsuit. Each worker also wore a hard hat and Slade needed both to blend in. There was no way he could walk up three flights of exposed stairs in blue jeans and a flannel shirt.

The door opening on his right startled him and he immediately ducked below some old oil barrels. Two men in hearty conversation walked out and past him. Slade moved to the door and tested the handle. A soft light spilled into the room before he entered the hallway.

The door let into a small lounge area and there was the smell of strong coffee. A smaller door led off to another room. The second room contained a row of lockers and Slade hurried to them and started opening each one. The ninth locker contained a blue jump suit and hard hat that fit. It took less than three minutes for him to slip them on.

This time, when he approached the stairs leading to the offices, he walked openly and started his ascent. When he was halfway up, he glanced out at the ship. The dry dock was lower than the main offices, but he was only about fifteen feet above the deck of the freighter. So far no one had paid him any attention. Quickening his stride, but not so much as to attract attention, Slade covered the remaining flight of stairs, his heart pounding.

Reaching out and seizing the door knob, Slade opened the door and stepped inside. As he moved through the door, Slade withdrew his Beretta and swung the weapon in a menacing arc. The office was vacant. Reaching back with his left hand, Slade locked the door and walked farther into the office.

The outer office contained only a small desk and several chairs. It appeared to be some type of meeting room. The drawers were unlocked, but contained nothing other than pads of empty paper and pens. A solitary phone sat on the desk.

There were two doors leading off the main lobby area and Slade selected the one on his left. It was already partially open and a light was on down the hall where he heard voices. Fate smiled on him; the hallway was carpeted and he was able to move silently down the padded corridor. When he was near the door, he could hear the conversation.

"And you're sure he's coming here?" asked Gunther Jacobs, night foreman overseeing the retrofit to *Quest 5*.

"That's what the teletype says. I printed it off not more than ten minutes ago. I even have a picture of him." Dustin Surface handed the picture of Slade across the desk to Gunther.

Gunther took the picture in his massive hands and scanned the image. A large Swede with a penchant for fighting, he was nonetheless an excellent ship foreman.

"And Kyle thinks he is going to sabotage the shipyard?" Gunther tossed the picture back to Dustin.

"That's what the memo says."

"But why? We have nothing here worth sabotaging. We're outfitting *Quest 5* like we did *Quest 1*. Unless he finds it interesting to see 50,000 gallon storage tanks inserted into the belly of a ship, I don't know what he would be looking to blow up." Gunther reached for a bottle of vodka, poured himself a shot and slammed it down. The warm liquid made him feel better. "Who is this man, this, what's his name?"

"Slade Lockwood."

At the mention of his name, Slade involuntarily stepped back, but stopped himself. How? How did they know he was here? But, more importantly, it told Slade he was on the right track. World Vision Quest was involved; he just did not know how. That meant the owner, Matt Kyle, was the suspect. Finally, a tangible piece of information to go on. The realization sent shock waves through his body, tingling every nerve, tightening every fiber. The resolve hardened in Slade's eyes and he moved back towards the door.

"This Slade Lockwood, what does Kyle say about him? Is he a terrorist? An ex-employee? Who the hell is he?" Gunther reached for the vodka a second time.

"I sent a query back to San Pedro and they told me he's an ex-cop trying to stir up trouble. Seems he has a hard on for Kyle. Already wanted for attacking a cop in California."

"I hate cops. This bastard sounds like he needs to meet with an accident. A permanent accident."

Slade was reeling from the information he was receiving. Kyle wanted him out of the picture but why? What did Kyle think he knew? What piece of information had Slade over looked? The slamming of the front door jarred Slade into action. Stepping across the hall, Slade reached for the doorknob opposite him. Twisting it, he realized it was closed. Too late, he knew he would be exposed.

Stuffing the gun into his waist band, Slade started walking down the hallway and turned the corner just as the door was opened and two heavy set men walked in. They both continued to talk about the weather and fishing as they walked into Gunther's office.

"You wanted to see us?" asked the heavier man.

"Yeah. Show him the memo from San Pedro." Gunther waited until both men had read the file and seen the photograph. "Pass his picture around and make sure we keep an eye out for him."

"I've seen this man," said Kelly Armagost. "He was in the restaurant last night drinking with some of the boys. I overheard him say he was up here to do some fishing."

"Shit!" roared Gunther. "That means the bastard could already be here on the sight. Lock her down!" yelled Gunther, lumbering to his feet. The bottle of vodka was knocked over, but the half-drunk shipyard foreman grabbed it by the neck and slammed it back down on the desk.

Slade had rounded the corner and forced his way into an interior office. Wasting no time, Slade moved to the file cabinets on one wall and started to search them. Nothing. Where would the plans on *Quest 1* be? What if they were not here? If Matt Kyle was so paranoid to notify the shipyard about his possible arrival, then the eccentric millionaire would have the plans with him. There was no way Kyle would leave the plans to fall into the wrong hands. Stop it! The man in the office said they were retrofitting the ship in dry dock like *Quest 1*. Find the plans to this ship, he would find the plans to *Quest 1*.

Recognizing a search was wasted energy, Slade turned his attention to escape just as a loud wailing siren sounded. The siren emitted three long signals and then went silent. A warning, no doubt, that the perimeter had been breached and an outsider was inside. And there was only one way up and one way down.

Not one to waste time, Slade moved towards the door. Just as he reached for the knob, the door was slammed open and Gunther filled the doorway.

"You dirty bastard! Come to my shipyard!" screamed the half-drunk foreman, swinging a roundhouse at Slade's head.

Slade had only time to react. Instinctively, he ducked and jabbed with his left hand, striking Gunther in the nose and mouth area. It was like hitting a side of beef; Gunther never flinched. Blood started to spread across the big man's face and a wicked smile touched his eyes.

Gunther bull rushed Slade and it caught him by surprise. Catching Slade in the upper torso, Gunther's momentum carried them into and over the desk. The impact of the larger man landing on him drove the wind out of Slade's lungs and he desperately tried to catch his breath. For his size, Gunther was surprisingly light on his feet and sprang up as Slade tried to roll out of the way. Slade was part way to his knees when Gunther attacked again. This time it was a boot to the right rib cage that sent Slade airborne towards the office chair. By luck, Slade had caught a hint at Gunther's intention before he saw the big man draw back his foot and he rolled with the kick or his ribs would have been broken.

Slade rolled over the chair and sent it hurtling towards Gunther, who was standing and staring predator-like at Slade. Gunther kicked the chair and sent it across the room. Slade moved slowly to his feet, the pain in his ribs resonating up his entire side. He could not last much longer against the larger man and he knew it. Surprise was his only chance.

Rising to his full height, Slade suddenly grimaced and went down to one knee, alertly keeping Gunther in his field of vision. Believing Slade was injured more than he was, Gunther closed to finish him. Slade waited for Gunther to close to within five feet when he attempted to scramble to his feet. Slade stumbled forward and feigned as if he was going to fall. Gunther's reaction was to reach out and grab Slade. The minute the big man's right hand touched Slade's left sleeve, Slade pivoted on his left foot, rotated his hips for additional torque and drove his right hand into Gunther's solar plexus as hard as he could. The jarring impact of the solid blow traveled all the way up Slade's arm to his shoulder.

Gunther had been caught by the unexpected and the impact of Slade's strike doubled him over. The drunken foreman started to slide to his knees and a wicked left hand from Slade finished the job. Gunther dropped unconscious at his feet. Not taking time to bask in his victory, Slade turned and ran to the door. So far, no one else had heard them fighting.

Moving into the corridor, Slade walked purposely back to the front door, pulling his hat down low. Reaching the entrance, Slade forced the door open and surprised Kelly Armagost, who was staring out the lobby windows with a pair of binoculars. When he turned and looked at Slade, his eyes riveted on the Beretta.

"What kind of modifications did you do to *Quest 1*?" The sound of the trigger being locked back had the desired effect.

"We put large, circular holding tanks inside of her. Five to be exact, each capable of holding 50,000 gallons of whatever you wanted." Kelly's eyes never left the gun. This was the first time a man had ever trained a gun on him. "You going to...to...to kill me?"

"Depends. Is there another way out of here?" Slade moved the barrel of the gun slightly. Fear was in Kelly's eyes and, so far, his gaze had not left the barrel of the Beretta.

"Out the back."

"Show me."

Kelly moved past Slade and entered the hallway he had just left. It was a short distance to the end and they turned right, down another corridor. At the back of this second hall was a recessed door.

"Out that door and the stairs will take you down to the yard." That was all Kelly remembered until he was transported to the hospital and revived. Slade hit him in the back of the head with the butt of the Beretta and the shipyard worker fell in a heap at his feet.

Footsteps could be heard rushing up the stairs near the front of the office. Help was on the way. Slade could not be quiet any longer. Snatching the door open, Slade scrambled through it and pulled it shut. Taking the stairs two and three at a time, he hurtled down the dimly lit stairwell until he reached ground level, breathing a little heavier than he would have liked.

Slowing down, Slade took the time to look around. No wonder he had not noticed this second set of stairs; they were behind a large rack of storage bins. He was hoping those same bins would provide cover.

Stuffing his gun into the front of his pants, Slade had covered about twenty yards when the first shot rang out and a bullet buzzed past his head. Not even taking time to look up, Slade hit the floor and rolled to his right. Other gunshots quickly followed and he could hear the bullets striking the barrels above his head. Instead of returning fire, Slade crawled on his hands and knees away from where they had last seen him.

The gunfire was intermittent and Slade stayed in the shadows. Finally assured he was no longer visible, Slade gained his feet. A cabinet was to his left and he eased the metal doors open, peering inside. He needed something to take the killers eyes off of him. On the top shelf Slade found his diversion. A row of flares in a water tight package, complete with a flare gun, was tucked inside a small canvas bag.

On the lower level, a search party was being formed and several errant shots were directed at shadows along the far wall. The bullets could be heard careening off of metal and concrete, buzzing around before coming to rest. Slade kept his head down and moved back towards the ship.

On his way to the stairs leading to the office, he remembered seeing some barrels. Undoubtedly, they contained oil or diesel. All he had to do was get close enough and the flare gun would do the rest.

The search crew was becoming more organized and they were fanning out and moving with purpose. It would only take them minutes to cover the area separating them from him. Aiming for the stack of barrels, Slade loaded a flare and squeezed off a round. The bright crimson glow of the flare arced menacingly towards the oil barrel and on impact the fuel burst into flames. Within seconds a second explosion followed the first and Slade became lost in the panic.

Rising to his feet, Slade walked quickly towards the exit, avoiding the people rushing past him. Glancing over his shoulder, he could see most of the men had abandoned repairs on the ship and were trying to help extinguish the fire, it now having been identified as the larger threat. A third explosion erupted closer to the ship and a large fire hose was brought to play, dumping water on the inferno.

Unnoticed, Slade left the ship yard and ran to the rear fence, slipping on his gloves and grabbing the wire. Heaving up and over the fence was harder this time, as his ribs screamed in protest from the brutal kick delivered by Gunther. Slade was about to drop to the ground when a series of shots rang out. Out of the corner of his eye, he saw the muzzle flashes from the area of the guard shack. A burning sensation hit his side, throwing him off the fence and to the ground. Slipping his hand down, he felt his blood soaked shirt, which was now all warm and sticky. He did not even have time to worry about how injured he was.

The guard was on the radio and was obviously excited. Putting the radio back down on the table, he sighted through his rifle sights and squeezed off several more shots at Slade. He was rewarded with seeing Slade drop back to the ground and flatten out.

Reaching inside his waistband, Slade withdrew his Beretta and turned towards the guard shack. The guard was about 150 feet away. Slade had no desire to kill the sentry, but he had no desire to be killed either. Sighting well above the eager guard's head, Slade squeezed off five quick shots, shattering the single window in the guard hut and hitting the light, casting the guard into shadow. The guard dropped his rifle and dove down behind the shack, his hands covering his head.

Regaining his feet, Slade staggered to the wood line and disappeared amongst the trees. Moments later, he had retrieved his backpack and had slipped it on, grimacing as a new wave of pain hit his right side. The bullet had done what Gunther had failed to do: slow him down. He would need medical attention, but he needed a way out first.

Skirting the ship yard, Slade worked his way back to the employee parking lot. On his approach, he had noticed a Jeep, much like his vehicle in Cedar Key, parked near the main road. It took Slade less than a blink of an eye to hot wire the sturdy truck and speed out of the lot. A check in the rear view mirror revealed the fire was still burning out of control.

Driving with one hand, Slade slipped his other hand inside his back pack and withdrew an old shirt. Folding it in half, he applied it to his right side. Much to his relief, Slade noticed his side had stopped bleeding, indicating the wound was not serious. If only he could hold out until he was able to obtain some help.

Getting through town was no hard task and finding the main road leading away was even easier. There was no way he could go to the room he had rented. If Kyle had alerted the shipyard he would have sent someone there to wait on his possible return.

Once out of town, Slade pressed on the accelerator and watched as the lights of Valdez disappeared. The fuel gauge indicated he had a little over three-fourths a tank of gas. That would be more than enough to get him to the next gas station.

Flipping on the high beams, Slade pressed harder on the accelerator and shot around each curve. His only goal was to now get to San Pedro and board *Quest 1*. Whatever Kyle was up to was on board the retrofitted freighter.

Cresting a hill, the head lamps from the Jeep fell upon a logging truck pulled across the road. Slade stood on the brakes and slammed the wheel to the right, going off the road and running over several small bushes. Only his familiarity with his Jeep back home kept him from flipping the vehicle. Too late, he realized it was a trap.

Careening around the truck, Slade maneuvered back onto the roadway, sliding across the narrow strip of asphalt, off the other side of the road and then back on before gaining control. All the while, the Jeep's tires were screaming in protest and the smell of burnt rubber filled the air. In his rearview mirror, Slade saw the truck driver talking on the radio and gesturing wildly. Someone must have seen him leave the shipyard.

Not bothering to slow down, Slade changed gears and slammed the gas pedal to the floor board. Time was his enemy and this road was his death trap. There was only one way to Valdez and he was on it. If they were going to set up another ambush, they would do it on this road, but where?

Reaching inside his waistband, Slade removed his Beretta and laid it on his backpack. Whatever Kyle had planned for him he would meet face to face. A knot formed in the pit of Slade's stomach and for the first time he realized he did not like Matt Kyle. He did not like him at all.

Chapter Twenty-Eight

The atmosphere was like a circus, complete with spectators, tents and the smell of food in the air. The only thing missing were the animals and trainers, a few clowns and a booth to charge admission. Still, it was a spectacle. Especially for a small town like Cedar Key, whose largest attraction was the annual Art Festival.

After convincing Shirley and Katherine his help was genuine and more was on the way, Professor Johansen had wanted to see what was left of Billy's lab. They had taken an immediate liking to the Professor, Shirley more so than Katherine because she understood the abstract world he lived in and could relate.

Once they had arrived at the remains of Billy's lab, the Professor had treated the sight like an archeological dig where ancient artifacts were hidden. Tape had been strung around the perimeter and only qualified people were allowed to enter. Your qualifications depended upon Professor Johansen classifying you as qualified. Initially, the list was short and the Professor had shown no signs of extending it. That all changed when the students arrived from Michigan.

After they had shared some brief stories about the drive, Professor Johansen explained to them the reason he had brought them to Cedar Key. It was not to study snails, but to find out what a young scientist by the name of Billy Waterbury had been working on and bring his work to the light of the world. The icing on the cake was when Shirley told them everything they had learned and how they believed her family had been murdered. The young girls could not help shedding a tear and several of them walked up and gave Shirley a hug. To the student, they pledged their help and commitment.

Events transpired fast after that. Tents were erected at the sight and the elderly couple, who were renting the home from Shirley, agreed to allow the scientists to use their facilities. Within hours news had spread throughout Cedar Key and people started lining up on the sidewalk to view the dig, as it was being called. Chief Singletee had to station an officer at the entrance to help with the crowd.

The sophisticated equipment was unpacked and everyone appeared to have a job, moving like busy ants on an awakened hive. Though it appeared to be chaos, there was laughter and a purpose to each movement, like a complicated choreographed dance where each participant knows their part and executes it flawlessly. It all started with the head man. There was a methodical ease by which the Professor instructed the students and they carried out his every desire. Billy's secret would yield itself to them soon.

The first part of the lab to be unearthed and sorted through was the roof. The fire had caused it to collapse and the students pried it off, one shingle at a time until the remains were left intact. There was not much left, or so it appeared to the untrained eye.

Each piece of evidence was cataloged and placed in a box, plastic container, or other suitable storage unit for safe keeping. It was all moving at an orderly pace, albeit slow.

"What do you think?" Katherine watched from the safety of one of the perimeter tents.

"It's like most field trips I've been on: hours of tedious work for seconds of initial discovery. Then you spend more hours in the lab verifying hopes and expectations. The problem is we don't have much time. I'm sure Slade could use a break on this end to help him."

Their thoughts were interrupted by the voice of an eager student. A young girl, supervising one area of the project, was motioning for the Professor. Professor Johansen moved quickly to her side.

"What is it, Angela?" Professor Johansen peered over the young woman's shoulder.

"I believe it's what's left of a file cabinet. The heat must have been intense on this side of the building, because the back portion is scorched. It seems to be lying face down and that may have saved the contents."

"Does it appear to be a fire proof cabinet? Or can you tell?" asked Professor Johansen. A break this early was more than he could have hoped for. Did the file cabinet contain Billy's notes? Were there complete reports inside?

"I don't know if it is fireproof or not, Professor. We'll have to turn it over to see," responded Angela, moving to one side to get a better view.

"Before we do that, let's think through this. We need to make sure the area around it has been checked. Let's get another crew over here to help." Professor Johansen motioned for several other students to assist. "Let's clear

213

the area around it in a four to five foot span. After that, we should be able to move it upright."

Katherine and Shirley watched each step as the students collected debris and sifted through the remains around the filing cabinet. It was agonizingly slow. Both women wanted to reach out and grab the cabinet, pull it upright and open the doors. But they both knew each piece of evidence around the cabinet would have to be checked. The smallest piece of paper could hold the clue they needed to unravel Billy's secret.

Several small pieces of paper were found and carefully placed inside bags. The fire had charred them to a dull grey or black, but, with the proper equipment, Professor Johansen was confident he could retrieve what had been written on them. Other than some pieces of wood and part of a chair, nothing else of value was found. Glancing at his watch, the Professor noted they had been going at it steadily for over three hours and lunch was near.

"Okay, let's take a break," smiled Professor Johansen, moving to the outer perimeter.

"Now? You want to take a break now? We're so close," lamented Angela, dirt streaked across her left cheek. Bright blue eyes stared at the Professor in disbelief, her hands dangling at her side.

"Yes. I want to take a break now. We have all been working for over three hours and need a rest. The most delicate and important part so far is about to occur and I want us to be fresh and rested." Professor Johansen slipped his arm around the shoulders of the young woman. "We will get to it today, just not right now."

Katherine and Shirley helped set up lunch and the work party drifted into conversation about Cedar Key. The students were an inquisitive group and asked countless questions of Shirley about the history of the buildings, industry, and anything else that popped into their mind. Katherine noticed Shirley slipped right in and mingled as one, her keen intellect allowing her to more than hold her own.

Lunch was sandwiches and iced tea. Most of the students lounged on the grass near the remains of Billy's lab, gazing occasionally at the work still to be done.

"Okay, let's see what secrets it holds." Professor Johansen stood and walked towards the filing cabinet. The metal rectangular box was lying face down, like a man who had fallen. Originally, the filing cabinet had been standing against the far wall, near the corner. Now it was lying closer to what had been the door, indicating it had been moved.

Assembling two work crews, Professor Johansen moved near the cabinet. Instructing two of the stronger young men in the group, they grabbed the top portion and slowly raised it to a standing position. Eager eyes watched as the cabinet was lifted upright, the students being careful not to allow the drawers to fall open. They need not have concerned themselves; the doors were so warped from the heat they would not slide.

Moving the cabinet to the safety of a nearby tent, Professor Johansen ordered the two young men to very carefully open the doors. The rest of the students he herded back to the site and had them continue their excavation.

Night caught them with only two of the five drawers open on the filing cabinet. Over half the folders were missing, but the other half was amazingly intact. The students had started at the top and were working their way down, going one drawer at a time. Luck had held and God had smiled on them: the filing cabinet was fire proof and when it had fallen the doors had slammed shut. The papers inside were in very good condition.

As each file was extracted from the filing cabinet it was given a number. A student would then write the same number onto the tab of a very large brown folder. The contents were placed inside and stored in a box. Billy had named most of his experiments and his notes were very detailed and descriptive. Topics from jet propulsion to animal science were in the top two drawers. It was hoped the bottom drawers would hold news on his later discoveries.

It was the earlier files they were going over in Slade's living room, moving through each one. Shirley, Katherine, Professor Johansen, his wife, Police Chief Bubba Singletee, and Angela Caruso were all seated on the floor in a circle. When one of them would finish with a folder, they would pass it along to the next. Professor Johansen's wife was kept busy refilling empty glasses.

"Your brother had an incredible intellectual mind," commented Professor Johansen, looking over a set of glasses perched on the end of his nose.

Shirley nodded in silence. The folders were having a profound effect on her. Here was Billy, so close, so alive it was if he was in the same room. At any moment, she expected him to walk out of these pages and take a seat amongst them. Many of these experiments he had discussed with her. How she wished she could have that conversation again.

"You have no idea, Professor. Billy was gifted."

"You think?" laughed Angela. "I'm due to graduate next summer and most of this is beyond me. I haven't even heard of most of this."

"Think how I feel. I'm an artist, not a scientist." Katherine joined in the laughter.

"You? We never covered any of this in the police academy, I can tell you that." Chief Singletee tossed a piece of paper towards Shirley. "This stuff would have flunked out half the class."

"But where does it take us from here?" Shirley let the laughter die down.

"It takes us forward, young lady. Ever forward. Billy will have notes or a clue as to what he was working on. Some of the stuff I have read already has value to business, especially the stuff on aerodynamics. I skimmed that folder, but if Billy is right about heat convection over a fixed wing at high altitude, the stealth bomber just became obsolete." Professor Johansen looked up and smiled his knowing smile. "Billy will lead us. I'm sure of it. I feel it in these old bones."

Everybody grinned as the Professor stretched his legs out to regain some circulation.

"What about the computer hard drive? Anything on it?" The chief had decided the chance to find some data from the hard drive outweighed the risk of holding onto it in the hope the case would be re-opened as a murder investigation. The hard drive may provide the only valuable piece of information.

"It is so damaged no data can be obtained with our current technology. That doesn't mean it won't prove to be useful in say five to ten years, but right now the information is irretrievable. It is of no help to us." Professor Johansen handed the last folder to Katherine.

"Where is it now?" asked Chief Singletee.

"The same place all of this stuff is going until we find out what is of value and what is not: Slade's spare bedroom closet," said Shirley.

"Interesting storage space," stated the chief.

"It's the safest place we have at the moment. Besides, I may want to look over these files when we have time." Shirley glanced at Katherine.

"What about the connection with World Vision Quest and Billy? Anything there?" The chief was probing, asking questions.

"No, other than they attended several science fairs Billy was in, but so did other companies. There is no record of them ever calling the house and I don't ever remember Billy mentioning them. Maybe Slade was wrong about them. I know they purchased the rights to ideas from other students. Science fairs are a small circle, but they never bought anything from me or Billy," said Shirley and the minute the words left her mouth, she wished she could have them back.

"He's not wrong," snapped Katherine, and then realizing she had raised her voice she sheepishly looked out at the back porch. "Sorry." Katherine reached over and squeezed Shirley's hand.

"It's okay. I didn't mean anything by it and I'm sure Slade must be on to something or he would've called." Shirley patted Katherine's hand before getting up.

"I say we all eat. The University of Michigan has a burning desire to buy everyone dinner at that seafood restaurant I saw on the pier. I say we take advantage of it." Professor Johansen patted his wallet as he spoke.

"They have excellent redfish." At the mention of food Chief Singletee had unconsciously rubbed his prodigious girth.

"Then lead the way, Constable, and we shall follow," quipped Professor Johansen.

Everybody joined in but Katherine, who was bringing up the rear. *Where was Slade? Why had he not called? Had something happened?* Forcing a smile where none existed, Katherine refused to think of the negative and focused on the future. When he got back she was going to take him on a long walk on the beach, hold him tight and tell him how much she loved him. That thought did lighten her spirit and she hurried to catch up.

On the back porch, an old pelican watched the merry little group leave. Where was the man who lived here? Somewhere in the dim recess of the bird's primitive brain, he knew the man was gone and had been for some time. Stretching out his wings, Old Clacker flew to the first piling on the pier and settled down for the night. The man had saved him and a peculiar bond existed between them. Until the man returned, the old bird had no intention of venturing out to sea to test the wind currents. He would wait.

Tucking his bill beneath one of his wings, he closed his eyes and went to sleep.

The three semi-trucks pulled into San Pedro and drove immediately to Pier 15, owned and operated by World Vision Quest. After clearing the guard house, security waved them past. They drove into a cavernous hanger and were directed to one end of the pier. Once parked, the drivers left their cabs and went to a small office situated near the end of the dock. Unlike the other piers in San Pedro, this pier was covered.

"I'll have Professor Klaus check the shipment once it is unloaded. You guys have just bought yourself some paid vacation time. Mr. Kyle has set you up with rooms at a local hotel. Enjoy yourself." Rodney Peters watched as the three confused truck divers were dismissed.

Rodney went outside and told a group of laborers to start unloading the trucks. Professor Klaus was seen hurrying over.

"They have arrived?" Klaus peered over horn rimmed glasses.

"That is what I need for you to tell me." Rodney did not like the meddling Klauss and had no intention of hiding his feelings.

"You unpack the merchandise, Mr. Peters, and I will tell you if the right stuff has arrived." Klauss ignored the younger man.

As each item was unloaded, Klaus checked it against his inventory sheet, making sure the valves and fittings matched the requirements he had sent to Dyno Technologies. *Quest 1* would arrive by midnight and they could start installation. It was all so close, so real.

Klauss was startled when the voice of Kyle echoed in his ears.

"I understand they have arrived. Is everything as it should be?"

"Yes. We can start installing as soon as *Quest 1* arrives."

"She'll be here in another hour or two. Captain Theopolous has made good time. How long before sea trials?" Kyle walked slowly through the valves and fittings being laid out on the floor in front of him.

"Give me two days. Everything else is in place. Two days maximum and we will be ready to begin tests." Klaus looked at Kyle for approval.

"Okay. Keep me informed." Kyle turned and left.

Klauss watched as his boss left the pier area and disappeared outside. Never had a man scared him the way Kyle did. There was a ruthlessness to him that was unnerving. Dismissing the chills going up and down his spine, Klauss went back to inventorying the valves and fittings.

Kyle walked back to his office and, once inside his air conditioned fortress, he called Randolph Myers.

"Do they have the fire under control?"

"They have it contained, but not under control. Lockwood stole a Jeep and was sighted on the road heading back to Anchorage. I have a team attempting to head him off." Randolph Myers shifted his grotesque bulk and continued to stare at the computer screens.

"What did he learn?" Kyle hid his anger. Lockwood was smarter than he had given him credit. The man had destroyed part of his dry dock facility in Valdez and had successfully escaped again. The ex-cop was getting too close.

"He was asking about the modifications to *Quest 1*. Other than that, we don't know. There were no papers or anything he could have taken."

"What about Cedar Key?"

"There is a Professor Johansen from the University of Michigan sifting through Billy Waterbury's old lab. This Professor has the blessing of Shirley Waterbury and the local Police Chief. He has a whole team of students helping him." Myers knew this latest information would push Kyle over the edge.

"Why in the hell wasn't I notified of this? When was I supposed to learn about this?" screamed Kyle.

"I just learned about it a few minutes ago. I was double-checking the information and just got it back. Relax, they haven't learned anything. The building was burned to the ground." Myers smiled to himself. Kyle was too high strung.

"Relax! I won't have anything screwing this up, especially a group of scientists poking around." Kyle had moved back to his chair.

"If they discover anything, I'll let you know. I have instructed our man in Cedar Key to call."

"I want to know the minute anything is learned." Kyle started to push the disconnect button on the phone, but added, "Let me know the minute Lockwood is dead."

"Will do."

Lockwood's death was imminent, mused Randolph. There was only one way in and one way out of Valdez by car and now they knew where Lockwood was. His death would occur in the very near future.

Chapter Twenty-Nine

The ambush came ten miles from where he had evaded the logging truck. A dense stand of trees crowded the road, their upper branches joining in a green arc. The dense growth lined the roadway for approximately three miles, circling around the lower portion of a small mountain before reaching the bottom. The road narrowed, the embankments were steep, almost sheer, creating a drop of a hundred feet.

The headlamps were already on, but he switched them to high beam. Instinctively, he slowed and became more alert. If he was going to be ambushed, it would be here, where visibility was difficult and colors mottled. He checked and evaluated every shadow or dip in the roadway.

The trees finally thinned and he pressed down on the accelerator. Slade had just entered the high point of the turn when he saw movement to his left. A boulder, slightly larger than the Jeep was tumbling down the embankment. Based on his speed and the path of the boulder, a collision was imminent.

A thousand thoughts raced through Slade's mind. He knew the boulder could not have broken loose on its own. The trap had been sprung. Slade steered the Jeep as far right as he could and pressed the pedal, trying to fuse it with the metal beneath. It was going to be close.

Jeremiah and William Henderson stood on the side of the mountain watching Slade race for his life. They had planted a small stick of dynamite beneath the boulder and when Slade had been spotted they had detonated it. Gravity had done the rest. It appeared as if there timing was impeccable as they watched the large granite ball race towards the Jeep.

Slade felt the rear of the Jeep start to lose control and he let up on the gas, allowing the tires to gain traction. The boulder struck a small ledge on his left about half way to the road bed, bounded into the air, and then resumed its deadly fall. Slade straightened out the Jeep and raced for safety. Every second was precious, every movement must be essential, every thought critical. There was no margin for error.

Options were slim as Slade evaluated his situation, remaining surprisingly calm with death rolling his way. Slade had to outrun the falling boulder or be crushed. Even if he stopped, the road would be blocked and he would be at the mercy of the killers. Better to take his chances and try to outrun it.

The next few seconds seemed like an eternity and everything appeared to slow down. The boulder hit the rock shoulder on his left that separated the road from the mountain and then careened into the air towards him. The Jeep swept abreast the boulder and Slade instinctively leaned towards the passenger door trying to place as much distance as he could between himself and the fragmented piece of mountain. Then the boulder hit the Jeep. The rear portion of the metal roof was torn loose and the Jeep staggered, much like a heavy weight fighter trying desperately to stay on his feet in the later rounds of a bout. Slade fought to regain control, the wheel convulsing in his iron grip. The right front fender of the Jeep hit the right rock wall and sparks flew, along with pieces of metal now littering the roadway. Snatching the wheel to the left, Slade tried to straighten the battered Jeep, but the damage was greater than he had feared. The weight of the boulder had crushed the rear suspension and the vehicle would not respond.

When the Jeep started to fish tail, Slade knew she was going to flip. All he could do was pick a flat spot if one appeared. Coming out of the turn, Slade saw where a portion of the mountain had been mined to build the road and tailings were left in a smooth grade. Aiming the Jeep that way, Slade jumped on the brake to slow her down. Luckily, the brakes held and the Jeep dropped to half her speed, but the swaying increased, over exaggerating until she dug her left front wheel into the loose gravel and went end over end. Later, Slade could not remember the flipping, just the mind numbing feeling of not being in control.

The sensation was short lived for Slade as he ducked and tried to avoid the shattered glass of the windshield. When the Jeep stopped rolling, Slade was upside down, at a forty-five degree angle. The head lights were shining into the night sky, casting a lonely beacon in the middle of the wilderness. Slade rolled out of the Jeep, landing heavily on the ground, his sense of direction and equilibrium thrown off. Another fifty feet and the Jeep would have plunged off the road into a small canyon. The loose tailings had allowed the left front tire to burrow deep, slowing the runaway vehicle before it started to somersault. When it landed, it was against a small pile of rocks and loose rubble.

Not wasting time, Slade surveyed his surroundings and retrieved his Beretta and backpack. Both items had been knocked to the passenger floorboard and had been wedged under the seat. Opening the backpack, Slade made sure he had all of his equipment. Slipping the shoulder harness on, he moved to the embankment and looked down. It appeared to be loose gravel and small rocks until he reached the base of the mountain. From there, it was about a half mile hike to the road, but the hike was through a thick stand of trees and underbrush. The road, from what he could see, stretched into a small valley.

Tucking the Beretta into his waistband, Slade stepped over a small rock and started to descend to the bottom of the slope and into the wood line. He would find cover in the forest and determine how many killers were after him. If he stayed where he was, he would be picked-off.

Reaching down with his right hand, he checked his side. The bleeding had stopped from the rags he had squeezed under his shirt. Too much exertion and he knew the blood would start to flow again. Slade also knew if he was out in the woods for very long, the odor of blood would attract bears and his Beretta was no match for a full grown grizzly. His problems were escalating, compounding by the minute.

When Slade took his second step, the loose rock caused his feet to slip out from under him and he was sent sprawling onto his back. There was a pause and then Slade felt the ground beneath him shudder. He was sent hurtling down the slope. Any chance at control was lost and he frantically tried to slow his descent by digging his feet into the loose gravel and dirt. Just before entering the outer portion of the wood line, Slade was able to orient himself and steer by his feet. Still, it did little to help him when he struck the small underbrush. A thick growth of small saplings caught him, spinning him like a top. When he finally stopped, Slade found himself against a large spruce, his backpack saving his skin from the rough bark of the tree.

For several minutes Slade did not move, as the pain in his side from the gunshot wound was re-aggravated. A warm sticky feeling was running beneath his shirt. Rolling onto his stomach was an act of supreme sacrifice as the pain coursed through his body, starting at his side and then touching every fiber up and through his right arm. With clenched teeth, Slade climbed shakily to his feet and looked back up the slope. Two men were standing on the edge of the grade, looking down and pointing to where he had slid. Slade started to step behind the large spruce and then realized the growth of thick saplings hid him from view.

Reaching for his waistband, Slade pulled the Beretta free and inspected the gun. Aside from some dirt lodged in the trigger guard which he removed, the weapon appeared to be fully functional. He would like to have had the time to field strip the weapon and inspect it, but knew he would not have that opportunity under the current conditions. He could only hope the Beretta would fire when called upon.

Staring back up the slope, he saw that the two men had disappeared. Where were they? Were they taking another route to the bottom? To drive around would take too long as the road serpentined along the base of the mountain. If he were the killers, he would look for more stable footing and move down the slope, one on either side to catch him in the middle. It was a standard tactic used to flush prey towards one or the other. One killer would probably lie in wait while the other moved towards him, hoping he would run into the waiting gun of the assassin. Unless there were more than two of them. Slade dismissed that thought from his mind. No need to complicate the picture. There was still plenty of time for that.

Jeremiah Henderson had moved north of Slade and had used a small growth of pines as hand holds for his descent. Once at the bottom, Jeremiah had cycled a round into his Uzi, swinging the weapon menacingly. A shoulder strap held the gun steady and the cold light in the killer's eyes belied his intention. Slade Lockwood was about to die.

William Henderson had moved south of Slade and, like his brother, had used some small trees to reach the forest. Unlike his brother, William preferred the reassuring feel of a twelve gauge pump shotgun loaded with double ought buckshot. His job was to find a secure place for an ambush and wait for Jeremiah to force Slade his way. The buckshot would do the rest and the grizzly bears would finish the carcass. Without any show of emotion, William slid between two large pine trees to wait.

Sounds on his left. Even, measured steps. It was one of the killers. It had to be. Slade knew the other one was on the other side, lying in ambush. There would be no mercy from either of them. They were trying to strike now, take him out while he was on the run, while they held the advantage. Their plan was simple: keep him running until he made a mistake or was forced into their gun sights.

Forcing the pain out of his mind, Slade eased down into the brush beside a pile of granite rocks and waited. The blood had been slowed, but he knew he was weakened. The lack of feeling was evident in his movements. His strength was vanishing, eluding him when he needed it the most. If he had not been in such outstanding physical condition, he would already have succumbed to unconsciousness.

When the two men had disappeared, he had moved. They had seen where his errant slide down the embankment had ended and that was probably where they would start their search. Moving as fast as his injured body would allow, and trying to erase his trail, Slade moved away but back towards the transition area of where the embankment met the trees. It was here where the excess granite boulders and small saplings were wrestling for supremacy of the slope. This was also the area where the underbrush was thickest, the densest, and offered the best chance of hiding.

Jeremiah paused as he walked, scanning the trunk of the trees in front of him and looking to his right and left for sign of movement. Why had he not heard a sound? The scurrying of rushing footsteps to retreat in a headlong flight had not reached him. Why? Was Slade Lockwood injured? Perhaps dead from the fall down the slope? It was possible.

Moving slower and constantly swinging his head in an arc from left to right, Jeremiah continued to move forward, the Uzi slung low and sweeping the trees in front of him.

Finally, he detected movement. The silhouette of a man was taking shape amongst the trees and moving closer. There was enough light to see by, but not much. The brief night was giving way to morning, but an ethereal darkness still clung to the forest, suffocating and close. Slade made no movement and was aware of his heart beating strongly in his chest. The killer needed to be closer.

Shifting his weight ever so slowly, Slade raised the Beretta and sighted down the barrel. His left hand supported his right in the classic Weaver firing position, his entire body one with the weapon. A few more moments.

Jeremiah had reached a stand of trees that were unusually thick in front of him. The trees would be a good place for an ambush, but so would the rocks and saplings on his right. There was no way he could cover both positions at once. The best plan of action was to clear the trees and then move towards the boulders and eliminate the possible threat, if any. It was the last mistake he would ever make.

Slade waited with a patience and ruthlessness he did not know he possessed. When Jeremiah filled his gun sights, he quickly fired two rounds from his Beretta, striking the killer in the right shoulder which spun him half way around. Slade moved forward, firing three more times. Each round struck Jeremiah in the chest and abdomen. Slade fired one last time into the killer's head.

Not bothering to dwell on the death of the man lying in front of him, Slade hobbled to the body and conducted a quick search. There was nothing of value in the man's pockets and no identification.

Slade removed the Uzi and two extra magazines of ammunition the killer had carried in a leg pocket. A long hunting knife was also taken and Slade slipped it into his back pack. Slade rolled the body over and took a long look at the man's face, committing it to memory for possible identification at a later time.

Reloading his partially empty magazine, he stuffed the Beretta back into his pocket and slipped the Uzi over his shoulder. Thumbing the safety to 'on', Slade turned and looked into the woods in front of him. Somewhere out there was a second killer.

An image of Katherine hit his eyes and he buried it in the dark corner of his mind. Slade had no thought of dying. It was because of her that he was in America's last frontier fighting for his life. And he would not have had it any other way. Slade Lockwood had finally found what he had been looking for on LAPD. By helping Shirley, whether he was successful or not, he had the chance to make a difference in one person's life. Maybe that difference was all he had, but at that very moment it was his most precious gift. That chance and the image of his beloved Katherine, who had forced him to help a wide-eyed young woman in search of the truth, was enough. For the first time, it all made sense: the right and the wrong, why people love and hate, and why unconditional love was not only the best kind of love, but the only kind of true love. Why are the things with the most meaning in our lives the hardest to find?

Slade looked around him like he was seeing the forest for the first time and sucked in a huge breath of air. The scent of the pine needles and the odor of the wild invigorated him, moved him, and he gazed in wide-eyed wonder. What was happening to him? Was this some sort of primeval transformation? Things were clear, almost translucent to his eyes. Never in his life was he more certain about what he was going to do and where he was going than now.

"I'm coming for you! You're next, you sorry bastard!" screamed Slade. His voice reverberated off the walls of the mountain and echoed across the small valley.

The hunted was now the hunter.

William Henderson sat silently, stunned into inaction. His brother.... dead...gone. But how? They were professionals, the best. This man was an ex-cop, a rank amateur in their deadly world. And now he was moving.

William straightened and tried to move to a better place to see, to gain a better vantage point. What was he doing? The man was coming towards him, but at an incredibly quick pace. He could hear the footsteps and movement as the man drew nearer.

Leaving his place of cover, William moved slightly down the slope, towards a large tree dominating those around it. Stepping as quickly as he could, he rushed forward. In his haste, his footsteps found several small dried limbs that crunched under his heel. Normally, he would never have made such a fatal error, but the death of his brother and the unanticipated reckless behavior of his prey had confounded him.

Reaching the tree, William moved around the base of it and a look of surprise registered on his face. Standing less than ten feet from him was Slade Lockwood with his brother's Uzi aimed at his chest. William attempted to react but his movement was no match for the ex-cop. The Uzi lifted William off his feet and flung him back against the tree, tattooing a trail of holes across his chest before stopping near his neck. Crimson stains spread across his upper torso, blanketing his shirt in sticky wetness. William slid slowly to the ground, dead before he landed.

Slade moved forward and searched the body. He took the shotgun and ammunition from the killer's pockets. Turning towards the dense forest, Slade moved towards the road and heard the deer he had surprised moving in front of him.

When he had yelled, Slade had started towards William's position. It was by accident he had surprised a young mule deer, still dependent on its mother as evidenced by the fading spots dappled across its coat, bedded down near a small thicket. It was the perfect hiding place from predators. The yearling had initially fled from him, but had stopped every so often to see if he was being pursued. Each time Slade drew closer, the yearling would run a short distance and stop, unsure as to what to do. It was the sounds of the yearling William had heard.

A renewed vigor was in Slade's step. It was a confidence he had been missing. It had been wrong for him to join LAPD. That was evident to him now. Initially, when he was a rookie and an outsider, he had envisioned himself as an avenger battling the forces of evil and, back then, he had believed he could make a difference or impact someone's life. When he had moved up in rank, he had lost his identity in the Big Blue Machine and became one of the members of the masses, spouting forth the ridiculous ideology modern society craved. No longer was his individualism required; just blind obedience. And it had slowly consumed him.

Slade fought back the pain and moved closer to the road. Never again would he succumb to the thoughts and wishes of a group threatening his identity. To lose the value of one's individuality was a crime greater than anything of which he could think; it was an offense against the person, a vanishing. Shirley Waterbury had someone who would uncover the truth even if he had to travel the ends of the Earth. And Katherine Wintergate had a companion who would love her forever.

Slade struggled through the last of the brush and stumbled onto the asphalt roadway, leaving behind the death and carnage in the forest. In the middle of a remote part of Alaska, on a lonely road, Slade Lockwood had found himself.

Chapter Thirty

The large freighter nosed into the dock on time and was tied fast. Captain Theopolous was the first off the boat and the first to shake the outstretched hand of Matt Kyle. The Captain of the vessel was beaming. *Quest 1* had been delivered a day early and Kyle had sounded surprised and pleased.

Captain Theopolous saw the long line of crates stacked near the dock and knew they were for his ship, and within the hour a crane was lifting the valves and fittings towards the deck where they disappeared into her massive hold. Hans Klaus dutifully stood by on the dock and checked off each load, nodding indifferently to each worker.

Within the interior of the massive freighter, a team of technicians and mechanics immediately started to unload the items. Within two hours they were busy assembling the parts based on diagrams supplied by Klauss. Kyle had ordered the dock foreman to work the men around the clock until the job was completed, being sure to mention overtime was not an issue, but that completion was. Kyle was rewarded with seeing their efforts doubled. Sea trials were to be conducted in less than a week and there were orders to fill.

When the last load was off the pier and moving towards the ship, Kyle approached Klaus. Captain Theopolous had disappeared back on board to consult with his crew.

"Are we on time?" Kyle craned his head to watch the freight being lifted towards the hold.

"We will make our schedule. The valves are exactly what we needed. Most of the other equipment was installed in Valdez. The design is so simple it should not take long." Klaus wiped at his glasses.

"Good. Then I will notify Sommer to send for our foreign investors. We will have them arrive in two weeks. That way, we'll have shaken all the bugs out of her." Kyle slapped Klaus on the back. The dream he had held since he was a little boy was coming to fruition. In less than a month, he would be the richest man on the planet.

Reaching inside his jacket pocket, Kyle punched in the number of Clyde Sommer. All that was left was to show the investors the product and take their orders.

"Well? What are they?" Shirley was unable to stop her curiosity from getting the best of her. They were examining the plants in the fifteen gallon buckets from Billy's lab.

"Black mangroves, I think, but I'm not sure." Angela responded slowly. "They have the genetic structure of black mangroves, but their cellular configuration has been changed. And, based on the information I can gather, these plants are only six months old."

"So what's the big deal? Six months or not, are they black mangroves?" Shirley failed to see the connection.

"The big deal is this—if they're only six months old, they shouldn't be this big, this far developed. These plants are the equivalent of a five to six year old black mangrove. Your brother discovered some way to alter their growth rate, to an unknown 'x' factor. I don't know how, but he did it. It's the same with the other four." Angela wrinkled her brow and looked at Professor Johansen.

"Amazing. Think of the potential to coastal communities. Mangroves play an important part in the eco-system in tidal and coastal fringes. They bring in an abunda-." Professor Johansen was cut off by Katherine.

"We know all that, but is that all that important? I mean, so Billy made them grow faster, so what? I don't think he was killed because he made a plant grow faster." Katherine looked over at Shirley and then back at the Professor.

Professor Johansen looked at the manicured lawn next to the tent covering what remained of Billy's lab. An afternoon shower had wet things earlier and they had to make sure everything was kept dry. The more he learned about this boy-genius the more he was convinced he had made the correct decision to come to Florida. They were close, but pieces of the puzzle were missing, just out of sight and beyond his grasp.

"I don't agree. You're underestimating the significance of this contribution. What if the cellular manipulation Billy successfully completed with the black mangroves was reintroduced to other plants and trees? Pines would grow at an alarming rate and would be able to feed the demand for lumber that is far outstripping the resources of the world. Native plants that are endangered could be reproduced in a fraction of the time…"

"Forests could be replanted and immediate results could be obtained in our lifetime," chimed in Angela, the excitement striking her voice.

For several seconds no one said anything, but each one of them looked around at the tents and the other students. Amazement registered on their faces, as the realization that something unique had just been discovered.

"But how did he do it?" Shirley was trying to reason through the puzzle her brother had left. "I know a little about biology and to manipulate cellular structure and alter growth rates to this extent has never been accomplished."

"Until now," said Katherine. "You said so yourself that Billy was 'off the charts' when it came to science. Obviously, he found a way. We need to know how he did it so we can know what to look for. The killers must have realized the potential of Billy's discovery and killed for it. I had never thought about forest reintroduction or the timber industry, but it makes sense. There are countries with little to no timber reserves. The ability to plant and harvest timber within a few years would be an incredible boon to their economy and way of life."

"We're forgetting about plants and trees that bear fruit. No longer would you have to wait three to six years as you currently do with most fruit bearing trees. Plant the tree and within two years you're harvesting, say, peaches or apples. The ramifications of the impact on a third world agricultural society could be far reaching." Angela looked at Professor Johansen and was rewarded with him nodding his head.

"This discovery could end hunger." Professor Johansen looked around at them again and his face took on a more serious note. "But what about accelerated growth? If not controlled, the introduced species could wipe out or overtake native plants and fauna. If unchecked, they could mature, seed, and grow, rapidly outdistancing other varieties. Depending on the species, they could pose a threat instead of a benefit."

No one had thought of that aspect of Billy's work, as evidenced by the look on their faces. They had been intent on focusing on the positive contributions of his work, not the negative.

"I don't believe Billy would have created something that would've harmed us." The note of defiance was in Shirley's voice. "He would've found a way to make sure the plants didn't reproduce. He would've made sure they could be controlled."

"It's not Billy that I was worried about." Professor Johansen met the eyes of Shirley and held them. "But whoever stole his creation may not be as prudent."

"Then we need to know what to look for." Shirley stood up and moved towards the remains of Billy's lab. "We need to know how he did it and the answer must lie somewhere in the debris."

Everyone was in agreement and people started to move back towards their respective assignments. The puzzle was coming together.

The whine of the engines was like music to his ears and the clouds were like welcome friends. June Stenger eased back on the throttle and let the *Pink Flamingo* start her descent. It had been an interesting flight up the coast of Alaska. Valdez, though a seaport, was half way up the state. Alaska was a big as a third of the continental United States and the trip was a long one.

When he had left Vancouver the air traffic controller had told him he might not be able to set down in Valdez. The primary source of transportation in and out of Valdez was float planes. June had told him he had a raft, but the humor was lost due to the serious nature of the man.

The *Pink Flamingo* had dropped to about 10,000 feet when he observed a light shining into what was left of the remnant of an alleged night sky masquerading over this part of the world. Odd, there was no settlement near here and he was still well outside of Valdez. June entered into a large circle while he consulted his map. Verifying there was no chance of civilization within miles, he eased the nose of the plane down to take a closer look.

On his first circle, he saw the Jeep turned upside down on the pile of rocks with the lights shining into the early morning sky like two bright beacons. On his second pass, June saw a man staggering down the roadway with a backpack on his shoulder. Even from his altitude he could tell the man was injured and in need of help. Saying a prayer, he hoped it was Slade.

Normally, the *Pink Flamingo* would need another third of the roadway that was rapidly filling his windshield. But he was in the heart of Alaska, so the ribbon of asphalt in front of him would have to do. Landing would be easier because he could rely on the brakes and reverse thrust. Taking off would be another matter all together.

June brought her in just over the tree tops. The whine of the engines caused the man in the roadway to stop and look up. June taxied the *Pink Flamingo* up next to him.

After opening the side door and stepping out, June Stenger stretched and smiled at Slade.

"Need a ride?" June took in Slade's appearance.

"Maybe. Where you going?" Slade smiled back at the ex-Navy pilot.

"The person who did that to you?" June motioned towards Slade's side that was wet with blood.

"Persons. They're both dead. Left 'em in the woods." Slade set his backpack down and dropped the Uzi and shotgun.

"Good place. Let's get you doctored up and you can tell me what you've found." June moved forward and picked up Slade's backpack and newly acquired weapons. After stowing them aboard, June retrieved a first aid kit and approached Slade.

"Take off your shirt and let's have a look," instructed June, opening the kit and pouring out the contents.

"I had always hoped a good looking nurse would tell me that," murmured Slade.

"I'm sure Katherine will play nurse for you when I get you back to Cedar Key. By the way, BJ's truck is being shipped back to him."

"The police found it?" Slade winced when June poured some peroxide onto his side.

"You'll need stitches. And yes, the cops found the truck and asked BJ some interesting questions." June applied a gauze to Slade's wound. "How much blood have you lost?"

"I don't know. Why?"

"Because you don't look good, that's why. You need a doctor." June retrieved the items in his first aid kit.

"I don't have time for a doctor. I'm going to San Pedro." Slade struggled to stand up. June reached out his hand and steadied him.

"What's in San Pedro?"

"Matt Kyle."

"Who's Matt Kyle?"

"The man who owns World Vision Quest and the man who just tried to have me killed. I don't know how or why yet, but I believe he's the man who killed Billy and his parents. Kyle is in San Pedro and that's where I'm going." Slade turned defiant on June and squared off, his eyes boring into the older man. "Will you take me?"

"Yes. But only on one condition."

"What is it?"

"We stop on the way and you see an old Navy doctor I know. Let her patch you up and then we'll fly down to San Pedro."

"Deal." Slade moved towards the door of the plane. It took June's help for him to get in.

Once inside, June moved Slade to the couch and told him to lie down. Before June could get to his pilot's seat, Slade was snoring comfortably. Apparently, his passenger had no idea how tricky it was going to be to take off.

The engines on the *Pink Flamingo* turned over on the first try and within seconds were purring. Easing the throttle forward, June taxied the plane to the far end of the road and down into the depths of the forest, all the way until the road started to curve. Deftly, he spun the *Pink Flamingo* around and pressed down hard on the brake. Smiling to himself, June revved the engines and watched as the rpm indicator climbed. The plane fought against the brakes. When the engines had reached a dull roar and the plane shook from the force, June released the brake and shoved the throttle to the limit. The *Pink Flamingo* shot forward like a rock from a sling shot.

Coming out of the forest, the twin engine speedster hungrily ate up the roadway and June watched with detached amusement as the plane raced toward where the road curved sharply around the base of the mountain.

There was no way the *Pink Flamingo* could take that turn at a high rate of speed and within seconds June would either have to hit the brakes and cut the engines, or hope she lifted into the air. He knew he needed another 200 feet.

Laughing out loud, June tapped on the throttle, hoping to edge a few more pounds of thrust out of her. The asphalt was running out from under him and, at the last possible second, June pulled back on the stick. The *Pink Flamingo* paused and like a dancer going into a slow waltz, started to lift. A set of trees started to loom larger in his windshield and June pulled harder on the stick. She was gaining altitude but way too slow. At the present trajectory, they would strike the trees about two-thirds of the way up the trunks.

Reacting with incredible ease, June leaned the twin engine rocket to his left, causing the left wing tip to point directly to the ground. With less than a foot on either side, the *Pink Flamingo* shot through a small opening in the stand of spruce and June leveled her back out. With nothing in her way, the small plane soared into the sky, answering the demands of the man at her controls.

Looking over his shoulder, he saw Slade, who was still wedged into the couch, had not awakened. Only he was able to appreciate the fine maneuvering of the aircraft that had taken place.

Reaching for a chart on his left, June rolled out a map of Washington and propped it up on the seat next to him. Flipping on the autopilot, June quickly read the gauges in front of him. He had more than enough fuel to make Anchorage. He could refuel on his way to Seattle. Dr. Emily Harris was an old girlfriend who lived in Seattle and who had married his best friend. They had all remained close.

A tinge of fear touched June and he stared at the man lying prone in the *Pink Flamingo's* cabin. Slade's injury was worse than either of them had let on. What had happened? He was sure Slade would tell him when the time was right.

June punched the new coordinates into his flight navigator and adjusted his course.

The flight to Anchorage was uneventful. June had encountered some bad weather, but Slade had slept through it. Dr. Emily Harris did not really live in Seattle, but just north in a small community called Silverado. Luckily, the town had a small airport.

June had called ahead and Emily and her husband John were waiting when they landed. June had asked for and had received a spot in the back of the airport away from the main terminal. It was dark when they landed and even though the airport was small, it was exceptionally busy. No one noticed the *Pink Flamingo* when she touched down.

Switching off the engines, June left the pilot's seat and opened the side door. Walking towards him was Emily and John. June jumped down the last several steps and hugged Emily when she walked up. John grabbed June in a bear hug and squeezed the breath out of him.

"How bad is he?" Emily moved past June. Slade had slipped into unconsciousness. The combination of loss of blood and fatigue had finally caught up with him.

"Not good. I think he has been shot and God only knows what else." June did not say anything as Emily took Slade's pulse and checked his breathing. Carefully, she removed the bandages from his side and inspected the injury.

"We need to move him. I have stuff at the house that will take care of this." Deftly, Dr. Emily Harris bandaged Slade back up and nodded towards the two men. "John, go and get the car. We don't want to move him anymore than we have to."

John pulled a dark blue Chevy Tahoe up next to the plane. June had already tied down the aircraft and returned to help John, who was inside the cabin and moving Slade to a sitting position.

Both men carried Slade to the SUV, depositing him on the back seat. After securing the door to the Pink Flamingo, all three jumped into the front seat and raced off, with Emily spending the bulk of her time constantly checking on Slade.

"He's lost a lot of blood, June," stated the Doctor, compressing her lips into a tight line.

"I know."

"How do you know him, June?" asked John, shooting through a caution light to the sound of blaring horns. Their house was less than five miles away.

"It's a long story and one I'll be happy to tell you over drinks tonight," instructed the ex-Navy pilot, turned adventurer.

The remainder of the trip was done in silence, the tenseness mounting as they neared Emily and John's house. When John drove into the driveway, he immediately turned the SUV around and backed into the garage. Normally, a Saab was also parked inside, but John had moved it when June had called, in anticipation of having to off-load an injured person.

After shutting the garage door June and John carried Slade into the house. The house was a two story colonial home, with a large basement. A portion of the basement had been transformed into a small medical clinic, including an operating table and all the instruments a doctor would need to conduct surgery.

Slade was laid out on the table and Emily started peeling his clothes off.

"Don't just stand there, help me," ordered the Doctor.

After removing Slade's clothes, Emily had them turn him over on his side so she could inspect the bullet wound.

"I wish I had an x-ray. It would help a lot."

"Can you operate without it?" June had concern etched over his face.

"They didn't have them in the old days, now did they? John, get me the IV over here and let me get a line started."

Both men moved back and watched Dr. Emily Harris at work. Slade's vein was found on the first attempt and she started an IV drip into his left arm. Next she moved over to the sink and scrubbed, carefully watching her patient as she did so. Satisfied she was sterile, she had John help her slip into a pair of gloves and she moved back to Slade.

"Both of you wash up and get gloves on. I'm going to need your help. Hurry it up," snapped Dr. Harris.

By the time June and John were scrubbed and in gloves, Emily had hooked Slade up to a heart monitoring device that also tracked his pulse and breathing.

"June, you watch that monitor. The minute something changes, you let me know. John, you're going to help me."

Without another word, Dr. Emily Harris moved alongside Slade and started to probe on his side where he had been shot. Reaching for a needle, she numbed the area and went to work. It was almost forty-five minutes later before she stopped and stepped back.

"He'll have a nice little scar, but he'll live. To his credit, he keeps himself in excellent shape. By the way, here's his souvenir." Dr. Harris dropped a bullet into the waiting palm of June. June closed his fist around it.

"No major damage?" June looked expectantly at the Doctor.

"None. Damn lucky, too. If that bullet would have traveled an inch or two either way, you would've never found him alive. He didn't lose as much blood as I thought, but he's still pretty weak."

"You want him over here?" John prepared to roll Slade over to the wall.

"Yes and cover him up. I gave him some medicine to make him sleep. He should be fine until morning."

"When can he leave?" June met the fiery eyes of Dr. Harris.

"You must be kidding?" Dr. Harris clenched her fists.

"No, I'm not," and then as if to offer an explanation, "You don't know him. He's dead set on proving Shirley's parents and brother were murdered. He has already done things and gone places I didn't think he could." June looked at the sleeping man and knew he spoke the truth. Slade Lockwood would not let a bullet slow him down.

"You have some explaining to do." John motioned for them to follow him upstairs.

Emily grabbed a mobile monitor, much like the kind mothers use to listen to sleeping babies, and followed. Before turning off the lights, she stole a quick glance at her patient. June must have a remarkable story to tell.

Once upstairs, John fetched some brandy and they all retired to the back upstairs patio. A small lake could be seen in the distance and sounds of nocturnal animals could be heard in the woods adjoining the property.

"It is a long story," confessed June, sipping from the brandy snifter.

"Well, why don't you start from the beginning. John and I aren't doing anything this evening." Emily snuggled against her husband. They were both seated in a porch swing facing June, who was in an old rocking chair.

"I met Slade through a police chief."

Emily and John listened intently to the story, June had to tell. A story far from over and destined to take still more unexpected turns.

Chapter Thirty-One

" Clyde, I need you to call the contacts overseas. The first demonstration will be in two weeks." Kyle was standing behind Randolph Myers watching the bank of computer screens projecting information to them. Slade Lockwood was no where to be found.

"Excellent! That means we're ahead of schedule. Do you want me to make any new contacts?" Clyde Sommer hugged his wife who was standing next to him. Their life had changed unbelievably in the last several months.

"No need to contact anyone else. I have a feeling we'll have problems filling our orders once the success of this project is understood and made known. Best just to sit back and wait. The moment is close, Clyde, the victory is ours." It was so easy manipulating those around him. It was a gift.

"Yes, sir, it is. I'll make the calls as soon as you hang up." Clyde squeezed his wife a second time. Who would have ever thought Clyde Sommer would amount to anything?

"Well you go ahead and make those phone calls. And, Clyde, call my secretary and she will help with travel arrangements. She has everything in place for their arrival."

"I sure will."

"Good-bye."

"Bye."

Kyle looked at Randolph. "So they found the bodies of Jeremiah and William. Perhaps I have underestimated this Lockwood. He has killed the last three men I've sent after him. All three professionals. I thought you said he was only a cop?" Kyle spit out the last sentence.

"Don't get pissed at me because your henchmen can't get the job done. I practically told them where he was and what he was doing. The Probability

Matrix doesn't lie. It was right then and it will be right now. Slade Lockwood is probably already in San Pedro. I would double security if I were you." Randolph punched the latest bit of information into the computer.

"How did he get out of Alaska?"

"I don't know." Randolph leaned back in his chair for the first time since Kyle had walked into the room. It was an enigma. Thousands of miles of untamed wilderness and Lockwood disappears, vanishes without a trace.

"The Jeep was found?" Kyle looked for confirmation.

"Busted all to bits."

"A plane?"

"No way. Not enough room to land a conventional plane and there was no body of water to land a float plane. Maybe a helicopter." Randolph let his voice trail off.

"That means he may have help. Check and see if anyone chartered a helicopter to Valdez and then didn't arrive. Maybe they stopped and picked up Mr. Lockwood and flew him down here." Kyle narrowed his eyes while talking, concentrating on the possibilities. If Lockwood had help, that meant he had shared his story with whoever had aided him. There was no information coming out of Cedar Key so Lockwood was keeping them in the dark. His sense of loyalty and love for his girlfriend would compel him to do that.

"No helicopters chartered to Valdez, other than the ones used to take tourists to ice flows and mountain streams."

"How can you be so sure so fast?" cautioned Kyle.

"Process of elimination. No helicopters. But," Randolph peered intently at the screen and then entered some more information. "N23961 booked a flight plan to Valdez, but never arrived. As a matter of fact, the plane turned around and flew back to Anchorage, re-fueled and then went to Seattle."

"I thought you said a plane could not land where Lockwood was last seen?"

"According to the reports I got from Alaska, it couldn't."

"Well, one did!" screamed Kyle. "How could they be so damn stupid? I must be hiring a group of amateurs." Kyle paced in the small room and only after he realized Randolph had not answered him or responded did he move back behind the computer wizard. "What have you found?"

"Look at this. N23961 belongs to June Stenger of Cedar Key, Florida. Mr. Stenger owns a 1984 T303 Cessna Crusader called the *Pink Flamingo*. Catchy name, a bit odd, but catchy. She has the range and the speed to get to Valdez and back."

"That's how Lockwood got out of Cedar Key without us knowing it. I bet if you check the flight records on file, this Stenger clown left Cedar Key when we lost sight of Lockwood. It all makes sense." Kyle had resumed his pacing.

"I already checked and yes, there is a flight plan out of Cedar Key on the same day Lockwood was discovered missing by your stooge in Florida. This

Stenger character has probably been flying Lockwood all over the place." Randolph slid back from his terminal and spun in his chair to face Kyle.

"Where are they now?"

"Just north of Seattle in a little town called Silverado. It has a tiny little airport and they landed last night, according to the flight records."

"Well, well. The bird has landed."

"Why don't we leave them alone? If Lockwood knew anything he would have already gone to the police. He has no information. We already know he didn't get anything of value from Valdez. He knows we're modifying a freighter. Big deal. He doesn't know for what." Randolph looked directly at Kyle and returned his stare. Most men withered under the direct glare of Kyle, but Randolph was not one of them.

"You are forgetting, my friend, that Lockwood is a fugitive. He's running from the police. Why would he go to the police now? I agree he knows very little, but of all the people curious about the deaths of the Waterburys, only Lockwood poses a threat. He seems to have the uncanny ability to appear in the most unlikely of places, asking the most intrusive questions. I think it is time I rid myself of Mr. Lockwood. Permanently. Besides, by this time next year, I could be the richest man on this planet and I'll be damned if I am going to let some stupid ex-cop screw it up!"

"If we kill him, then it raises the question of our guilt. We also know he notified his girlfriend of his belief we were involved in the death of the Waterburys. Maybe we should just set back and wait."

"That is where you and I differ. Obviously, this Stenger chap knows someone in Seattle and probably went there with Lockwood. If everyone is killed, I'm sure the media can be led to believe Lockwood flipped out, killed them all and killed himself. Remember, this man is a fugitive."

"Be sure about this," warned the computer geek.

"I never doubt myself. Do you know where they went?"

"Yeah. Stenger called a number in Silverado and I've already cross checked it and gotten the address. Make sure they don't miss this time," sneered Randolph, turning back to his computer screen.

Kyle never heard the sarcastic response as he was already up the stairs and out the door on the way to his office. Some 'friends' had to be called to take care of an issue in Seattle. The Lockwood problem was about to end.

"Okay. This isn't what I expected." Angela moved back from the microscope and motioned for Professor Johansen.

Professor Johansen adjusted the magnifying glass and after careful scrutiny leaned back. Before answering, he took a second look and sat back down.

"Well? We're all in the dark here." Katherine stared at the Professor and Angela.

"They're not the same," mumbled Professor Johansen.

"What's not the same?" Katherine looked over at Angela who had her eyes glued to the microscope again. "Someone had better start making some sense."

Professor Johansen was looking out towards the street and his mind seemed to be wandering. "Yesterday, my wife said she would like to retire here. She loves the weather and the community. I can see where you get your inspiration for your art." The Professor smiled at Katherine and then looked back at Angela. "Is it different?"

"Yes." Angela slid a fourth slide beneath the powerful lens of the microscope for examination and promptly popped back up after giving it a quick viewing. "It's different. That means all five black mangroves have been genetically altered, but why and for what?"

"I thought you said they were altered to grow faster?" Katherine was so totally confused—science.

"They were, but that wasn't all. Angela discovered additional engineering had been done. In addition to growth enhancement, the trees have been altered genetically on the sub-cellular level. One tree has an incredible amount of nitrogen in its cells, another has a high amount of sodium, and another has a high level of carbon dioxide. What is peculiar is how high the levels are. Billy found a way to have the cellular structure in the plants go after a particular element or substance, seize it and transport it into its system."

"And?" Katherine arched her eyebrows.

"How did he do it? There are so many chemical reactions taking place at the cellular level and at such minute quantities and at different times, it would be impossible to know which one to alter, change, or enhance. It's impossible to calculate the possible combinations," stammered Angela.

"Not anymore," replied Professor Johansen.

"But we only have the end product, not the methodology. Without the code, we're looking in the dark without a light." Angela held her palms up in defeat.

"Perhaps. We need to move backwards. We know the trees were altered, we need to learn how. Angela, we'll need an unaltered specimen to compare to these. Get with Chief Singletee. I'm certain he can point you in the direction of where to find some black mangroves, and of course, we'll pay." Professor Johansen touched Katherine on the shoulders. "We'll find the answer."

"I know you will. I'm just impatient. I want the answer now." Katherine let the older man lead her away from the site.

"You will get it soon enough and not before." Professor Johansen smiled and moved away from her and back to the tent covering the remains of Billy's lab.

The remains of the building had been removed and the students were carefully sifting through what was left. Each item was examined, labeled for identification and then the work would resume. They were almost done with the excavation. The professor had said they would go back and evaluate each piece.

238

Katherine left them working and went to find Shirley. There was nothing she could do at the site that was not already being done. At times, she felt she was in the way.

Reaching into her pocket, she pulled out her cell phone and flipped it open. No missed calls. She folded the phone and placed it back in her pocket. Why had Slade not called? Was he all right? Katherine knew she should have gone with him. Her woman's intuition had told her to go, but she had allowed Slade to talk her out of it. That was a mistake and when he got back, she would be sure to tell him.

A tear ran down from her left eye and she wiped it away. She missed him. Missed him more than anything in the world.

The sleep had been a sound one and it had delivered a much needed rest to his battered and bruised body. When he moved, Slade became aware of the throb in his right side and when he ran his fingers over the wound, he was surprised to find stitches there. A dim light lit the room several feet in all directions and it appeared he was in a hospital recovery area. He could discern monitors tracking his body's heartbeat and respiration in green letters. The IV in his room confirmed his suspicion.

"Well, I see you have joined the living." Dr. Harris flipped on a light and walked into the room. John and June were close in tow.

"It beats the alternative. I don't believe we've met. Slade Lockwood." Slade extended his hand.

"Emily Harris. I believe you know this guy." Emily motioned towards June. "And this is my husband, John."

"You're a load to carry." John shook Slade's hand.

"Sorry about that, but I don't remember much. Where am I, by the way?"

"In our basement. I was a doctor in the Navy for over twenty years. The medical field never leaves you." Emily checked the stitches on Slade's side.

"Nice set up," countered Slade, wincing when Dr. Harris probed a little harder.

"It serves its purpose, especially when you keep the kind of company we keep." Dr. Harris did not offer any more in the way of an explanation. "You ready to get up and get about?"

"You bet. You remove the IV and I'll be out of your hair," smiled Slade. The smile was not returned.

"You move too soon and you will tear those stitches loose. Then you'll spend the next two weeks in a real hospital, because you will have serious loss of blood." Dr. Harris had removed the IV in Slade's arm and placed cotton gauze over the puncture, using a piece of tape to hold it in place.

"How long before I can move and be fully functional?" Slade looked directly into the Doctor's eyes.

"I can remove the stitches in four to five days depending on how fast you mend. The internal healing will take longer, say three to five weeks. You don't want to test it too much too soon." Dr. Harris looked back at Slade and smiled. "June has told us what you're working on. Why don't you get dressed and join us upstairs. Maybe all of us can put our minds together and come up with a solution."

Without saying another word, John dropped Slade's clothes onto his lap. Slade noticed his clothes had been washed, pressed, and folded. All except for his heavy undershirt. It was clean, but it had also been sewn where the bullet had entered his body.

Once he was dressed, Slade found his way to the first floor where everyone was seated around the kitchen table. A large plate of food was strategically positioned in front of a chair and Emily motioned for Slade to sit. Thanking her and John, he wasted little time in emptying the plate.

"That was very good." Slade sipped from a second cup of coffee.

"I think you were very hungry." Dr. Harris admired the appetite of her patient. "You would've eaten cardboard with maple syrup on it."

"Probably."

"Why don't you catch us up with what you found in Valdez? Maybe we can make some sense of all of this." John smiled reassuringly at Slade and shoved some pastries his way. Slade took one and then seemed to become lost in thought for a second.

"Okay, let me start at the beginning from when I left BJ Watson's." For the next thirty minutes, Slade talked non-stop. When he had finished, he looked around the room and noticed the puzzled expressions on their faces. "Any ideas?"

"The worker in Valdez never said what the modifications to *Quest 1* were for?" June asked.

"No. I don't believe he knew. Seemed real surprised when I asked. The scary thing is they knew I was coming. How, I don't know, but they knew." Slade asked for and received a third cup of coffee. The pain in his side had lessened, but was still a dull throb.

"That is puzzling. I didn't even know you were going to Valdez until the cops showed up at BJ's and started asking questions." June looked over at John.

"Someone is tracking him through automation. Probably monitoring police channels and all other electronic media." John closed one eye as he spoke.

"Is there that much information available to them?" Emily looked at the men as she asked the question.

"More than you could ever realize. During our last deployment in Hawaii, I met one of the intelligence guys when you were working late shift and he told me it was scary the stuff they could pick up on the electronic airwaves. In addition to learning everything about you from cradle to grave, they can write a program to monitor your activity by referencing your name, nick name, driver license number, or a host of other data. It's virtually unlimited the amount of information they can glean." John looked directly at Slade.

"But that's the military. How does a citizen get the information?" asked Emily. The world of cyber-space was still a fourth dimension for her.

"Don't forget, Uncle Sam has trained some pretty smart people that have left and gone into private business. Some corporations have the money to track someone. With the stroke of a computer key, they can learn more than ten detectives going door to door. Cyber-space is the new information frontier and whoever can access it and control it, wins." John looked back at Slade.

"Then you're not safe." Slade spoke slowly to let his words sink in. John had already come to that conclusion, but it took Emily a few seconds to process. "Did you file a flight plan?" Slade looked over at June. June nodded his head and a worried look crossed his normally calm features. Slade knew what it was. He had brought danger to the home of his friends.

"Don't worry, we'll handle it," consoled John, reading June's face.

"We need to be prepared," stated Slade, a sudden toughness hitting his voice that sent chills up and down their spines. "June, did you bring my duffle bag with all the toys?"

"Yup. You want them?"

"Yeah. If I'm right and, based on their prior actions, they'll act right away. I don't know what they think I know, but they've shown diligence in trying to kill me. We better expect the worse."

"Do you really think they will come here?" Emily arched her eyebrows.

"If I'm right, they're already on the way." Slade slid back his chair and motioned for June to join him. The battle was about to begin.

The next several hours found the house alive with activity. Slade inspected the weapons and made sure they were working properly. The Uzi and assault shotgun he had taken off the killers in Alaska were in excellent condition. When they were fully loaded, he had given June the shotgun. June hefted it with his right hand and then snapped it to his shoulder, centering the sights on a picture on the far wall.

"This damn thing is balanced." June looked over the stock at Slade.

"Yes it is. The Uzi is, too. By the way, if that shotgun is like the Uzi, it has a hair trigger."

"I'll keep that in mind." June placed the shotgun down as John and Emily walked in.

"I have two handguns, Slade, and that's it. I never thought I would need more than that." John had a helpless look on his face.

"That'll be more than enough. Our goal is to funnel them into the house to a position of our advantage. If we can keep them in our territory, then we have a chance. My only concern is communication. The cell phones will never work."

"Well, we will just have to improvise." Emily hid her nervousness.

"I want you and John to take the upstairs, but stay away from the windows. There is only one way up and that's the stairs. Guard the stairs and the balcony and you should be okay. June and I will handle things down here." Slade looked at the ex-fighter pilot.

"I'll take the front door." June picked up the shotgun.

"They'll probably try stealth first and then a distraction if that doesn't work. You two stay upstairs when you hear the shooting. If I don't yell or come and get you, then we're dead. Call the cops and wait till they arrive." Slade carefully stood up and slid his Beretta into a shoulder holster. The Uzi he let drop around his neck.

Emily walked over and gave him a hug. For several seconds, she looked into his eyes and then turned to walk away. After taking two steps, she stopped and glanced back at him. "You're not afraid, are you?"

"No. I can't explain it, but I'm not. I just don't believe I've come this far to be stopped." Slade moved the Uzi to a quick retrieve location on his hip and then looked over at John and motioned for them to go upstairs. John grabbed Emily by the arm and led the way.

"Turn out the lights," reminded June. "I'm moving to a comfortable position. See you when the fireworks start."

Slade moved towards the living room area at the back of the house. This would be the hardest area to cover. The entire back of the house was windows. Two sets of French doors led out onto a wooden deck that stretched into the backyard. John and Emily had designed the house to take advantage of the view. It was tough to defend, but Slade did not think they had that in mind when they built their dream home.

Turning off the lights, Slade slipped down beside the couch and leaned against the wall. He could see the rear of the house and he would be able to recognize a darker shadow from the surrounding vegetation bordering the back yard. Now, it was a waiting game.

Matt Kyle had been true to his word. A quick phone call to a man of dubious character he knew in Seattle had assured him a 'team' of thugs would remove his problem. Like all big cities, Seattle had its problem of gang violence and corruption, especially in the inner city. The Asian gangs were the most violent and in exchange for this job, Kyle had guaranteed the 'businessman' a percentage of the computer market in Taiwan. Money always cemented deals, even when brokering death.

Five Chinese hit-men had been dispatched. They had already killed a policeman, robbed several jewelry stores and heisted an armored truck. With each day, they grew bolder and more violent. All five killers had criminal records. Why they had not been deported was a mystery to the local police. Each had committed a murder; two had killed repeatedly.

Upon arriving in Silverado, they went straight to the target. The house looked no different than the many others they had passed. Rich Americans living out their dream of retirement in the quiet hills, with the picturesque landscapes and manicured lawns.

They had squeezed into a small Nissan Sentra, their weapons piled in the trunk. Once they had found the address of Emily and John they had parked a half mile from the house and walked through the woods. The homes had not been built close to each other and there was sufficient under-brush and trees to hide their approach.

When the last light had been turned off, they had waited another full hour before moving. Their surveillance had not revealed a dog, which made the approach easier. Surprise was essential. According to their information, there were four people.

The leader of the group rose from behind a bush where he had been lying and brushed off dirt and leaves. Without a word he removed a Smith and Wesson .45 semi-automatic. The others did the same.

When the leader was near the backyard, he stopped and waited, atten-tively watching for any sign of movement. After another half an hour of scan-ning the house, he finally moved forward, but not before waving two of the members towards the front.

The three killers fanned out onto the deck and approached the house from different vantage points. The leader of the group was in the middle and reached the center set of French doors. Testing the lock and realizing it was locked, he turned to the side and elbowed the pane of glass just above the door knob. A shattering of glass was heard and he reached inside and opened the door. The other two killers followed.

Slade had waited patiently by the couch, fighting sleep and fatigue. He was still not feeling one hundred percent and he knew it would take a while before he regained all of his strength. There was, however, no doubt in his mind Matt Kyle would send a killer after him. Whatever information the eccentric millionaire thought he possessed was his death warrant. When dark-ness had descended, Slade had begun to think he may have over-reacted. After all, he was in a strange house in a small town on the outskirts of Seattle. Who would look here? Who could find him here? Then the movement. A darker silhouette against the background of trees and he knew he was not alone.

Sliding to a kneeling position, Slade trained the Uzi on the back door and watched with rapt fascination as the five men approached, weapons held at the ready. Two of the men peeled off and moved towards the front. June would have to deal with them.

When the lead killer broke the glass, Slade waited until all three piled into the doorway, all in close proximity. It was a foolish mistake and one Slade capitalized upon. Professionals would have moved in one at a time, clearing a path for their partner, until the last team member had entered.

The third man had just stepped inside when Slade popped up from behind the couch and opened fire. The Uzi was held in steady hands and he sent a line of lethal lead screaming towards the three would-be assassins. They never had a chance. The front man dropped in his tracks, quickly followed by the other two. The man bringing up the rear squeezed off a shot that went harmlessly into the wooden floor, shooting splinters up.

Slade dropped the empty magazine and quickly slammed another one home. Spinning away from the couch, he moved towards the front door, yelling to June as he moved.

"I got three down back here! You got two coming your way!"

Nothing. Had he missed something? June should have responded. Slade started cautiously down the hall, the Uzi held waist high and ready. Straining his ears, Slade heard a scraping sound to his left. What was there? A sitting room? An extension of the foyer? He could not remember, because he had spent all of his time memorizing the layout of the back of the house.

Just as he neared the door to the room where he had heard the sounds, a shotgun blast sounded and a man was slammed through the door near Slade. Hitting the floor, the man slid down the hall to the front door and crumpled near the place mat. A large gaping hole in his chest, with blood spreading in all directions. June had found his target.

"Where is the other one?" yelled Slade.

"About to meet God," answered June and two rapid shotgun blasts punctuated the night.

Slade heard a man scream and rapid shots from a handgun were heard. Forgetting his own safety, Slade hooked around the door jam into the room, his Uzi searching for a target. Backing towards a window, was the last of the killers, buckshot wounds to his upper torso, seeping blood, and a look of fear in his eyes. He was desperately trying to find the man with the shotgun behind the wooden desk on the far side of the room. Slade swung his weapon towards him and opened fire at the same time June jumped up and pumped three shotgun rounds towards the would-be killer.

Their bullets struck home, spinning the killer in a circle and propelling him through the window. He was dead before he hit the ground.

"We need to let Emily and John know we're okay and we better leave. The cops are still looking for you." June looked over at Slade. Sliding the breech down on the shotgun, he started to unload his weapon.

"Good point. I'll round things up."

"Don't be long. I'm sure somebody heard the shots, even if we are in the country," yelled June.

Slade cast one last look at the dead killer before moving into the house to retrieve his backpack. How many more surprises did Matt Kyle have for him?

Chapter Thirty-Two

The excavation of Billy's lab was almost complete. Only a small portion of the interior remained and several students, led by Angela, were busy removing items. Still, they were no closer to the truth.

Moving over to one of the smaller tents shielding several tables from the sun, Katherine smiled reassuringly at Shirley. Remains of the file cabinet were lined in neat rows on top of the tables and some stuff was stored neatly beneath them. It was all very orderly and precise, much like you would expect to find at a scientific field research expedition.

"Almost done." Shirley glanced over at Katherine. It was obvious both women had expected to find more.

"I know," answered Katherine. "Not much left. What do we do from here?"

"I don't know. We'll talk to the Professor tonight and see what he thinks." Shirley slipped a pair of sunglasses onto her face to cover her eyes against the rising sun. There was a sense of apprehension in the air. This site had become special to the students, even though they had never met Billy they were intent on re-discovering his work. The passion was in their eyes, in the intensity in their voice, and in the determination in their features.

In another couple of days when the work was done and there was no chance for discovery, Shirley knew she would have to step forward and console them. For a split second, a blank look worked across Shirley's face and then was replaced by an inner smile beginning somewhere deep within her. That was something her mother would have said and done. It was the warmest feeling Shirley had known in quite a while and a new life entered her for she knew she had never been alone. Somehow, some way, unexplainable as it was, her mother was guiding her, leading her on the difficult journey to becoming a woman. It was clearer than ever this path she had been thrust down had not happened by chance. Finding Slade and Katherine had not occurred by luck either and she looked over at the older woman who was staring intently at her.

"You okay?" Katherine moved near Shirley and placed her hand on the young woman's shoulder.

"I haven't felt this good in a while. I'm so lucky I found you and Slade to help me." Shirley leaned over and gave a surprised artist a hug. "Come on. Let's go see what secrets Billy has left."

Katherine's spirits were lifted by Shirley's enthusiasm. The young woman was growing. She wished Slade were here to see it.

Shirley led her to the edge of the work area and Angela looked up.

"Your timing is good, real good. Look what we found," beamed the young girl, the excitement contagious.

"What is it?" Katherine was always the first to ask.

"I'm not sure yet, but I think this holds the key to what Billy was working on." Angela moved back and waved for Professor Johansen.

Three large wash tubs were placed next to each other and were connected by copper lines. Two of the lines had melted, flattening out in places, but were still intact. Inside each tub were several hanging wire baskets containing a fibrous sponge like material, rectangular in shape. Each one was about three inches thick, a foot long and six inches wide. There were four to each tub. A re-circulating pump was attached to the first wash tub and pumped water through a two inch hose to start the cycling process. A return hose led from the last tub back to the pump to complete the circuit.

Professor Johansen walked up and looked at the site and then quickly dropped to his knees to get a closer look.

"How come this is just now being found?" His irritation was evident.

"It was under a pile of burnt shingles and boards. We didn't know anything was here. It looked like it was going to be the hardest to move, so we saved it till last," explained Angela, moving alongside the Professor. Of all the students, she was the only one who would approach him when he became irritable.

"What's in the hangers? Have we identified it yet?" The Professor was asking questions in rapid fire.

"Not yet. We also have not identified what substance was in the tubs. As you can see, almost all of the fluid is gone."

"Let's get pictures and move this stuff to a work area." Professor Johansen was trying to keep the excitement out of his voice, but failed. Everyone was aware this may be the break.

In addition to the pictures, the entire scene was videotaped. It took time for them to move the wash tubs and contents to a table under a hastily erected tent. Space in the back yard of the old house was becoming a premium.

Angela was the first to pry a piece of the dried substance from a metal hanger in the first tub and slide a sliver beneath a microscope. Another student cut a small piece and started soaking it in a solution of water to make it more pliable.

"I believe it may be some type of plant or shrub." Angela adjusted her microscope. "There are a lot of plant fibers here, but they are interwoven very tightly, almost compacted." Angela stepped back and let the Professor have a look.

"Angela, look at this," called Julie, one of the young assistants. Everyone turned and looked at her and noticed she was pointing to a small glass bowl where she had placed a piece of the plant-like substance. The water was almost gone and the fiber had swollen to four times its original size.

"How much water did you put in there?" Professor Johansen wrinkled his brow. What type of plant would suck up water like a sponge?

"I placed a quarter cup of water in there and five grams of the material." Julie looked at the Professor as if she had done something wrong.

"Very good, young lady. It's always imperative to measure and record when conducting an experiment." Professor Johansen placed a reassuring hand on her shoulder. "The color has changed, Angela. It's now a dull greenish-brown. Also, the fibers have fattened up considerably. Get a piece of it under your lens."

There was silence as a small piece was sliced and placed onto a slide. Angela adjusted the eye piece, took a look, which was followed by a quick intake of breath.

"Professor, take a look at this. The fibers are still absorbing water. I've never seen anything like this! They're doubling in size again!" Angela stepped back and allowed the Professor to take a look. The fibers were soaking up any excess water on the slide, swelling to abnormal proportions.

Professor Johansen shoved himself away from the microscope and looked at the glass bowl on the table in front of Julie. All of the water had disappeared, absorbed by the fibers.

It was Shirley who broke the silence. "What type of plant do we think it is?"

"I don't know." Professor Johansen looked from the microscope to the glass bowl and back again. Whatever it was, it had a healthy appetite for water.

"I say we check it against the black mangroves with which Billy was working ith. We already know he was manipulating their cellular structure. This could be another modification of the host plant, this altered material." Angela looked through the microscope.

"Very good theory, Angela. Let's go ahead and eliminate that as a possibility, but keep in mind, Billy may have been working on several different types of experiments simultaneously. Never rule out that possibility." Professor Johansen nodded to his eager staff and they immediately started snipping off pieces of the substance from the first tray in an effort to identify the material.

The effort did not take long. Within the hour, the material was identified and Angela had been correct. The fiber in the hanging baskets, were genetic offspring of black mangroves. It was unlike any black mangrove they had ever seen, as the cellular structure had been altered.

"Okay, now that we have identified the species, we need to learn all we can about it. For instance, why did Billy have the black mangrove fiber absorb so much water? Was it to live in a limited water environment where the absorption of as much water as the tree could find would dictate survival? That's a possibility. Come on ladies and gentlemen, we have a lot of work to do." Professor Johansen breathed a sigh of relief when all of the students started moving as one, intent on learning the secrets Billy Waterbury had left behind. Just hours before, he thought all chances of learning anything about the young genius were gone. Now, a new light was shining, growing brighter with each step they took. True discovery was calling.

"See, I told you it was going to be a great day." Shirley grabbed Katherine by the arm.

Katherine smiled back at Shirley and looked one last time at the glass bowl holding the small piece of fiber. All of the water was gone, absorbed by the tiny fragment lying in the bottom, now swollen to many times its original size. But why? Why would Billy genetically alter a plant to absorb so much water?

Turning her attention away from the plant, Katherine watched as two engineering students examined the three wash tubs, evaluating how the apparatus was put together. Another group of students had already removed the hanging baskets and were examining the contents and placing the remains into containers for safekeeping. Katherine could feel the answers were near.

Shirley and Katherine both turned their gaze towards the outer perimeter of yellow tape and watched police Chief Bubba Singletee make his way towards them. The large man parked himself directly in front of them and dispensed with any pleasantries.

"We have a problem. Slade and June have been involved in a shoot-out in Seattle. Five people are dead and we don't know where they are." The police chief was watching the two women intently. "Have you heard from Slade?" The chief looked directly at Katherine. He could not keep the lid on all of this much longer.

"No, I haven't," whispered Katherine, her heart pounding wildly, thoughts racing out of control in her mind. What was going on?

"Tell me everything you know." Shirley took charge. This day had been a success and she was not about to let it slip away into chaos. The young woman reached out, took Katherine's hand and squared her shoulders towards the chief. Her mother had always confronted problems immediately and head on. She would be no different.

"I don't know that much, but I've called LAPD Commander Rick LeFluer to give him a heads up. He already knew about Seattle. Our two heroes have vanished again. Whatever they're up to, they seem to be holding their own. I'm sure they'll contact us when they need to."

"You said we had a problem," countered Shirley, getting directly to the point. "What's the problem?" The young woman's jaw was set tight, her eyes hard.

Chief Singletee looked at her for several seconds before responding and when he did his voice was softer, more deep. "You look and act a lot like your mother." He smiled at her. Placing his hands on his hips, the chief turned and looked at the students busy at work. "The problem, Miss Waterbury, is that we're running out of time. We don't have much time before this story goes public."

All three of them looked at each other. They had all been through so much, come so far, and now, with a possible answer to Billy's work looming closer, time had become the enemy. There was nothing they could do but wait, and pray.

The *Pink Flamingo* had moved to 15,000 feet and was cruising at over 230 miles per hour. June was humming as he flew, glancing out at the clouds. Slade was in the co-pilot seat, seeming oblivious to what was going on. June knew better.

"You still think it is a good idea filing a flight plan straight to San Pedro?" June stole a sideways glance at Slade.

"Yeah. It'll put Kyle on notice we're coming. At the last second, we will divert and land at LAX. I can rent a car to San Pedro. The element of surprise will be mine." Slade looked back out the window, shifting uncomfortably to alleviate the pain in his right side. The stitches were holding, but the wound was beginning to throb, shooting up his side to his shoulder. Reaching inside his pocket, he shook out a pain pill and gulped it down.

"Your side hurting again?" June received a nod.

After the shootout at Emily and John's house, they had gathered their gear and borrowed Emily's SUV. Slade had instructed them to call the police and told them to tell the truth about what had occurred. June had told Emily to tell the police he had threatened her with harm if she did not treat Slade. By law, all gunshot victims were supposed to be reported to the police.

"I've never been a fugitive before." June flipped on the auto-pilot.

"Neither have I. We're getting pretty good at it." Slade leaned back in his seat to get some sleep. There was plenty of trouble waiting in San Pedro.

Ten large trucks pulled into the hanger at San Pedro and parked near *Quest 1*. All of the valves and fittings had been installed and this was the final and most important part to be added. The trucks had originally been designed as dump trucks, but the beds had been removed and water containers had been added. Inside the containers were four large rectangular wire-mesh sleeves, twelve feet long, seven feet high and over a foot thick. Inside the sleeves was the black mangrove fibrous material Billy Waterbury had created.

The fibrous material was kept inside the water tanks and an armed detachment of security personnel were hovering nearby. Hans Klauss and Matt Kyle were standing beside the trucks, staring at the containers.

"The growth of the material is amazing. It took less than two weeks to grow these." Klaus looked at Kyle. "We're ready for installation. Any last minute requests?"

"Nope. Get them on board. I want to be at sea by morning. I want a full week of sea trials before I have our guests arrive. I want to be absolutely certain this works to our expectations."

Jumping into a golf cart near the hanger entrance, Kyle rode back to his administrative complex. Bypassing his office, he went straight down to see Randolph Myers and found him in front of his screens, a half eaten hamburger with a large amount of onions stinking up the place.

"Do something with that. It stinks."

Randolph ignored him. "Your bright idea back fired in Seattle. They got away, but not before killing the men you sent." Randolph leaned back in his seat to observe the impact this information would have on Kyle. He was disappointed when he got no visible reaction.

"Where is Lockwood now?"

"Headed to San Pedro."

"How do you know?" Kyle moved towards the computer screens.

"The *Pink Flamingo* filed a flight plan to San Pedro last night. This morning, he changed the plan and landed at LAX. A car was rented by Lockwood at the Hertz counter and I would guess he's either in San Pedro or well on his way." Randolph was ecstatic when he saw the color drain from Kyle's face.

"How long ago did he rent the car?"

"About an hour ago. Paid for it with his Visa, which means he's not interested in hiding his whereabouts. This is a vast departure from his earlier behavior." Randolph looked over at Kyle and was rewarded with seeing him start to pace, which was an indicator he was worried.

"Well, I've already added additional security and I think that will be sufficient. I hope Mr. Lockwood does come here, because I would like to meet the man. Keep me apprised of his movements as best you can. The man has proven to be very resourceful." Kyle turned and left without waiting on a reply from Randolph.

Picking up his heavily laden onion filled hamburger, the fat computer analyst bit a large portion off and started to chew, much like a cow chomping on its cud. The game had changed and Lockwood had grown bolder, much bolder. Where was he now?

Randolph let his fingers fly across the keyboard, inputting data to track down the man.

Chapter Thirty-Three

The revelations were coming quickly, almost too fast to grasp and comprehend. Initially, they had thought the recycling pump had been used to filter and circulate water to all three wash tubs to keep the plants alive, but that theory evaporated in face of new evidence. The two inch hose leading from the pump to the first wash basin did carry water, but the return hose never hooked back to the initial water source. That meant the two inch return hose or overflow hose, had hooked up to something, but what? There had been no other metal basin where the water had been deposited.

The startling discovery was made by the least experienced of the team, a freshman undergraduate who made the trip because he was a friend of Angela's. Where the wash tubs had originally been placed, there had also been a series of plastic containers the return hose had fed into. The fire had completely burned all of them except one and only the base of it was left. Still, it was enough.

Because of the foot traffic inside Billy's lab, where the plastic containers had originally been set was obliterated. Professor Johansen had them play back the video tape and they were able to make out indentations in the debris where the containers had been aligned. By inspecting the concrete floor, they were able to find the residue left from the burnt rubber containers. There had been five of the plastic containers adjacent to the wash tubs.

Another discovery had been made by accident. Julie had continued her research to determine how much water the fiber could absorb. She had placed five small glass bowls, each with different amounts of fiber in them, and had added various amounts of water. Later in the day, she had checked on the fiber and had been startled to learn the fiber with the most amount of water had not only absorbed all of the water, but was already beginning to

252

grow. The plant had added an inch to its overall growth, which was confirmed by the new sprouts and cellular reproduction.

The last tidbit of information was extracted from the wash tubs themselves. The fluid in the bottom of the tubs was none other than common sea water, which made perfectly good sense, because mangroves grow in areas high in salinity.

Armed with all of this information, the Professor had the students gather around to discuss the findings.

"So, we know the growth rate of the altered black mangrove is alarming and rivals that of some bamboo found in China. Based on our calculations, a full grown tree could develop in less than ten months. The ability of the tree to absorb water would aid in its development in high saline environments and would give it the edge of other species, thereby ensuring its survival."

"But is that all there is?" Shirley was still not convinced. "I just don't believe someone would kill my brother to gain growth secrets of a black mangrove."

"You're forgetting Billy enhanced these species. We haven't run all of the tests. What if he did find a way to have them remove toxins from eco-systems like we have discussed? That, together, with the enhanced growth rate would make this species attractive to investors, developers, and ecologists. And what about the impact on other species? It could have a significant climate changing impact on existing eco-systems as Professor Johansen has said," said Angela.

"I do think you're overlooking the financial gain this proposal could have," said Chance Rivers, one of the young engineers who had discovered the return hose did not lead back to the recycling pump. "I got on the internet last night and checked on the impact of mangroves on the coast line. The largest problem they're having is waiting on the species to develop when they're re-introduced into an area. We have already discussed the impact they have on the environment, but it takes time for this to happen. Your brother found a way to replace what it has taken mankind years to destroy and Billy's mangroves can repopulate an area in less than a year."

"And, I'm fairly certain the plants are sterile, meaning they cannot reproduce," added Angela.

"I think we're on the right track. Any other ideas?" Professor Johansen looked for comments.

Before anyone could respond, the cell phone on Katherine's belt rang. She grabbed the phone and placed it to her ear.

"Hello?"

"Katherine! This is Slade."

"Slade! How are you? Where are you? What happened? Why haven't you called?" said Katherine, all in one quick vocal burst that immediately started to crack. Within seconds, tears were streaming down her face and

Shirley moved to her side. "I've been so worried about you," sobbed Katherine, not caring who was around.

"Slow down. I'm okay. How is everything going?" Slade had his heart torn apart by hearing her cry. The next voice that came over the line was not Katherine's, but Slade recognized it immediately.

"Slade, this is Shirley," the young woman had pried the phone from Katherine's ear and was holding it so both of them could hear. "Where are you?"

"San Pedro. Shirley, I'm convinced World Vision Quest and a Matt Kyle are behind the death of your family, but I need more information. He's tried to kill me on three separate occasions. Have you learned anything on your end?" Slade took a moment to look around him. He was at a public phone booth near the harbor. If Kyle was as efficient as he believed, he would already have a trace on the call.

"Yes, our original idea that Billy had altered black mangroves to impact eco-systems may have been correct all along. We have found some stuff at his lab that could be used as evidence." Shirley squeezed Katherine who had regained some of her composure.

"What type of evidence?"

"Billy created a fibrous mat of black mangrove material that has an accelerated growth rate and the ability to absorb vast quantities of water. These two combinations would make it an ideal candidate to survive in a hostile environment and to reintroduce itself in a short period of time where it has become extinct due to development."

"But we'll need proof that Kyle got this technology from Billy," countered Slade.

"Yes." Katherine spoke for the first time since Shirley had joined the conversation.

"But this doesn't make sense." Slade's mind was racing. He was not a scientist, but a cop, and an investigator had to make sure all the pieces fit. "Why would Kyle need to modify a freighter to grow Black Mangroves? Why not do it on land where he would have more room?"

"What are you talking about, Slade?" asked Shirley.

"Kyle owns a freighter, *Quest 1*, and had it modified. In the hold of the ship are five, fifty thousand gallon tanks all in a row, or so I was told. Why would he need that?"

"Probably to grow this fibrous mat I told you about and conduct further research. Billy had the mats in wash tubs where he could pump water to them." Shirley paused.

"But why on a ship? Why not on land?" Slade saw a brown pick-up truck pass him for the second time. The man in the passenger seat looked his way and spoke rapidly into a cell phone. Time was up. "I have to go. I'll call when I can. Katherine, I love you." Without another word, Slade hung up the phone and disappeared into a group of tourists.

"Slade! Slade!" screamed Katherine. After several seconds, she closed the phone and slipped it back onto her belt, slumping against Shirley for support.

"He'll be okay. We both know him and what he can do," comforted Shirley. After Katherine nodded her head in agreement, Shirley looked over at Professor Johansen. "Slade thinks he has found who killed my family. He also told us about a freighter that has been constructed to carry five, fifty thousand gallon holding tanks in her hold. I believe it may be to develop more of the fibrous material Billy cultivated from the black mangrove."

"Based on that information, I would say we are right on target," beamed Professor Johansen. "Let's get everything stowed away for tonight, because I want a fresh start tomorrow. And Shirley, I want you and Katherine to tell me everything Mr. Lockwood told you about this ship…er, freighter…whatever it is. The more information we have the better."

By the time the pick-up circled the block a third time, Slade was gone. The security guards called in to report to Randolph that Slade had eluded them. Randolph told them to go to the pier and await further orders. There was no way they would find him in the sea of humanity walking the streets.

The information on the telephone call Slade had made was coming in. While he did not have the message in front of him, he had learned Slade had called Katherine, as he had verified the receiving phone number as hers based on her monthly statement from AT&T. The way in which he had gleaned the information was illegal, but Randolph was confident the criminal act could not be traced.

Picking up the phone, Randolph called Kyle.

"Lockwood was seen in San Pedro, but our men missed him. He made a telephone call to a Katherine Wintergate in Cedar Key, but was cut short when he saw our men. Do you want me to activate counter measures in Cedar Key?" Myers leaned back from the bank of computers and stretched in his chair. A two day old mustard stain was on the front of his shirt and finally noticing it, he dipped a napkin in a glass of water in a vain attempt to wipe it off.

"No. Leave the woman alone in Cedar Key until we learn what Mr. Lockwood knows. I want you to reduce security around the pier and if Lockwood is seen, let him have access to *Quest 1*, but don't make it obvious."

"Come again?"

"If we have him on board the ship, he is confined and he can't run or hide, now can he? We can then interrogate him at our leisure."

"Will do." Randolph hung up on Kyle and dialed the chief of security for World Vision Quest.

Night had fallen before Slade made his move. He had spent the afternoon visiting the docks and obtaining a layout of the vicinity. *Quest 1* was housed inside a metal building covering the pier. In casual conversation with workers on the dock, he had learned Kyle was a fanatic about privacy.

Under the cover of darkness, Slade was certain he could slip inside without being seen. The answer to the puzzle was inside the ship.

Based on his surveillance, the easiest way to enter the building would be near the sea doors that closed when *Quest 1* was inside. It meant he might get wet, but he had been wet before.

Walking casually down the pier, Slade moved ever closer to the structure, being careful to watch for any alert security guard. Detecting none, he dropped down onto a walkway paralleling the pier and ran to the sea doors. When he neared the doors, he checked for cameras, but failed to find any. He did not think the doors protruded all the way to the bottom, but probably were only in the water four to five feet. The depth of the channel to move the ship inside would have to be considerable, probably twenty-five to thirty feet, if not more.

Slipping off his clothes, Slade placed them inside a plastic bag and zipped them shut. He was careful to make sure his Beretta was placed near the top of the bag in case he needed it when he surfaced.

Dangling his feet over the side, Slade touched the water and winced. The Pacific was not as kind as the Gulf of Mexico and he found himself wishing for the warm waters of Florida. Steeling himself for what he knew was about to come, he lowered himself into the water and felt the air rush involuntarily out of his lungs. He tried his best not to gasp, but failed.

After becoming somewhat accustomed to the temperature, he reached up and grabbed the plastic bag containing his clothes and gun. Whatever company had designed the bag, he owed his thanks. The bag had a strap and he slipped it over his shoulders which made it easier to hold. With several deep breaths behind him, he drew a lungful of air, flipped over and dove for the bottom, keeping one hand in constant contact with the sea doors. Slade had to equalize the pressure in his ears several times as he swam deeper.

Being somewhat familiar with depths from all of his free diving, Slade knew he was coming upon thirty feet, maybe a little more and still the metal doors reached down into the channel. Just when he was about to turn back towards the top, Slade felt the steel run out from under his hand and he detected a small current ebbing beneath the door. He moved the bag from his shoulder and shoved it beneath the door, turning it loose, but holding onto the strap. Grabbing the door, he had to wedge himself beneath it and with a powerful tug Slade pulled himself through and started up the other side.

When his head broke the surface, Slade looked around. The hanger was expansive, far more so than he would have thought. The bow of *Quest 1* loomed over him, dwarfing him. Multiple lines ran from the huge ship to the concrete pilings, holding her in place. A gangway ran up her side and a land mounted crane, idle now, was situated near the center of the ship, undoubtedly to unload and load cargo.

Not detecting anyone on the deck of the ship, Slade swam towards the pier and eased up onto the safety of the concrete. Scanning the area, Slade did not see anyone and that made him uneasy. There should have been someone around, especially if the cargo inside the ship was as important as he believed. Slade dressed, drying off the best he could with a small hand towel.

Discarding the bag, Slade walked towards the guard shack. A light was emanating from beneath the door and when Slade looked inside the little window, he saw the guard sitting in front of several video monitors. The guard's chin resting on his folded arms told Slade he was asleep and, after watching him for several seconds his suspicions were confirmed.

If only his luck held. Slade turned for the boat, the Beretta tucked inside his waist band. His walk up the ramp to the ship was uneventful and when he stepped onto her deck, he was once again awed by the sheer size of the vessel. She was at least three, maybe four football fields in length and at least a football field in width. The bridge was another ten to twelve stories over the deck.

Committing the layout of the deck to memory, Slade moved towards an open door leading into the bowels of the ship. Stepping inside, Slade allowed his eyes to become adjusted to the limited lighting and then moved forward.

Seven levels later, Slade moved through a set of double water tight doors that emptied him into the hold. A catwalk now encircled the area and five huge tanks were lined up in a neat row, each massive in its own right. Walking around the nearest tank, Slade saw that a two foot pipe had been installed near the top, but a larger, possibly three to four foot pipe, was near the bottom.

An overhead movable crane on a trolley system, capable of rolling over each of the tanks, was tied off near the center of the ship. Walking around to where the pipe emerged from the lower portion of the tank, Slade checked to see if there were any doors leading to where it might terminate. Finding none, Slade moved back to inspect the other, smaller pipe. This pipe seemed to originate beneath the tank, even though it entered at the top, so again Slade looked for and this time found a door that would lead him to the pipe's origin.

The termination of the smaller pipe occurred one flight beneath the tanks. Slade found himself in an area equal in size to the one immediately above him only this one did not have large tanks. Instead, there were a series of smaller rectangular shaped boxes, each with several wire mesh containers hanging down in them. Each box was full of sea water and he estimated them to be over twenty feet long.

Moving closer, Slade climbed up on a small ladder and leaned over to inspect the wire mesh containers hanging inside the metal boxes. There was a fibrous material inside them and he realized this was probably the material

Katherine and Shirley had told him about. But what was it doing here? And why? Any further thoughts he may have had were cut short.

"Good of you to join us Mr. Lockwood. I have been expecting you," droned the irritating voice of Matt Kyle.

Initially, Slade had been startled, but he calmly turned and looked at Kyle. A half dozen guns were leveled at him and Kyle stood there smugly, knowing he held the winning hand. Slade knew there was no escape.

"You're shorter than I thought you would be." Slade tried to regain the upper hand.

"Humor will get you nowhere, Mr. Lockwood. But I bet your curiosity is killing you, isn't it?" Kyle laughed hysterically.

Slade noticed a short, fat man move alongside Kyle and he immediately did not like him.

"You're a hard man to track Lockwood, but I found you." The short man wiped a greasy palm across a mustard stain.

"Why don't you come down from there and one of my men will take your weapon," instructed Kyle.

Slade stepped off the ladder and walked forward, but was stopped by one of the guards. With several weapons trained on him, he stood still while one of the men removed his weapon and deftly searched him. After finding nothing else, other than two additional magazines for his Beretta, the guard turned and nodded towards Kyle. When Kyle nodded back, the man spun and buried his fist in Slade's stomach, doubling him over. Before Slade could fall, a second punch caught Slade right behind the head on the side of the neck. Stars raced before his eyes and he fought to remain conscious.

When the guard had removed his weapon, he knew he was going to be beaten. He had tried his best to tense his body in preparation for the blow he knew was coming, but had only partially succeeded. The breath was driven from him and he knew he was at the mercy of the men around him. Like a pack of hungry wolves, they moved in, kicking viciously at his face and upper body, intent on damaging him as much as possible. Slade curled into a fetal position and covered his face and front part of his torso as best he could, but he knew he could not sustain the effort for long. An errant boot caught him in the nose and blood quickly flooded his face.

The area he was most concerned about was his right side and he had managed to land on that side, using the floor as a shied to hide his injury. If not, they would quickly exploit his weakness and several blows there could cause serious damage. Mercifully, Kyle called to them and the men backed off, the bloodlust still in their eyes.

"Help him to his feet," ordered Kyle.

Two of the ruffians moved forward and snatched Slade to a standing position. Slade was still blinking, trying to remove the stars from his eyes, while trying to pump oxygen back into his lungs.

Kyle moved up in front of him, but well out of striking distance. "One of my men in Alaska said he thought he shot you in the right side and I noticed you seemed particularly careful to protect that area." Before the words had died on Kyle's lips, the man on Slade's right ripped his shirt up, exposing the stitches and redness of the injury. "I was right."

Kyle stepped back and one of the men to Slade's rear moved up and swung a vicious blow to Slade's right side, just above the stitches and right below the rib cage. Slade felt like he had been hit by a train and all the energy left his legs and he crumpled to the floor. When he landed, the man who had ripped his shirt delivered three successive kicks to Slade's right side, causing the ex-cop to make a feeble attempt to roll away. Unconsciousness came to him like an angel in the night, when he was kicked the third time.

"Take him to a holding area. I'm not done with Mr. Lockwood." Kyle turned and walked away.

Two men grabbed Slade and dragged him down a hallway to a dimly lit portion of the ship. Opening a door to a storage room, they dumped him inside, but not before one of them kicked him in the ribs a fourth time. They closed the door, plunging the room into darkness.

The remainder of the night would be one of indescribable pain.

Chapter Thirty-Four

The hour hand moved with agonizing slowness, tracking slowly across the face of the clock before moving on. Shirley had lain in bed watching time slowly pass by, her thoughts everywhere and yet no where. Something was wrong. The rest of the day had been spent by the Professor and the students analyzing and researching Billy's project, trying to prove their theory. Shirley did not share their enthusiasm.

Billy had a gift they still did not comprehend. To alter the growth of black mangroves was one thing, but she just did not believe that was what he was trying to do. She knew Billy had messed with cellular manipulation in the past. He had done it with her mother's roses and had created a hybrid that bloomed brighter than the others and held the flower three times as long. Cellular manipulation was old hat to Billy.

The arrangement of the wash tubs and the location of the rubber containers still bothered her. Why had Billy located them like that? She did not believe Billy was trying to enhance growth rates. Plus the arrangement of the containers was wrong. Nobody knew Billy like her. What was he trying to tell her? Come on Billy speak to me, muttered Shirley.

Leaving the bedroom, Shirley walked out into Slade's living room. Ever since Slade had killed the man in her house, she and Katherine had been living at Slade's. Shirley had taken the guest room and Katherine had taken the master bedroom. They had agreed to the arrangement until things got back to normal. Normal. What was that? Shirley shook her head and walked to the kitchen.

Trying to be quiet, Shirley selected a glass, grabbed a handful of ice and poured some iced tea. Sitting down at the table, Shirley took a spoon and measured off some sugar and dribbled it into the glass. Fascinated, she watched as some of the sugar fell slowly towards the bottom. Dumping the rest of the sugar into the tea, she used her spoon and stirred the contents before drinking. When she took her second sip, her eyes shot wide open and in her haste, she spilled half the glass on the table in front of her, trying to set it down. Not bothering to wipe it up, she jumped up, ripped open the refrigerator door and filled the glass back up. Grabbing the sugar dispenser, she started to pour some into the glass and watched again when some of the white crystals settled towards the bottom and the other part dissolved. That was it!

Shirley started to leave the room and then turned back. Billy! A true genius! No wonder Matt Kyle wanted the invention! Matt Kyle and half the world would want the invention!

"Katherine! I figured it out!" shouted Shirley, running towards Katherine's room.

Katherine met Shirley at her door and grabbed the young woman. Terror was in Katherine's eyes and she frantically looked around, wondering if they were going to be attacked. The murderer who had come for them was still a vivid picture.

"Shirley, what is it? What's wrong?"

"I figured out what Billy was working on! Come on! Get dressed! I knew he was smart! I knew it! We have to get the Professor!" screamed Shirley. Before leaving, Shirley kissed Katherine on the cheek and disappeared into her bedroom, running towards the room and discarding her robe as she went.

A knock at the door. Katherine froze. A second knock, this time louder.

"Is everything okay?" asked the young officer stationed outside their house.

Katherine slipped on a robe and answered the door. "Yes, it is. Do me a favor and have someone contact Professor Johansen. It's urgent."

"Ma'am, it is three o'clock in the morning."

"I don't care. Have him and all the students meet us at Billy's lab." Katherine slammed the door before he could reply.

It took Katherine and Shirley less than twenty minutes to get to the lab. When they arrived, the Professor and students were already there. Portable lights were on.

"Shirley, what is this all about?" asked Professor Johansen.

"The answer, Professor. My brother was smarter than any of us realized. He was using black mangroves, but not for habitat reconstruction, but for another more noble purpose. Come on and I'll show you." Not waiting on a response, Shirley moved forward.

Several students were standing around and she started to give orders. "Angela, we're going to recreate Billy's experiment and I think you'll be surprised. Bring me one of the wash basins."

For the next three hours, Shirley had them set up an abbreviated version of Billy's experiment. Instead of three wash tubs, she used one. The other two were used in place of the original rubber containers. Relying on the engineering students, Shirley directed them on how to place the pump, the connecting hoses and the overflow hose. She had already sent four students to bring fifty gallons of sea water.

Once everything was in place, Shirley asked them to bring her four of the fibrous mats, the metal screens and the tray used to hold them. Once again, directing the engineering students, Shirley had them suspend the three mats into the tub.

"Now, here is what confused me," said Shirley. "See this residue along the sides of this metal screen? I couldn't figure out what it was, but then it hit me. It's what was left over."

"I'm not following you, Shirley. I don't know about them, but you've lost me," said Katherine.

"Look here at the tray the mats are in. There is a hole near the bottom. The excess is allowed to run out of there. Remember when we found the five plastic containers? We assumed they were all hooked up in sequence, one right after the other. I don't believe that's accurate. They were hooked up separately, two at a time. I'll show you."

Shirley moved forward and connected an overflow hose to the bottom of the tray and placed the end into one of the wash tubs. Taking the other hose, she connected it to the upper portion of the tray and dropped it into a different tub.

Turning to one of the engineering students, she said "Did you place the hose in the sea water and attach it to the pump." When he nodded yes, she continued, "Start the pump, but go slowly. The mats have been dry for some time."

Flipping the switch and adjusting the rate of suction, the sea water ran through the hose and filled the screens holding the fibrous mats. For several seconds, nothing happened as the plant material absorbed the sea water, swelling before their very eyes. Then, water started to flow out of the screens, but not uniformly. Some flowed towards the bottom and out the hose into a wash basin. Some of the water flowed across the tops of the screens, out towards the top hose and into the second tub.

"I'll be damned." Professor Johansen looked over at a smiling Shirley Waterbury, who had tears in her eyes.

Katherine stepped forward and slipped her arm around the young woman's waist.

"I told you he was a genius. I told you," repeated Shirley, wiping away a tear.

"You're not too bad yourself, kiddo." Katherine hugged her.

When the realization of what they were seeing struck them, the students burst into shouts and applause. Cheers and yelling erupted from them and they danced wildly, laughing, with all of them trying to talk at once. This was a moment in science like no other and they may never see it again. It was unique, special and only happened once in a lifetime. History was being made before their very eyes. It *was* a discovery that rivaled Einstein's in physics.

Billy Waterbury had discovered the impossible.

The remainder of the night and most of the next day was spent in agony. When Slade regained consciousness, the pain in his right side shot lightening bolts of torment throughout his body, starting in his right rib cage and ending with pinpoints of light behind his eyes. There was no way he could get comfortable and after several hours, gave up trying. His nose was not broken and he had been able to stop the bleeding.

He knew they were moving. Even as big as she was, *Quest 1* still rolled with the movement of the sea. How long had they been under way? Slade had no way of telling, but figured it had been sometime.

Slade could detect sounds coming down the corridor and stopping outside his door, where he could make out muffled conversation. Through the steel, he could hear the sounds of conversation and a key being inserted into the lock. Moments later, the door was thrown open wide and light spilled into his cell. Squinting he tried to adjust his eyes, but two pairs of rough hands grabbed him and snatched him to his feet, causing new sensations of pain to rack his body.

Slade was half carried, half dragged to a freight elevator and pushed inside. The two guards shoved him against the far wall and Slade leaned heavily against it. He knew he was hurt, but he wanted them to think he was more injured than he was.

When the elevator stopped, he was propelled out the door and stumbled down the hallway, being guided and shoved by his tormentors. One of the guards opened the door and he was pulled inside. Matt Kyle was standing in the middle of the room and a metal chair had been placed near him.

"Ah, Mr. Lockwood. I hope your night and most of the day went well. You don't look too good." Slade was shoved down into the chair. A set of handcuffs were snapped onto his wrists and he straightened himself when the guard moved away.

"We need to talk." Kyle moved over to a desk and sat half on it, but kept one foot on the floor.

"What about?" Slade fought back the pain in his side.

"Your side bothering you? Sorry about that, but you have proven resourceful, especially in killing the people I've sent after you," retorted Kyle. "Now I need to know what you know, Mr. Lockwood. It can be an easy conversation or a tough conversation. You get to decide."

Slade turned and looked at the two men guarding the door. A third man was in the room and he was immense. By the size of his shoulders and arms he was used to heavy work. There was no doubt he would break bones if given the opportunity.

"I know you killed the Waterburys. And I know you hope to market Billy's idea. And I'm not the only one who knows." Slade looked the egotistical man in the face.

"Really. What do you know about Billy's idea, as you call it? Do you know how much money is involved with his invention? Do you have any idea?" Kyle moved to the front of the man. Kyle enjoyed an audience and was relishing in his role of dominance. In a one-on-one fight, Slade would have the upper hand. He was bigger, stronger and probably more athletic.

"It could never make you enough money to validate killing them," snapped Slade. "Besides, the reintroduction of black mangroves is already being done in certain eco-systems. So you have one that grows quicker and absorbs pollutants faster, so what? Others will do the same." Slade let his voice trail off when he saw Kyle stare at him.

"What did you say? Reintroduction of black mangroves to eco-systems." Kyle started to laugh and became so hysterical, tears streamed from his face and he lost his breath. Slumping into a sofa on the far wall next to a window with a view of the ocean, Kyle finally regained his composure, stood up and walked back over to Slade.

"You really are a dumb cop, aren't you? I've been worried about what you knew and you know nothing. All the wasted time and effort to have you killed and all I had to do was let you stumble around in the dark." Kyle shook his head in disbelief.

"You deny you killed them." Slade was cut off.

"I don't deny anything! But I didn't have them killed because of some eco-system rehabilitation project. Are you crazy? I can see you're not a businessmen Mr. Lockwood. When an entrepreneur goes into an endeavor, they do so by weighing all the variables. Most of these variables include cost of production, potential markets, labor, competition, and a host of other factors that can eat into your bottom line. What I and my counterparts look for is a product no one else is manufacturing or an idea no one else has. Are you with me so far?" Kyle realized he was enjoying this lecture.

"So far." Slade moved his wrists. He could not become so caught up in the conversation with Kyle that he failed to plan for his escape.

"Well, you see, Billy Waterbury discovered something everybody wants Mr. Lockwood. Something people have fought over, are currently fighting over, and is in short demand and growing shorter. By and large, Mr. Lockwood, Billy Waterbury may have solved a Twenty-first Century problem. And you know what, I now have that solution to mankind's problem, but unlike Billy and his ignorant father, I'm shrewd enough to market it to the highest bidder." Kyle turned smugly and walked back towards his desk.

"So, Hank wouldn't sell it to you?"

"That idiot didn't even know what Billy had. He was stumbling around in the dark worse than you. At least Billy was not your son and you came in on this at the end, so that is somewhat of an excuse." Kyle looked at Slade. "What is the largest problem facing your state, Mr. Lockwood?"

"I don't know. I guess it would be the influx of people."

"You are partially correct and you don't know how close to the truth you are. The problem facing your state is the same one facing any populated area. Drinking water, Mr. Lockwood, drinking water."

Slade slowly nodded his head in agreement, recognizing the importance of what Kyle was saying. "You're correct in that regards, but the shortage of water affects farmers, ranchers, and many others. Not just a state with burgeoning populations."

"Correct again, but once again you're short-sighted. What about the arid regions of this planet? What about those areas where the desert is encroaching or where ninety percent of the country has land that can't be farmed? What if there was an economical, inexpensive, yet simple solution to this problem? Do you think it would be worth something, Mr. Lockwood? Try billions!" Kyle moved away from his desk and started to resume his pacing.

"So you killed Billy and his parents for it." Slade let his voice grow cold.

"Spare me the guilt, Mr. Lockwood, because I don't feel any. They stood in the way of progress. If Hank Waterbury had accepted my proposal, then he and his family would be alive and worth millions. As it is, to the victor go the spoils." Kyle held his hands palms up and shrugged.

"Humor me," said Slade. "How did Billy do it? I know about the accelerated growth of the black mangroves and the rapid absorption capabilities he enhanced, but how does that translate to a water making machine."

"What covers over seventy-five percent of our planet? The oceans and they're full of sea water. For years, scientists have wrestled with a way to desalt the oceans and make the water fit for human consumption. We can't keep drilling wells and tapping into underground reservoirs, because they're ceasing to exist. Salt water intrusion is entering some of them. Florida is a prime example, especially the lower half of your state. However, the problem of desalting has been a cumbersome one, until now."

"And costly," added Slade.

"Precisely. The cost of building a desalting plant costs upward of sixty to seventy million dollars and then there's the NIMBY concern—Not In My Back Yard is the response of most residents, because the plants are large, noisy, and ugly. Most desalting plants have been opposed. Plus, the cost of the produced water is still very high."

"Tampa, Florida, just approved a desalting plant after years of debate and funding problems."

"That's correct, but they approved it because they had to. There was a referendum about to be placed on the state ballot that would have allowed the voters the opportunity to choose where their water was to come from to quench the thirst of Tampa, Sarasota, and other cities. A lot of people in the central urban sprawl have targeted the rivers in North Central Florida. They want the water diverted south to quench their appetite and that would have set off a war with environmentalists and politicians. The politicians knew it was a political nightmare and they moved to get the necessary funding to head off a nasty voter issue. My water desalting plant will solve that."

"Billy's desalting plant," clarified Slade.

"You're beginning to bore me, Mr. Lockwood."

"You haven't told me how the plant works. Surely, you can do that." Slade mustered all the sarcasm he could.

"I have a better idea. Why don't I show you?" With that last statement, Kyle motioned for the two guards to get Slade.

Waiting for just the right moment when the nauseating businessmen was in front of him, Slade mustered all of his strength and leaped out of the chair crashing into Kyle and sending him sprawling to the floor. Slade stumbled into Kyle's desk as the smaller man shrieked in terror. The two guards immediately pounced on Slade and drove him to the floor. One of the guards pulled out his weapon and placed it to the back of Slade's head and looked questioningly at his boss, who had regained his feet if not his composure.

"Don't kill him here. I have a far more interesting death for Mr. Lockwood. Bring him along," sneered the eccentric millionaire, not looking back as he left the room.

The two guards snatched Slade to his feet and pulled him to the door. Slade kept his fists tightly clenched and moved reluctantly with them. Kyle had never been the object of his attack, but he had needed the businessman as a diversion. Slade had seen a large paper clip lying on Kyle's desk and he knew he needed it to pick the handcuffs around his wrists if he had any hope of freedom.

Slade was shoved into the elevator and taken down to the rectangular tanks where the hybrid black mangroves were suspended in seawater. Matt Kyle was already there.

"You see, Mr. Lockwood, the hybrids are already working. Billy was able to alter the cellular makeup of the mangroves, but in ways he could not have possibly imagined when he started. Initially, he was just experimenting with cellular manipulation, but stumbled upon the sequence where he could enhance the mangroves ability to go after a particular substance. In this case, he altered them to focus on hydrogen and oxygen, which, in its proper combination becomes H_2O, or water. What Billy discovered was quite simple. By enhancing the ability of the mangroves to detect fresh water the hybrid cells absorb as much as possible in the blink of an eye. The beautiful part is this: they don't stop absorbing when the cells are full, but continue to do so, shedding the excess water to take on more. They become tiny water purifiers, working at alarming speed, turning out an incredible volume." Kyle was already looking at the rectangular boxes in front of him and motioned for the technician to turn on the pumps.

"How long do they last?" Slade moved forward to watch the demonstration.

"That's the beautiful part. We have original hybrid cellular mats still functioning after processing billions of gallons of water. They obtain their nutrients from the sea water, but do not pass along anything except fresh water. They're a living organism and function quite well."

"Do they reproduce?"

"No. Billy made sure they could not proliferate. Also, this is the maximum size we have been able to grow. When they reach about twenty feet in length they stop. Apparently, he wanted them controlled, which is good for us, but bad for competition. We control the only supply of hybrid cellular mats, so you could say we have cornered the market."

"So you don't know how to make the hybrid, you just continue to produce what you stole from Billy?" asked Slade, seeing the fire hit Kyle's eyes.

"You continue to mock me, Mr. Lockwood? Very well, you will die soon enough. At least you can appreciate the invention Billy left for me," Kyle smiled when he saw the anger cloud Slade's face. "By the way, did I tell you that one of these units the size of a tractor trailer could supply enough water for a city the size of San Pedro? What a gift. I may win the Noble Prize for this invention."

Despite himself, Slade started to step forward, but the barrel of a handgun shoved into his chest stopped him.

"Come, come, Mr. Lockwood. Let me give you a first hand demonstration." Kyle motioned for the guards to bring Slade along, but made sure not to go near the ex-cop.

Slade found himself on the catwalk overlooking the five huge holding tanks. Water was pouring in from the two foot pipes and quickly filled each reservoir.

"Each tank is hooked up to one of my desalting units. It takes a little over two minutes for them to fill. Each tank holds fifty thousand gallons of water. Unlike conventional desalting plants, we have no high and low pressure pumps, no costly membranes, and we don't have to rely on current reverse osmosis technology. The mats extract what we want and send the waste back to sea."

Each tank was full and a technician dipped a vial of water from each one and screwed a cap on it, before placing it in a tray. Once that was complete, the technician then spoke into a radio and a trap door leading to the three foot pipe was thrown open and the water rushed out.

"What are they checking for? I thought you said the water was pure?" queried Slade.

"It is pure, but our clients will want to see results." Kyle motioned to another technician who activated an overhead crane.

The crane moved to where Slade was standing and for the first time, he saw a small platform that carried workers. The two guards directed Slade onto the platform and gave the thumbs up. The crane operator lowered the hook. Within moments, they were airborne and were swung out over one of the holding tanks. The crane operator deposited them on the floor of the third tank, where Slade was directed to get off.

In the center of the tank was a small round steel eyelet that had been welded into place for this occasion. One of the guards moved Slade towards the eyelet and removed a piece of chain from the platform. Looping the chain over Slade's handcuffs, the guard ran the chain through the eyelet and then locked it into place with a very large padlock. Slade was left standing in the bottom of the tank as the two guards were lifted out.

"How long can you hold your breath, Mr. Lockwood? Two minutes?" laughed Kyle. "I have so enjoyed our conversation, but now it is time for us to say goodbye."

"Go to hell, Kyle."

"I expected a better retort, really I did." Everyone burst into laughter except Slade. "Let's see how fast she fills up."

With that last statement, Kyle motioned for the technician who immediately radioed the operator. Slade could hear the rush of water coming and he looked up just as the door to the two foot pipe was sprung open and gallons of ice cold water poured in. He had just enough time to clear his lungs and suck in a deep breath of air. The water almost took his breath away and he was whipped around by the force of the water pouring in, the chain acting as a tether to hold him in place.

Frantically, he moved the paperclip into the palm of his hand as the force of the water subsided and he was able to manipulate it. There was no way he could pick the handcuffs when the water rushed in as he was beat around too much. He would have to do it during the break between filling and evacuation. Prying the paperclip open, he quickly bent it into the desired shape, more from feel and memory than sight. Just as he was done, the three foot door sprung open and he was sucked towards it with startling force. Once again, Slade was whipped around like a ball on a chain and his wrists became battered and bruised.

The only positive for him was the pain in his side had been numbed by the icy cold water, but he could also feel his strength being sapped away. When he could get his head above water, he did so and let out a loud gasp, more for Kyle than anything else. Two minutes was child's play for a skin diver. When all the water was gone, Slade fell to his knees over the eyelet, his hands working to undue the handcuffs. His fingers were numb from the water and they were not responding like he desired.

"Not bad Mr. Lockwood. Are you ready for round two? Sure you are." Kyle motioned the technician.

Slade heard the water rushing through the pipes and braced himself for the onslaught. The handcuff was sticking and would not come loose. Behind him, he heard the door springing open and he knew the water was coming down. The cuff was free! Slade sucked in a huge breath of air and held onto the eyelet. If he turned loose, he would be thrown to the top and Kyle's men would finish him off.

The water hit him square in the middle of the back and drove him to a prone position. Slade had expected the hammer like blow and had prepared himself for it as much as he could. His grip on the eyelet had been partially torn loose and he desperately tried to regain his grip. The swirling water was making it difficult and he watched the water rise with eager anticipation. The turbulence slowed and was coming to a stop. In moments, the trap door to the three foot pipe would spring open and the evacuation of 50,000 gallons of water would commence.

Slade looked down to make sure the handcuffs were loose. His right hand was free, but the left hand was still in the handcuffs, however he had already slipped that loose of the chain. His bigger problem was the three foot pipe. With the water rushing in, he would be swept along and would not be able to control his flight. If he struck the pipe at a bad angle, he could be knocked unconscious or a bone could be broken. He did not know where the pipe went, but he was hoping it vented the water out of the ship. He did not even want to think about the possibility of a grate at the other end.

The water had stopped and Slade turned to eye the three foot trap door, his body rigid and tense. The door sprung open and Slade released the eyelet, his body was caught by the out rushing water and he was hurtled towards the pipe, all sense of control lost. Steering as best he could, Slade entered the pipe head first and had almost cleared the opening when he careened into the pipe, striking his right side on cold steel. Even though he was under water, it brought tears to his eyes.

The men on the catwalk had been caught by surprise and they stared in disbelief as Slade shot towards the discharge tube, vanishing from sight within seconds. Kyle's mouth dropped open and then he regained his composure.

"Get topside and kill him! Move!" screamed the mad billionaire, following his men up the stairs as they elected to bypass the elevator.

Slade's journey inside the tube was brief. He discerned a change in color ahead and then he was shot out of the man-made tunnel into mid-air. The discharge tube was located thirty feet above the water line of *Quest 1* and Slade fell the entire distance, striking the water with a resounding thud. Regaining the surface, he spit water and sucked in lung full after lung full of air.

Later, Slade would tell Katherine two things saved his life: *Quest 1* was moving and darkness was descending. The mighty ship was traveling at a leisurely eight knots and Slade was soon left in her wake. By the time Kyle got the Captain to stop the ship and smaller crafts were launched, the distance between them had grown to over three miles. Darkness helped, because as he rode each swell to its height, he could see some lights in the distance and it was to these he swam.

The feeling in his right side was all but gone and he primarily swam with his left arm and kicked with his feet. Despite the turbulence and the headlong rush through the tube, he had held onto the paperclip and it had only taken him moments to send the handcuffs on a journey to the bottom. Slade had also taken his pants off and made an emergency life vest out of them. By tying them around his neck, he was able to keep his head above water and by lying on his back he could paddle with his feet and make some progress. The looming concern was blood. He had no way of telling if he was bleeding again. If he was, then sharks would hunt him down.

As hour after hour passed, Slade had to fight to stay awake. The lights were farther away than he had first thought and he was in danger of being swept past them due to the current. He realized the lights were on an island, probably Catalina, and that was the last stop before thousands of miles of open ocean. Slade kicked harder and tried to angle his approach. The island was still two miles away.

The moon had dropped into the night sky, which meant morning was near. With daylight, the hunt for him would resume and Slade knew they would come in earnest this time. Fighting fatigue, Slade continued to kick towards the island, the rhythm of his feet splashing the water the only sound.

Chapter Thirty-Five

Morning had finally streaked across the sky, subtle at first and then with more authority as the rising sun burned away the envelope of darkness. The heat had not yet arrived, so they were in the in-between time, when light was met with a cool ocean breeze.

They were still huddled around Billy's invention, measuring water flow and being awed at how such a simple mechanism could produce such a volume of fresh water. The break through had been with the cellular manipulation of the black mangrove. Billy had taken one of nature's gifts and enhanced it. Black mangroves derived their water from sea water and excreted salt through its leaves. Billy had enhanced the effect by discovering the firing sequence of the individual cells, causing them to take in vast amounts of fresh water and exclude the other minerals.

"Shirley, your brother does not disappoint." Professor Johansen stared at the simple device in front of him. They had added two more wash tubs and had upped the sea water to over 150 gallons. The fresh water machine handled it with startling ease, separating the fresh water from the salt, channeling each to respective holding basins.

"One hundred percent pure," announced Julie, holding up the latest cup of water.

"How does it know which is which?" asked Katherine.

"The sea water is heavier than fresh water so it sinks. I won't know this until further research is conducted, but I believe the fibrous mat channels the sea water to the bottom of the vertical column, thus leaving the fresh water, since the plant is only interested in the non-mineral laden fluid. Billy took advantage of Isaac Newton's law of gravity and the weight of the water to solve what scientists have been using low pressure and high pressure pumps

271

to attain. The simplicity of the design is the greatest engineering marvel I have ever been privy to witness." Professor Johansen stood back like a proud parent and beamed.

"Here comes Chief Singletee. I called him a few minutes ago and asked him to come over. If we're to take the next step and have the killers prosecuted, we need to make sure he's on board." Shirley watched the chief walk up.

"Good morning, all. Tell me what you've found."

It took less time than anyone would have thought for the chief to be briefed, which was done mostly by the Professor and Shirley. In the end, the chief stood silently for several minutes looking at the invention and then he turned to address the group, focusing primarily on Shirley.

"Shirley, I've been in contact with a friend of mine in the State Attorney's office. She was very pointed in telling me what to expect. Right now, as it stands, we don't have a prosecutable case."

"You must be kidding?" snapped Shirley.

"Where is the link between World Vision Quest and Billy? They attended some science fairs Billy was at, but there are no phone records showing they called your house, no correspondence, nothing to establish a link," said Chief Singletee.

"But what if they show up with this invention? Don't you think that's a little too coincidental?" The Professor moved over towards Shirley. The symbolic gesture was not lost on the chief.

"I'm not trying to take sides, but present the case as it must go forward in a court of law. I asked Denise about that very issue. Competing businesses discover things simultaneously all the time and they fight in court to determine who has patent rights. Of course, there're also patent laws and whoever files first has the proprietary rights. Just so you know, I checked and Billy, Hank or Mary never filed for any patents."

"Well, we need to file a patent for Billy." The enthusiasm once again entered Shirley's voice.

"I already have that ready. Harry Sloan has an attorney waiting in the wings to file a patent when we're sure you want to proceed. I would suggest we're ready and I'll give him a call if that's okay with you."

"Yes, it is and thank you. I can see you have been as busy as we have."

"So the killers get away with it?" stated Angela.

"I didn't say that. We need some type of evidence we can sink our teeth into and present to the State Attorney's office. We don't have that," responded Chief Singletee.

"What do we do next?" Professor Johansen spoke for the first time in several minutes.

"I need for all of you to get this ready for a patent application and I'll contact Harry and have the attorney come over. I'll also need everything you have done here put in written form. I will need copies of videos, audios..." the chief was cut off by the Professor.

"Hold on a minute, Chief. Angela, Julie, get some paper and pencils so we can write down what is needed. Our job is not done until Billy Waterbury is vindicated and his killers are behind bars." Professor Johansen waited while the young women grabbed the necessary items. "Go ahead."

"In addition to the audios and videos, I'll need one master report from the person who is the project lead and then I'll need briefer reports from everyone else chronicling their involvement. Any questions?" Chief Singletee was impressed by the efficiency of the young minds assembled in front of him.

"I'm sure there will be, so don't go anywhere," replied Professor Johansen. "Angela, you prepare the master report and Julie you will be her back-up. Any questions?" Seeing none, the Professor added, "Then let's get started."

The students dispersed, moving to the sections of the work-site where they had been laboring, excitedly sharing ideas and conversing. Lap-top computers appeared out of backpacks and notes were brought forth. The young man in charge of the video tapes was already setting up his equipment to make copies.

"Damn impressive," muttered Chief Singletee.

"You going to call Harry?" Shirley moved closer to Chief Singletee.

"Yes. By the way, Shirley, unless you come up with something here, Slade is our last hope." Chief Singletee extracted a cell phone from his pocket and dialed Harry Sloan's number.

"Slade has always been our last hope, Chief." Shirley turned to watch the students scurrying to record and format all the work they had done.

Now more than ever, they needed Slade Lockwood to find a link in a puzzle that was taking shape.

His body had been pushed to the greatest physical limits he possessed and beyond. Slade had nothing left. If he did not make landfall in the next few minutes he would die in the cold, lonely sea.

The first twinge of sun poking over the horizon found him closer to the island. By altering his course during the night it appeared the current would wash him towards shore. Now, for the first time, he could hear the sound of waves crashing onto rocks, their thunderous roar ever closer.

Movement. A darker shadow had flashed through the swell near him and was gone. A shark? Slade continued to kick, glancing continuously over his shoulder to line himself up with the shoreline. There it was again! Closer this time.

Slade turned and looked at the shore. It was two hundred yards away, but extremely rocky. Boulders the size of small cars welcomed the violent kiss of each wave. It would be difficult to avoid being crushed by the surf pounding him into the rocks if he had all of his energy and the use of his limbs. He could no longer move his right arm, the pain being too unbearable, and it hung useless at his side.

The distance was narrowing and Slade found himself swimming through some giant kelp. Several times he had to stop and untangle the vines from around his feet. His breaths were now coming in gasps and he found himself panting despite efforts to control his breathing.

Less than a hundred yards and it seemed forever. This time, the shadow in the swell came within fifteen feet. It was long and streamlined and darted with amazing velocity, looking like a torpedo on an errant mission. Slade felt the hair on the back of his neck stand on end. If it was a shark, it was probably sizing him up for the final rush and he knew the attack would come from behind and below. Judging by the size of the shadow, he would not stand a chance.

Slade could feel the surf picking him up and carrying him forward before dropping him into the trough between waves. The frequency was becoming shorter, more violent, as the water became shallower, accenting the turbulence.

A change in color out of the corner of his eye! This time the shadow was coming straight for him and showed no sign of stopping or slowing down. Slade instinctively moved to a vertical position in the water and waited—that was all he could do. If it was an attack, the momentum from the creature would knock the wind out of him.

Slade set his teeth and waited, his legs continuing to scissor kick to keep him vertical. The shadow moved to within five feet and then turned towards his left and surfaced. A sea lion stared at him with large brown eyes, his thick, fat neck disappearing into the water. His sleek brown coat was matted tight against his body and the whiskers on his snout twitched repeatedly.

Unable to control himself, Slade burst into laughter but it did not scare his new found swimming companion. The sea lion circled Slade three times and then dove back down towards the kelp bed, hunger winning over curiosity. Realizing there was no danger Slade flipped over onto his stomach and began swimming again towards the rocks, which were now less than fifty feet away.

Timing would be crucial. Slade would be given one opportunity to land near the boulders. A mishap and his head would be crushed on the rocks or his body mangled. Riding to the crest of the wave, Slade picked his landing spot. Two boulders, slightly smaller than their brethren, was his best chance. Where they came together, a small opening was created and the water rushed through them. If Slade could slip between them, he could be washed past and wedge himself behind them when the backwash tried to pull him out to sea.

Tensing his body, Slade rode to the crest of the wave that would carry him to shore and attempted to guide his arrival. The surf rushed him forward, a headlong dash faster than he could handle. The water struck the shoreline and Slade could feel the water vanishing beneath him as it threw him towards the boulders. Rolling to his right to streamline his approach, the swell carried him past the boulders and through the opening. The water swirled around him, pausing before rushing back. Slade shoved himself over and lashed out with his feet trying to stop from being pulled back out to sea. His left foot struck some submerged rocks and he thought he was safe, but the relentless strength of the water pried him loose. With one last act of desperation, Slade grabbed the nearest boulder with his left hand and held on. The water ebbed past.

Slade pulled himself to the cover of the boulder and waited. The next watery assault rushed through the opening and swirled around his legs but he was in no danger. After catching his breath and timing the waves, Slade crawled to safety and collapsed, his strength gone.

It was mid-morning before he was able to move. Every muscle in his body ached. He was suffering from dehydration and exhaustion. What he needed the most was sleep.

Gaining his feet, Slade stumbled up the shoreline to where the landscape flattened out. It was an island he was on and he was certain it was Catalina. In the distance, he could see some houses and he started that way.

The first house he came to was a small cottage, with a commanding view overlooking the Pacific Ocean. Slade knocked on the door and an older gentleman answered.

"Yes?"

"Hi, I was wondering if I could use your phone?" Slade watched as the man took in his battered appearance.

"You don't look good. What happened?" The man ushered Slade inside.

"It's a long story. But if I could use your phone, I'll share it with you," countered Slade.

"Come on in. Michelle! We have company," yelled the older man.

A woman in her mid-fifties appeared, took one look at Slade and immediately hurried to the kitchen. She returned with a steaming mug of coffee.

"George, go and get some clothes for this man to put on, you can see he is shivering," ordered Michelle.

"Thank you," said Slade.

Michelle ushered Slade to the bathroom to change and George supplied a change of clothes. After toweling dry, Slade walked back to the living room, massaging his right arm where feeling was beginning to return.

"Is this Catalina?"

"Yes, it is. We're on the other side of the island. The port and all the shops are on the California side. We like the Pacific side." Michelle looked at Slade.

"Can I borrow your phone?"

Slade called June Stenger and talked quietly to him for several minutes. Finishing, he handed the phone back to Michelle.

"Have you eaten?" asked Michelle.

"No, I haven't, but I don't want to impose. You've already done enough."

"Nonsense. George and I don't get many visitors. Let me make you something to eat." Michelle disappeared towards the kitchen.

After a hearty lunch, Michelle handed Slade his dried clothes and he changed back into them and thanked them again.

"Do I follow the road to get to the port and airfield?"

"It's quite a walk. We're going into town, so why don't you ride with us?" said George.

"Thank you."

By the time George and Michelle dropped Slade off at the airport, June Stenger and the *Pink Flamingo* had landed. Bidding them farewell, Slade met June and they were airborne within minutes.

At cruising altitude, June looked over at Slade and asked him to bring him up to date. Slade explained everything and June slapped his passenger on the shoulder.

"Do we have enough?"

"You mean for an indictment?" When June nodded yes, Slade continued, "I don't know. It's flimsy at best and it's my word against his. If they have any evidence in Cedar Key, we may have a shot, but it's a long shot."

"Damn. You took a chance on calling me. I mean to come and get you on Catalina. What if Kyle had intercepted the call?"

"I didn't think that was likely. I took a chance he was not tracing your cell phone. And I figured you could get there first. I had faith in you."

"We'll be in Cedar Key late tonight. You want to get some sleep?"

"Yes, but first I need to talk to Katherine, Shirley, and Chief Singletee. We need to present a case to the authorities." Slade reached over and picked up the radio headset and was patched through.

For the next hour, Slade, June, Shirley, Katherine and Chief Singletee were on a conference call. At times, they all tried to talk at once and they would have to start over. By the end of the conversation it was agreed the State Attorney would meet them at Slade's when he arrived. Shirley and Katherine had told him about their discovery, which matched what Slade had seen and learned from Kyle.

"Now go and get some sleep. You look like you have been dropped over a cliff," smirked June, checking his fuel gauges and other instruments.

"Thanks. I can always count on you for a word of support."

Slade climbed into the passenger compartment, folded out the couch and was asleep before his head hit the pillow. When June was sure he was fast asleep, he used his radio to contact Katherine a second time. Their conversation was brief and when June hung up the phone, he started to hum.

Everything now depended on a State Attorney and the evidence they could present.

Chapter Thirty-Six

Slade slept through the flight and was awakened when they were thirty minutes from landing. The approach to the airport was flawless and the *Pink Flamingo* taxied to her hanger.

Rejoining June in the cockpit, Slade was amazed at the number of people at the tiny terminal. Katherine, he immediately recognized, Shirley, the chief and some others, but there was a large group of people he did not know.

When the engines had quieted, June opened the door and was the first down the steps to be greeted by Chief Singletee who pumped his hand in thanks. Slade was close behind and the minute he stepped onto the asphalt, Katherine was in his arms, sobbing against his chest and kissing him all over the face. Shirley was standing close by and Slade hugged her, too.

Introductions were finally made and Slade met Professor Johansen and the students and Denise Boyd, the State Attorney.

"I hope we have enough to prosecute," said Slade.

"So do I. I'm interested to hear what you have to tell us." Denise was a large woman, with blond hair cut short and piercing green eyes.

"Before you go anywhere, you're going to the hospital. June told me you've been injured." Katherine gave Slade the 'don't argue with me' look and he scowled at June.

After getting his right ribcage bandaged and additional pain pills, Slade was released, but not before the doctor had pointed out he had now fixed both of his sides.

At Slade's, everyone met in the living room and sitting space was at a premium. Slade relayed the entire story of his ordeal to Denise Boyd, who had a notepad and pen, making frequent notes.

"I'm going to call my boss. Your case is purely circumstantial, although a good one. I learned yesterday that World Vision Quest had already filed for a patent for a desalting machine exactly like the one Billy invented." A loud intake of air could be heard throughout the room. Denise looked directly at Shirley. "I didn't want to tell you until I heard from Slade because I was hoping he would bring us more with which to work."

"I need to get on the phone as well," said Chief Singletee. "I think I can get the charges dropped against you in California with regards to the assault on the officer and the incident at the library. Your old friend Commander Rick LeFluer said he would help. I'll let you know what happens."

"Thanks. You mean what I've told you is not enough in combination with what they have discovered?"

"I didn't say that. Kyle is going to claim you were the one trying to steal this invention from him and I'll bet he has a hundred people who will testify on his behalf. We have zero records indicating he ever contacted Billy or his parents and I'll bet he denies it. As far as him confessing to you, so what? You know as well as I do it would never be admissible and he'll have another group willing to testify he made no such statement. As it stands right now, this case is purely circumstantial and I'll have to see how far my boss is willing to go. I understand why you took the course of action you did, but by not going through the proper process you hurt us." Denise saw the wrath hit Slade's eyes.

"Don't give me that line of bullshit!" snapped Slade. Every head in the living room turned and marveled at the intensity in the ex-cop as he rose to his feet, shrugging off Katherine's restraining hand. "I was a cop longer than you've been an attorney and I know how assholes like Kyle hide and manipulate the system. There's no way we could have gotten the information any other way and you know it."

"If you know the system, then you won't be surprised if my superiors elect to do nothing." Denise gathered up her things and walked to the door. Looking over her shoulder, she added, "I'll be in touch."

Silence reigned in the room.

The next two days were the slowest in Slade's life. Chief Singletee had gotten charges of assault and setting off a fire alarm against Slade dropped in California, as well as burglary and a host of other crimes. Matt Kyle, however, wanted to press charges against Slade for burglary, arson, and destruction of property.

The eccentric billionaire had been interviewed by LAPD and like Denise Boyd surmised, he had alibis and witnesses. To add insult to injury, Kyle had publicly stated he had never met a Billy Waterbury or his family, and had offered any assistance he could give to the grieving sister, a move which infuriated Shirley.

To aggravate the situation, Kyle had launched a media extravaganza touting his new water desalting invention and foreign heads of state were lining up like it was an auction. Kyle had already been interviewed a dozen times on national news and his face seemed to be everywhere.

Finally, word from Denise Boyd was not good. Matt Kyle was now a multi-billionaire and her boss was scared to bring charges against him on a purely circumstantial case. Without a connection tying World Vision Quest to Billy Waterbury the case was dead.

That night Chief Singletee, Professor Johansen and his wife stopped by for dinner. Shirley was the quietest one of the group and was more of a spectator. When dinner plates had been removed and everyone had retired to the living room, Slade retrieved a bottle of brandy.

"I think it's time we all shared in a drink." Slade held the bottle up to the light and looked at the contents. "After all, we've all been through a lot."

"Are you allowed to drink with the medication you're on?" Katherine had concern etched on her face.

"I think I'll make it. It might even help," joked Slade.

As if on cue, there was a scraping sound at the screen door and everyone looked around to see Old Clacker peering inside.

"He wants some, too," quipped Professor Johansen.

Shirley got up and gave him several pieces of fish, which seemed to appease him and he waddled back over to a corner of the porch.

"He doesn't roost on the piling anymore?" Slade looked at Katherine, but it was Shirley who spoke up.

"Sometimes, but most of the time he likes it right there," answered Shirley.

"Likes to keep an eye on what's going on," commented Katherine.

Professor Johansen asked how Old Clacker had taken up residence at Slade's and Katherine was telling the story when the doorbell rang. Slade motioned for her to continue.

A young woman was standing on the doorstep, with a questioning look on her face.

"Are you Slade Lockwood?"

"Yes, I am." Slade remembered a little over a month ago when he answered the door and Shirley had asked him the same thing.

"I was told Shirley Waterbury was staying here. I'm Mandy Chambliss, her college roommate." Mandy offered her hand and Slade invited her in.

Slade walked her to the living room and when Shirley saw her college friend, she jumped up and ran to her, giving her a hug. Quick introductions followed.

"I'm so sorry about everything that has happened, Shirley. I tried calling but no one answered at your house." Mandy looked around the room at the people gathered there.

"I've been staying here for awhile. It was nice of you to come and see me."

"Not a problem. Hey, I finished my last chemistry class this summer and got a 'B'. I could have used your help, though." Mandy looked for approval in her ex-roommate's eyes.

"See, I knew you could do it." Shirley hugged her again.

"Also, my parents bought a condo in Gainesville and I was wondering if you wanted to room with me. They didn't like the sorority house." Mandy noticed Shirley had changed. She was stronger, more set.

"Not now. I have to figure out what I'm going to do." Shirley tried to keep her voice up. "Have a seat." When both of them had rejoined the group, Mandy spoke again.

"Well I didn't know what you were going to do, so I left your clothes and your computer at the sorority." Mandy let her voice trail off as Shirley leaped to her feet, spilling the glass of brandy down her shirt.

"Oh no!" Shirley's hand flew to her mouth. "Slade! Slade, I may know where the proof is we need. My computer! Billy would e-mail me about the projects he was working on, especially if he thought it was really a good one. He always wanted my advice. With everything going on, I totally forgot about it."

Slade was now on his feet and moving towards Shirley. The excitement filled the room and a buzz was in the air.

"Where's the computer?" Slade was standing directly in front of her.

"In Gainesville. The computer is in my sorority room. We can be there in less than an hour." Shirley glanced at her watch.

"I can do better than that," said Chief Singletee, "Let's go."

It was a mad scramble to Chief Singletee's patrol car and when they realized everyone would not fit, Professor Johansen grabbed the keys to the rented minivan he was driving and the remainder piled inside. With blue lights on and the gas pedal imbedded in the floorboard, Chief Singletee led them out of Cedar Key and to Gainesville.

The trip was done in under forty minutes as they slid to a stop in front of a red brick sorority house. Chief Singletee was the first to make it to the door and found it locked.

"I have a key." Mandy moved past the chief.

Once the door was opened, they all streamed in like an invading army storming the last castle. Young women in nightgowns were watching TV and they screamed when they saw all the men walking in.

"Relax. Police," yelled the chief.

"It's on the second floor," instructed Shirley, taking the lead by running up the stairs.

Mandy opened the door and Shirley raced to her computer. Fumbling with the power switch, they all waited expectantly as she turned it on. Shirley had a message flash across her screen that she had unopened mail. Deftly, she positioned the arrow on mail and clicked. The screen filled with unread mail. Shirley scanned towards the bottom and found several that read 'Waterbury, Billy.' Selecting the first one, Shirley clicked on it and the screen filled with text.

Everyone in the room stood in silence when they realized they were reading e-mail from Billy to Shirley. The date was two days before he was killed.

"*Hi, Sis.*

> *Hope you're doing well. Is Chemistry kicking you? Mom said you were having to study a lot. What are you going over in class? Send me some information, I might like to read it. If it gets too tough, let me know and I will help…. ☺ Just kidding!*

> *Hey, I wanted to tell you about something really cool I'm working on. I mean, this is so totally cool it is way off the cool meter. It is out there, Sis. You're not going to believe this, but I found a way to make fresh water from mangroves. I knew I could make them grow bigger and faster, but during my research in the lab, I found a way for them to make fresh water from salt water! Is that cool or what? I called Professor Gordon, she got me entered into the science fair at the University of Michigan. That is the National Science Fair and that is so cool. She wanted to know what I was working on, but I told her it would be a surprise. You're the only one, besides mom and dad that know. Well actually, there is another person, but he's not a scientist. This guy from a company called World Vision Quest wants to buy my water invention. Might make a lot of money so you better be nice to baby bro! ☺ He heard me talking about it with Dad at the Orlando Science Fair and has been bothering us ever since. Dad had to get tough with him and tell him it was not for sale until I had finished my research. Goofy looking guy with a beard and glasses. I don't know his name, but when I was taking a picture of my exhibit in Orlando, he's in the background. I'll send it later and tell me if you think he's a geek!*

> *Well, I got to go. By the way, Sis, I have a favor to ask—I know, I know, I'm always asking for favors—what are brothers for? Will you look at the specs I'm sending you on the water purifier? (I'm calling this the Oasis Project! It makes water where none exists, a true oasis! Get it? Pretty cool, huh?) I have calculated how much water Oasis can produce, but I want you to verify my data. Thanks, Sis, I owe you.*

> *Till next research,*
> *Your Bro*"

At the end of the e-mail was a picture of Billy's face on Superman's body.

"Billy," said Shirley, reaching out to touch the image of his face on the screen. Shirley heard several people cough and was aware she was not the only one crying.

"Open up the next one, Shirley," said Slade, blinking rapidly. Billy Waterbury had been a very unique young man. And as Slade rubbed Shirley's shoulder, he reflected that so was his sister.

The second e-mail was the schematic of Oasis. Billy had labeled each part and described how it worked. There were seven different pictures of the Oasis unit he had constructed in the lab, taken from a variety of angles. One was taken with Billy in the background watching as Oasis processed sea water into fresh.

The third e-mail was a set of several pictures taken from the Orlando Science Fair. In two of the pictures, Matt Kyle was prominently featured in the background and on one of the pictures, Billy had typed, "Sis, is he a geek or what?" An arrow pointed straight at Kyle's head.

"What now?" asked Professor Johansen.

"We call Denise Boyd, get a warrant and arrest the sorry bastard," snapped Chief Singletee, reaching for his cell phone.

Three weeks later…

Matt Kyle was behind bars facing murder charges and his empire had crumbled. In exchange for a suspended sentence, Randolph Myers had turned State's evidence and implicated Kyle in everything, along with Hans Klaus. All charges against Slade had been dropped and all the orders for the water purifying machine now belonged to Shirley Waterbury.

It had been over three weeks since they had rushed to Shirley's sorority house to check her computer for possible evidence. Since that time, she had gone from a local Cedar Key girl to the richest woman in the world. The deposits given to World Vision Quest had all been transferred to her, more to ease International tension than anything since foreign countries were clamoring not to be left out, and, in a rare move for a court of law, *Quest 1* had been transferred to her since it possessed so much of Billy's stolen technology.

The authorities in California had seized all of Kyle's assets and were shipping everything to her that had to do with Billy's invention. Shirley was on the news, in magazines and had been interviewed more in the last three weeks, than most heads of state. She handled it all like a seasoned pro.

Clyde Sommer had come to her and explained how the contracts had been obtained and who had deposited what amount of money and what they expected to receive. It also helped that he had copies of all the contracts he had negotiated. After convincing herself Clyde was an innocent pawn used by Kyle, she hired him and placed him in charge of sales and marketing.

Shirley had acted swiftly to incorporate and made sure she was protected by the law. Sleeping little and working late, she had been able to accomplish a great deal in a short amount of time. Her hardest task would be assembling a team around her.

Willard Mayes had also stopped by with a gift for Slade. He had spent his time refurbishing the *Fair Rose* and she was as elegant and graceful as ever. Willard had refused payment and told Slade it had become a matter of giving back. He never offered any other explanation.

When tied to his dock, Katherine had told him he finally had the power boat he wanted. Slade would not accept the gift until it was offered to Shirley and she asked him to keep it, in memory of her father. When he got well, Slade had promised to build a boat house for the *Fair Rose*.

Chapter Thirty-Seven

Cedar Key, *three months later.*
The signs of activity were everywhere and impacting everything. Near downtown and commanding a large tract of seashore property, land was being cleared, stakes were being driven into the ground and change was in the air. A large sheet of plywood had an artist's drawing of what the new building was to look like. The new structure took its design from buildings of the turn of the century, but on a far larger and more grandeur scale. It was the centerpiece of a beginning, a rebirth of sorts.

To those who took the time to look closely and read the lettering on the plywood, the new building would house Waterbury Enterprises, Inc. A picture of Shirley Waterbury was prominently displayed in one corner of the billboard and identified her as owner and CEO. The youthful exuberance that had dominated her face only months before was still present, but there was a mature, knowing hint in the eyes and face. The young girl had grown into a woman. The change was subtle, yet distinctive. Next to the construction area a large wooden and metal platform had been erected, complete with a canopy to cast the people sitting on chairs into shade. Those standing before the stage had no such luck and tiny beads of perspiration eased down their face. Still, the courtyard and surrounding streets were packed.

Slade squeezed Katherine's hand and was rewarded with her tightening her grip. Turning his head slightly, he looked down at Katherine. "She seems to have everything under control."

"She looks so calm and in charge. Who would have thought she could have done this other than us?"

Shirley was seated in the center of the stage, flanked by the Governor of the State of Florida, a congressman and senator. The Mayor of Cedar Key was presently speaking, extolling the virtue of the young woman who was the cause of all the attention and fanfare. Every time her name was mentioned, the crowd would burst into applause, shouts, and whistles. Shirley was the darling of Cedar Key.

"What do you think her next move will be?" Katherine turned back to Slade. "Headquartering Waterbury Enterprises here is a major coup for the local economy. With Billy's invention and the right marketing skills, there is no telling how large her company can grow."

"I don't know what the immediate future for her holds, but here comes someone who can tell us." Slade nodded towards a small elderly man moving towards them with a large smile on his face. Slade had not seen Harry Sloan since the whole affair with Matt Kyle had started. The little man parked himself in front of them and seemed to grin broader, if that was possible.

"You look happy," returned Katherine.

"Young lady, I'm beyond happy. I'm so glad Shirley took my advice and contacted you, Slade. Without you, the truth would never have come to light and we would not be standing here today. She owes you a great deal," beamed Harry.

"Shirley doesn't owe me anything. I owe her. More than she will every know." Slade had turned to stare back at Shirley who seemed to be looking their way. Katherine and Slade were on the edge of the crowd, near the rear. The last six months had changed him, probably forever. Slade knew now that life's journey was a never ending series of loops, trials and difficulties as one moved down the path of discovery.

"Maybe so, but Matt Kyle is behind bars where he belongs. Without you, it would have never happened." Harry had not picked up on the softness in Slade's voice.

"I hope she surrounds herself with good people," commented Katherine. "She has so much to do."

"Oh, she has, Katherine. As a matter of fact, you and Slade are on the Board of Directors of Waterbury Enterprises." Harry laughed when he saw their surprise. "I've been retained as Chief Financial Officer and a friend of mine I knew from my college days, is her chief legal advisor. He's one of the shrewdest men in the legal profession."

"Sounds like a lot of chiefs to me," grinned Slade. "Who's handling security?"

"The ex-police chief of Cedar Key, Bubba Singletee himself. Shirley accuses him of smothering her, but you can tell she has complete trust in him."

"He's a good man. Shirley will be safe with him." Slade nodded to emphasize his point.

"Shirley said you would say that. She values your opinion very much. I believe you, in her eyes, have taken the place of her father with regards to matters like that." Harry smiled when he noticed Slade shifted uncomfortably. "And she talks about you all the time, constantly comparing you to her mother." Harry had reached out and touched Katherine on the shoulder when he had spoken directly to her.

Despite her best efforts, Katherine felt the mist hit her eyes and her vision clouded. Removing her glasses, she wiped at the tears, losing the battle and not caring. "Thank you for telling me that. I love that girl. She is so special. If I ever have a daughter I hope she turns out like Shirley Waterbury. I can only imagine what her brother must have been like. Not to mention her mother and father."

"Well I did know them and they were the nicest people you would have ever met. They were the perfect family. Shirley is intent on maintaining that feeling of family, which is why I believe she has reached out to all of us to whom she is familiar and comfortable. By the way," paused Harry, looking directly at both of them. "We're talking about the richest woman in the world. In just under four months she has amassed over $7 billion dollars. Billy's invention is not only what he claimed it to be, but has exceeded all expectations. Countries all over the world are clamoring for it. We're already backlogged on orders for the next two years and that doesn't even skim the surface. With patent rights and marketing, Shirley could be worth well over $100 billion by this time next year."

Katherine and Slade looked at each other, neither able to comprehend that kind of money.

"No wonder Matt Kyle was willing to kill to get his hands on Billy's invention," said Katherine.

"Billy brought water to places on Earth where none would have existed. A fourteen year old boy stumbled onto the greatest invention in the history of the world in a garage in Cedar Key. Billy's invention could end hunger by allowing deserts to support life. His invention could increase productivity, solve problems with pollution. The benefits are too great to name and growing every minute. Not a day goes by without another discovery being made where Billy Waterbury solved a problem confronting humankind. If only Hank had been a businessman and recognized what Billy was doing, they could have been marketing his ideas years ago. To Hank and Mary, Billy was a kid genius playing with his experiments." Harry shook his head in disbelief.

"Who is handling research for Shirley?" asked Slade, forgetting the numbers.

"Professor Johansen. He called the University of Michigan and resigned. He and his wife have already bought a house and a boat." They burst into laughter. "Professor Johansen is committed to finishing Billy's work. Interestingly, his secretary and most of the students have moved down as well. I think the science wing of Waterbury Enterprises is in good hands."

"Sounds like everything is in good hands at Waterbury Enterprises," smiled Katherine. "What did Shirley finally name Billy's invention? I heard there was some debate over it."

"Shirley named the invention the same thing Billy called it: Oasis. It is truly an oasis of water to humankind, a fountain of life. Billy's discovery brings hope, with no pollution. There is already discussion about a solar powered model."

"You people have been busy the last three months," said Slade, twisting his upper torso to stretch still healing muscles.

"You have no idea. Shirley is like her mother: she can go on very little sleep and is constantly alert and sharp. We know she has to slow down, but she is hard-headed, definitely a Waterbury."

Harry looked at the young woman on the stage and Slade could see the care for her in his eyes. Shirley had assembled the Dream Team for her company and Slade hoped it would all go as planned. The next year would be one of change, not only for Cedar Key, but for Shirley. Slade knew he and Katherine would be there to help. Shirley had lost one family and gained another.

"I heard she is giving Cedar Key an Oasis to help alleviate the dependence on well water and their current treatment facility," stated Katherine, moving against Slade.

"It will not assist Cedar Key with its water problem, but solve it. A small Oasis unit will produce enough fresh water for everyone on the islands and then some. It is an incredible gift." Harry smiled like a proud parent showing off a new toy. "Have you seen the designs for Waterbury Enterprises' new headquarters? The office complex is going to be incredible."

"I hope she picks the right colors," laughed the artist.

"Oh, I'm sure she will. She has already told the architect you have final say on the color scheme and she is commissioning you to paint murals on the interior in the lobby." Harry laughed out loud again when a stunned Katherine Wintergate could find no verbal response.

"Looks like you're going to be busy," smiled Slade, sliding his arm around her waist.

"One last thing before I have to go," said Harry Sloan, reaching into his breast pocket. Harry extracted two small savings passport books and handed one each to Slade and Katherine. He waited until they had opened them. "It's Shirley's way of saying thank you. She wants you both to know she will be there for you, like you were for her. She wanted to give them to you herself, but knew it would be impossible. She is flying out of here when this is over to meet the President of the United States."

Katherine grabbed Slade's arm and fell backwards into him. Slade, after opening the passport book was equally stunned.

"Slade, this is for one million dollars! I have never dreamed of having this much money!"

"Mine, too." Slade could think of nothing else to say.

"To a woman with billions, a couple of million is nothing. Especially for you two."

"Tell her thank you. And tell her she had better take time to come and see us when she gets back from the White House," instructed Slade, looking directly at Harry.

"I'll tell her. By the way, there are two tickets to a concert in the back of your book."

Slade opened the back of the book and removed two tickets to a concert in Tampa Bay Stadium. The tickets were for front row seats, center stage.

"Who's playing?" Katherine craned her neck to see.

"The Bee Gees." Slade folded the passport savings book with the tickets inside and slipped it into his pants pocket.

"Shirley said you're a big fan. I didn't know they were still doing concerts." Harry looked at Slade.

"I've been waiting to see them for years. One of the brothers died, but the other two succumbed to the wishes of the fans to see them perform again. Tell Shirley thank you again." For some unknown reason, Slade looked toward the stage and saw Shirley was looking directly at him and Katherine. Slade placed his fingers to his lips and blew her a kiss. Shirley smiled and nodded her head slightly, acknowledging the gesture.

"Will do." Harry turned and started to walk away, but stopped after several steps. "By the way, I've been meaning to ask you something." Harry paused and looked at Slade.

"Go ahead."

"Slade Lockwood. You have an interesting name. I've never heard of anyone else with a name like that. Were you named after someone?" Harry canted his head as he studied the taller man.

"Yes, I was. I was named after an uncle." Slade said no more and Harry smiled, before walking away.

"You never told me you were named after your uncle," chided Katherine, looping her arm through his as they started to leave.

"There are a few things I haven't told you. Man's prerogative. Sort of like a woman's intuition," laughed Slade, moving his shoulder as Katherine playfully slapped him.

"Would I have liked him? Your uncle, I mean."

"Yup. He was an outdoorsman. Loved to hunt and fish and was a good family man." Slade looked down at her and smiled. "You would've liked him."

They both stopped and turned to look back at the stage as the crowd burst into a huge roar, their clapping and screaming deafening. Shirley Waterbury had been introduced and had moved toward the microphone. With a grace and confidence distinctly hers, she waved to the crowd and started to address them. Silence reigned as everyone tried to hear.

Katherine and Slade turned and resumed walking, moving slowly and carefully, like only two lovers entranced with each other's presence can.

Overhead, a large brown pelican circled, his large outstretched wings catching the rising updrafts of warm air, his eyes searching for two familiar faces in the crowd. Spotting the two lovers, he glided lower and circled a second time. Satisfied they were heading home, Old Clacker flapped his massive wings. It was about time. He was hungry.